A TYLER ZAHN NOVEL

SCORCHED

BURN ME ONCE...

CAM TORRENS

Black Rose Writing | Texas

ISBN: 978-1-68513-468-6
PUBLISHED BY BLACK ROSE WRITING
www.blackrosewriting.com

Printed in the United States of America
Suggested Retail Price (SRP) $22.95

Scorched is printed in Minion Pro

*As a planet-friendly publisher, Black Rose Writing does its best to eliminate unnecessary waste to reduce paper usage and energy costs, while never compromising the reading experience. As a result, the final word count vs. page count may not meet common expectations.

PRAISE FOR
SCORCHED

"Cam Torrens once again proves he is the master of suspense!"
–Lena Gibson, bestselling author of *The Edge of Life: Love and Survival During the Apocalypse* **and the** *Train Hoppers* **series**

"*Scorched* is a blazing hot conflagration of art thieves, powerful families, sizzling romance –and especially, in Tyler Zahn, a hero with heart and soul."
–David Shawn Klein, award-winning author of *And the Dead Shall Live* **and** *The Money*

"Zahn puts it all on the line to solve the murder and art heist, and Torrens will leave you guessing until the final pages who is guilty, and who is an innocent victim caught up in horrific circumstances."
–Gary Gerlacher, bestselling author of *Last Patient of the Night*

"Tyler Zahn is back, and this time he's playing with fire –in more ways than one. A riveting page turner to the end, *Scorched* keeps Tyler pinned between a rock and a hard place, and the reader glued to their seat. Do not miss this latest thriller from Cam Torrens!"
–Chris Riley, author of *Went Missing*

"The third installment in Cam Torrens's Tyler Zahn series may just be the best one yet. *Scorched* is twisty, action-packed, and unexpected in the best possible ways. This is one thrill ride you don't want to miss."
–Brooke L. French, author of *Inhuman Acts* **and** *The Carolina Variant*

"Cam Torrens strikes it hot again with a protagonist who can't stay away from trouble – a must read!"
–A.J. McCarthy, bestselling author of the *Charlie & Simm* **mystery series**

"Cam Torrens has done it again. *Scorched*, the third book in the Tyler Zahn series, is a must-read mystery/thriller that takes the reader inside the world of art heists, NFTs, and Colorado wildfires. Part locked-room mystery and part outdoor rescue adventure, *Scorched* will keep you guessing all the way to the surprising finish."
–Travis Tougaw, author of the *Marcotte and Collins Investigative Thrillers*

ACKNOWLEDGMENTS

The further I get into this writing business, the more I rely on others to produce a book. Somehow, I thought the more I learned, the more I could do on my own. Ah, so wrong. Again…

Linda, your patience is infinite. Thank you for allowing me the time to write, the encouragement to pursue my dreams, and honest (very honest) beta reads.

All my thanks to:

The family—mother Susan Torrens, sister Amy Torrens-Harry, sisters-in-law Sandra Rose and Donna Mosely. Grandpa Fred and Grandma Joan. My go-to first readers when I need a lift. Grandma Liz for the inspiration.

The beta tribe—the originals: Terry Williams, Penny Martin, Brooke Dillon, Kathy Bowen, Sue and Ben Paganelli, Alta Beren, Mary Riley, and Joy Knight. And talented recent additions: Sarah Greenberg, Lynda Carraher, Jason Brooks, and Kristy Beardemphl.

The SAR team—Shane Bumgarner for keeping me honest. Rebecca Hinds for constant support. And the entire team at Chaffee County SAR-North for inspiring me every day.

Central Colorado Writers (aka Critique Group)—you're still the ones who get first crack at everything I write. Everyone else gets to read the improved version you inspire.

The team at Black Rose Writing—not just the crack publishing team who has my back, but my fellow BRW authors. Thanks Brooke L. French, Gary Gerlacher, Lena Gibson, David Shawn Klein, John Lenoir, Barbara A. Luker, AJ MCCarthy, Gail Ward Olmsted, Chris Riley, and Travis Tougaw for beta reads. You're a talented group and provide so much support. Keep writing!

I still read a ton. Miles and miles of long, slow runs include hours and hours of audiobooks with my favorite authors. *Scorched* definitely benefitted from the following writers I consider mentors: Kelley Lindberg, for inspiring me to get my first words down for our CCW seminar; David L. Robbins, for changing my writing (for the better, I hope) and your service to veterans nationwide; Agatha Christie, Lucy Foley, and Ruth Ware—if I'm ever in a locked room, I'll depend on you all to save me!

Finally, a special thanks to sister-author-editor MaxieJane Frazier who proved her editing talent endures, even in the face of an older brother who still can't resist giving her grief every chance he gets. You took *Scorched* to the next level.

Readers—thank you for picking up *Scorched* and joining Tyler Zahn on another adventure!

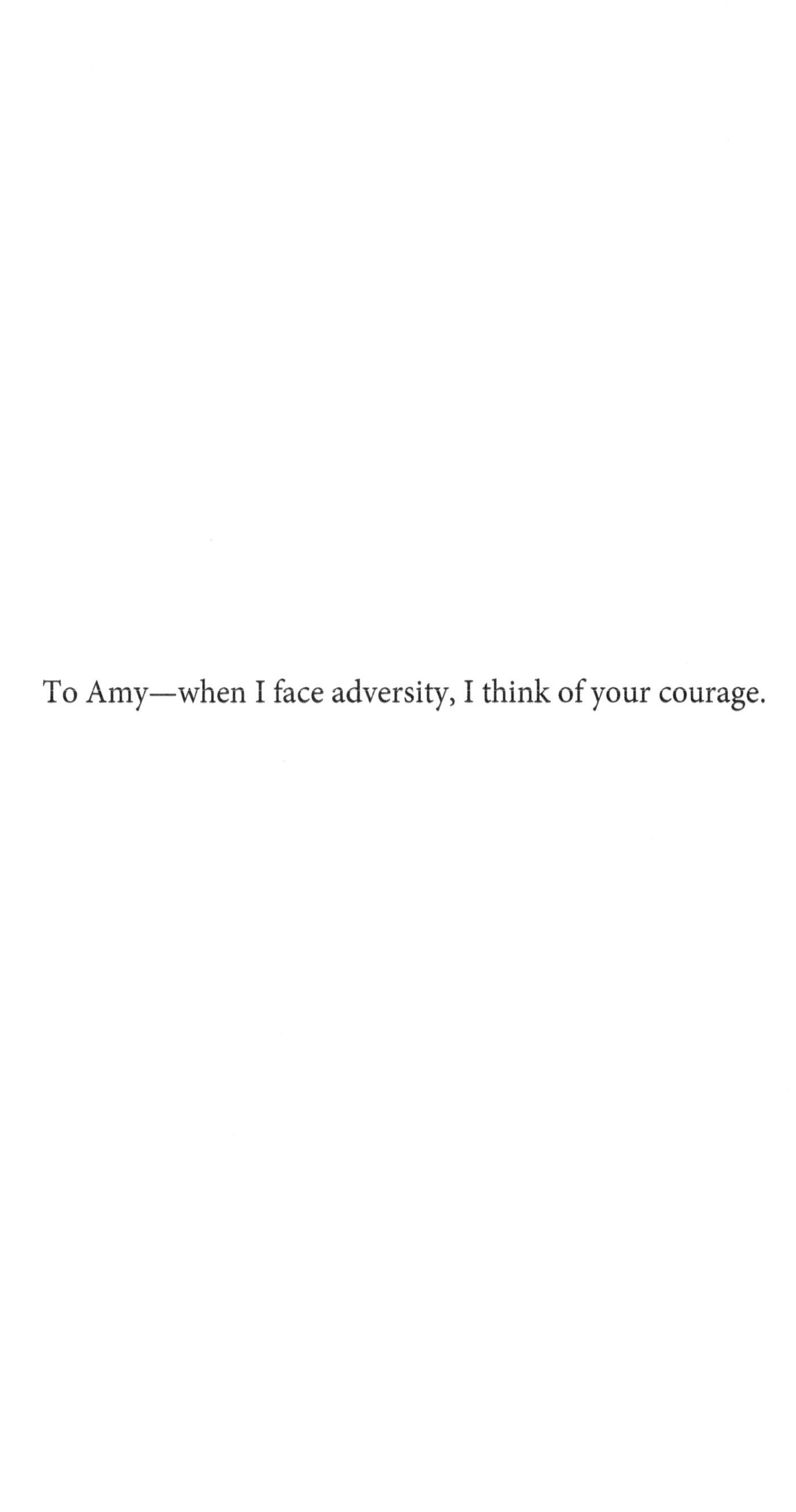

To Amy—when I face adversity, I think of your courage.

SCORCHED

CHAPTER 1

The digital radio on the Search & Rescue (SAR) command desk crackles. I jerk in my chair.

Command, this is Team 1. We're back at the Cottonwood Pass parking lot, loading the patient into the ambulance. We've got a problem.

My pulse quickens. I don't answer right away. Instead, I swivel my chair, and stare at the map on the big screen. Why is it always me involved with the non-standard missions? Usually, by the time we're turning over a subject to the EMTs at the ambulance, the mission is practically complete. Tonight is the wrong night for an extended mission—I've got a date.

I key the mike. *Team 1, Command. What's up?*

Yeah, Zahn—Lauren was taking care of business off the side of the parking lot and took another look at that panel van we told you about?

When my teams arrived at Colorado's highest paved pass, the parking lot was practically empty, except for the panel van we assumed belonged to the person the hikers found. My team lead's voice is raspy. He's either getting sick or the smoke from the fires down south is bothering him.

Copy. What'd she find?

We've got blood. Blood on the rear door. Blood on the bumper. Blood all over the ground. If this was our guy's vehicle, it looks like he was hurt before he ever left the parking lot.

My chest constricts. I pause before answering, considering how the rest of this night will play out.

The only reason I'm running command down here in Buena Vista instead of leading a SAR team in the field is because I'm recovering from injuries indirectly related to a previous SAR mission. Not from the mission itself, where we spent days unsuccessfully searching for my close friend Kristee Li, but from my personal investigation afterwards, which resulted in me getting knocked out by two drug dealers.

A month later, and I'm back to yoga with Ruth three times a week. I consider myself recovered. Unfortunately, the SAR leadership doesn't share my optimism. They have me riding the desk until they're sure I'm ready to go out on missions again.

So here I sit—the guy known most recently around our town as "Conspiracy Zahn" after my muddled attempt to investigate Kristee's disappearance—and the shit is hitting the fan again.

Team 1, this is Command. I copy. If you haven't already, pull your team away from the van. I say again, move back from the van. There's a roll of yellow marking tape in the Tech Rig. Use the traffic cones in the back and the tape to mark off the area. You copy?

I tug the Events Log binder toward me while transmitting and scan the entries. The Sheriff's Office will probably collect our reports later for evidence.

Command, this is Team 1. We're way ahead of you. They're doing it right now. Treating it like a crime scene. I'm guessing you want us to stay here until the Sheriff's folks arrive?

My breath releases in a whoosh. I should have guessed my team would be all over this.

A different voice crackles across the radio. *Command, this is Dispatch.*

I key the mike to answer. Dispatch is the communications center at the Chaffee County Sheriff's Office.

Go ahead, Dispatch. I poise my pen over the binder, ready to record.

Roger. We copied the last transmission. Deputy Morrissey is departing Johnson Village at this time and estimates she'll be on scene in 25 minutes. Confirm the name of the SAR Incident Commander.

This one's easy. I press transmit. *Copy. The IC is me, Tyler Zahn. Break-break. Team 1, did you copy that last transmission from Dispatch?*

Team 1 copies. We'll wait.

I scan the Injured Party-Known Location checklist, even though I know the last item by heart: *Account for all SAR members and resources.* We failed to do that when we lost Kristee.

Nothing in the procedures will tell us what to do about the blood around the vehicle. Which means I have time for a quick call to Laura Coker Long to explain why I'm ducking out of my first date in eight years.

She answers on the first ring. "Relax, Tyler. There's no way you could've known you were going to get a SAR call tonight. It's probably for the best, anyway."

Laura's calm voice eases my tension—right up until that last sentence. *For the best?*

"What do you mean?" I say. "We can reschedule—"

"Of course we can." She laughs. Relief washes over me. "I just mean I've got an issue going on, as well. I've been on the phone for an hour trying to find out why *Broncho Buster* hasn't arrived."

Broncho Buster. Laura's textured oil painting version of the iconic Frederic Remington sculpture. I'm so wrapped up in a SAR mission gone weird, and me canceling our date, I forgot about Laura's painting.

"I thought it was scheduled for an afternoon delivery?"

"So did I. I gave them until four before I started calling. I've got the cell for one of the security guards, but he didn't answer. I called the transport company and they haven't made contact either. They talked about cell reception in the mountains, but come on…five hours late?"

"I'm sure—" the radio interrupts me just in time, because I'm not sure about anything regarding Laura's issues. I just want to hear the smile she usually carries in her voice. "Hang on, Laura, I have to listen to this."

Dispatch, this is EMT 1.

The Sheriff's Office dispatcher answers: *Go ahead.*

Yeah, we're off the pass and headed for the hospital. Got some info for you to pass to Deputy Morrissey.

EMT 1, Dispatch—ready to copy.

Subject's name is Bruce Davis. He's got a gunshot wound. He regained consciousness a minute ago and said someone tried to kill him during a robbery.

I pull my phone back to my ear to reassure Laura I'm still connected. She's already talking.

"—said his name was Bruce Davis? A robbery?"

"Laura, I'm back with you. Can I call you back?"

"No!" Laura's voice shrills with alarm. "Bruce Davis. That's my contact's name with the painting. The security guard. Did I hear that right? There was a robbery?"

I pause as the radio cuts in again.

EMT 1, Dispatch copies. Subject was a robbery victim. Any other details?

Dispatch, that's affirmative. And not just your run-of-the-mill carjack. Mr. Davis claims to be a security guard for high-value art transport. Someone stole the paintings he was guarding. They shot him and his partner.

I turn from the radio to my phone.

"Laura?"

There is no answer. She has disconnected the call.

CHAPTER 2

SAR's role in the Cottonwood Pass mission ends well past midnight. When my cell phone rings at seven the next morning, it jolts me awake like a dormitory fire alarm. I even smell smoke. I flop my hand across my nightstand, grabbing for anything to make it stop. Finally, I find the phone. I swipe open the call at the same time I read *Laura* across the screen. My dog, Amore—actually Kristee's dog until she disappeared—stands at the end of the mattress. He aims for the unused pillow at my side, curling into a ball when I answer the phone.

"Hey," I say. "Sorry I didn't call back." Technically, it wasn't me who hung up, but I figure leading with an apology is a safe bet.

"Not a problem, Tyler." Her voice sounds bright, the opposite of what I expect from an artist whose prize-winning painting is missing. "I've got good news."

"They catch them?" My team turned the van over to the deputy sheriff last night after returning to the parking lot with the injured security guard. When Deputy Morrissey opened the rear doors, she found a dead body. The injured guard in the ambulance had been right. It was an art heist. But also a murder.

Laura pauses, her voice somber. "I don't know. That poor man. I'm talking about good news a little closer to home. They found *Broncho Buster!*"

I rub my eyes with my free hand. I'm unsure what this means. Laura's painting is called *Broncho Buster*. But she told me something about other paintings with the same name. "How's that? Where?"

"It was still in the van. There was a Buena Vista shipment—mine—and separate crates for the stuff going to Texas. They took the Texas stuff."

I tap the phone's speaker button, returning it to the nightstand before reaching for a pair of sweatpants. "I don't get it. If you're going to all that trouble to steal valuable art, why just take part of it?"

"Uh, Tyler? Do you remember what the exhibition was?"

"I do. *Rethinking the Masters*, or *Maestros*, or something like that, right?" I might not remember the title, but I knew Laura's latest exhibit because I'd looked it up in anticipation of our dinner date. No way was I going to show up unprepared in front of Buena Vista's favorite artist. The Los Angeles show was all about promising new painters adapting the works of the American West masters. Artists like Charles Russell, Frank Tenney Johnson, and others.

"Right. You're close. *Reimagining the Masters*. And my 'master' was Frederic Remington. The *Broncho Buster* sculpture. But part of the exhibit was to bring in originals. There were three Remington paintings in the van, including his *Bronco Buster* oil painting."

Now I remember her explanation. Laura's oil painting is spelled *Broncho Buster* in homage to Remington's iconic bronze sculpture. Which makes sense, because Laura's signature style is all about texture. She slathers her oil so thick in some places, viewers see her paintings as three-dimensional–like a sculpture. Remington's *Bronco Buster* oil painting, his own version of the sculpture, is more of a traditional oil painting–and it drops the "*h*" in the name, per modern convention.

And just to confuse non-art connoisseurs like me, the pronunciation of both title versions is the same. "They stole the Remingtons? So now this theft is big time. Like nationwide news, right?"

Laura coughs. I reconsider my words. Did I imply that having her painting stolen wouldn't have been news?

"I mean—"

"No." Laura exhales. "I mean yes. You're exactly right. The theft of the Remington works is huge.

I relax. "So, what about your painting? Any damage?"

"None." Laura's voice switches back to chirpy. "The Sheriff's Office towed the van down to Salida last night. They called me this morning with the news. They just need to hang on to it while they're doing the initial investigation."

"What about your local exhibition? At The Lodge? Will they be done in time?" Laura and I might not have enjoyed our first date yet, but she's already given me a ticket to her show four days from now. The exhibition at the small mountain hotel and wedding venue will be her largest local event.

"They assured me they would have it back in time. Not only that, they offered to bring the painting up to my gallery. I don't have to find transportation to get it back from their Salida office.

I glance out the window at my black Toyota Tundra pickup. Laura's framed *Broncho Buster* is too big for the back seat of any vehicle. I had almost offered to help with the transport. Somehow, I'm guessing hauling Laura's painting in my truck's bed wasn't what she had in mind.

"So, let's talk dinner. You owe me now after standing me up for drinks last night," she says.

I haven't known Laura that long, but I recognize she's teasing me. "Sounds like it wouldn't have been the best night for you, either. How about tonight?"

"I'm having dinner with my sisters tonight, but—" Her voice trails off, as if she's considering a decision. "No, wait. That would be perfect. They're going to want to hear about the art heist and the shootings and stuff. And you were the guy in charge. Come join us."

I don't answer.

Laura fills the silence. "Will you?"

Although I'd never admit it out loud, I want to see Laura alone. Last week, I hit The Lariat to hear an Americana band out of Boulder. I was sipping Coors Light in an effort to throttle back my Kristee-induced drinking surge, but the woman next to me was less inhibited. After moving to the back of the bar and talking for two hours straight, I drove a tipsy Laura back to her house. The longest interaction I've had with a woman my age in—well, since I was still married almost a decade ago. One thing led to another; we ended up making out like teenagers on her porch. I slept in my own bed that night, but took her to breakfast the next morning on the way to picking up her car. I'm looking forward to getting to know this woman who has occupied my thoughts every day since. Now I have another chance. But a family dinner?

"Do you think that's—"

"Please, Tyler? We'll do another dinner, just me and you, but come join us. Los Rancheros at six, OK? Maybe the smoke will have cleared some by then."

Smoke. I smelled it when I woke up and wondered if it was from the neighborhood. If Laura's smelling smoke as well, it must be from the recent fires down south.

I grab the phone as I move toward the kitchen. I've lived in this town for four years. Long enough to hear about the late Dwight Coker and his three daughters. It was one thing to agree to a date with one of the Coker women—Laura. Now I'm signing up to meet all three? And I'm still waiting for that first date.

I take the phone off speaker, releasing a sigh before returning it to my ear. My ex-wife Sheila was a strong woman as well. I like strong women. Most of the time.

"Yeah, Laura. See you at six."

* * *

An hour later, I step from my truck and feel a jolt of adrenaline as the scent of the Elkhead's freshly brewed coffee envelops me. I'm unsure if it's an anticipatory reaction to impending caffeine or because of my meeting with my closest friend, Deputy Sheriff Rick Perez.

I'm early and order my tall—the size of the smallest serving offered these days—cup of black coffee before grabbing a table in the rear facing the door. I nod at a couple of locals on my way to my seat. I could have ordered for Perez—the same coffee order as mine and his favorite wedge of quiche—but he likes his breakfast warmed and he's still not here. Sipping my drink, I take in the view of Mt. Princeton dominating the western side of our river valley, the summer winds wisping the north-side snow from the top as if Mother Nature was spinning cotton candy.

Perez and I usually convene for coffee once a week; today is our second meeting in four days. The SAR mission last night pivoted from standard rescue to a crime scene in minutes. Although I have a rough idea what went down—art theft resulting in one dead and one injured—I'm hoping for more details.

But how much will Perez share? He and I have a mixed history of collaboration resulting in what I like to think of as a 2-1 record. We were undefeated until this last go, when I couldn't solve Kristee's disappearance. I'm sure Perez doesn't consider that a loss. He thinks I went rogue on investigating Kristee. If we were simply acquaintances, he would have told me I approached the investigation from the wrong direction. Because we're friends, his comments were more along the line of, "you fucked this all up, Z-man."

I've moved past Perez's criticism. I wish I could say I've done the same with Kristee's disappearance.

Still, the residual friction between Perez and me hasn't disappeared. He'll be cautious with what he shares. I dropped my Reserve Sheriff slot at the Law Enforcement Academy during the Kristee thing. Actually they asked me to take a leave of absence. If I'm going to return to my training–which I definitely want to do–I need to demonstrate calm judgment and rational analysis when dealing with situations like these.

A bell jingles. Perez blows in, aiming for the counter while nodding at me. I raise my cup before returning my gaze to the mountains.

"Late night, huh?" Perez sets down his coffee and quiche. He pulls out a chair. "I was tracking your SAR mission on the mutual aid channel."

"Yep. Turned crazy fast. Did you talk to Regina at all?" Regina Morrissey is Perez's coworker, the deputy who responded after we found the blood.

"You weren't the only one out late, Z-man. Soon as she opened that van and found the other guard, I was pulling on my boots and on my way. Not like we get a ton of murder cases in Chaffee County."

"And?"

"Best we can tell, it went down the way your subject—the injured security guard—said. The guards pulled their van over at the pass for a bathroom break and got jacked as soon as they turned off the ignition. The thieves pulled them out of the truck at gunpoint and had them unlock the rear. One of them checked the crates while the other held a weapon on the guards. As soon as the guy in the van called out, 'we're good,' the gun guy shot the first guard in the chest. Davis bolted from the parking lot and they fired another three shots. One of them creased his head. Guess you guys already know that."

"Not really. We treated him for a head injury on the trail, but assumed he'd scraped it falling on the rocks where we found him. Nobody recognized it as a gunshot wound."

"Well, the docs did. I stopped by there this morning and they confirmed it."

"Something sounds off about what you just told me."

Perez smiles. "Tell me. What's off?"

I sip my coffee before answering, not wanting to appear too eager. I can tell Perez has already guessed what I'm about to say, but he's not being an asshole about it. It's like he's extending a hand and letting me ease back into the law enforcement business.

"The whole Cottonwood Pass parking lot thing. Taking a leak and then getting jacked by those guys. Seems a little too convenient. How would the thieves know the guards would stop?"

"You don't miss a trick, do you? So, what do we need to find out?"

I consider delaying my answer again, but can't help myself. "Who had to take the piss? That's what you need to know. Whoever suggested the stop was likely in on it."

"Bruce Davis—the injured guard—says it wasn't him, so what do we do now?"

"You talked to him?"

"Yep. After I saw the doctors, I dropped by his room. He's going to be there a few days while he recovers. He says the other guy—a John Jacobson—was the one who suggested it."

Now I see Perez's problem. Jacobson is dead and we have no way of knowing if Davis is telling the truth. Either Jacobson was in on the heist, or Davis was lying and in on it. After all, he's alive and Jacobson isn't.

"Or both," Perez says, like he's reading my thoughts. "They could have both been in on it."

I turn back to the window. My search and rescue role is over for this case. It's unlikely Perez will ask me for help. But I'm curious as hell. Perez is right. There aren't many murders in our county. And an art theft? I'm not sure they've ever had one of those.

"So what's the office's plan?"

Perez inhales a forkful of quiche, his eyes twinkling as I wait for him to speak. Finally, he says, "We've got an investigative plan, but I doubt we'll get to use it."

"Why's that?"

"Because of the art. Did you hear about what got stolen?"

"I heard it was stuff by Remington."

Perez nods, then stops.

"What?"

"Before yesterday, I thought a Remington was a gun. Had no idea about the art thing. But you're all over it. Didn't realize you were an art guy."

"I'm not. But I've been talking with Laura Coker Long…"

"The artist whose work was in the van with the famous stuff?" Perez pushes back his chair.

"Yes, we—"

"Listen, Zahn. I need you to stop with the questions. You can talk to me, but I don't want you going around involving yourself in this case like you tried to do last time. That's a non-starter."

I raise my hands, ready to explain to Perez about the whole me and Laura and the planned date thing, but he's having none of it.

"That includes that guard down in Salida. Davis. Do you hear me? You don't need to be talking to him. We got this." Perez strides toward the door. I know he's pissed because there's still a quarter wedge of quiche left on his plate. After Perez disappears, I wrap his leftovers in a napkin. I've got a dog at home who doesn't think I'm a screwup.

Coffee with Perez leaves me unsettled. It's not like I'm the one who invited him for our morning get-together. We're friends. We always talk these things through. But this is the first real case of interest since Kristee disappeared. He's not over what happened with me during those screwed up weeks of searching for her.

CHAPTER 3

Back home, I switch to running clothes. I should probably call my attire walking apparel or jogging gear, because it's hard to describe my neighborhood workouts as runs. My Elk Trace community nestles against the Collegiate Peaks foothills. Flat spots are few and far between. Any venture outside results in a workout. And for me, none of them are fast.

Amore splays across the mudroom door threshold, just in case I have any illusions about running solo.

"Ahhh-more-ay," I sing, in my best imitation of Dean Martin's version of Volare. Amore leaps to his feet. I grab his leash and two plastic bags for cleanup duty. The half-mile jog to my mailbox takes less than five minutes. No packages. I shuffle fifty steps of the first hill before slowing to a power-hike. My conversation with Perez replays in my head. Like last time, he had said.

This is bullshit. It's not like my frantic investigation into Kristee's disappearance yielded nothing. Bucking Perez's guidance to slow down, I had put together a convincing theory that someone made Kristee disappear. I helped put people in jail. But, in the end, they weren't the ones who made Kristee vanish. The satisfaction of putting away criminals didn't outweigh the look of pity Perez gave me as I recovered in the hospital.

Cresting the hill, I break into an easy jog on the short downhill before the slope increases again. Amore is off leash, tucked in tight by my side. As my breathing slows, I use the respite to scan the mountains jutting up from the Elk Trace boundary. The wind eases, making room for the heady scent of pines. With a side whiff of smoke. Mt. Princeton, Mt. Yale, and Mt. Columbia thrust against the hazy blue sky like nature's billboard advertising a challenge. I've summited all three, but usually spend my time halfway up these peaks helping carry injured hikers to a helicopter or lost hikers back to the trail.

Screw Perez. I haven't told him about my delayed date with Laura yet. And I don't like him telling me who I can and can't talk to. Even if he can. Why would I want to talk to the security guard? That one was weird.

After returning home to shower, I spend the afternoon on my laptop. I already checked out Laura Coker Long online after our Lariat experience because I'd heard she was a well-known artist in this part of Colorado. Nothing creepy like cyber-stalking. I was just trying to get a sense of who Laura is. I'm self-aware enough to know my major interest in Laura is because she seems interested in me.

And it worked. Laura Coker Long turned out to be my age, a 49-year-old long-time resident of Buena Vista, divorced for three years, and a local artist known for her unique style. Her niche is the American West, as it might have looked in the late 1800s. That's how her current work relates to Frederic Remington's pieces.

Today, I check out her sisters. Just for situational awareness. So I don't stick my foot in my mouth like I might have done when I met Laura the day after our unexpected night of PG-13 romance.

I type in *Julie Coker* and *Buena Vista*. Julie Coker is actually Julie Coker Keller and is widowed. She's 47, and a certified public accountant. When I click on *Images,* a newspaper photo pops up: Julie handing a certificate from the Optimist Club to a local high school student. A scholarship award. Julie resembles Laura—both with long blond hair, and distinctive smiles. Laura is lean and built like a runner, whereas Julie's more full-bodied.

My search for Monica Coker tells a different story. The top news results are from the Chaffee County Tribune's police blotter. Monica is

44 and has a record. When I search by image, there's no doubt she's the Monica Coker Laura mentioned. She's got the same blond hair and a long body. But her features are hardened. Not chiseled like a model, but brittle—like if she smiled, her face might fracture. Unlike Laura or Julie, Monica is gaunt. She wears tight creases around her eyes and mouth and her pressed lips form a horizontal line. I skim her background before guiltily closing my screen. No husband. A couple of DUIs. She's been arrested for possession of a controlled substance. And that is just the first page. Too much information.

Dinner should be interesting.

•   •   •

I show at Los Rancheros ten minutes early and request a table for four. It's not just my military training in customs and courtesies driving my early arrival—I'm a tad nervous as well. I'd rather meet Laura's sisters one-by-one, than be the last to arrive with all the attention focused on me.

The server introduces himself as Jason. He guides me to a table after I let him know I'm expecting company. A voice rings out just as I slide into the booth.

"Tyler! Not there."

A woman stands at the restaurant door, waving her hand for me to join her. I recognize her from my internet sleuthing as Julie Coker Keller, the middle Coker sister. She points her finger toward the back of the restaurant.

I offer my hand. "Tyler Zahn. But I guess you already know that?" We haven't met. I'm unsure whether she just assumed a middle-aged man in a booth that seats four had to be me, or if she has done some sleuthing of her own.

Julie laughs. "I recognize you from the newspaper. You know, from that missing girl's case." She grabs my forearm. "I can't believe that was happening right here in our valley. We're lucky to have you."

I'm about to try to change the subject when Julie turns toward Jason.

"The Cactus Room please. We're with Laura Coker Long."

Jason's eyebrows raise. He turns to me. "So sorry, sir."

I shrug. "I didn't know either."

We follow him to the rear of the restaurant. Julie glances back at me. "Laura always reserves the private room at Los Rancheros. It's a thing with her."

I say nothing. I didn't even know there was a private room.

We settle in at the round table across from each other. Suddenly I'm questioning my plan to meet the sisters one at a time. I wasn't expecting the private room. Jason serves us waters and tortilla chips with salsa before taking our drink orders. Julie goes for the house margarita. I try to order an IPA before I remember why I'm so ambivalent about Mexican restaurants. Usually great food. Always mediocre beer. I nod when Jason offers a Tecate with salt. After he disappears, I realize I should probably try to fill the silence.

"So," I start. "What do you—?"

"Tyler. We've probably got two minutes before Laura or Monica get here. Do you want the Coker sister brief, or do you really want to know what I do all day?"

I grab a chip and aim for the red salsa. "I guess you go for the direct approach?"

"No. That's Laura's technique. But you won't hear what I'm going to tell you from her." She sips her water. "OK. Here we go. Have you heard of Dwight Coker?"

"Your father? The football field is named after him, right?"

"Right. Our daddy. His father was David D. Coker, founder of the Coker Ranchlands. Ring a bell?"

I nod. The Coker name is all over the valley. I recognize her grandfather's name.

"We've got a long history here in Buena Vista and the valley. But the Coker men are all gone. It's just us three Coker daughters. And we're not doing a very good job of preserving the family name." Julie shakes her head. "Or the ranch."

I wrinkle my brow, trying to guess what Julie is getting at.

Julie's laugh sounds nervous. "You're a polite one, aren't you?"

I'm unsure why I'm getting the lesson on Coker family history, but it's information I don't know, so I bob my head, figuring the more nodding I do, the less responsibility I'll incur to pick up the conversation.

"I lost my husband some years ago. We never had kids. Laura is divorced, as you obviously know. There was no way she was ever going to let kids get between her and her work."

Julie's last remark catches my attention. The first thing I noted about Laura was her backside in denim. Couldn't keep myself from noticing. But the second thing that stuck out was her interest in me. She certainly hasn't come across as self-centered.

Julie continues. "Her art? That's her work. You know how artists are, right? I mean, it takes a bit of an ego to devote your life to producing things that other people can look at and say, 'Wow! I wonder who made that?'" She laughs again, but I don't join her.

Maybe Julie is trying to show me a side of Laura I've missed, but her delivery is off. All I see is a younger sister who seems jealous of her older sister's success.

"And then there's Monica." Julie sighs, a sure sign this story won't get any better.

"Is Monica an artist, as well?" I ask, more to show I'm still engaged in the conversation than out of any real interest. I have no doubt Julie's going to tell me.

"No. Monica is special. She's the main reason I wanted to get here early and talk to you."

A tap sounds at the door. Jason enters, holding the door open with one hand and a tray with our drinks in the other. Laura steps into the room behind him, closely followed by a woman I recognize as Monica.

"Shit. Guess we'll save this conversation for later," Julie mutters.

I stand and step forward to greet Laura. We've talked once in her gallery and on the phone, but last night was supposed to be our first date. So, I'm not really sure about protocol with someone I've kissed after a beer too many, but never met in public. A kiss on the cheek? That double European kiss? Or is it triple? At a loss, I tentatively offer my hand.

Laura laughs and does a half-curtsy, before thrusting her cheek up so close to my face, I have no choice but to connect with my lips.

She steps back, turning to Julie with a smile. "Hi, Jules. Sorry we're late. Did you and Tyler get all introduced? Give him the family history?"

Julie glances over Laura's shoulder at Monica, before stepping forward to give Laura a hug. "We were just talking. That's all."

"Can I get you and Ms. Monica anything?" Jason offers.

Laura points to Julie's margarita. "Can you bring us two of those? Virgin though." She turns to Monica. "Sound good?"

Monica remains silent, her lips a tight line. Laura turns back to Jason, but my eyes linger on the youngest Coker. If Monica's glare was a superpower, it would stab Laura in the back.

My first thought is the story Julie didn't finish. Her version of the self-centered Laura. That might explain Monica's obvious animosity. But I'm not seeing it. The Laura I see almost had her art stolen during a robbery and murder, and now she's introducing her new male friend to her family. I'd be uptight. And ready for a drink. Instead, Laura has been nothing but magnanimous even to the point of helping her sister by not drinking in front of her.

Jason serves me my beer before leaving for the rest of the drinks. I thank him, grabbing it and holding it down by my leg, so it's not obvious.

"It's OK," Laura mouths.

She introduces me to Monica, who gives me a short "Hi." We take our seats. Julie pushes the basket of chips toward Monica. I don't blame Monica for staying silent. She seems to draw a lot of attention from her older sisters.

Julie asks some get-to-know-you questions. I describe my work with Search & Rescue, and my volunteer duties at the library. Laura joins in with questions she hasn't asked before. They dig deeper, and I sum up my 20-plus year Air Force career as "a lot of flying beans and bullets around the desert." I tell a few stories about buzzing a desert airstrip to clear sleeping Marines off the runway so we can land. Using steep, spiral approaches into tight airfields to avoid missiles. They don't need to hear about my son's death, the loss of my aircrew, and my years of wallowing in depression. Hell, I don't even want to think about it.

When they ask about family, I tell them about my daughter Daria, and her studies at CU Boulder. I don't bring up my work I've done with the Sheriff's Office over the last couple of years. Julie has hinted she already knows, and Laura is very aware of my reputation in Buena Vista. I also don't mention the Law Enforcement Academy course I was taking to become a Reserve Sheriff, nor the fact they asked me to leave when I got caught up in the recent search for my SAR partner, Kristee.

Jason returns with our two additional drinks. As soon as he's out the door, Laura taps a spoon against her margarita glass.

"Do you guys mind if I propose a toast?"

Julie rolls her eyes. She glances at Monica, so I do too. Monica's eyes shift between her sisters' margaritas. I'm unsure she's caught up with the toast proposal.

"*Broncho Buster* is safe and sound back in my gallery. The Sheriff's Office delivered it this morning."

"Cheers," Julie says. I notice that, while she tried to hide her eye roll, her voice sounds sincere.

"That's not all. I've also confirmed that the exhibition at The Lodge will continue as planned." Julie raises her glass, but Laura uses her free hand to motion her to put it back. "And you all are invited to the grand opening." She looks at Julie, then toward Monica. "Will you come, Monica? I'm sure you realize how important this exhibition is for our family."

Monica does the lip press thing again. Her eyes harden, but she nods.

Laura raises her margarita. "Now we can toast."

We clink our glasses together. Laura turns to me. "You already have your invitation, Tyler. Will you be joining me?"

"I'll have to check my schedule." My voice trails off as Laura squints. I realize my lame attempt at some *I'm retired* humor is falling flat. She has no idea I'm joking. "Just kidding. I'll be there."

Monica speaks for the first time. "What about Duane?"

Laura and Julie's smiles drop. The tension at the table rises like the water in an overloaded hot tub.

Laura cocks her head. "Are you asking if he can come to the exhibition?" Her voice is tight, but she wears a smile.

"Yes?" Monica's voice sounds pleading. I'm unsure who Duane is, but he's obviously important to Monica.

Laura reaches for Monica's arm, and Monica flinches. "Can we discuss it later?"

"You've never liked him." Monica's voice sounds choked.

Laura moves her hand to Monica's shoulder and squeezes. "I'm trying, Monica. But after what almost happened to *Broncho Buster* the other night?"

Monica's response is immediate. "It wasn't his fault."

Laura shakes her head. "I'll never trust him again."

CHAPTER 4

The next day, I'm still sorting out the almost-dinner with the sisters while doing work around the outside of my house. My landlord and I came to an agreement two years into my lease. She'd stopped by while I was cleaning the gutters. She noticed the paving stone walkway I'd put in around the house and checked my work after I replaced the gas valve on the furnace. We decided she'd cut my rent by ten percent if I continued to provide upkeep on the house.

That's why when my phone rings, I'm in the middle of planting Russian sage between my house and the walkway. The benefits of high altitude living include no lawns to mow. Pine trees and cheatgrass do okay—but not much else. I'm not a flower kind of guy, but when my neighbor June stopped by with peach pecan muffins after the Kristee mission, she'd suggested I jazz up the front of my simple home. So here I am, putting in flowers and trying to ignore the smoky haze from the southern fires.

I glance at the phone screen before answering, looking—OK, hoping—for Laura's name on the screen. Last night's event resulted in a hoo-ha after Monica started arguing with Laura about her boyfriend, Duane. Laura was obviously upset about something involving Duane and her art. Which has me a bit curious as well. I haven't seen Laura in a conflict before, but after meeting jealous Julie and misguided Monica, I'd say she's definitely the most grounded of the sisters. That night at The Lariat, her body pressed against mine–the memory still stirs me.

Then our time on her porch. Not just the kissing—it was also the way she listened to what I had to say. Hell, I'll gladly put up with her sisters for another evening like that.

We'd cut the dinner short, but it wasn't a total failure. Laura confirmed my invitation to the exhibition's grand opening. I hope we'll get a chance for a one-on-one date before then.

But the screen reads *Alex,* not *Laura.* Alex is our SAR equipment/facility coordinator.

"Z-man, you got time for a question?"

My first thought is that Alex has already asked a question—so really, he's asking if I have time for two. I missed the whole dad-jokes-phase during my absence from my daughter's childhood, so I keep my thoughts to myself.

"Hit me."

"Yeah, I'm cleaning up the bay and doing some vehicle maintenance. I had some people down here dropping off a cell phone. They think it's from the mission you ran the day before yesterday. Up on Cottonwood Pass?"

I turn away from the house, toward the surrounding pines, my phone pressed against my ear. SAR's not usually the first place hikers take lost and found items.

"How did they even know about the mission?"

"They said they read about it. They saw the blood where you all found the guy. They mentioned the blood in the parking lot. And they didn't look like hikers—maybe they're like crime junkies or something?" Alex's voice is clipped, like this phone call isn't his top priority of the day. "So I took it. It was dead, and I plugged it in. Powered it up in case someone called looking for it."

"Good idea." If I remember right, Alex still uses a flip phone. I'm surprised he found a power cord that fit at the SAR bay.

"Of course, now I'm not really sure what to do with it. I was going to call Will or someone over at the Sheriff's Office, but figured I'd ask you first since you were the incident commander."

I nod, even though Alex can't see me. If I were in his shoes, I'd probably have a deputy swing by and pick it up too. Perez's admonition about what I could do and couldn't do on this art theft case runs through my head. *That includes that guard in the hospital in Salida…*

Perez pissed me off with that one. He had switched from a friendly conversation to an abrupt reminder that I'm on law enforcement topic probation because of my overreaction to the Kristee case. Except now I have a pretty good excuse to talk to the guard, assuming he's still in the hospital. Sure, I probably shouldn't just hand him the cellphone if he claims it's his, but I can at least find out if he lost one. And it wouldn't be my fault if he started talking about what happened that night.

Why did the thieves pick Cottonwood Pass for the heist? How did they know the van would stop? Why the violence? And why not take all the art instead of just the Remingtons? It's not just my new relationship with Laura bringing up these questions. I'm an inquisitive guy. I've found over the last couple years that the Sheriff's Office doesn't always think of the same questions I do.

"Good call, Alex. Giving it to the Sheriff's Office, I mean. Probably the right thing to do. Tell you what, though. I'm heading to Salida today and can drop it off. You going to be around for another twenty minutes or so?"

Alex likes my plan. He's almost done with work, and doesn't want to wait around for the closest deputy to swing by. I grab my Tundra keys from the hook on my mudroom wall.

•   •   •

Lights in my rearview mirror force me to pull over on my way to Salida. Fire vehicles whip by my truck, and then turn toward the mountains a half-mile ahead. In the distance, I see smoke billowing close to the hatchery where the treeline meets the valley. A brush fire, maybe.

Pulling into the hospital parking lot, I note the smoke hangs heavier here than in Buena Vista. Salida is closer to the southern fires. I walk through the hospital's main entrance expecting to talk my way into

Bruce Davis's room, or argue about visiting hours. I'm wrong. Evidently, anyone with a pulse can roam the halls.

"Mr. Davis? Yes, he's still here. Last door on the right," the nurse at the general care desk says.

I head down the hall, tapping my pockets to remind myself which one has my cell phone and which holds Mr. Davis's. As I approach the door, two men step from the room. The first is short and stocky. He wears a baseball cap with a Colorado Corrections patch on the front and khaki cargo pants with tan combat boots. He's dressed exactly like the ubiquitous contractors from my flying days in Iraq. The guys who did everything from running independent scouting missions to emptying the portable latrines.

The second man is dressed in jeans and a polo shirt. While the contractor man ignores me, the preppie guy gives me a nod. I nod back. He eyes my Search & Rescue cap with what appears to be the same interest I'd shown toward the contractor guy's Corrections hat. I glance over my shoulder after they pass. The preppie guy looks back at me.

Bruce Davis sits on the edge of his hospital bed, fully clothed. When his eyes focus on my SAR hat, he breaks into a smile.

"Man, you guys are awesome! First, you save my life. Now you're checking up on me?"

"Tyler Zahn." I thrust out my hand. "You're Mr. Davis?"

"Bruce. Call me Bruce." He shakes my hand.

"You don't look like a patient," I say, eyeing his street clothes. "I take it you're recovering? Or recovered?"

"Yeah, your timing is perfect. I'm checking out in an hour or so. Thanks for stopping by. You guys do that for all the people you rescue?"

"Not really. I came by to find out if you lost a phone up there?"

Davis's smile disappears. I watch his eyes shift to the door behind me. I turn, but the door remains shut.

"You with Duane and his friend?"

"Who?"

"Duane. Those two guys who were just in here. He was the short one built like a fireplug. Everyone's asking about my phone today." He squints at me. "And here I thought you were just checking up on me."

"Don't know Duane. But I do have information about your phone. Some hikers dropped it at our SAR building. They came across it yesterday near where we found you. I need to give it to the Sheriff's Office, but thought I'd stop by first and confirm you lost one."

Davis pushes off the bed's edge and stands. "You got it? You got it with you right now?"

I pull the phone from my pocket, and hold it up. "Look like yours?"

"Let me see the back of it." Davis grabs the phone from my hand.

"Hey–" I step forward.

Davis takes a step backward, twisting the phone in his hand. "Looks like mine. Let me check the code."

I nod, certain I've just made a mistake, but a tad uncertain at the protocol for this scenario. We rescued Mr. Davis on a standard search and rescue mission. Injured party in our jurisdiction. It was only after we loaded Davis into the ambulance that we found he had nearly died escaping a crime scene. I know the Sheriff's Office should decide when he gets the phone, but now he's already got it. And I'm not sure I have any authority to take his phone back from him.

Davis taps his fingers on the phone.

"Yours?"

Davis nods, his fingers still tapping.

"Yeah, I need to answer an email. Been stuck here for two days. It's not like I have anybody's cell phone number memorized.

"Bruce. I need it back. It's part of a crime scene. This needs to go through the Sheriff first."

"Just a sec." His fingers still work the phone. I step forward. He leans back. I debate physically taking the phone from him. He taps a button and thrusts the phone at me. "Sent."

I scan his phone in my hand. The screen is dark. I hit the button on the side and it asks for the code. I look at Davis, but don't have the nerve to ask.

"When do you think I'll get it back?" Davis smiles, almost like he recognizes my dilemma.

"Not sure about that. They're still investigating the case as far as I know. Bringing in the feds too. But I guess you know about all that, right? They've been talking to you?"

Davis nods. "Oh yeah. Been over that story enough times. They sent in three different interviewers to have me tell the same story. Two guys. One shooter. The woman in the van. My dead partner." He lets out a sigh. "Hopefully I'm done with that."

"What woman in the van? I thought it was just you and the other guard." Davis may not be interested in talking anymore, but he's just grabbed my attention.

"Not our van. Ours was a cargo van. These guys had one of those Sprinter vans. She was in there. Chinese maybe? Or Korean. I couldn't tell. She was staring at us from the center of the front windshield of their van."

"I'm not tracking. I thought there were two suspects. Now you say there were three people involved in the heist? And this all went down at night, right? How could you see into their vehicle?"

"Oh shit. Here we go again. When people ask, I'm going to tell them the cops interviewed me four times, OK? Can I count you as a cop?"

"Whatever."

"So we're parked up in the pass parking lot. The only other vehicle was the Sprinter at the other end of the lot. Of course, we weren't suspicious—people sleep in those things everywhere, right? We assumed it was hikers."

I nod and say nothing. Which is hard, because I want to know more about what this woman looks like. He said maybe Chinese?

"We haven't been there thirty seconds, and that Sprinter turns on its lights right behind us. Like it creeped across the lot and blocked us in. Now, I don't want to get into the details about what happened next. Already told the cops. Me and Paul fucked up. They got the jump on us and we gave up our weapons. They corralled us at the back end of our van. One guy's got his gun on us and is making us open up crates so they can see the art. The other guy is walking the parking lot to check for cars coming up either side of the pass. You know how those switchbacks are, right? You can see who's coming in either direction by walking twenty yards across the lot."

He's right. If you want a spot where you can monitor arriving traffic, the summit of Cottonwood Pass is perfect.

"So the guy calls out that a car is coming. The gun guy says 'get the lights.' The lookout guy moves back to their car and kills the lights. He turns on a flashlight and that's when I see the Asian gal. She's crouched between the seats. I can see the other guy talking to her. The gun guy looks away from us and yells to the lights guy, something like 'she's your problem—make her stay in the back,' or something along those lines. I nudge Paul, my partner, the other guard, to let him know now's the time to run. I bolt. But then—"

Davis chokes a little. "I mean, I didn't know Paul all that well. First time we've done a job together. But he breaks toward the front of the van while I run the other way. I hear the shots but just keep running. Didn't find out until later they killed Paul."

This is way more detail than Perez shared with me the other morning. The more Davis talks, the more his body tenses. I'm not really that interested in the whole gunshot sequence. It's this Asian girl in the van that has me laser focused.

"Why do you think they didn't want the girl watching if she was with them?"

"I'm not sure." He tilts his head. "The cops didn't ask me that one. I guess I didn't get the sense that she was in on the whole thing. The thieves were acting like they hadn't planned to have her along or something."

I've spent weeks getting over Kristee Li, trying to understand how one of probably four Asian women in their mid-twenties in the entire county could vanish without a trace. My talented but troubled friend disappeared only six miles from the summit of Cottonwood Pass.

I know she's gone. I know it's a month later. I know I have a tendency to see conspiracy in coincidence.

But they never found her body.

CHAPTER 5

When I drop off the phone at the Sheriff's Office, Perez is sitting behind his desk. I realize I've never seen him in an office environment. Salida is the county seat and where the Sheriff is headquartered, but Buena Vista is where Perez and his Tahoe spend most of their time. I hold back on the "desk jockey" jokes. Things aren't going as planned today.

"Davis know you found this?" Perez holds up the phone.

"I swung by on the way here. He knows you guys have it." Shit. Now I have to tell Perez about Davis sending the email.

"I thought I asked you not to get in—" A warbling tone fills the room. Perez turns to the radio console.

Attention all units. Attention all units. The fire at the hatchery has jumped. All units respond for evacuation enforcement.

The hatchery. That's the fire I passed on the way to Salida.

"Got to go." Perez walks past me toward the door. As he grabs his gear, he turns. "Stay out of this shit, Zahn. You're not law enforcement."

I intend to explain how right he is—to tell him about my mistake in letting Davis handle his phone. But Perez leaves before I utter a sound.

On the drive home, I try to shove thoughts of Kristee away. There's no way Davis saw her on the pass. Crazy thoughts. It's a good thing Perez is busy. If I'd revealed these Kristee musings, he might have locked me up and thrown away the key.

Twenty minutes out of Buena Vista, my phone buzzes in its dash mount. I read Laura's name on the screen.

I stab the answer button, heart pounding. *She's calling.* "Hey! Got you on speaker. Driving back from Salida."

"Hi, Tyler. Just checking in after last night. Sorry about the little argument there at the end. What'd you think of the Coker gals?"

I thought leaving before dinner was downright awkward. But I see no reason to share this with Laura. She and Monica can figure out their problems with this Duane guy on their own.

Duane. Same name as the hospital dude. I file that away for future reference.

"Really appreciated the invite, Laura. Always great to meet family." My daughter's sarcastic response "Not" pops into my head. I ignore it. "But we're still due a dinner for just the two of us, right? Any thoughts on that?" My voice involuntarily pitches up at the end of my questions. I cringe at my obvious desperation.

"Just about all I think about, big boy." Laura switches her voice to sultry.

I stifle a laugh and inadvertently let out a snort. We're both closer to fifty than forty, and this kind of stuff makes me laugh now. I pull myself together. Laura might not share my off-brand humor.

But Laura laughs too, before switching to her normal voice. "Can't be tonight, though. I've got a guest in town, and a favor to ask."

"What's up?"

"Tristen LaFrance just checked into his room at the Surf Hotel. He's my dinner date tonight. Can you believe it?"

I say nothing; my habit when I have nothing to say. I've never heard the name.

"*The* Tristen LaFrance. The owner of LaFrance Gallery in Ft. Worth?" Her emphasis on *The* indicates the man is important enough that Laura thinks even an art cretin such as myself must have heard of him. I'm prepared to continue the silent technique when Laura spills the beans.

"He's the owner of the stolen Remingtons."

Relieved from the pressure to guess, I follow on with the logical question. "Law enforcement made him travel all the way out here to interview? Why didn't they have someone from Dallas ask him questions?"

"No. That's not why he's here. He's already been through all that. He's coming out to see where it happened. To 'walk the ground,' so to speak." She lets out a small laugh. "Sounds kind of military-like, doesn't it? Did you do that stuff when you were in? Survey the battlefield?"

"It's a thing." I leave it at that. I've walked the beaches of Normandy with Army battalion commanders and studied Gettysburg with military historians. But I need to let Laura get to the point.

"It's kind of funny. Tristen is as far from the stereotypical warrior as you can imagine. He's exactly what you'd expect from someone named Tristen."

I'm not a hundred percent sure what she means, so I don't say anything.

"So what's the favor?"

"Can you take him up to Cottonwood Pass and show him where it happened? I told Tristen I would ask the Sheriff's Office if they'd do it. He didn't like that idea. He said he's had too much time with law enforcement lately. When I told him about you, he liked that plan better."

The whole time Laura's talking, I know I'm going to say yes. Not because I have the slightest interest in playing tour guide for this Tristen guy, but because I'm interested in getting Laura to do that sultry voice thing again.

"Sure, I can do that. When are we talking about?"

"He's got the whole day free tomorrow. Maybe longer after that if I can talk him into staying in town for my exhibition. What works for you?"

I glance at my watch. Plenty of time to knock out this task today if Tristen can deal with a change of plans. I need to get home and let Amore run around outside first. My gut tells me Tristen won't be a dog guy. Especially with a dog accustomed to roaming around my truck's interior. I survey the back seats in my rear-view mirror. Tristen might not be a guy who likes riding in trucks like mine, period. I'll need to do a quick clean up.

"I'd just as soon go today if he's up for it. I figure if I pick him up in two hours, I'll still have him back in time for his dinner with you. What do you think?"

"I'll give him a call. And, Tyler?" Laura switches back to that voice thing again.

"Yes?" Shit. My voice sounds like a frog's croak.

"Did I mention how much I'm looking forward to our own 'me-and-you' dinner?"

• • •

Tristen staggers when he steps from my truck at Cottonwood Pass. I grab his arm and turn to his photographer for some help. Nate, wearing an ear-to-ear grin, is already aiming for the parking lot's edge, snapping pictures on the way. From the guard rail, the switch-backed road winds like an alpine snake toward smoky Buena Vista—on a clear day it's one of the more iconic photos in this part of the Colorado Rockies.

"You OK?" I say to Tristen, even though I know he's not. He was gasping for air when I picked him up at the hotel, unaccustomed to the 8,000-foot elevation in Buena Vista. Now we're 4,000 feet higher. He still seems to be in shock from the twisting climb to the pass.

Tristen takes a pill, chasing it with the water I provided him and Nate. I don't ask what he's taking, but I doubt it is altitude sickness medication. Tristen rolls his eyes at me before speaking.

"You know I'm not. I always feel like a fish out of water back home in Texas. But obviously I'm not meant for Colorado either."

I smile at that. I haven't spent much time in Texas, but I'm guessing he's right. Tristen wears a light blue polo shirt and tan khakis without pockets. His shoes are polished leather and he's wearing a visor like I've seen golfers use. Not that I watch a ton of golf, but I've spotted the visors before while channel surfing. I worried about my truck smelling like dog when I offered to drive them, but now it smells flowery or tangy, like some kind of man spray, I guess. Tristen's definitely not the ten-gallon hat, Levi-wearing, belt-buckle-flashing stereotype I've come to expect from the largest state in the Lower 48.

Tristen turns a circle in the lot. "So, where did it happen?"

I point to the opposite end of the lot from where Nate snaps pictures. "This way."

We walk toward the sign marking the Colorado and Continental Divide Trails on the Gunnison side of the pass. Halfway across the lot, Tristen stops. I pause, waiting for him.

"We need Nate," he says. "We want pictures."

I turn toward where Nate disappeared to shoot pictures of the view. The young man is nowhere in sight. Tristen follows me back to the truck, where I check the back seat in case Nate climbed back inside. Nothing.

"Nate?" Tristen's voice rings shrill against the wind.

"Here." The voice comes from the guardrail. I move toward the edge, scanning left and right for the missing photographer. "Down here. I slipped."

Eight feet down the near vertical slope, Nate clings to a clump of grass while his designer sneakers scrabble for a purchase on the disintegrating slope. It's not like he's in mortal peril, but the pitch doesn't begin to level for another thirty feet. If Nate loses his grip, it's going to hurt by the time he stops sliding.

"Hold tight." I race back to my truck, where I open the rear canopy. I yank out my 24-hour bag used on SAR missions. Rummaging in the back pouch, I pull out one of two 15-foot cordelettes I use for a variety of purposes on our rescues.

"Oh my God!" Tristen's breath is ragged. "Should we call 911?"

I glance at the man before securing one end of the rope to the wooden post anchoring the guardrail to the pavement. I have to remind myself that these two see the situation differently than I do. Nate's waiting for a rope, feet dangling from the side of a 12K-foot mountainside. Of course these men are frightened.

What they don't realize is that I could climb down the slope to Nate and push him back up to the parking lot. I'm using the rope because I have it and…well, because I don't really want to go down there after him if I don't have to.

Three minutes later, Nate sits against the guard rail, feet splayed straight ahead in the parking lot, sipping the water I offer him.

"Oh my God, Nate. Are you alright? What the hell?" Tristen gives the young man a mini-lecture on safety. I decide to let them catch their breath while I put my ropes away.

When I return, I extend my hand to Nate. "Ready to go take a look at the scene?"

Nate looks at Tristen, then at my hand, as if he's unsure what to do. Tristen turns to me. "Do you think it's safe to move him?"

"Are you hurt, Nate?" I want to smile at Tristen's misplaced concern, but don't.

Nate shakes his head. "Just embarrassed is all."

I pull him to his feet. "Let's go check out where the van was parked."

Cleaning blood off asphalt is not a top priority in central Colorado. Drivers crash into elk, deer, and even moose, every day out here. It's hard for the road crews to keep up. So I'm not surprised bloodstains still mark the spot where Brandon radioed in the incident on our SAR channel.

I run through the robbery timeline with Tristen and Nate, weaving in the story of SAR's part in the rescue. Our organization didn't have much to do with the theft, but I never pass up an opportunity to promote our SAR work, especially in front of a potential donor.

Nate takes pictures of the blood-stained asphalt. He steps back for an angle, which puts the trailhead signs in the background.

"You might want to talk to law enforcement, Tristen. They might share some of their photos with you." I step backward so I'm not in Nate's crime-scene pictures.

"Do you think they would? Do you think they would give us digital copies?"

I figure Perez and his guys would show Tristen the pics, but I'm unsure if they would give them to him. "Are you planning on running your own investigation?"

"NFTs," Nate calls from behind his camera. "We're going to make NFTs."

Tristen looks at me and tilts his head toward Nate. "He's going to pick a single shot of the robbery scene and mint it."

"What do you mean mint it?"

"Nate, you want to explain the details or risk me screwing up the explanation?"

Nate looks up from his camera. "We're going to turn the picture into a non-fungible token, or NFT."

I consider myself a technology neophyte, but I have learned about the cloud, apps, and crypto over the last several years. I've heard of NFTs. Non-fungible tokens. I read an article about pictures of cartoon monkeys being sold for thousands of dollars. Something to do with an image that can transfer ownership through a digital ledger–called a blockchain. Because of the blockchain thingie, each NFT can be unique—and therefore, rare.

"But there are tons of pictures of this pass," I say. "I'm not sure why your picture would be unique."

Nate's smile fades. "Nothing is going to replace Tristen's Remingtons. And he's expecting to recover those." Nate glances at Tristen, who nods. "But in the meantime, Tristen is helping me with a side hustle. Sort of like squeezing opportunity from a crisis. This is the opportunity."

Nate looks at me like he's expecting to see a flash of understanding. He gets nothing.

"Our picture, after we mint it as an NFT, will be unique in several ways. It will be a picture from immediately after the theft of Tristen's art. But more importantly—" Nate stops speaking and waves his hand where he wants Tristen to stand near the trailhead sign at the end of the parking spot. Nate lines up the shot so that he gets the blood-spattered pavement, Tristen, and the view looking down from the pass.

Nate presses a button and the camera whirs as it takes multiple shots. He looks back at me and continues. "Most importantly, it will be the only picture in the world of the owner at the scene where his art was stolen."

"So you're going to make money off your boss's misfortune?" I turn to Tristen. "And you're OK with that?"

Tristen laughs. "More than OK. I'm Nate's angel investor. If his plan works, I'll make more money than he will."

I look from Tristen back to Nate, then shift my gaze to the mountains I've grown to love.

The mountains might be unpredictable but at least I understand them.

Art connoisseurs? Not so much.

CHAPTER 6

I drop Tristen and Nate at the hotel in time for their dinner date with Laura before pointing my truck toward home. Amore has been cooped up in the house for a couple of hours. He'll need dinner and a walk. But I'm hungry too, and the home fridge holds nothing but beer. Not as much beer as it held while I dealt with Kristee's disappearance. But enough for nutritional purposes. I squeeze into a parking spot at Rocks, Rapids, & Eats for a to-go order.

The line is three couples deep. I recognize the woman ahead of me. Laura's sister Monica nudges the man next to her. When he turns, I recognize him—the short, stocky guy I bumped into at my hospital visit to Bruce Davis.

"Duane, this is Tyler Zahn. Laura's friend."

Duane gives me an I-know-something-you-don't smile, like he's just passed gas and isn't going to admit it. His eyes dart from me back to Monica, then back to me before he thrusts his hand forward.

"Duane Dahl."

We shake while I try to guess if anything would be gained by mentioning our earlier meeting at the hospital. He hasn't brought it up in front of Monica, so I stay silent.

The line shifts. Monica moves forward, then turns again. "Tyler's the one who caught that asshole taking little girls last year." She looks at me. "Right?"

"Well, I was working with the Sheriff's Office." I don't go into the details because she got it right. Monica's already said more words in my presence than she did during the entire dinner the other night.

Duane appears interested. I'm unsure why. "You're with the Sheriff's Office?"

"Not yet. I'm working toward becoming a Reserve Sheriff." I don't tell him I'm on an indefinite leave of absence from the Law Enforcement Academy after the episode with Kristee Li. "I was just a liaison in that case from last year that Monica's talking about."

"Lee-ayy-zawn." Duane sounds like he's trying the word on for size. He turns to Monica. "He's friends with the law. Maybe he can get someone out to take a look at our problem."

"Shut up, Duane. He's Laura's friend—that's it."

"What's your issue?" I probably can't help, but I can't help asking.

Monica tugs on Duane's shirt, trying to turn him back to the counter, but Duane doesn't get the signal.

"Monica got her computer stolen last week. Her laptop. She called it in to the cops, but they haven't even sent anyone out."

Monica turns away, her body rigid. This is clearly a topic she does not want to discuss. I consider asking Duane more about the specifics of the theft, but decide I'd be better off preserving my new relationship with Laura than making friends with Duane.

"Been a busy week for law enforcement." I throw my comment out as a platitude. Duane recognizes it. He squints, waiting for me to speak again.

I don't.

"Well, it's sure been nice meeting you, Mr. Tyler Zahn." There's no mistaking the sarcasm in his voice. To seal the deal, Duane cuffs my shoulder before turning to Monica. I wait for her to lay into Duane again, but she stands as stiff and motionless as the rock formations on the outskirts of town.

I check behind me, curious if our awkward conversation has drawn interest from other customers. A woman outside the restaurant window waves at me. I shade my eyes from the glare of the interior lights. Julie Coker Keller, Laura's other sister, waves again. She points in my direction, then beckons me outside. I lift my hand toward the line, but she doesn't stop motioning for me to join her. Duane and Monica pay me no attention. I give up on takeout and head for the door.

Stepping outside, I scan both directions for Julie. She's nowhere in sight. A car flashes its lights in a slot three spaces down the street. I squint in that direction and it flashes its lights again. As I approach, the driver's side window lowers. Julie does that beckoning thing again. She must be good at it because here I am.

I lower myself into the passenger seat. Julie shifts into reverse.

"Where are we going?"

"Away from here. I still owe you the Coker sisters briefing."

Just when I've almost suppressed the awkward dinner, the jealous sister returns for another round. And I've made myself a captive audience.

•　•　•

Julie drives two blocks down Main Street before easing us down the gravel road to the River Park. She pulls in behind the public restroom. I flash back thirty years to my high school sweetheart, also named Julie, slipping the car behind the Brady Grange for a stolen hour of groping and professed love.

"Uh, Julie?"

Julie parks and turns off her headlights. I rest my hands on my knees, uncertain what else to do with them. She lets out a laugh.

"Relax. Just give me five minutes and I'll have you back to your car."

My smartass instinct is to say I might be late forties, but I'm good for more than five minutes. I don't. I'm pissed at finding myself "parking" with my would-be girlfriend's jealous sister instead of feeding my dog. Besides, I have no recent proof about the five-minute thing.

"Go." I debate glancing at my watch, but decide that might be too rude.

"You like Laura, right?"

I nod.

"OK. I'm not getting into the details about her. You can figure that out yourself. But I need to talk to you about Monica if you're going to pursue Laura."

I say nothing. Not because I can't think of anything to say. In fact, I want to ask if dating a Coker sister is a package deal or something? Call on one and you get the other two for free? But I've learned to save my off-the-top-of-my-head comments for Perez. And Williams, my US Marshal friend.

"Monica has issues. She always has, and I guarantee you, she always will. With three sisters growing up in the same household, you would think the whole nurturing thing would override nature. But not with Monica." Julie pauses, as if to make sure she has my attention. "Bad men, bad drugs, and no money. That about sums it up. She's never been married, and she's never stayed sober. She relies on Laura and me to pay for her house."

My online search for Monica hinted at drug and alcohol use, but this is more than I expected. Sure, I noticed Laura not drinking around Monica. Yes, things went off-kilter when Monica mentioned Duane. But I assumed these were normal family squabbles. I never guessed Monica was in such sad shape.

I'm even more concerned about why I'm sitting in a car down by the river with Julie talking smack about the family. Why do I need to know? "Julie, Why is this so important to share with me?"

Julie opens her mouth to answer. In a flash of self-awareness, I recognize she could misinterpret my question as uncaring. I keep talking. "Don't get me wrong. I'm sorry your sister suffers from addiction. It's obvious you and Laura must care deeply about helping her. I guess my question is, why do you feel the need to share this with me? I just met Laura. This is only the second time I've talked to you."

Julie nods. "We do care. Laura and I. But we care in different ways. I'm not trying to convince you which way is better. I'm just here to warn you that Laura's and Monica's relationship is not healthy. Laura provides support to Monica with conditions. Monica struggles with that. It can turn explosive at times." She stares at me like she's trying to see a glimmer of understanding. I figure she's coming up empty because she sighs instead. "I'm screwing this warning up. Let me cut to the chase."

"OK."

"Laura gives Monica a monthly subsistence check. Monica blew through the money Daddy left her years ago—all she has left is her share of the ranch property. I give her money too, but the bulk comes from Laura. I could give you some details about our outlays for rehab, times two, but that story is unrelated to your situation." Julie taps on the steering wheel, eyes straight ahead. "Laura's check comes with conditions. Monica has to show up sober to lunch with Laura once a week. Monica has to introduce Laura to any men in her life. Monica has to provide proof she's working. If Monica fails any of these tasks, Laura takes it out of the monthly check. Like she's docking her allowance or something."

Julie's story unnerves me. She's right about the analogy of the allowance. It sounds like Laura is treating Monica like a child. But who am I to judge? I don't know Monica. I barely know Laura. I'm still waiting to see how this affects me.

"Here's what you need to know. Monica has her problems, but she's also a fiercely independent woman. Headstrong. She might run with bad men, but she won't let any of them take advantage of her. And she doesn't take Laura's direction well. Let me give you an example. Two years ago, Laura was dating Drew Thompson, the town planner. Both divorced, both available, normal relationship. Until Monica wormed her way into bed with the guy."

I hold out my hand to pause this one-way conversation. I'm not interested in Laura's previous relationships. Even if I was, I'd expect to hear about them from Laura, not Julie. Sister rivalry? Save it for someone else.

But Julie seems to sense me withdrawing.

"And in case you think this might just be some inter-sister rivalry thing, where they both like the same guy? Guess again. Laura walked in on the two of them in Laura's bed…not Monica's."

My eyes widen, even though I'm trying to remain implacable.

Julie obviously notices. "There're other things too. None as obvious as the sleeping with Drew thing. Nothing that can be proven. But things that have Monica's fingerprints all over them if you know what to look for."

"Like?" I can't help myself. Julie has successfully wrapped me into this story.

"She started rumors about Laura's gallery. There was another sabotaged date for Laura—they came out from dinner and the guy's tire was slashed."

Holy shit. Now, I'm laser-focused on Julie's narrative. I can see why Laura might choose to be somewhat directive with Monica. She's obviously more than a handful.

I find it hard to imagine Laura dealing with all this. When we talk on the phone, she acts like I'm the most important thing in her life. Now I realize she's a lot like me—a master at compartmentalization.

But I'm a tad nervous about stepping into a long-running sister feud. Especially if I'm a potential target.

Julie seems to realize she's finally made her point. "Do you have any questions?"

I sure as hell do.

CHAPTER 7

I'm out of bed early the next morning, Amore at my side on a walk-run around the neighborhood. At almost nine-thousand feet elevation, I still spend more time on the walk part than the run part. Another man looking for excuses might blame it on my concussion last month, but I know better. It's just getting harder to run these days. Getting old sucks.

Something is different about the smoke today. It's not just a haze like before. Today it's heavier and has a taste to it. I'll check the news when I get back, but I suspect this might be from the hatchery fire. Or a new one. It's probably not the ideal day for exercise, but I can't afford to let myself slide. Besides, I owe it to Amore.

Laura interviews today with an FBI agent in the Art Theft Division. She's asked me to join them for lunch. I'm unsure why the FBI is talking to the owner of the only painting that didn't get stolen, but Laura seems unfazed. She assumes I'll be interested in talking to the agent because of my past, but I'm beginning to wonder if Laura is just afraid to have a meal alone with me.

One thing I'm sure of is that I'm not bringing up my conversation with Julie last night. I'm still processing everything Laura's sister shared with me about Monica and Laura and the family drama, but I'm certain that starting a conversation with Laura with the words "your middle sister told me your relationship with your younger sister is toxic" will be a non-starter.

Call me socially savvy.

•   •   •

I tap my phone on the way to town and glance at the warning about the new fire. They're calling it the Chalk Creek Fire and it's burning within two miles of the Mt. Princeton Hot Springs. Reports say it's under control. My wheels drift toward the shoulder while I'm reading and I chastise myself for multitasking.

I miss Laura on my first scan of the Surf Hotel's dining area. When I finally catch sight of her, I realize why. I'd been looking for a man and a woman, or specifically, an FBI male in a suit and Laura. Instead, Laura sits across from a tall, slender woman who stands as I approach. She's younger than I am—maybe mid-to-late thirties. I'm disappointed in myself for stereotyping this meeting.

The woman offers her hand. "I'm Agent Emma Frazier, Art Crimes Division."

We shake and I note Agent Frazier's calm confidence in her grip. No perceived need to out-squeeze me on the greeting. But no limp grasp, either. First impressions matter. Emma Frazier has made one on me.

"Tyler Zahn, retired," I say, pulling a chair between the two women.

"Doesn't sound like it. Laura's told me a bit about you. Seems like you stay busy."

I used to adopt the "aw shucks" look when people brought up my reputation. Before Kristee disappeared, I was known for assisting the Sheriff and the Marshals in stopping a terrorist operation, and later, for helping take down a child trafficker. But lately I'm wary about people bringing up my past. I'm unsure whether they've heard about the terrorist and kidnapper work, or the period where I unsuccessfully chased false leads, trying to discover what happened to Kristee Li.

"I try to help where I can."

No one speaks for a moment. The silence turns awkward, so I fumble for something to get us talking again.

"How did the interview go?" Oops. It's unlikely an FBI agent is going to share interview results with a civilian. Let alone one she just met.

But my question seems to trigger Laura because she jumps in, taking the lead in answering.

"Oh, Tyler, it was so interesting. We should have had you sit in on it. Emma here really knows what she's doing." Laura flashes a smile at Frazier, whose amused eyes tell me she's happy for Laura to answer my question instead of her. "Emma, can Tyler see what you showed me on your computer? Your lost painting program?"

Frazier reaches toward a case at her feet. "The missing art database?"

"Right, I want to show him where you have the Remingtons."

Frazier opens the laptop and jabs at a couple buttons. She turns the computer toward Laura. I scoot my chair closer to hers and look at the screen.

Laura presses her fingers on the screen and spreads them like she's trying to enlarge a cellphone image. "The font's too small." She swivels the computer toward Frazier. "This is why I don't own one of these things. Can you bring it back up and make it bigger?"

Frazier takes the laptop back. I reach into my pocket for my reading glasses and offer them to Laura. She refuses.

"I don't need those." Then she winks at me. "Not yet anyway."

Frazier hands the computer back to Laura. I keep the glasses at the ready, but Frazier has fixed the issue. Laura shows me the first Remington, the original *Bronco Buster* painted from the sculpture the artist had created of the same name.

"So the FBI has all the provenance listed for each missing item. Everything you would want to know about each piece is in their database." Laura glances at Frazier. "The arrow key, right?"

Frazier nods.

Laura brings up the other missing pieces, one at a time, and I nod as if suitably impressed. Actually, I am—I knew the FBI investigated art theft, but had no idea the resources they had at their fingertips.

Laura returns the laptop to Frazier before turning to me. "Isn't that data thing fascinating? I'm not really sure whether anything I had to say to Emma was helpful, but we really got to know each other. And, guess what?"

I don't have a clue, but I bite anyway. "What?"

"Emma's coming to the exhibition tomorrow. At The Lodge."

I raise my eyebrows at Frazier. "I guess one of the requirements to work in Art Theft is to be an art fan?"

"Not a requirement. But a lot of us are—including me. That's not the only reason I'm going. I'm supposed to interview Tristen LaFrance during this trip. We got our dates crossed. The rest of my team left today. I'm leaving tomorrow night, but he's committed to the exhibition. So we're interviewing while we're out there." Her head tilts. "Will you be there, Mr. Zahn?"

"You can call me Tyler. Yep. Wouldn't miss it." I smile. "Why? Do you need to interview me as well?" I throw my questions out as a joke, but Frazier nods before I finish my sentence. I continue, "You know I wasn't there, right? I'm sure Laura explained to you I was the SAR incident commander back at the office during the theft. I didn't actually go to the site until yesterday, after law enforcement processed it."

"And you can call me Emma. I'm aware you weren't on scene, but I have some questions for you about how the SAR call originated. Timelines, radio calls, and such. Are you OK with that?"

"Sure. I'll need to pull the SAR logs off the shared drive if we're going to talk about communications and times. Not a problem."

"People are buzzing about the show, Tyler. God, I hope that Chalk Creek Fire stays contained." Laura rests her hand on my forearm. "Almost everyone RSVP'd. Now we've got Tristen and Emma coming.

Rumor is, there's a big-name buyer coming too. Martin Algood. It's going to be so much fun."

Fun isn't how I'd describe any event requiring me to dress up, make small talk with strangers, and pretend to understand paintings. But I am looking forward to the exhibition. It means so much to Laura. Seeing the artist side of her doing her artist thing will help me understand her better.

And I don't have to worry about standing in a corner with no one to talk to. The FBI has let me know they have questions for me.

CHAPTER 8

The route from my place in Elk Trace to The Lodge where Laura will display her art takes only fifteen minutes, a quick drive south along the Collegiate Peaks foothills. Normally, I see Mt. Princeton on my way out of the neighborhood and turn right at the first paved road toward Cottonwood Pass. Today, wildfire smoke obscures our iconic mountain and I navigate by rote memory.

Laura has overcome so many challenges to put on this show. Her painting was almost stolen, just thirteen miles up the pass from her planned exhibition. Then the Sheriff's Office held her painting while they investigated the thefts of the Remingtons. The scent of acrid smoke seeps into my truck, a reminder of the third factor that almost canceled the exhibition—the two-day-old Chalk Creek Fire. Although the fire started in the next mountain valley over from The Lodge, it still rages only five miles south of the venue. Laura had to plead her case to the Joint Fire Team to approve the exhibition. Prevailing winds in the valley typically run from the mountains toward the Arkansas River; the firefighters don't have reason to think the fire will burn north up the mountain range. In fact, they're hoping it will stall out today as it crawls down to the treeless Upper Arkansas River Valley.

I drive through The Lodge's ranch-style entry arch, noting the parking lot is only a quarter full. Small cabins dot the perimeter, reminding me The Lodge is more than just an event venue. They host guests, as well.

Laura asked if I could arrive a half-hour before the opening to help set up. Not the one-on-one time I've been angling for with her, but a step in that direction. And I'm always up for lending a hand. I've shoved away all of Julie's backstory on her sisters. This is Laura's day. And she needs my help.

I pull my phone from the dash mount and jam it in my front pocket. I've scanned the SAR events log onto my phone's Files app for the FBI. Stepping from my truck, I pat the sides of my pants for my wallet before remembering I'm in jeans today. When Laura suggested I wear denim, I thought she was passing judgment on my standard utility-oriented 7-pocket pants that went out of style a decade ago. But when she also proposed a cowboy hat, I realized she was trying to clue me in on the exhibition's western theme. I agree to the jeans. The cowboy hat is a non-starter. Not because I don't herd cows or horses; although that excuse crosses my mind. I simply don't own one. The only thing appealing about a hat is it hides my bald spot and most of my increasingly graying hair.

Laura waits in the entryway. She greets me with a light touch of her lips on my cheek.

"Everything's on track, Tyler." Her eyes glow. "The caterers are all set up. The guys from the gallery are with Julie, positioning my pieces. I even found a hundred masks people can wear if they're worried about the smoke. They're stacked on the table inside if you want one." She looks past me at the haze smothering the parking lot. "I can't believe we have to put up with this.."

I smile. "I can't believe they let you go on with the exhibition with a fire this close."

Laura shifts her eyes back to mine and frowns.

I realize my lack of faith sounds more like I didn't believe Laura could convince the authorities than it does concern for her safety. "I'm glad they did, though," I add.

Her expression softens. "Will you stand with me? Here? When the guests arrive? I'd like the company."

My heart swells. Asking me to help greet her guests is like a public announcement that we're dating. We're not, of course. But if Laura is willing to let the public think we are, she must be entertaining thoughts of us spending future time together. I just hope that eventually includes some one-on-one time.

"You bet. We can practice right now. Here comes Monica."

Laura's gaze shifts from me to the lot. The softening in her expression freezes. "Oh, no. I thought I was clear about Duane." She squints. "Who's the other guy?"

I follow her gaze and recognize Bruce Davis exiting from the rear door. Laura hasn't met Davis, as far as I know.

"That's Bruce Davis. The security guard from the panel van. The one who survived—" I stop speaking, realizing how stupid my statement sounds. Of course he's the one who didn't die. Laura must recognize the name. It was his name on the radio that alerted her to the fact that her *Broncho Buster* was involved in the art heist. "I guess they're friends. Did you know that?" What I'm really wondering is whether Agent Frazier knows about this relationship. If she doesn't, I'll need to fill her in.

"Duane recommended Davis for the job. They used to work together. This is my first time seeing him in person." Laura appears pensive. "I'm not making a scene, or sending Duane away. We'll just deal with it. But let me ask you something."

"What?" My response is automatic. I'm still stuck on *Duane recommended Davis for the job*. No wonder she's pissed about Duane's involvement in the almost-theft of *Broncho Buster*.

"Do you think I'll be expected to mention Mr. Davis during my speech? I mean, is he considered a hero in this whole thing?"

I ponder that. The art thieves held-up Davis. He escaped, allowing the theft of the property he signed up to protect. I don't fault him for that—if they had killed my partner, I'd have run too. But nothing Davis did explains why the thieves ignored Laura's art.

"I think it's up to you. You certainly don't need to make him a hero, but you could acknowledge his recovery. Say how happy you are to see him here."

Laura smirks. "Look at you with the politically correct advice. Such depth. I thought you were just the local town hero."

I protest, but Laura lays her hand on my forearm. "Just teasing, Z-man. Good advice. I'll use it."

I nod without answering, wondering where she heard my SAR nickname "Z-man."

Monica and the two men approach the entry. "You remember Duane, right, Sis?"

I'm struck at how confident she sounds compared to the restaurant where Laura influenced what Monica drank and tried to dictate who she could bring to the exhibit.

Laura takes the high road. She steps forward, accepting an awkward hug from Duane before turning to Bruce Davis.

"And you're the survivor. Mr. Davis. I'm so happy you're recovering. Thanks for joining us today."

I note how she shapes Davis's expectations. He's welcome to attend but shouldn't expect a hero's reception.

Davis thrusts his hand forward. "Thanks for having me. You can call me Bruce." He turns to Duane and shrugs before turning back to Laura. "I just—well, Duane and me know each other. From our security work. And I told him I wanted a chance to see something else that made it through that night besides me. I wanted to see your painting."

Laura's smile appears bemused. "My painting survived because it wasn't valuable enough to take. I hope that doesn't say anything about why you made it through that night."

I glance from Davis to Laura. My daughter's college friends would have called Laura's remark a "burn."

Davis squints. I'm pretty sure the gears in his head are turning fast, trying to decipher what Laura just said. Or what an appropriate response might be.

Finally, he shakes his head. "The doctors gave me a clean bill of health. I'll be heading back to Denver tomorrow."

The three guests continue into the lodge. Laura whispers into Monica's ear, loud enough for me to hear, "Stick with the fruit punch, honey. It's on the right."

Monica doesn't even turn her head.

"She seems different from the other night," I say. "More sure of herself or something." I pause for a moment. "You too. Nice little dig you gave Davis."

Laura sighs, ignoring my last comment. "Monica's tripping on something. I'm not sure what she's taking, but I can always tell when she's on something."

We return to the doors to greet the steady flow of arriving guests.

"There's Emma." Laura points at the FBI agent striding toward us. "I like her."

I nod. I like her too, but don't voice my opinion. Just like yesterday, Emma Frazier radiates an aura of professional competence that reminds me of my friend Kristee. Like a Kristee ten years older. Frazier smiles as she approaches us and shakes our hands.

"Thanks again for accommodating my schedule," Frazier says, as if Laura had the option of turning down a request from the FBI. "Is Tristen here yet?"

"Not yet," Laura says. "But he promised he'd come. His photographer volunteered to shoot footage for me."

"Did you know Bruce Davis is here?" I offer. "Maybe you can knock off two birds while you're asking questions?"

Frazier gives me a nod as if she appreciates the heads up. "Interviewed him yesterday morning before they released him from the hospital. Didn't know he'd be here today, though. Thanks."

"Are you Laura Coker Long?" The voice comes from behind Frazier. She turns and steps to the side, allowing a short, heavyset man to step forward. He positions himself in front of Frazier.

Frazier looks over his head at us and mouths, "I'll go on in."

Laura lowers her eyes to the man before reaching out and grabbing his hand. "You're Martin Algood, right? Thanks so much for coming."

Algood nods, pulling his hand from Laura's. I'm momentarily curious at Laura's obvious deference to the man. Then I remember—Martin Algood is the potential buyer. He's traveled from Jackson Hole, Wyoming, to decide whether to purchase *Broncho Buster*.

Laura opens her mouth. I presume she's introducing me, but Algood speaks first. "Where's the painting?"

"Inside—" Laura begins, but Algood interrupts, rolling his eyes.

"I know it's inside. This is an exhibition, so I assume there will be other pieces, as well. So either give me directions to the *Broncho Buster*, or take me there yourself."

I've yet to see Laura flustered, but the next ten seconds are pretty close. Two more groups of visitors are walking in our direction. She turns to me, raising her eyebrows.

I'm about to volunteer to take Algood to the painting—even though I'm not sure where it's at—when Laura turns to him. "Mr. Algood, of course I'll take you. Follow me." She grabs his elbow and steers the man inside. She turns back to me as she crosses the foyer and tilts her head at the parking lot. Translation? *Tyler, can you greet the guests while I'm gone?*

I can, and I do, providing a tight smile while grinding my teeth. Acting as the sole greeter for a ritzy art exhibition was not on the list of things I imagined I'd do when I woke this morning.

Ten minutes later, I'm conflicted about my duties. Laura hasn't returned. The exhibition is supposed to have started five minutes ago. It's not that we don't have plenty of guests—the inside of the lodge is packed. But Tristen and his photographer haven't arrived yet. I wait another minute before Julie tugs my arm.

"Laura says you're probably out here waiting for Tristen?"

I nod. "And the photographer, Nate. Last expected guests, I think."

"She says forget him. Come join the party. She wants you up front by the podium for her speaking part. Follow me." Julie turns and walks into The Lodge. I follow. The masks for the smoke are still stacked high on the table. Either the ventilation is good inside the lodge or no one is too worried about the smoke.

Julie glances back at me. "Watch yourself, today."

"What do you mean?"

"Laura's wound tight as a clock. Monica's tripping on something. I'm not saying anything is going to happen, but the conditions couldn't be worse."

I don't respond. I've almost decided Julie might be the sister I should worry about. Of course Laura is nervous. Who wouldn't be for an event like this? Monica looks like she's having a great time. We pass by her, Duane, and Davis, and she toasts me with a glass of something clear. Not punch. So really, the only person forecasting doom and gloom—again—is Julie.

Laura steps to the podium. No mask for her. Maybe everyone is following her lead. I know she's stressed about this event, but I wonder if anyone else picks up on it. Her hands are firm as they grip the lectern. She surveys the audience for a good thirty seconds before beginning. This is a woman accustomed to public speaking.

"I'd like to welcome you all to The Lodge and thank you for—" she stops, at the sound of commotion in the rear of the room. I look past the last row of seats. Nate, Tristen's photographer, is squeezing between audience members to photograph Tristen's arrival.

I turn back to Laura. She's doing that lip pursing thing again. But then her eyes meet mine, the corners of her mouth turning up. I raise my eyebrows. She turns back to the podium.

"Thank you for taking the time to come see our little exhibition, especially after the tragic theft that occurred last week and with the nearby wildfire causing all the smoke. And a special thanks to Mr. Tristen LaFrance, the owner of the stolen Remingtons, for attending today."

Laura nods toward the back of the crowd. The audience turns as one. Tristen gives a small wave as applause ripples through the crowd. Laura gestures to the empty chair on her left. Tristen works his way up front.

Laura's magnanimous gesture doesn't surprise me. This is her day, her event, and her painting. Tristen has suffered a substantial loss, but it's a loss of personal property, not his first-born child. Laura is allowing the entire attention of the crowd to shift from her to Tristen. The same way she did the night I met her, when she ignored my questions about her and got me talking about myself. Something I rarely do.

The way she joined Monica in abstaining from alcohol at dinner. Because she's a caring soul.

I was first attracted to Laura's physical appearance. No, that's not how I usually start a relationship, but it's true in this case. The moment I saw her, something stirred in me. And not just in my heart. That she seems interested in me also played a role. I'm unsure how middle-aged romance works for others. I'm new to it myself. I'm guessing that finding someone who likes you back is probably half the battle.

"But most of all, I'd like to say thank you to the residents of this valley, from Leadville all the way down to Salida." Laura pauses, scans the crowd, and then points at someone in the back, and laughs. "Some of you came from even farther than that. Thank you for your support for my gallery and for putting up with the smoke to join us today." Laura's smile widens. "I declare the exhibition officially open. Enjoy!"

Applause fills the room. Laura steps from the podium, her eyebrows lifted in a *how'd I do?* expression. Not that there is more than one answer to that unspoken question, but I'm still flattered she values my opinion.

"Fantastic, Laura. I mean, I knew you were a special artist. Your paintings are really good." I fumble at my words because Laura knows I'm clueless as to what caliber of artist she is or how to judge her work. But she just gives me that smile, like she expects me to keep stumbling forward. So I do. "I just didn't realize how much respect this community has for you. Or how natural you look up at that podium talking to them." Laura nods. I've hit the right tone. "You had them eating out of your hand. Total control."

Crash. Laura's smile freezes. She squints at me. I scramble to rephrase my last sentence, but she reaches out and grabs my forearm before I can speak.

"Tyler, that's not how you see me, is it? Someone who has to be in control?"

I say nothing, swaying my head in a "no" like a cow avoiding flies.

"Let's just stick with the part about how you liked my welcoming remarks."

I nod, still silent. Laura is like chocolate-chip cookies—or beer. The more I have, the more I want. And I want to spend more time with her.

I just need to work on my conversational skills.

CHAPTER 9

Agent Frazier stands beside me, admiring the small sculpture of a tired cowboy slumped on a horse that appears as worn out as its rider. She turns toward me. "What do you think?"

The bulk of the audience mills around the main attraction: the *Broncho Buster* painting. Avoiding the crowd, I'm checking out some of Laura's lesser-known pieces.

I nibble at a pastry filled with spinach and bacon, and read the name of the piece. *Still Standing.* "If you're asking me about quality, you're asking the wrong guy. The best I can do is tell you I think this is bronze."

Frazier laughs. "You're right, it's a bronze. Do you see how she imitates her painting style in her sculpture? Everything for Laura is about texture. Her work makes you want to touch it." Frazier looks at the crowd surrounding *Broncho Buster.* "I'm surprised she doesn't have more issues with that. People touching her work."

"I didn't even know she did sculpture. I thought she just did paintings."

"What about the exhibition? How do you think it's going?"

I take a last glance at the piece before shifting my gaze to the crowd. "I'd say it's a success. Especially when you consider how close it came to never happening."

Frazier nods. She turns to the window next to the main entrance. Smoke still blankets The Lodge. The cars in the lot are barely visible. The ventilation proves somewhat effective in the exhibit area but the lobby smells like a Boy Scout campfire. "Right. Art thefts aside, I'm surprised they let the event proceed with all the smoke from the fire. I guess they know what they are doing."

"Did you interview him?" I nod toward Tristen LaFrance across the room. He stands to the side of *Broncho Buster*, talking to Martin Algood. Nate bobs in the crowd, trying to capture a shot of Tristen, Algood, and the painting.

"Not yet. Mr. LaFrance is one of those people who likes to do things on their own timeline. I'll give him another fifteen minutes before I remind him of our appointment."

"You think it's a money thing? Like those kinds of people purposely make your job hard because they want you to know who's in control?"

Frazier furrows her brow. "I know what you're saying. I've seen that before." She glances at me. "Obviously you have as well."

Laura must have shared more with Frazier than just my Colorado time. Frazier's not wrong. I've seen it in the military. Not so much the money part of it, but how people with power, or those close to it, use it to remind us who's in charge. We would get 20-year-old civilian aides to the Secretary of State or Commerce or something, and I swear, they would demand schedule changes because they could. But Frazier doesn't want to hear my stories. I say nothing.

"I don't think Mr. LaFrance is doing this on purpose," Frazier says. "My first impression is that he just marches to his own drummer."

She's probably right. The typical billionaire who had his most expensive art stolen wouldn't personally travel to the crime scene to check it out for themselves. They would hire someone to do it for them. Your average wealthy art owner wouldn't agree to be interviewed at an art exhibition. They would have told Frazier to "have your people coordinate with my people." Frazier's quick assessment of Tristen LaFrance seems spot on.

"Agent Frazier, let me ask you something."

"Emma, please."

"OK. Emma. Did you already know Duane Dahl and Bruce Davis were friends?

"We did. Not so much the nature of their relationship, but we're aware of it." She pauses. "And looking into it."

I nod and move to my real question. "You said you interviewed Bruce Davis, right? About the heist?"

"Yes."

"Did he mention anything to you about a third person involved in the theft? Someone that never got out of the vehicle."

Frazier tilts her head. "Where did you hear that?"

"I stopped by the hospital to talk to Davis after someone dropped off his cell phone at our SAR headquarters. He told me about the woman."

Frazier winces. "Ah, I see. You're the one who let him have his phone before we had time to look at it."

"No. I mean, I took it to the Sheriff's office after I talked to Davis." I'm unsure why I don't immediately admit she's right. It's like I'm in junior high wanting to say *it wasn't me.*

"Right. But Davis had his hands on the phone. You gave it to him? Then took it back?"

She's busted me. "Yeah, he said he sent an email."

Frazier presses her lips together, but says nothing.

She doesn't have to.

CHAPTER 10

My phone buzzes. When I step from the exhibit hall to the lobby to take the call, Julie makes a beeline for Laura. I glance back at Frazier, who has her phone pressed to her ear. I tap "accept" on my phone. The initials "RP" tell me who's calling. Deputy Sheriff Rick Perez.

"Hey Rick."

"Yeah, Z-man. Are you still at that art shindig at The Lodge?"

"Yep. What's up?"

"Your artist friend isn't answering her phone."

Across the room, Julie is showing her phone screen to Laura. "I'm not surprised. She's hosting her show. Kind of busy."

"Any law enforcement up there with you?"

I review the guests I greeted at the door. No uniforms. Didn't recognize any cops. "I don't think so." I reconsider. "Wait. We've got Emma Frazier. The FBI agent."

"Why's she there?"

"Interviewing Tristen LaFrance. You going to tell me what's up or make me guess?"

"Nothing too serious." Perez goes silent for a beat. "I hope. The wind shifted on the Chalk Creek Fire. We need you all to shut down that art show. Get folks back to Buena Vista. I'm a little short-handed right now. I called the BV Police, but they say they'll be another hour at least. Could I talk you into making the announcement? Make sure people start moving?"

"Got it." It's a simple request—a tough one to screw up. "What about the permanent residents? The folks who take care of this place?"

"Let them know what's up. I think we're talking another day or more if the winds stay the same. They can wait a while longer if they need to get stuff out of there, but make sure they have connectivity to Wi-Fi or a landline to Chaffee Fire to follow the status." Perez's voice trails, like he has more to add. "I'd recommend they come out with everyone else, though."

"Got it. I'll give you a holler with an update after I get folks moving."

I return inside. Laura stands by the podium at the front of the room, looking from side to side as if she's missing something.

She zeroes in on me, eyebrows rising as I approach."Did you hear about the fire?"

I nod. "Sheriff's Office wants me to get everyone moving. I'm going to use the microphone, alright?" I point to the podium.

"OK." Laura grabs my arm. "Will you stay and help me load my art?"

How could she think I would leave her? "I'm not going anywhere without you or your work. Let me get folks notified and heading the right direction first. Of course I'll stay."

"Attention. May I have your attention please?" Heads turn in my direction. Conversation stops. "We have received a message from the Chaffee County Sheriff's Office. The Chalk Creek Fire has shifted." A low murmur begins as the visitors turn to each other, deciphering the news. "Although it has started moving this way, it likely will shift again based on the wind forecast. Even if it doesn't shift away, they estimate it would take more than a day to reach this location."

"Are the roads clear?" A voice from the back of the room calls out.

I nod, scanning the crowd. "They are. As a precaution, the exhibit is closing. We are asking all attendees to depart immediately." The murmurs morph into a rumble. "In an orderly fashion."

Patrons surge toward the main doors. Unsure if I've injected the right amount of calm into my announcement, I lean into the microphone again. "I repeat, this is a precaution. Not an emergency.

Please take your time. Gather your belongings and proceed to your vehicles. If you would like, you can grab a mask for the smoke on the way out. You should move with a purpose, but there is no need to panic."

Heads nod, but eyes still flare like a bronco who's smelled a grizzly, as the visitors surge toward the front entrance. Agent Frazier appears at my side. "Anything I can do to assist?"

My smile is tight. "Guess you're not getting that interview with Tristen, huh?"

Frazier shakes her head. "I can't find him. His photographer is still here. He doesn't know where he went, either."

"That's not good." I fix my eyes on Frazier. "Why don't you keep looking for him? And anyone else who might have left the main exhibit area. I'm helping Laura pack her art. I'll come back to you when we're done for a final sweep of the place."

Frazier nods, turning toward the staircase by the foyer. I walk through the kitchen, heading for the service entrance at the back of The Lodge. I push the door open. Laura paces the rear access road, her hands out to the side.

"They're gone. You made that announcement and everyone just bolted. I can't find the caterers."

"Caterers?" I'm unsure why she's worried about the food.

"They're the ones who unpacked and displayed my artwork. It's part of their contract to pack it up at the end."

I check the access road. Two cars remain parked on the shoulder. "Are you sure? Maybe they just moved their vehicles after everything was loaded inside."

Laura's face is slack. "What am I going to do, Tyler?"

A couple of days ago, I had almost volunteered my truck to haul Laura's art from the Sheriff's Office in Salida to Buena Vista. Now the idea doesn't look so crazy.

"Wait inside. I'll bring my truck around and we can load the stuff in the back." I point to the crates at the bottom of the stairs. "We don't have to pack it perfectly. But we can use the same crates they used to deliver it here. We can recruit some folks to ride in the back with it to make sure it's secure." I pause. "Hell, I'll ride back there. You can drive the truck."

Laura meets me halfway on the stairs, giving me a quick hug before moving inside. I continue to the road and loop around The Lodge to the front parking lot. My tan Tundra is barely visible through the smoke, one of only a smattering of vehicles left in the lot. I pull out and circle the lot to the access road leading to the back of The Lodge.

Back at the service entrance, I reverse into the loading area. The crates I suggested for Laura's painting still sit by the stairs. I stride through the kitchen into the exhibition room, where I stop in my tracks.

Later, I won't remember whether I froze because of sound or sight. A high-pitched wail, something less than a scream but more than a moan, fills the exhibition. A small group of people—Monica, Julie, and Tristen off to one side—surround a figure kneeling on the floor. Even from the other side of the room, I recognize Laura. The easel by her side is empty.

As I rush toward her, Agent Frazier lowers to a knee, resting a hand on Laura's shoulder.

"What's going on?" I step into the gap between Julie and Monica, trying to decide if I should join Frazier at Laura's side. Laura doesn't appear injured. I can't understand what's happening.

Monica turns to me, her head shaking. "It's *Broncho Buster.* Someone took it."

My eyes shift to the empty easel. In the scramble to leave The Lodge, someone has taken advantage of the chaos to steal Laura's most-prized piece of art.

I whip my head around the room. It's not like this is a big city exhibition. I can count the number of attendees.

Who stole *Broncho Buster*?

CHAPTER 11

I thank God FBI Agent Emma Frazier is here.

Not in an actual prayer—just a momentary flash in my head. I'm still working out the religious side of my life. My second chance with my daughter, and my new life in the Rockies, isn't luck. It's something more powerful. I just haven't paused long enough to ponder what that something is.

What I do know is I can't handle a wildfire evacuation and an art theft without Agent Frazier.

I scan the room. Duane has his arm around Monica, who shudders into his shoulder. Julie's eyes shift between her sisters, as if she's positive one of them is at fault. Bruce Davis is former law enforcement—maybe he can help Frazier. But he lacks a certain credibility after running from the art heist on the pass. The prospective art buyer, Martin Algood, stands to the side shaking his head and checking his watch, while Tristen appears to be waiting for me to speak. Nate is head down, fumbling with his cell phone. I'm unsure why these last three men haven't left like everyone else.

The only others in the room wear black slacks and white shirts. I'm guessing these are Laura's caterers with additional duties as movers of art. They hadn't left after all.

Frazier looks up. "Can you sit with Laura? I need to talk to everyone here."

I kneel on Laura's other side. Her back quakes under my hand. I lean forward, whispering in her ear. "Hey, it's Tyler. I'm here." Laura's sobbing continues. She gives no sign she's heard me.

Frazier moves to the front of the fireplace. "Here's the deal, folks. Normally, in a situation like this, we would lock this place down until we could log all the attendees' contact info and do some preliminary interviews." She looks around the room. "This scenario is going to play out a little differently. You've all heard about the wind shift and the fire."

Heads nod. Everyone knows about the fire.

"So we're going to need to leave. Mr. Zahn will help me with your names. I'm asking you to reconvene down at the police station after we depart here. Does everyone understand?"

More bobbing heads. Except for one.

"Uh, no." Martin Algood shakes his head. "I don't believe I have time for that."

"My God, man," Tristen LaFrance interjects. "You, of all people, should understand what's happened. Do your part."

Algood provides LaFrance with a tight smile before facing Frazier. "I didn't see who took the painting." He sweeps his hand toward the small group of people. "And just like everyone else in this room, I doubt I'm a suspect. After all, they have just stolen it in the last minutes and they took it frame and all. We're all still here. Unless you think one of us has it under our jacket?" He coughs a dry laugh. Even from where I kneel, I can tell no one laughs with him.

Algood has a point about *Broncho Buster*. It's the size of a card table in the frame. Even if someone cut out the canvas, the rolled-up painting would be over three feet long. And what about Laura's thick, textured style? I'm not sure you can roll *Broncho Buster* without destroying it.

I'm sure Frazier wasn't expecting arguments, so I marvel at her poise. She clasps her hands. I detect zero tension in her posture.

"Mr. Algood, correct?" Frazier says. It occurs to me the two probably haven't yet met. She had wisely ducked inside when Algood made the scene at the door about seeing *Broncho Buster*.

Algood nods.

"You both have a point," Frazier continues, glancing from Algood to LaFrance. "You are correct in your assumption that you all are not suspects. But you all are potential witnesses."

Several people nod, but not Algood, who seems to wait for Frazier to continue.

"But Mr. LaFrance also has a point. I am asking everyone in this room to do their part so we can track down this painting. We don't have time for me to ask the right questions here. So I'm asking—not demanding—you to agree to meet me at the station where I will arrange an interview schedule. Does that sound reasonable?"

"No." Algood says. "I'm not doing it."

"I will." LaFrance dips his chin toward his photographer. "And so will Nate."

"I'm in," Davis says. He glances at Duane and Monica, who both nod.

"Thank you. Mr. Algood, find a pen and paper and leave me your contact info. Do it now."

Algood stiffens, obviously unaccustomed to taking orders. He heads toward the reception desk to follow Frazier's instructions.

Frazier's eyes follow Algood for several seconds before focusing back on me. "Do you know everybody else?"

I survey the group surrounding Frazier, pausing at the staff members in the rear. "I'm sorry. I don't know your names."

"I'm Mike. Mike Ove." A bearded young man, who looks a couple years older than my college-aged daughter, swings his hand toward the two women beside him. "These are my coworkers—they're my friends, too. They can leave their contact info." The women raise their hands in a motion so tentative, I wonder if they are certain of their own names. "The Lodge's owner, Mr. Harris, isn't here today. We're the set-up crew. And the caterers. Mr. Harris gave us the keys. He told me I'm in charge of the premises. I can be the last out and lock up."

Frazier nods. "Did you all ride together, or do you have your own cars?"

"Own cars," Mike says. "We're parked out front. My coworkers have been loading the food trays in the van."

No wonder Laura thought the set-up crew had deserted her.

Frazier points to the two women. "You all leave your contact info, then head out. I want to minimize the number of people staying behind. Mike, you provide yours as well. I want you to stay. Can you help us load the art and close up behind us?"

"Yep."

"Mike. You said you're responsible for The Lodge?"

"That's what Mr. Harris said."

"Do I have your permission to search The Lodge?"

Mike rolls his eyes. "Yeah. Of course."

Frazier eyes the crowd. "I want the rest of you to leave." She turns to me. "Get Laura in your truck, then you and Mike load the art. I'll do a walk-through of The Lodge while you guys are packing and see what I can find."

She turns to the cluster still surrounding her. "I've given you instructions. Move out." Frazier has added a sharpness to her tone that seems to penetrate the audience's inertia. I watch as Tristen, Nate, and Algood head for the door.

Duane grabs Monica's hand. "Let's go."

Monica resists momentarily, glancing at Laura, but Julie steps to her side and nudges her toward Duane. "I'll help with Laura. You go."

Two minutes later, it's just five of us: Frazier, Julie, Laura, Mike the caterer, and myself. Julie helps me get Laura on her feet.

"Let's get you out of here." Julie wraps her arm around Laura.

Her voice seems to snap Laura out of her shock. "What do you mean *out of here*? We're not going anywhere until the cops get here. I want my painting."

Julie raises her eyebrows in my direction. Laura's voice carries a tone I've never heard. I step forward, but Frazier intervenes and approaches Laura.

"Law enforcement isn't coming, Laura. Not until this fire warning lifts. We need to load the rest of your work into the truck and get out of here."

"You expect me to leave *Broncho Buster*? To just let it burn?" Laura turns to me, as if expecting support.

Frazier looks like she's thinking the same thing I am—that The Lodge is the last place we'd expect *Broncho Buster* to be. Odds are, someone took advantage of the evacuation turmoil and bolted with the painting.

Frazier explains this to Laura in a quiet voice, assuring her she will search the building while we're packing. Laura's shoulders shake again.

"Take care of her." Frazier grips Julie's arm before heading for the stairs.

I turn to Mike. "Let's move the packing material from the pantry out here. We can decide how much wrapping we're going to do."

He joins me as I stride across the exhibition area.

A voice stops me in my tracks halfway across the room. "You know she did it."

Laura stands in front of Julie, shaking her finger.

Julie backs away. "Who?"

"Our little sister and her crooked boyfriend. They knew about that thing on the mountain. They are in on this. I don't know what's going on, but I know they're involved."

Mike seems to recognize family drama when he sees it, continuing through the door to the kitchen. I am mesmerized by the venom in Laura's voice. Obviously, she remains in shock.

Julie has made the bad blood between Laura and Monica very clear, as if she's trying to use their relationship to drive a wedge between me and Laura. But this is the first time I've seen Laura say a bad word about Monica.

And it's more than bad words. Laura just accused her sister of robbery.

CHAPTER 12

Mike and I wedge among the crates of paintings shelved in the bed of my truck. Smoke drapes the loading dock in an orange haze, like an Iraqi sandstorm from my Air Force days. I twist toward the cab, slapping the truck's side.

"Ready back here," I call to Laura, who grips the steering wheel. She's not happy about leaving without *Broncho Buster*, but Agent Frazier has searched The Lodge and come up empty. We have no reason to think the painting's still here.

Laura shifts into gear. We pull from the loading dock and maneuver around The Lodge. My truck decelerates as we skirt the front parking lot on the access road. Just past the junction at the parking lot exit, a line of four vehicles clogs the single lane to the main road. I stand between the crates, resting my hands on the cab's roof. Monica and Julie are in what appears to be a heated discussion with Martin Algood. I tap the side of the truck again. Laura brakes.

"I'm getting out. Be right back."

Laura doesn't answer. I hop from the truck bed to the ground. "Stay here with the paintings," I direct Mike. I'm not exactly sure who would hijack Laura's remaining work during an emergency evacuation, but I wasn't prepared for the theft of *Broncho Buster* either. I err on the side of caution.

"I don't care. If it won't start, push it out of the fucking way." Algood isn't screaming at Monica and Julie—yet—but he's definitely not using his milk and honey voice either. His shoulders and upper body are so rigid, I wonder if he's considering striking either woman. Tears stream down Monica's face. Julie has positioned herself so she's partially blocking her sister from Algood. As I approach, I look past the small group and spot the issue.

The back end of a quad-cab Dodge 1500 pickup angles toward me on the far side of the bridge. The front end folds around an upright log framing the small bridge's exit. The base of the bridge is splintered, and a section has fallen into the ravine below. Vehicles can't cross because the truck has both blocked and damaged the bridge.

I scan the parking lot for alternatives, even though I already know the answer. The rear of The Lodge borders a lake. A mountain blocks the view up Cottonwood Pass. This creek, an outlet from Aspen Lake two miles up the basin, wraps around the parking lot before flowing into Middle Cottonwood Creek. Both creeks have to be crossed to get to the main road.

Unlike Middle Cottonwood Creek, which is really more like a river, this first one is shallow enough to ford—if it didn't run through a steep gully. No one is leaving The Lodge in a vehicle until someone from the other side of the bridge moves this truck.

Julie's eyebrows raise as I approach. She flicks her eyes back to Algood, as if signaling, "we have a problem here…a little help, please?"

"What happened?" I pause next to Julie, facing Algood. It doesn't really matter what happened; what matters is how we're going to fix it. But I'm trying to defuse this confrontation.

"These fucking—" Algood starts. I cut him off.

"Is it your truck?"

"No," he sputters. "But—"

I interrupt him again: "Then let them tell me."

I turn to Julie and Monica, but can sense Algood fuming at my side.

Julie rests her hand on Monica's shoulder. "Are you OK? Can you tell Tyler what happened?"

Monica takes a breath like she's steeling herself to speak. She pauses, breathes out, and takes another one. Julie pulls her sister closer.

"Duane was driving. Bruce was in the back. I had my head down because he'd asked me to find his pen he'd dropped on the floor. I didn't even see him hit the bridge. I mean, it felt like we were driving fast, and then all of a sudden, we crashed. My head was down. I slammed into the space under the glove box."

I had assumed Monica's tears resulted from the shock of the accident—or maybe the pressure from Algood. There's no blood on her. But definitely a scrape near her eye. I nod at Monica and turn to the truck. The impact was on the passenger side. She was lucky.

The door to the driver's side of the Dodge hangs open. I search for Duane, expecting to find him working on a solution to clear the bridge. I don't see him.

"Duane?" I turn back to Monica. "Where is he? Did he get hurt?"

Monica doesn't answer.

"What about the security guard guy? Bruce?"

Monica sobs again. Julie answers. "Duane went to get help. Like a tow truck or something. At least that's what Monica said, right, honey?"

Monica nods. "He's OK. He saw the problem right away with how no one can get out. He went up to the main road to get a ride into town for a tow truck. Bruce is over there by the truck, trying to get it going."

I glance back at the crashed vehicle. I don't see Bruce. "Why didn't Duane just call one?" I check my phone for service. Nothing. The only reason I could get calls in The Lodge was because I was connected to their Wi-Fi.

"There's no service here." Algood rejoins the conversation. He's still pissed, but seems to have recovered from me shutting him down.

"There's Wi-Fi back at the lodge," I say, looking at Monica.

She shrugs. "I don't know. It all happened so fast. He said he'd be right back."

"Not if he's hitching a ride into town, finding a truck, and bringing it out. Does he not have a phone or something?"

"He's got one," Monica says.

"What's going on?" Frazier's voice makes me turn. She glances over my shoulder. "Oh."

I nod toward The Lodge, two-tenths of a mile away. "Want to take a walk?"

"What's the plan?" She falls in step with me.

"The truck's got us blocked in. Monica's boyfriend, Duane, went to go find a tow truck. I'm going to try to call for one from the lodge." I turn to Frazier. "Was wondering if I could talk you into staying out here and keeping the peace? And maybe monitor my truck—you know, the rest of Laura's paintings?"

Frazier stops. "You mean Algood?"

"Exactly."

"We're not really blocked in, right? I mean, we could walk across the bridge and have someone pick us up on the other side." She squints toward the bridge. I follow her gaze. The heavy smoke almost obscures the bridge from this distance.

"We could. I'll make some calls while I'm inside. Check what's happening with the winds and the fire. If we're in danger, then yes, I recommend we walk out of here. I'll arrange for someone to pick us up."

"Sounds like a plan. You make the calls. I'll be in charge of law and order."

Inside, I call Gunbarrel Towing and ask if anyone's called for a tow from The Lodge yet. Paul Berenger runs the service. I've had plenty of opportunity to get to know him and his trucks over the last several years.

"Nope. Slow day today. You need one?"

I explain to Berenger what's happening and that he might get another call from someone named Duane. "Paul, we're kind of in a pinch up here. The Chalk Creek Fire has shifted and Rick Perez says it's coming our way. I've got 7-8 people trapped up here in this parking lot and would like to clear them out."

"Yeah, I'll drive up myself. See you in twenty, Zahn."

I speed dial Perez.

"Where you at?" he says as soon as he answers.

"Still at The Lodge."

"Dammit! I told you—"

I interrupt. "You want to give me a chance to explain?"

Perez sighs. "Sorry, Z-man. Got all my folks out trying to warn the ranches between Mt. Princeton and where you're at. Working up some evacuation options. What's up?"

I explain, but Perez can't get past the stolen painting.

"Are you fucking kidding? Are you sure someone wasn't just helping as you guys were evacuating?"

"So someone left all the other art and just decided to help out with the show's main attraction?" I suggest.

Perez's breath releases again. "Shit. Since when has Chaffee County become the fucking nexus for art theft? I can't believe this."

"It gets better." I tell him about the bridge and our current predicament.

"You're not thinking the bridge thing is related to the theft, are you?"

I say nothing because the thought of a connection between the painting and the bridge hasn't even crossed my mind. What motive would a thief have to keep us at The Lodge if they had the painting? And it's Duane's truck, so if they were involved—no…it wouldn't make sense.

"Zahn?"

"Yeah…I mean, no. I don't see how they can be related. It's probably coincidence." As soon as the words leave my mouth, I want to pull them back. Perez doesn't believe in coincidence. Every time he's said that out loud to me, he's turned out to be right. "OK. No, I don't think they are related. But I hadn't considered a connection until you asked me about it. I'll bring it up to Agent Frazier."

"Shit. That's right. Forgot she was there."

I'm surprised by this. Not because it's Perez's job to monitor every law enforcement official in his jurisdiction, but rather because I'd expect that if something drew the FBI to Chaffee County, the Sheriff's Office wouldn't let them take a crap without someone close by. Like a turf thing.

"She's out keeping everyone calmed down while we wait for the tow truck."

Perez says nothing for a moment, as if he's absorbing all I've shared with him. Finally, he says, "The winds haven't shifted. The fire's still heading in your direction. How long until Berenger gets there with the truck?"

"He said twenty minutes."

"I'm going to put a bus on standby for you guys. In case Berenger has problems clearing the bridge. I'll get the Polar Express, or a bus from the prison ready to come up. Sound like a plan?"

I agree. "How long do we have if the winds don't shift?"

"There's plenty of time. Maybe 36 hours or so. But the smoke is going to get worse. How bad is it now?"

I glance out of the foyer through the tall windows. There isn't a vehicle in sight in the parking area. Smoke obscures the line of cars I left waiting at the bridge. "It's bad. Putting a bus on standby is a good idea."

"Stay in touch, Zahn. I'll let you know if anything changes with the fire. You let me know if you run into problems with the tow and need the bus."

"I don't have service out by the bridge. I'll check in with you in thirty minutes. We should either be out by then or needing help."

"Sounds good. And Z-man?"

I recognize the tone Perez uses. He's getting ready to piss me off. "Yeah?"

"You know I don't believe in coincidences, right?"

"Yeah." Here it comes.

"Whoever took that painting is likely long gone. But there's a chance they're sitting in that parking lot right now with you."

My mouth drops. I've missed this possibility. Perez is right.

"Don't go all Lone Ranger on me up there. Get the people out and then we'll investigate what happened. Got it?"

It pisses me off that our mutual trust in each other has slipped, like a shifting ice shelf on one of our nearby mountains. I hope the slip doesn't start an avalanche.

Perez doesn't want me to get involved, because it's not my job. The last time I was in a situation like this–Kristee's disappearance–he had to clean up several of my messes.

But it's not only Perez making me angry. I'm disappointed with myself. I missed the possibility of a connection between the bridge and the painting.

When they released me from the hospital after my concussion, I followed the doctor's orders, walking instead of jogging. I complied with SAR leadership's direction to stay out of the field until I was recovered. This month after the Kristee case was supposed to be all about healing myself. And sharpening my mind.

Instead, I've been following my hormones and my heart. My preoccupation with chasing Laura has dulled my thought process.

I'm pissed Perez is the one who noticed. He's right–the culprit in this case might still be here. I don't plan on missing any more leads.

Not on my watch.

CHAPTER 13

I pull Frazier aside to update her on the tow truck.

"Maybe I should go inside and make another search for anything related to the theft," she says. "I've got Mike's permission. If there's evidence inside, it's in imminent danger from the fire. I think I'm good to search."

I hadn't even considered the fact that Frazier was searching without a warrant. "What about the cars?" I point to the four vehicles lined up behind the blocked bridge, then sweep my hand toward the two remaining vehicles in the main lot—Laura's 4-Runner and a Subaru Impreza. Probably Mike's. "I mean, we can't assume just because all these people know Laura that they had nothing to do with the theft, right? Should I poke around and see what I find?"

Heck. If Frazier is doing a warrantless search, maybe I can too.

"I like the way you think. But neither of us really have the authority to do that. Why don't you head back inside to the Wi-Fi. I'll follow you in a few."

"I can do that. Let me check in with Laura first." I like the way Frazier thinks, as well. She's sending me inside while she checks the cars.

I angle toward the wrecked truck first, working my way in reverse order down the line, assuring each driver the tow truck is fifteen minutes out. Bruce Davis stands next to Monica, slapping dust off his pants, and comforting her. I'm relieved to discover Algood has moved back to his car. He purses his lips before giving me a curt nod at the update. Tristen and Nate stand outside their car, the only guests remaining who opted to grab masks on the way out. Nate still snaps pictures of the wreck, the surrounding haze, and the faint outline of The Lodge.

Laura is exactly as I've left her. Not exactly catatonic, but definitely experiencing something. Her hands grip the steering wheel, eyes fixed on Tristen and Nate.

"Laura."

She squints at me as if trying to focus. "Where have you been?"

"Trying to get Duane's pickup out of the way. Tow truck is on its way." I reach through the driver's window and lay my hand on her forearm. "Don't worry. We're going to get you and your paintings out of here."

"I just wasn't expecting it. For *Broncho Buster* to disappear like that. I don't see how it's possible. I was keeping close tabs on Monica." Laura shakes her head. "She must have had Duane do it. Have you talked to him yet?"

I'm unsure why Laura is convinced Monica or Duane stole her painting, but I'm sensitive enough to recognize telling Laura that Duane is no longer anywhere near The Lodge won't go over well.

"Not yet. But Agent Frazier's here." I nod toward Tristen's car in front of us, where Frazier stands in front of a popped trunk. "I'll remind her about Monica and Duane, OK?"

Laura's head stiffens in what might be a nod of understanding. My first thought is to get her out of the truck and take her on a walk. She needs comfort. But Frazier asked me to return to The Lodge. Laura is safe here–I need to focus on what I can do to help Frazier's investigation before we evacuate.

I pass Frazier on my way to The Lodge. She's definitely innovative. She's asking each vehicle owner if she can check their trunks for emergency equipment, like ropes, chains, and flares, in case the tow truck is delayed.

I've spent six or seven minutes talking to Laura and Frazier. The tow truck should be here any minute. As I enter the foyer my phone rings. I glance at the screen—Berenger from Gunbarrel Towing—and accept the call.

"Tyler? It's Paul. We got a problem."

"What's up?" My voice catches. Paul Berenger isn't calling me to tell me he's planning on arriving early. "Let me guess. It's going to be longer than twenty minutes?"

Berenger coughs, loud at first, then muffled, as if he's covering the phone with his hand. "Oh, you got that right. I'm not sure we're going to get up there at all."

"Any recommendations on anyone else I can call? It's kind of important that we get everyone out of here." I don't ask the reason for the delay. If he could get here, he would—so it must be important.

"No one else can do it either. County Road 306 is closed right past the hot springs, about two miles short of where you're at. Nobody can get through."

Closed? I tilt my head back. A large crystal chandelier dangles from the ancient ceiling above me. If this were a normal Colorado day, sunlight would reflect off the crystal pendants and dance light upon the walls. Through the window, I survey the smoke swirling around The Lodge. Of course the road is closed.

"Any idea what's going on? How long will it be closed?"

Berenger is slow to answer, as if he's carefully picking his words. "Well, it's closed for the fire. So I guess until they get it under control."

"Fire?" Even as I speak, I realize my voice approaches a shout. "The guys over at Chalk Creek said the fire is 36 hours away. 24 at its fastest. Why are they closing 306 now?"

"Not that fire. The new one."

CHAPTER 14

"Everyone inside. Leave your cars here. There's a change of plans." I try to strike a tone of urgency mixed with *everything's under control*, but the glances thrown between our remaining parking lot party tell me I'm fooling no one.

"Where's the tow truck?" Davis says, when I make it up to the front of our stalled convoy.

"Road's closed for a new fire, so it can't get up here right now. I've got the Sheriff's Office working an air evacuation." I'm telling Davis the truth. As soon as I had hung up with Berenger, I called Perez and gave him the situation. All of a sudden, we're at the top of his priority list. He's working to get us out of here ASAP. But I have my doubts about the helicopter option. Not with this damn smoke.

I told him my plan to move everyone back into The Lodge. He promised to have a status report for me in ten minutes, or less.

Monica, Davis, and I work our way down the line of cars, until we reach Laura, still sitting behind the wheel of my truck.

Mike leans against the truck's bed. "What's up?"

I explain the situation.

He waves his hand at the crated art stacked upright in my truck. "What about this?"

I realize we've saved the most complicated part for last. The helicopter can't fit the art, and Laura isn't going anywhere without it. I look from Mike to Laura, who remains expressionless. The only way

I'm going to get her into The Lodge, let alone into the helicopter, is to assure her we are protecting her work.

"Let's unload it back at the dock where we picked it up. Move it inside. The firefighting teams prioritize structures—The Lodge is the safest place to put it."

Frazier steps forward. "I'll make sure everyone is inside. The smoke is getting worse."

I peer over her shoulder toward the bridge. She's right. In the short time since the bridge incident, the smoke has thickened. And it's different. The smoke from Chalk Creek had advanced on us like the tide was coming in. Steady. Almost predictable. The smoke from the new fire swirls like a matador with a cape who has lost sight of his bull.

I know where the bridge is supposed to be, but I can't see it. A breeze sways the branches of the trees closest to us. I can't determine which way the wind is blowing. Which means I can't tell whether the new fire is heading our way or not.

Laura scoots to the passenger seat when I open the driver's door. She glances my direction after settling in her seat.

"What's the delay?" she says.

I realize she didn't hear my explanation when we approached the truck. "They can't get the tow truck up here. We're moving inside until we get our departure squared away." I'm hesitant to share the helicopter plan, uncertain if Laura will connect the dots about having to leave her art. "They're sending a helicopter. The ventilation in the Lodge will help with our breathing…and your art."

"Will the helicopter take my paintings?

Shit. "No. Probably not."

"I need to get my work out of here. I'm already upset about *Broncho Buster*, which you assure me is no longer on the premises. Now you expect me to leave the rest of my art in a place which might burn to the ground."

A moment before, Laura appeared catatonic. She just spent twenty minutes staring out my truck's front window, ignoring the delay, her sister's accident, and my reassurances. Now the alert Laura I'm used to is back–but she's pissed. And I have zero good news to offer.

After we return to the service entrance, Laura supervises as we unload the truck. She designates a space off the kitchen for the crates–one Mike can lock. When Mike and I finish, we join the others in the lobby area.

Algood paces near the foyer, his cell phone pressed to his ear, while Tristen and Nate talk by the staircase. Monica sits in a chair next to the unlit fireplace, Julie at her side holding her hand.

My phone rings. Perez.

I press the green handset button. "What you got for us?"

"Good news and bad news." Perez doesn't give me a choice of which I want first. "I've got two different helos on standby to get you out. The primary already headed up your way, but had to turn away for smoke. How bad is it where you're at, Z-man?"

I turn and scan the foyer windows. Smoke obscures the outside of The Lodge. No vehicles are visible in the lot. "It's bad."

"That's what the pilot said. The winds are shifting to the east. Blowing the fire away from you. The helo is on standby to see if the wind will clear the smoke out a bit, but right now, I can't get anyone up there. The road's still closed. Fire on both sides of it. The fire guys say it's probably jumping the road."

"So, what are we supposed to do? You want us to hike it out?

"No!" Perez's voice is sharp. "Where would you go? The fire is blocking the route to town. It's thirteen miles up to Cottonwood Pass and another fifteen down the other side before you run into civilization. You going to hike almost thirty miles in this smoke with folks gussied up for an art exhibition?"

"Can you send someone over the pass from the other side to pick us up?"

"Thought of that already. I don't feel comfortable sending a ground vehicle your way in that smoke. Not yet. Our fire guys don't think the new fire will blow your way. The same winds slowing the Chalk Creek Fire are keeping this one from you as well."

I pause before asking the question he's already indirectly answered. But I need to hear the words. "So what you're saying…" I let my voice trail off.

"You know what I'm saying, Z-man. For now, you're trapped."

CHAPTER 15

Mike helps me gather everyone near the fireplace. I break the news about the evacuation delay. Most of them instantly grasp the situation. It's not really a delay, but more of a *we're not sure we'll be able to save you if we need to* scenario.

"Bullshit is what it is," Algood fumes. He walks away from the group before I've finished talking, pulling his cellphone from his pocket. Laura's eyes follow Algood. I wonder what's running through her mind. She seemed so hopeful that Algood would purchase *Broncho Buster*. For the prestige, maybe? Through a bizarre series of events, she now has a captive audience…but no painting. Or maybe what worries her is the fate of the rest of her art. Here's what doesn't sit right with me. The Laura I've briefly known seems to care more about people than anything else. I understand her concern for her art–it's her life's work. But where is her concern for all of us who now find ourselves trapped in the path of an oncoming wildfire?

Frazier appears contemplative. I should have talked to her before announcing our situation to everyone. My connection with Perez and the announcement about the rescue delay makes it look like I'm in charge. I'm OK with stepping up to the role—in a crisis, a small group needs a leader to keep things from spinning out of control—but I don't know if Frazier is all right with it. And I shouldn't try to run the *Broncho Buster* theft investigation. That's all Frazier.

"The smoke isn't likely to dissipate before dark. So I think we should plan on figuring out dinner." I glance in Mike's direction. "And maybe take a look upstairs at the floor plan. Figure out how to divvy up the rooms."

Someone groans, and I sense a collective resigned sigh as everyone realizes we're going to be here overnight.

"What about those cabins out by the parking lot? Can we use those?" Monica says.

"I wouldn't." Mike points to a ceiling fan above us. "The Lodge has a ventilation system with filters. Those cabins don't. You'll suck in a lot of smoke if you stay out there."

No one says anything.

"I'll come up with a dinner plan," Mike offers, heading for the kitchen. "And I'll stay in Mr. Moore's living area out back, so don't worry about saving me a room."

"How many rooms are there?" Julie says.

Mike turns his head from the kitchen door. "Six. Some of you are going to have to double up."

I watch as Julie glances from Laura to me and then toward Monica. She's probably assuming Laura and I will share a room. I've spent the last week unsuccessfully trying to get Laura alone on a date, but her sister already thinks we're sleeping together? This should be interesting.

Monica appears to have missed Julie's raised eyebrows, signaling a willingness to share. Instead, she grips Bruce Davis's elbow and steers him for the stairs.

"Let's grab the singles while the getting's good." Monica's initiative seems to energize the group. Tristen and Nate unmask and follow them to the stairs.

Laura seems to snap out of her trance, standing and following the others to the stairs.

"Share?" she says to me over her shoulder, as she walks away.

Really? Laura's question surprises me.

Algood walks in from the foyer. If I share a room with Laura, and none of the people in front of us share rooms, then there's one room left. Julie, Frazier, and Algood are the only remaining guests without a place to stay. Julie's head is already shaking.

"Where's everyone going?" Algood says, joining me in the line moving up the stairs.

"Spending the night. They're picking rooms."

"I'll need the one with the best connectivity," Algood says. "I've got business."

This isn't my first rodeo leading small groups. All it's going to take is one person to mention to Algood that he's doubling up and he'll spin through the ceiling.

I let Algood pass. When he's out of earshot, I tell Julie, "You share with Laura. I'll room with Algood."

Julie pauses on the landing. "You stay with Laura. I'll room with Monica."

"She said she was grabbing a single."

"She'll stay with me. Trust me."

I don't answer. The Coker sisters remain a mystery to me.

•   •   •

Mike has a flair for presentation. He's created an intimate dinner ambience with wine and lighting—maybe to make up for the simple meal. The Lodge operates as a small hotel between events, and Mike has raided the meager supply of fresh vegetables. Pasta primavera, garlic bread, and Caesar salad grace our plates. The rustic chandelier casts a golden glow, illuminating the table with a sepia tint reminiscent of times past. The large dining-room windows face the lake, but all we can distinguish are two orbs guarding the gangway to the dock, struggling to shine through the swirling smoke.

Frazier and I met before dinner and agreed on our responsibilities. She'll continue to deal with anything relating to the painting theft, including interviewing the remaining folks here in The Lodge. I'm in charge of our logistics and extraction. In other words, keeping us fed and functional, and arranging for us to get out of here.

I survey this odd gathering of strangers. It's like I'm living a cliché. As if we're trapped in an Agatha Christie novel where everyone knows someone in the room is guilty, but only the villain knows who it truly is. Hell, we even have a missing painting.

I sip a wine that Mike has suggested from the cellar—a 1975 Mirassou Vineyards Pinot Noir. Mike has assured me that The Lodge is stocked for a week and he'll keep track of what we use, but I'm still uneasy about that. Just because we keep track doesn't mean it's going to be easy at the end when we figure out how much everybody owes. If I was in charge…shit. I should have suggested the house wine for dinner. And a beer for me.

Table conversation is quiet. I'm unsurprised. Except for the sisters, we're strangers, brought together through Laura's art. Now we're stuck together by an act of God. It's not like we're enjoying a family Thanksgiving with each other.

Laura and I sit side-by-side in the middle of the table facing the windows, seats she chooses after we serve ourselves buffet-style from Mike's kitchen spread. We had barely spoken in our shared room, Laura sitting on the edge of the double bed closest to the bathroom, and me taking the other by the door. Her sisters sit across the table from us, leaving the outsiders on the ends. Bruce Davis and Frazier face each other on our right, Tristen and Nate do the same at the other end of the table. Algood and Mike sit to our left.

I pick up my fork, but hesitate before starting. "Are you going to eat?" Laura hasn't touched her food or spoken since sitting. Her eyes train straight ahead as if her sisters have something on their plate that she wants. Then she blinks.

"Still flying aren't you, Sis?" Laura ignores my question, fixing her eyes on Monica. "You think we got enough booze here to keep you buzzed until we get home?"

My mouth drops. I know Laura is under considerable strain. But this can't be the same woman who drank virgin margaritas in a show of solidarity with her alcoholic sister.

"Laura. Not now." Julie places her fork on her plate. "Let it go."

Monica had been reaching for her wine glass when Laura called her out. Her hand still hovers above her plate as if Laura's question has paralyzed her.

Monica gulps from her glass before she says, "I don't think a little wine with dinner is going to hurt anything. And I don't really think it's your job to bitch at me while I enjoy it."

What little conversation happening at the table stops as tension blankets the room. Laura rolls her eyes. "We'll see."

Frazier clears her throat to draw attention away from the drama. "So, Martin, tell me a bit about your collection."

Martin doesn't even look at her, holding up his hand as if to block all future questions. Bruce Davis sits next to Monica. He shifts after Monica's rebuke to Laura, like he's holding her free hand under the table, or pressing a leg against her, or something.

Julie flicks her eyes from Laura to Monica and back. "Here we go."

"No!" Laura shoves back in her chair, rising to her feet. "No! Not *here we go*." She points to Julie, then shifts her finger to Monica. "And no *quit bitching at me* from you, either. This was supposed to be my day, Monica, and you've ruined it. Like always, you've figured out the perfect way to fuck things up."

If it wasn't for Laura's sisters acting like they've had these arguments with their oldest sister before, I'd be convinced Laura was having a fit.

Monica stands so abruptly her chair falls behind her. Julie whips her head toward her younger sister in shock, like she's never seen this reaction. Davis is so surprised, he jerks away from Monica's chair, his hand flailing now that it has nothing to grasp.

"Really? You want to go there?" I've not heard Monica use this voice before. She was so nervous and tentative at dinner the other night, and so distraught after the truck accident on the bridge this afternoon that this Monica sounds foreign to me. She speaks quietly and evenly, but because no one at the table even dares to take a breath, every syllable she utters is clearly audible. "You want to blame me for two forest fires? Like I'm a telepathic arsonist or something? Maybe you ought to finish your wine, Sis? Take the edge off?" She steps forward and raises her glass. "It works for me."

The Coker sister dynamics still baffle me. But it doesn't take an expert to realize that calm, cool, and collected Monica is not the version Laura enjoys talking to. Laura's arm is still outstretched, her finger pointing, and as Monica finishes, Laura's hand quivers.

"Not the fires. It's not the fires, and you know it. It's my art. It always has been. You can't handle the fact that I can make a living from it. And you can't survive if I don't." Laura's voice oscillates in time with her quivering hand. "You're in on this somehow. The thefts on the pass. Taking *Broncho Buster* today. I know you're involved. Just like before."

I glance around the dining room, partly to avoid watching Laura's meltdown, but also to observe our fellow guests. When Laura mentions the theft on the pass, Tristen whips his head toward Monica. I'm not surprised. He's the one who lost a cool $4.5M in the Remington heist.

Most of the room seems focused on the two sisters. Except for Frazier. She's got her eyes on me, like she's gauging my reaction to Laura's histrionics.

I'm embarrassed. Mostly for Laura, but a tiny part of me feels like Frazier is judging my taste in women. And I'm coming up short.

Monica seems not to care who watches. "Actually, Laura, I don't give a fuck about your art, so long as you keep helping with the rent." She steps away from her chair and walks to the credenza where Mike has two bottles of wine sitting in reserve for dinner. She grabs one before turning back to the table. "Bruce, I think I've lost my appetite. You want to join me for a nightcap?"

"Hell, yeah." Davis swallows the last of his wine. He pushes from the table and follows Monica. The silence that graced our meal's beginning returns. Entertainment over, Algood turns to Frazier. "So you were asking about my collection?"

Laura walks toward the kitchen. Nate leans across the table in conversation with Tristen, probably trying to decipher what Laura was talking about with Monica and the art theft. I shift my eyes to Tristen's right, to the empty chair Bruce Davis vacated. Something niggles at the fringes of my thought process.

And then it hits me. When Laura implicated Monica in the theft on the pass, Tristen's reaction was immediate and involuntary. But the man sitting next to him—the same man responsible for guarding the art on that pass, nearly losing his life while protecting it—didn't even blink.

CHAPTER 16

The Lodge's Wi-Fi drops offline just past midnight. I'd been lying in bed, charging my phone, and exchanging texts with Perez about the status of the fires. And asking him to see if he can call someone to feed Amore and take him for a walk.

Then my phone's Wi-Fi symbol disappears. The word *SOS* replaces it. The same word I get on SAR missions when I have no signal.

Laura and I share a room designed to sleep four in a pinch. Two double beds. Our relationship had been progressing toward a night where we might share a bed, but between the inconsistent start to our dating status and the ordeal Laura has undergone today, we both understand that tonight's not that night. In fact, I'm not sure I'll sleep at all.

I slip downstairs to poke around the main floor for the router, or a server, or something that looks like it has to do with Wi-Fi. The Lodge's power is still on. I figure that means there's either an issue with the provider, or an equipment problem here on the premises. Maybe a slight chance there's something wrong with my phone. I can check if it's my phone by finding someone else awake. Unfortunately, the cracks under the doorways remain dark. The downstairs lobby is empty. I squint out the window at the caretaker's building. It's dark as well. Mike is getting some well-deserved rest.

I consider waking him. Wi-Fi is the only thing connecting us to the outside world. My 24-hour SAR pack sits in the back of my truck, but my text-capable GPS locator is charging on my nightstand at home. The exhausted part of me recognizes that a couple more hours of sleep won't hurt any of us. We can figure it out in the morning.

I round the banister to the upstairs hallway when a door clicks shut. I pause, not because I don't want to be seen, but in case the person who made the sound is trying to avoid detection. We're all under a lot of stress. If late night trysts ease shaky nerves, who am I to judge? I peer around the banister and spy a figure walking away from me down the hall. I can't tell who it is in the dark.

It's not like I've mapped out everyone's room choices, so I'm uncertain whose room the person came out of, nor whose room they entered. I don't even know whether they're coming or going. The figure disappears in the dark. A door clicks shut.

I shrug, take the last step up the staircase, and return to my room.

Sleep comes easily this time. I wake up at half-past five in the morning feeling like I've gotten a full eight hours. I glance over at Laura, who still sleeps in the other bed, then reach for my cell phone to check connectivity. No messages. No service.

Mike already has coffee going when I walk into the kitchen. This young man is squared away. He didn't sign up to serve nine strangers trapped in a lodge. I doubt this is even a full-time gig for him. But he's embraced the role of caretaker for The Lodge and caregiver for our group. I shouldn't be surprised at youthful initiative, but it's so easy to assume every person under the age of thirty in our valley cares about nothing but riding the Arkansas River rapids or scaling our plethora of 14ers—our valley's iconic fourteen-thousand-foot mountains. And it says a lot about me that approaching fifty, I'm starting to be cynical about our youths' work ethic. I wasn't this way in the Air Force, where our young airmen worked their ass off every day. Just because I'm aging doesn't mean I have to act like it.

I thank Mike for the coffee and ask him about the Wi-Fi situation.

"Easy to check. I've done a lot of gigs up here and know this place pretty well. Follow me." He leads me through the kitchen and into the lobby. Instead of turning upstairs, he veers to the left, pointing to a hallway leading to the west wing of the first floor.

"What's back here?"

Mike flips on lights as he walks down the corridor. "Conference room and gym." He pulls a key from his pocket, then opens a door. "All the Wi-Fi stuff is in the conference room."

I wait next to a long, wood-stained conference table while Mike pushes into a storage room. He flips on another light switch and disappears inside.

I wait a minute—probably closer to thirty seconds—and hearing nothing, I call out, "Any luck? Can you reboot it?"

Mike sticks his head out of the closet. "You know anything about Wi-Fi?"

"I know how to put in a password. And if there's a problem in my house, I usually unplug the router and plug it back in. That's about it." I pause. "You trying the router thing?"

Mike curls his finger at me. "Come look at this and tell me what you see."

He steps from the closet to make room for me to poke in my head. A wheeled carousel with a computer on top, and two empty shelves underneath sit against the closet's back wall.

I twist my head back to Mike. "Does the Wi-Fi run from the computer? Like a built-in router or something?"

"No. The router was on the second shelf. It's not there anymore. See that rectangle shape where there's no dust?"

I stick my head back in the closet, crouching to peer through the empty shelf of the carousel. Mike's right. It's empty and there's a cluster of wires nested on the floor like they are just waiting to be plugged into whatever used to occupy the shelf. Someone has decided we don't need Wi-Fi anymore.

•   •   •

On a typical Colorado summer day, the morning sun angles its way up past The Lodge, spotlighting the steep mountainsides funneling anglers to the lake three miles farther up this valley. Last summer, my daughter

Daria and I fished that lake. Today, the smoke from the fires blocks the sun's rays. The view from the lobby windows reveals a diaphanous pink haze. Even if I could call Perez, I doubt he would have good news about a helicopter evacuation.

Frazier sits across from me, our chairs angled to the unlit fireplace. I've shown her the empty Wi-Fi shelf. She appears to be processing our situation. Trapped in a mountain lodge. Surrounded by fires. A stolen painting. And now we've lost communication with the outside world.

"It doesn't make sense," Frazier says. "Any one of these things by themselves is odd. Another stolen painting in a county of twenty-thousand people, two weeks after your first art heist in a hundred years? Weird. Us trapped in a mountain resort because of fires? A first for me. You?"

I nod.

"And now, you're saying someone in our group sabotaged the only means of communication with the outside world? That's messed up." She shifts her eyes to the fireplace. "What the hell is going on?"

I'm as bewildered as Frazier. "Should we line everyone up and start interrogating them?" I don't possess this kind of authority. But Frazier does.

"I'd have to interview you too." Frazier smiles. "But you're right. It's definitely an option. Alternatively, we can attempt to get ourselves out of here. Wait until we get back to find out who's behind all this. If I go into full investigative mode here at The Lodge, I'm not sure we'll find out who it is."

"So, what do you propose?"

"How about we try another meal together? Everyone's going to discover we lost Wi-Fi. It'll be the main topic this morning. We'll let breakfast play out and see what happens. If we don't have any leads after that, I'll start interviewing people about the stolen painting. See what I can discover." Frazier sighs.

"What?"

"I still need to interview Tristen about his paintings. The originals stolen up on the pass."

She heads to the conference room for another look at the Wi-Fi set-up. I check in with Mike. He's already working on a breakfast plan and assures me he'll have something on the table in thirty minutes. I don't share what Frazier and I discussed with Mike. He doesn't have a need to know. As impressed as I am with the young man, it doesn't mean he couldn't be responsible for the Wi-Fi. Or the painting. He had direct access to the painting during the evacuation. And who would know better where to hide the painting if it was still on the grounds?

Upstairs, I tap on doors, beginning with the one I saw someone exiting last night.

"Morning. We're having breakfast together in thirty minutes. Wanted to let you know." No one replies. I knock again. Nothing. I move to the next door and tap. Before I can open my mouth, a voice answers.

"We heard you. We'll be there."

I repeat my tapping at the next door.

"Everybody hears you, Tyler," a muffled feminine voice answers.

At Laura's door—mine too, I guess—I tap, then crack the door open. My sheets remain twisted upon the mattress closest to the door. I didn't make my bed because I was concerned about waking Laura. Her side of the room is pristine. I note a sliver of light under the bathroom door.

"Laura?"

"Be right out." I recognize Laura's voice, but can't read her mood.

"Breakfast will be ready in about twenty minutes. I'm going to wake everyone else."

No answer.

"I'll meet you downstairs," I announce, figuring she'll be more comfortable emerging from the bathroom if I'm not there.

It's another thirty minutes before we're gathered around the table. Stacks of French toast serve as the centerpiece. Orange juice sits at the two o'clock position of every plate while utensils rest on paper napkins next to stoneware plates.

"Hash browns will be out in five," Mike assures us.

I suppress a smile when everyone seats themselves in the same position as last night. My weekly yoga class at the community center–

where everyone rolls out their mat in the exact same spot as the previous week–has taught me the same thing. We humans are creatures of habit.

The tension from dinner still lies thick in the room. Algood reaches across the table for the French toast, obviously not shy about eating first.

The chair next to Monica remains empty. Bruce Davis hasn't joined us yet. I want to talk to him today, especially if we remain on standby for an evacuation. I have more questions about the Asian woman he says he saw during the theft on the pass.

"Bruce running behind?" I say, trying not to focus my question on Monica. Last night Julie had said Monica would sleep with her. But Monica left the table with Davis.

Tristen and Nate turn toward Monica. Monica glares at them. "How would I know?" She looks around the table. I follow her eyes. Everyone appears to be waiting for her to continue. "We finished a bottle of wine. He had a headache. I wouldn't sleep with him, anyway. I'm in a relationship." She focuses her eyes on Laura. "With Duane."

I instinctively glance at Julie. She meets my gaze and nods. Guess I was wrong.

"I'll get him," Monica says, sliding her chair from the table.

Algood raises his phone in his left hand, his right still curled around a fork stabbing a piece of French toast. "What the fuck's up with the Wi-Fi? It worked last night. This morning I don't have shit." He looks down the length of the table. "Anyone else have any?"

"Mine's been out since we woke up," Julie says.

Tristen, Nate, and Frazier pull out their phones, I assume to check for themselves. Laura continues nibbling at her breakfast.

Mike walks in, carrying an aroma of fried grease and a platter of hash browns. He pauses at the sight of everyone's cell phones out.

"The Wi-Fi's out." He sets the plate on the table. "Didn't Zahn tell you? Someone—"

A scream interrupts Mike. All heads turn toward the staircase. I push back from the table and head for the stairs. Steps pound behind me; Frazier, I assume.

I'm halfway to the landing when Monica wheels around the upstairs banister, panting, her face white.

"What—?" I start, but Monica interrupts.

"It's Bruce." Monica's voice rings shrill. "He's not breathing." She takes a breath. "He's cold. Oh God…I think he's dead."

CHAPTER 17

Monica teeters at the edge of the stairs. I lunge forward, grabbing her shoulders and pulling her onto the landing. Her hands shoot up like a bank teller in a hold-up—as if she can't bear the thought of anyone touching her. She backs away from me, pressing against the wall.

Steps thunder up the stairs behind me. Frazier pauses, apparently unsure if she can step between me and Monica. Mike and Julie pause two steps below.

"Which room?" I say. "Show us!"

Monica points to the closest room in the hallway. The same room someone exited from last night. A wedge of dim light from the open door reflects on the hallway floor.

I turn to Julie. "Help her." I nod toward Monica. "Get her downstairs and sit her down." When I turn back, Frazier is already entering the room.

I step through the doorway. Frazier presses her fingers against the side of a figure lying on the bed. I join her on the opposite side and look down at the body's face. Davis's open eyes remain frozen.

"CPR?" I say.

Frazier's eyes are focused on the window, as if she doesn't want anything to distract her from her search for a pulse, but her head shakes. "He's been gone for some time. No pulse. He's cold."

Davis's body lies stiff, still covered with bedsheets. He looks like he simply died in his sleep. I think about Frazier's list of coincidences last night. There's no way this is an accidental death.

"What do you think?"

Frazier glares at me, but not like she's angry. More like frustrated. "I've been in this room five seconds longer than you. What do *you* think?"

"Sorry." I am sorry. "How do you want to handle this?"

Frazier grabs the sheet, pulling on it to expose Davis's body. He wears a white T-shirt, and a pair of snug-fitting blue boxer briefs. I run my eyes up and down his body. Frazier is doing the same. Davis shows no signs of blood or injury, save the healing head wound from his art heist escape.

"Stand back, Tyler."

I step away from the body. Frazier snaps pictures with her cell phone.

"Can you roll him?"

I step forward again, grasping Davis by the upper arm and thigh. I roll him onto his stomach. As I step backward, I scan his body again. Nothing unusual. Frazier takes more pictures.

"OK." Frazier lowers her phone and fixes her eyes on mine. "This time I'm being serious instead of snarky. What do you think?"

"I don't see any signs of foul play, do you?"

"No."

"I still don't think it's an accident." I run my fingers through my hair. "Between the painting, the bridge, and the Wi-Fi? And now this. It's just too much stuff for it all to be a coincidence."

Frazier nods. "I agree. Something's going on, and the person—or persons—behind it are still here." She lets out a breath. "Which means we've got a problem."

"We already had a problem before Mr. Davis died." I nod toward the corpse. "We need to figure out how to get out of here before we burn to death."

"You're right. But this problem makes that problem worse."

"How's that?"

"We now have a murderer among us. If we don't figure out who it is and how to neutralize them, then we're all in danger." Frazier pauses like she's unsure I'm keeping up. "If we do find out who it is, our evacuation is complicated by bringing both a body," she nods at Davis, "and a criminal, out with us."

"You carrying?" I shift my eyes down from hers. I haven't noticed the bulge of a weapon.

"Not right now. It's in my bag." She hesitates. "Which is totally unprofessional. What about you?"

"Locked in my glove box." I pause, considering whether Frazier needs more information about my firearm experience. "I have a permit."

"Tell you what. How about you rally everyone downstairs? Tell them what's happened while I arm up. When I show up, you can go out to your truck and grab yours.

"Sounds like a plan. What do you want me to tell them?"

"The truth, mostly. Tell them Davis died. We don't know why, but there's no sign that he died of anything unusual. Remind them he just got out of the hospital with a head injury." She glances at Davis again. "Hell, who knows? That could be it."

She's right. That could be it. But I doubt it. I glance at the door, remembering last night. The person leaving Davis's room. I tell Frazier what I saw.

"You couldn't tell if it was a man or a woman?" she says.

"No. Just that it was someone from one of the other upstairs rooms."

"What about Mike? And how do you know it wasn't Davis himself? Going to another room."

She's not wrong. I haven't considered either of these options. "I guess it could have been either of them as well. But the person went into another upstairs room. I'm not sure which one, but that would have been odd for Mike, don't you think? It almost would have implied that

Mike was working with someone else. I'm not sure he even knows anyone else up here."

Frazier nods. "And if it was Davis, that means he went to someone else's room before he died. Would be nice to know who was the last one to see him alive."

•   •   •

"You've got to be fucking kidding me," Algood glances at Monica, who is still panting from the shock of discovering Davis. "You can't honestly think one of us did it. Fucking why? He was a two-bit security guard. What motive could anyone here possibly have?" He keeps his eyes on Monica. "Unless it was a crime of passion."

I disagree with Algood, but say nothing. Someone in this room is responsible for Davis's death. But now is not the time to get into that. I need to keep everyone in this room until Frazier returns with her weapon.

As if on cue, Frazier enters the lobby from behind the group. I flick my eyes from her back to Algood. "I didn't gather you all here to point fingers, Algood. And there's no sense in you doing it either. We don't know how he died." I scan the group. "You're here so that everyone knows what happened. We need you to stay away from Davis's room." I acknowledge Frazier standing behind the others. "Agent Frazier will be asking you all some questions having to do with Davis. When you last saw him. How he looked. That kind of thing. Once we reestablish communications, she can pass the info on to law enforcement and the medical folks."

Frazier tilts her head at me, a small smile crossing her face. I realize I'm talking outside my box. Who am I to tell these people what kind of questions Frazier will ask?

"Agent Frazier?" I extend my hand toward her.

"Thank you, Mr. Zahn." Frazier reciprocates my formality, but there's just a hint of humor in her voice. I'm unsure anyone else notices it. She strides to the front of the room. I exit through the kitchen toward the service entrance to retrieve my Glock 26 and holster from my truck's glove box. I mentally kick myself, approaching my Tundra. I've been so worried about valuable paintings and looming fires that I haven't even bothered locking my truck.

Relief washes over me after I twist the glove box key and pop the compartment open. I glance up at the kitchen window as I strap on my concealed shoulder holster. Mike's face is framed in one of the panes. I adjust the holster before pulling on my jacket. When I check the window again, Mike is no longer there.

I'm in no hurry to return to The Lodge. Frazier's armed. I'm not worried about her. What I need now is some thinking time. Now that I'm carrying my Glock, I don't need to carry my keys. I toss them under the passenger seat. Leaning against the truck's metal frame, I gaze toward The Lodge's small lake. I know the water is there because I saw it yesterday during the exhibition. But now a heavy layer of haze blankets everything within twenty yards.

If I'd planned on staying outside, I should have grabbed a mask. I snort, then cough from the smoke. Where there's smoke there's fire—I should be more worried about the flames than the smoke.

This is a first for me. We're trapped in a crime scene that might burn to a crisp within twenty-four hours. So, crime scene preservation—both for the art theft and the suspected murder—has dropped in priority. The number one thing we need to do is get our people out of here before they die.

Without communication, we have no idea if conditions are improving for a helicopter evacuation. We also lack information about whether things are getting worse. Perez said thirty-six hours. But that was yesterday. Now it could be less than a day. I'm unsure about the others, but I'm uncomfortable simply waiting to see what happens.

But here's another problem: if we all leave together, whatever route we take has to succeed, or we'll all perish. And if we leave together, we'll be trying to work our way back to civilization with a murderer among us.

Alternatively, Frazier or I could scout out a route. It's got to be one of us two. She's the only one I'm positive wasn't responsible for Davis's death. I mean, I'm pretty sure Laura or Julie didn't have anything to do with it either. But I'm not positive. So it's me or Frazier for scout duty. Whoever doesn't go has to serve as security while the other is gone.

I take a deep breath. It needs to be me. I don't have the authority to keep order if Frazier scouts a route. I have no badge, no position, and no right to pull a weapon if things get out of line. I have no problem doing so—but some of the others might have an issue with me being in that position.

I return to The Lodge to discuss this with Frazier. Raised voices greet me from the lobby as soon as I walk through the kitchen. Women's voices. The Coker sisters are at it again.

"Laura, please stop." I recognize Julie's voice before I enter the lobby. I'm beginning to reevaluate my first assessment of Julie. When we met, I labeled her the jealous sister. Now I'm seeing her as the peacemaker. And the peacemaker is hard at work again.

"I will not. I said it last night, and I'll say it again." Laura's finger shakes as she points it toward Monica. "She is responsible for what is going on here."

Monica's head is buried between her hands, her fists balled at her ears like she's trying to block out Laura's tirade. Laura paces in front of the fireplace hearth as if holding court. She points at her sister, but doesn't appear to realize Monica isn't listening. Julie rests her hands on the back of a chair, her head swiveling between her sisters like a Wimbledon spectator.

My first instinct is to lower the tension in the room. Like Julie, I'm a peacemaker. I'd rather help lower others' heart rates than raise my own. But inserting myself between these sisters? I don't think so. The last thing I want is to rile up Laura even more.

Julie and Laura turn to me as I enter. When Laura stops talking, Monica lifts her head. No one says anything, and a spark of hope kindles in me. Maybe I've stopped the argument just with my presence.

"Any of you seen Agent Frazier?"

Monica shakes her head. Laura gapes at me as if she can't believe I have the audacity to interrupt her while she's on a roll.

"She's upstairs, I think." Julie offers. "With…you know—"

I assume Julie means Frazier is in the room with Davis's body. "Thanks." I give a weak smile in Laura's direction before heading for the stairs.

"Tyler?" Laura's voice is shrill. I hesitate before turning. "What's going to happen now? Now that we've had all these things happen? Are the police coming? Or are we just going to leave?"

I glance at Monica and Julie, who both seem as interested in my response as Laura. "Until we get communications back, I don't know the answer to that question." I point out the lobby windows at the smoke draping the parking lot. "But judging from the visibility out there, I don't think anybody is flying in or out any time soon."

Julie nods. Laura doesn't even look out the window. She closes the distance between us, speaking softly as she approaches.

"I don't know whether I should be talking to you or to Frazier about this, but I'll say it right now. When this thing gets investigated? The robbery. The death…or, should I say, murder?" Laura sucks in her breath. "I'm done ignoring the obvious. I will no longer cover for my sister's actions."

"Laura—" Julie's voice sounds reproachful, but I don't get to hear the end of her sentence because suddenly Laura staggers. I reach forward to catch her from falling. Monica stands behind her, arms retracting from the shove she gave Laura.

"You take her, Zahn. Keep the bitch." Monica's breath is ragged. "I've had about all I can take from her." She stalks back to her chair. Laura struggles in my arms. She's not hurt—she's furious and attempting to escape my grasp so she can retaliate against her sister.

I hug her tighter. "Let it go," I whisper, in my best I-know-how-you-must-be-feeling tone. Which I instantly realize must sound patronizing. I'm not privy to these sisters' history. How much will Laura be *letting go* if she chooses to ignore Monica?

Laura strains against my arms. When I tighten my grip, she suddenly sags. I steer her toward the conference room hallway.

"What were you thinking?" Julie admonishes Monica, as Laura and I disappear down the corridor. Her voice turns indistinguishable as we keep walking.

My job is the evacuation, not the stolen painting, or Davis's death. Those are Frazier's problems. But Laura seems so certain about Monica's involvement. I sense she needs to let her thoughts loose on someone besides her sister.

I open the conference room door and wave to the chairs at the table. "You want to talk about it? About why you're so upset with Monica?"

Laura is having none of it. "Did I stutter? Was I unclear? The stuff going on here? She's behind it. If she's not doing it, she knows who is."

I say nothing. Laura has never used this tone of voice with me.

Laura doesn't drop her eyes. I see exasperation written all over her face. After what feels like minutes, but is likely seconds, her expression softens. She pulls a chair out and sits at the table. "I'm sorry, Tyler. I misread your intentions."

"What do you mean?"

"I thought you were just trying to get me to talk, so I could get things out of my system and feel better. But I don't think that's the only reason, right? You're curious. You're trying to solve this thing, aren't you?"

I want to remind Laura that I don't have a badge—solving is Frazier's job—but Laura appears more willing to talk if she thinks I'm investigating rather than providing comfort. She's not completely wrong about my desire to get answers. Our impending evacuation will be a lot easier if we can figure out who is behind what's happening here. So I do want to know.

"Anything you can share with me would be useful. I'm not law enforcement. But I can make sure the right people hear what you have to say if I talk to them before you do."

Laura waves at the chair I'm gripping. "Grab a seat. You can't understand Monica's actions without understanding our history."

I lower myself into the chair, hoping my face doesn't show the wariness I feel. As attracted as I am to Laura–and I'm giving her recent outbursts a pass based on the circumstances–I've learned from these Coker women that perspectives vary. I have no way to tell which woman is telling me the truth about their complicated relationships.

"I'm not going to give you the scarred childhood sob story–that *Mommie Dearest* crap or stories of Daddy locking us in the closet." Laura reaches out, laying her hand on my forearm. "Here's the deal: Monica is an addict. You know that by now, don't you?"

I nod. Julie has shared Monica's drug history with me. Plus, I saw it online, and read between the lines when Perez raised his eyebrows at me after finding out I was hanging out with the Coker sisters.

"Because of her problems, she was my father's sole focus growing up. When he passed away, our other sister, Julie, was already dealing with the death of her own husband. And the load of debt he left behind. I was the only one with the time and the means to help Monica. People always assume Daddy left us girls a ton of money and a family legacy." She snorts. "He left me two things. The snarled mess of his ranch. And, of course, the responsibility for cleaning up after Monica's messes."

Laura shakes her head. "This is the part that's going to sound snarky. Self-centered. But I have to share it with you so you can understand how it relates to what's going on right now. OK? Try to understand."

I start to nod, but stop. I'm nodding so much and talking so little that I look like a bobber with a trout on the hook.

"Julie ran track in high school. She was good. You might not see it in her now, but she still holds records in Buena Vista for long distance running. She was on her way to Colorado State on a full-ride. Then Monica tried to kill herself. Daddy asked Julie to take a gap year and help me with Monica while he worked the ranch." Laura purses her lips. "Not like he was going to be much help in the teenage girl angst department." She pauses. "And Julie never went to college. At least not on a full-ride track scholarship. She did a two-year program with Colorado Community College and moved on from there."

This is news to me, but only dredges up new questions. Why isn't Julie the one so pissed at Monica? What drives Laura's passionate hatred of her youngest sister?

Laura seems to read my thoughts. "That time. That period where she was so-called recovering? That's when it started with her and me." Laura's face pales. Her hand quivers on my arm. "She just took. Piece by piece, little by little, she took whatever made me happy, and co-opted it."

"What do you mean by co-opt?" I know what the verb means, but don't understand the context. Normally, I would stay silent and figure it out as I go. But I want to show Laura I'm engaged in this conversation.

"She took my father's love. He was not an easy man, but he loved his girls. He'd show it in little ways: rides across the ranch, a tiny flower on a pillow for a birthday—or, sometimes, with a quick smile. Just because." Laura's eyes mist. She pulls her hand away to wipe at them. "That all stopped after Monica's incident. It's hard to describe."

Laura has no idea. The father she describes? It's a description of my hapless efforts as a paternal figure. My ex-wife Sheila and I lost our son Jacob to the flu. Then I lost an aircrew under my command in the Iraq War. I sunk into a grief so profound, I literally deserted my family. Sheila and I divorced. I allowed my daughter, Daria, to drop from my life. My Air Force performance plummeted—the military didn't try to convince me otherwise when I left the service. I wallowed away five years as a defense contractor before staggering to the Colorado Rockies in an attempt at a new start. So this Dwight Coker, the father Laura describes? I know him. I was him.

But I just nod again.

"The rest of it, when we were in high school, sounds so petty. But it matters. She confided about her problems to my boyfriend, then slept with him. She accidentally destroyed my senior art project. She overdosed the morning of my high school graduation—I spent that day in a hospital in Colorado Springs instead of walking across the high school stage."

The tears flow now. When she reaches again to brush them away, I intercept her arm, grabbing it softly. She reaches for my free hand with her own. I lean forward, attempting to pull her into a hug, but our swivel chairs make it impossible. Instead, I press my knees against hers. She presses her forehead against mine. I lace my fingers together behind her head holding it against my own while she sobs.

"Shhh." I'm still processing everything Laura has shared with me. I can't claim to understand it all. But the woman I care about is in pain and I want to help make it go away.

"So you think she's pulling the same stuff now? The same type of antics she did in high school?" Laura stiffens as she pulls away from me. I realize I should have let her cry some more. Allowed her to decide when the conversation should continue.

I brace myself as she opens her mouth, but we're interrupted by a rap on the door.

"Yeah!" I call.

The door opens. Nate barrels into the room, swiveling his head left and right like he's playing hide-and -seek. "Where's Agent Frazier?"

"Not sure, Nate. What's up?" I say.

"It's Tristen." Nate lets out a moan. "He's gone."

"What do you mean by gone? Like you can't find him? Did you check your room?"

"I mean like he's trying to make it out. He took his bag. I think he's going to try to walk through the fire."

CHAPTER 18

I expect Frazier to push back when I tell her I'm going after Tristen. Instead, she agrees with my logic.

"I don't see how Tristen can be our thief or murderer. So you're the right guy to retrieve our lost guest—not me. You can scout the fire while you're searching. Just be careful."

"I don't think he's guilty either." Tristen owns, or owned, some of the most expensive American art in the world before the Cottonwood Pass theft. Why would he steal Laura's work? I wouldn't voice this question out loud to Laura, but she's likely self-aware enough to recognize her work is worth much less than a Remington. And murder? Not only does Tristen look like the last guy you'd expect to take a life, but why kill Bruce Davis? For failing to keep Tristen's Remington from disappearing? Not likely.

"Right." Frazier glances at the lobby. "I'll stay here. Try to keep law and order while you retrieve our wayward art baron and see about finding a way out of here." She pauses. "Before you go, any word on the Wi-Fi? Any comms with the outside?"

"Don't you think you would've been the first person I told?" I smile, so she knows I'm teasing.

"That's the part making me nervous. We've gone more than twelve hours without an update. The cops don't know we've had a probable homicide. We don't know what's happening with the fires. This is all fucked up."

I snap my head toward Frazier. A casual dropping of the F-bomb is common among the law enforcement officers I know. But this is new from Frazier—the first potential sign she might be rattled. As dazzled as I've been with her professionalism and confidence, it's a relief to see some of her humanity as well. Hell, I'm rattled too.

"I'll have my cell. Even if I don't get through, I might get enough signal to call Perez or someone working the fires."

Frazier leaves for the lobby, her new central point for keeping tabs on our group. I head up to the room I share with Laura to grab my SAR backpack, which I'd retrieved from my truck the previous night. When I enter, Laura sits on the edge of her bed, her fingers working her cell phone. This is the first time since the theft of her painting I've seen her doing anything besides staring at nothing, or blaming Monica for our situation.

Laura glances at me, then taps a button before sliding the phone into her purse on the nightstand.

"Wi-Fi back?" I pull out my own phone to check the screen. No connection.

"No. Just looking at my pictures."

I give her my best expression of confusion. We're in a hell of a predicament here. It's an odd time to take a trip down memory lane.

Evidently, Laura reads my thoughts. "I was checking to see the last photograph I have of *Broncho Buster*. The police will ask for that when they investigate Monica."

I say nothing. Laura's right about what the cops will ask for, but I'm still frustrated at her insistence Monica stole the painting. High school antics don't seem like enough grounds for her accusations. Some of the more recent things that Julie told me about her sisters? Maybe. But I'm still uncertain Julie was telling the truth.

Laura must misinterpret my silence as disapproval because she continues. "You probably wonder how I can let my own sister go down for this. But you don't know us well enough to judge." She pauses. "So don't."

"Laura, I came up to grab my bag. I'm going after Tristen."

I watch as Laura's eyes seem to clear, like finally something I've said has gotten through.

"You don't think Tristen did it, do you? Stole my painting and killed Mr. Davis? There's just no way."

"I'm going after him because he's in danger. He doesn't know his way around here. The fire's between the town and us. I was going to scout us a way through, anyway. Now I've got an additional reason to go."

Laura stands and hugs me. I sense her slipping back into the same stupor from yesterday. Our fledgling relationship is in jeopardy. I wrap my arms around her. Here I am wondering if I'm ever going to get that first date with Laura when I should be asking myself if any of us will survive this predicament.

•   •   •

Five minutes later, a mask covering my nose and mouth, I thread the gap between Duane's truck and the undamaged side of the bridge to cross the river. I'm not a professional tracker—hell, I'm not even an amateur tracker—so I have little hope of following his trail toward town. Even if I see prints, I won't be able to distinguish between Duane's tracks from yesterday and Tristen's. Instead, I try to put myself in Tristen's head. He told me he's a city boy, but I suspect he's savvier than he lets on.

When Tristen crossed the bridge, he had three choices–assuming he recognized his location. He could turn left and try to hike thirteen miles up Cottonwood Pass to where his paintings were stolen, and fifteen miles down the other side. At least a two-day hike, unless he caught a ride on the far side. Straight ahead, a steep ridge blocks anyone from trying to hike north. The Colorado Trail snakes over a pass next to Mt. Yale only a mile or two up the pass from here, but I doubt Tristen knows that. Turning right is downhill. Tristen's most likely choice. Even Tristen is likely to recognize water flows downhill, and that's where the valley and Buena Vista must sit. It's also the location of the fire trapping us in The Lodge.

Tristen knows the road to Buena Vista is closed because of the fire. My guess is he'll try to follow the creek instead.

Smoke shrouds the creek, burning my nostrils, as I pick my way along the bank. The current runs swift, more like a river than a creek. If I hadn't taken the bridge, I'm unsure I would've found another crossing as I worked my way downstream alongside the roiling water. Climate change is supposed to be a century-long process, but it's crazy that Colorado got enough snow over the winter to keep this river high while the lack of rain over the last three months is keeping fire danger in the red. What the hell?

I'm only a half-mile from the bridge, picking my way through stream-side cottonwoods when I hear the crack of tree branches. My first guess is wildlife, because the noise is familiar from my hiking. My second is Tristen. It wouldn't surprise me if I'd caught up with him. The sound gets louder, branches cracking.

I round the bend of the river at the same time I realize what I'm hearing. It's not someone or something trying to escape the trees lining this river, but rather the fire trying to devour them. The fire that closed Cottonwood Pass burns before me.

I'm not in immediate danger. The flames aren't roaring in my direction. Instead, the burn is steady, like the fire is trying to make sure it uses all the fuel it touches before leaping forward to the next log, branch, or tree. I can't tell which direction the wind is blowing because the flames create their own wind. The Lodge's side of the stream is pockmarked with clusters of fire. Downstream—toward town—is blocked. I watch the burn for another minute, trying to gauge the fire's direction. It's definitely moving north, paralleling the Upper Arkansas River valley. Which means it is possible to scramble that direction off the river bank and work my way over to the paved road to Buena Vista before the flames reach it.

Using tree roots and rocks as hand and footholds, I pull myself from the creek basin, threading my way up toward the road. Behind me, the fire continues its cacophony of cracks and pops, as if waiting for an audience reaction to decide which direction to go next.

At the road's shoulder, I'm reduced to a crawl. I slip twice on the loose gravel leading to the roadside before finally reaching the pavement. The visibility here is no better than in the creek bed—about twenty yards in either direction. I aim toward town, shuffling down the pavement when the roaring in my ears brings me to a stop. Everything to my right sounds like it's burning. The noise has turned deafening. If I continue straight, there's a chance the fire will pass behind me. I'll lose the option of returning to The Lodge.

All thoughts of catching Tristen disappear. Now I'm just trying to assess where I'll be the most useful.

I left The Lodge with dual objectives. Find Tristen. Scout a workable escape route in case we need it. If I make it through the flames facing me, I'll only save myself. And I have no way of telling the others not to come this way. I've got to turn back.

I turn back and start hiking uphill. A loud crack, followed by a scream, overrides the fire's roar. I whirl just as a thirty-foot pine crashes to the pavement, a patch of red flashing among its branches. A shower of sparks explodes from the fallen tree.

The noise is all-consuming. But I have no doubt I heard a scream. I run toward where I saw the red among the branches.

The tree's fall has smothered the fire that engulfed the dry needles. Flames search for purchase among the unburnt branches. I step between the black smoldering limbs, searching for the source of the scream.

"Here!" A muffled cry escapes near the tree's tip in the road's center. The branches near me reignite. I skirt the flames, lifting at the few remaining green limbs while searching for the voice's source.

"I'm burning!" The high-pitched call morphs into a scream. Rounding the tip of the tree, I spy Tristen's head near the pavement, twisted my direction. He lays face down on the road, a torn mask next to his head. The burning treetop covers the backs of his legs.

If I grab the burning mass with my hands, I'm going to burn myself. Badly. Tristen screams again as the embers settle against his legs. I don't have time to find anything to pry off the tree.

Tristen reaches behind his backpack, pounding on the tip of the tree, trying to assuage the pain.

"Stop!" I yell, ripping off my mask. "Stick your hands out in front of you. Straight ahead." I crouch in front of Tristen, but he ignores my commands. I grab his head, turning his face to me. "Listen to me! Give me your hands."

Recognition registers in Tristen's eyes. He thrusts his arms forward. I grab his knapsack, first tugging on it, then ripping it over his shoulders and up his arms. When I have the bag in my hands, I yank the zipper open, spreading the flap open so I have a two-foot swath of open Gore-Tex in my hands. A tangle of clothes, a water bottle, and various electronics drop to my feet. I step around the moaning man and wrap the open backpack around the very tip of the tree. The embers immediately burn through the backpack material, but I only need a split-second. I tug the burning end of the tree away from Tristen.

"Crawl!" I can't move the entire tree, but the tree's tip is narrow enough to flex it like I'm aiming a slingshot. I need Tristen to move because once I release the tree, the burning mass will fling right back to where he lays. "Move it, now!" I grunt. Searing pain engulfs my hands.

Tristen uses his burned hands to push himself to his knees. He crawls forward a few feet before collapsing. The material in my left hand burns through. Raw coals sear my palm.

"Shit!" I release the end of the tree. It whips toward Tristen. The burning end smacks his ankles. He lets out another scream.

I leap to my feet. Tristen's no longer pinned to the ground. I roll him over and drag him away from the burning tree.

Lowering Tristen's head to the ground, I kneel beside him. "Are you OK?"

His head shakes back and forth in a rhythmic motion. "My legs. My legs are burned."

I don't have to roll Tristen on his stomach to check his leg wounds. I watched the flaming tree press into his hamstrings. The roar of the ongoing fire envelops us. I turn in the direction from which Tristen came. Toward town. The situation has changed. Tristen needs medical attention. Buena Vista has a clinic. If we can get through, we should go for the town.

But the fire has jumped the road. The pavement leading to town is lit like a Sunday school cartoon memory from my childhood depicting the approach to heaven's pearly gates. But instead of a path to redemption, this is a gateway to hell. We have no hope of making it to town on foot.

Tristen's open backpack lies in a smoldering heap where I left it, only ten feet away. It almost looks like Tristen, but without legs. Now that I've caught my breath, I reflect on why Tristen left in the first place. When he bolted from The Lodge, just as we discovered Bruce Davis's body, Tristen became my number one suspect. If he didn't kill Davis, why did he run?

I turn back to Tristen, lowering my face close to his. "Can you walk?" It's not a useful question, because his answer doesn't matter. If he stays here, he's going to burn to death. So he'll damn well be able to walk.

"No—"

"Wrong answer. We're moving." I glance in the creek's direction, wondering if it might provide safety if the flames overtake us. The cold water would soothe Tristen's burns if we stopped to treat them.

No. The road is faster. The sooner I can get Tristen back, the sooner we can do something for him.

We haven't gone ten steps, Tristen's arm slung around my neck, before he crumples to the ground, moaning. I make sure he doesn't hit too hard before turning to scout the fire still raging on both sides of the road. It's no longer advancing on us, but definitely blocking the road. We're committed to returning to The Lodge.

"Let's go, Tristen." I tug on his arm. He yanks it from my hand.

"I can't." He coughs.

I step back and look at him. "You didn't have a problem battling a fire to get away from us."

Tristen groans. "It just seemed stupid to wait in that lodge to die in a fire. That's all."

"Really? You decide to bolt an hour after we find a dead body near your room? You don't even take your friend Nate with you?" I've already determined Tristen is unarmed. I'm pretty sure I could kick his ass even without his burned legs. So I'm needling him a bit for a reaction.

Tristen struggles to his feet. He gives me a look of what looks like disgust before staggering up the road. I move in beside him, reaching my arm around his waist to help keep him standing. He lurches forward. "You don't know anything. You didn't lose 75% of your net worth overnight."

"What, you weren't insured?"

"That's just money. The Remingtons are priceless."

I've got him going now. "So you took it out on the security guard? Come on, Tristen…" I intentionally pause, hoping Tristen will fill it with an explanation. But I hadn't counted on the way *come on, Tristen* would roll off my tongue. I can't decide if it's just bad poetry, an alliteration, or a connection with Dexys Midnight Runners's hit *Come on, Eileen*, but now the song is stuck in my head. I snort.

Fortunately, Tristen misses my mental sidebar. "You think I had anything to do with that?" He staggers forward another ten feet. I need to keep him talking because that's when he makes the most progress toward The Lodge. He looks sideways at me. "Do you honestly believe I would kill a guard because he failed to prevent my art from being stolen? Disregarding his poor judgment, I thank God he wasn't murdered like the other guard."

Tristen speaks with passion. I'm unsure if that's his normal style or whether second-degree burns and a nearby raging fire play a role. But he sounds sincere.

"If you think someone murdered Mr. Davis," Tristen says. "I'd suggest you ask yourself who would benefit from his death."

No shit. Like I haven't been asking myself this question already. Tristen's stagger morphs into a consistent gait. Either his legs are loosening or the motion masks his pain.

"What did you mean by poor judgment?"

"What?"

"You said *disregarding his poor judgment* when you were talking about Bruce Davis. What did you mean by that?"

Tristen stops and faces me, his mouth opening to reply. But he says nothing. He closes his mouth and starts walking up the road.

"Tristen, we're going to figure this all out, eventually. Don't you want to be the cooperating guy instead of the aiding and abetting guy?"

He whirls. "I am not helping anyone. If you want to talk to someone about Mr. Davis's decisions, talk to Monica. Or her friend Duane."

Whoa. Not that I had totally discounted Laura's accusations against Monica, but I thought it was a little over the top. The whole *she slept with my boyfriend in high school* thing wasn't lining up with a motive to steal a semi-valuable piece of art and sneak into a room and kill a security guard.

"Monica? You think she had something to do with Mr. Davis's death?"

I'm talking to Tristen's back because he resumes his lurch up the road. The trees on the left start to thin. Although the smoke still reduces our visual range to meters, I sense we are approaching the turn to the bridge at The Lodge.

"I didn't say that. I didn't say she killed him. And Duane couldn't have—he was already gone. But those two knew Mr. Davis before this all started. They're knee deep in all this. And Mr. Davis knew Monica stole *Broncho Buster*. You figure it out from there."

I stop in my tracks. "Wait a minute. You think Monica stole her sister's painting?"

"No. I don't *think* she stole the painting. I *know* she stole it. She told me."

CHAPTER 19

I'm like a mule team driver for the remainder of the trek back to The Lodge. Tristen's adrenaline surge seems to fade. As he slows his gait, I try to coax more information from him.

"Where is *Broncho Buster*? There's no way Monica sent Duane away with it, is there?" I fall in next to Tristen, adjusting my pace. The noise from the fire fades, and the smoke seems to be dissipating just a bit.

"Duane doesn't have it. She told me she hid it, but she didn't tell me where."

"Why would she tell you? How are you involved?" I rush my questions, worried he might pass out before I get answers.

"I'm not. She was wasted. We were talking about art. I mentioned something about how her sister's paintings were good but not great and—oh my God, Tyler—it's like that one remark opened the floodgates. She was all over the negativity, saying, 'I knew they weren't that good. I've always told her they were just okay…' stuff like that. I don't think those two like each other very much."

"That's the understatement of the year," I offer.

"But then she added something that didn't make sense. She said, 'I'm making her painting more valuable. It's my pet project.' Something like that. She said now that she had it tucked away, the value would increase even more."

"Whoa. Are you saying—?"

A woman's shout interrupts my interrogation. "Zahn!"

"Frazier?" I call. "Is that you?"

We approach the bridge. A figure materializes from the smoke at the opposite end next to where the truck still blocks the exit.

"It's Julie," the voice answers.

I expect Julie to meet us, maybe help with Tristen, but instead she stands, as if paralyzed, on the far side of the bridge, a mask hiding her expression.

Tristen crosses the bridge. He pauses in front of Julie. She steps to the side, her eyes searching for mine. Tristen continues toward The Lodge. He and I have a conversation to finish.

As soon as I step off the bridge, Julie grasps my hands, her eyes locked on mine.

I wince. The burns from rescuing Tristen are minor. But they sting. "What's wrong? What happened?"

"It's Algood. The guy who came to buy Laura's painting?

"What happened to him?"

"He's got a gun. He used it to make Agent Frazier go with him. They left. He said he was tired of being forced to stay at The Lodge against his will."

Now it's my turn to lock eyes with Julie. Algood's been nothing but an asshole since we arrived, but he hasn't been high on my suspect list. What motive would he have to kill Davis? Why would you advertise your interest in buying *Broncho Buster*, and then steal it?

Unless he's got something going with Monica.

I can't make out The Lodge through the smoke. "Did you see anybody else with a weapon? Back at The Lodge?" Tristen's accusations against Monica flash through my head.

Laura was right. Monica has something to do with what's going on here. "What about Monica? Did she give anything to Algood?"

"No. But that's what I'm trying to tell you. It's not just Emma with Algood. Monica went too."

"Why? I can see why Algood took an FBI agent. To keep her from following him. But why take Monica?" I take Julie's arm, steering her toward The Lodge.

Julie stops and tugs her arm away. Her voice raises to almost a wail. "That's the thing. He didn't make Monica go."

"What?"

Julie nods. "As soon as Monica heard what was happening—that Algood was heading back to BV—she was begging him to take her with him. So he did."

"Let me guess. Did she have a big painting with her?" This is the only reason I can guess why Monica would risk the dangerous route back to town. She was fixated on the painting and wanted to get it away from the rest of us.

Julie looks at me with what appears to be confusion in her eyes. "No. No painting." She narrows her eyes. "You don't believe all that stuff Laura's been feeding you about Monica being behind all this, do you?"

"Let's get back." I don't reach for her arm this time. I take three steps across the parking lot, then turn to make sure Julie follows. She does.

"Did the Wi-Fi come back?" I know the answer before I even ask. It's not like a router walked through the door.

"No."

Now isn't the right time to grill Julie about what happened. The funny thing is that I didn't believe Laura's accusations about Monica until I met up with Tristen and he implied Monica took the painting. Why would he lie about that?

I need to get back inside and count heads. Figure out exactly what happened and what I'm going to do. It was easier when Frazier was here. With her in charge, I could focus on figuring out how to get all of us out of here. She was the one concentrating on the murder and the theft. Now that the FBI is out of the picture, I figure I'm the only one left who can get us out of this predicament.

•   •   •

"I need each of you to tell me where you were when Algood took Frazier. Tell me what you saw." I've got the remaining members of our party in the lobby next to the unlit fire. The same place we started yesterday when we found out we were trapped in The Lodge. Mike stands between me and the kitchen. Laura and Julie share the sofa facing me and the fireplace. Nate sits in the armchair angled toward the hearth. Tristen is absent. He's upstairs, face down on a bed after Nate helped me dress his wounds with first aid material Mike dug up from one of the storage rooms.

I don't like leaving people alone right now. Not until I have a better idea of what is going on. But I also can't picture us circling Tristen's bandaged backside discussing our situation. Nate stands to my right next to the sofa where the sisters sit. Five of us remaining—six, if I include myself.

I've switched holsters, now carrying my Glock 26 at my hip instead of concealed against my chest. It made sense to keep it hidden while Emma was here—a backup in case she needed help. Now that she's gone, I need the remaining people to recognize someone is in charge. I might not have the legal authority, but the Glock should keep anyone from asking about that.

"You start, Mike." I direct my question at the young man first, intending to move clockwise around the room. I'm pretty sure the art thief isn't sitting in this group. Nor the murderer. Now that I've confirmed Algood's carrying a gun, he's moved up on my murder suspect list. Bruce Davis didn't die from a gunshot. But a gun could have forced him to ingest something fatal.

"I didn't see them leave. I was in the kitchen prepping lunch. Didn't even know what had happened until Ms. Julie told me. You can ask her." He looks at Julie. I follow his gaze. Julie gives a curt nod.

"Laura?" My heart sinks as I turn in her direction, trying to imagine a scenario in the future—assuming we make it out of here alive—where our nascent relationship survives. I'm not seeing it. "Were you here?"

Laura's eyes focus directly on mine for the first time since we got the calls about the fire. I'm unsure what grief stages she has experienced but from my angle she started with shock, then grief, then anger, and now—well, I'm unsure what you would call it, but she looks a bit like the Laura I first met. Her chin juts, her eyes engage mine, and she appears to be listening to everything I'm saying.

"Yes. We were all here." Laura sweeps her hand to the left, indicating Julie and Nate. "Emma—Agent Frazier, I mean—and Monica too. Agent Frazier was talking to all of us when Algood walked into the room with a tote bag. He asked if he could sit. She pointed toward that empty chair." Laura glances over at the chair next to Nate. "I'm not exactly sure what happened next because I had turned my attention back to Agent Frazier—"

Nate cuts off Laura. "I saw him. I was sitting right here in the same spot. He sat down, bent over and stuck his hand in his bag, and pulled out a gun. He pointed it at Agent Frazier and said something like, 'You can stop talking now. Give me your weapon.'"

Nate turns to Laura. "Sorry. I saw that part. Do you want to tell the rest?"

"Right," Laura continues. "He said 'stop talking now and give me your gun.' That's what I heard." She turns to Julie. "Right?"

Julie nods, but says nothing.

Laura continues, "Agent Frazier puts her palms down like she's trying to calm a dog or something and that's when Algood just loses it."

I'm unsure my one-at-a-time story technique is going to work because Nate jumps in again.

"Right," Nate says. "You guys correct me if I get this wrong, but he basically leaps to his feet. He walks straight toward Frazier screaming, 'No. That's not how it's going to go. Give it to me now, or I'll blow your fucking head off.'"

Julie and Laura nod their heads. I wait for Nate to continue.

Nate pauses, like he's disappointed at my reaction, before continuing. "Agent Frazier took a step backward. She moved her hand toward her holster. That's when Algood pressed the barrel against her head. Frazier froze. Algood took her weapon and made her sit in the chair he was sitting in. That's when he apologized."

This time, I can't stay quiet. "What do you mean, apologized?"

Laura chimes in. "I know. We all knew him for like one day and I don't think any of us can imagine him apologizing for anything, right?" She glances at Julie, but her sister's face remains blank.

It occurs to me that Laura and Nate are doing all the talking while Mike and Julie are just watching. Mike's got a good excuse—he wasn't in the room. But what about Julie?

"Julie, can you describe how the apology looked to you?"

"It was—" Nate tries to interject, but I hold up my hand, palm out.

"I'd like to hear Julie's observations."

Julie's voice starts out soft but grows in volume as she relates what she saw. "It was like he flipped a switch on and off. It turned on when he pulled out that gun and started screaming. But after he had Agent Frazier's gun, the switch turned off. But instead of turning back into the asshole we all knew, he started explaining himself."

Laura nods. I glance in Nate's direction. He's doing the same. "Go on," I say to Julie.

"He starts with Agent Frazier and says something like 'I know this looks bad, like I'm the bad guy in this situation. But that's not how it is. This is something else.'" Julie looks at her sister, who still bobs her head in agreement. "He says 'I can't stay here. I can't just wait for some act of nature to take me out. That's not what Martin J. Algood does. I move.' I can't remember the exact words he used after that, but he referred to how Tristen tried to leave and you," Julie looks directly at me, "were out tracking him down. He said that if he left, he had no doubt Frazier would do the same for him. So that's why he was taking Frazier with him. Frazier argued then, but he made her shut up."

"Because that's when our crazy sister barged into the scene," Laura says. "She's laughing, and it's not her sober laugh. She was high on something, right Julie?"

I look at Julie, expecting her to counter Laura's statement like she has every other time Laura puts down Monica in public. But Julie nods. "It wasn't a normal laugh. I think you're right."

"I know what she looks like when she's high," Laura says. "So she interrupts Frazier with this laugh, then moves toward Algood. He raises the gun at her and asks what she's doing. And she just keeps right on walking toward him. She stops right in front of him and says, 'I'm going with you, Marty boy. I'm going with you.' Algood is shaking his head, all confused-like, and Monica keeps talking. 'I've just been waiting for someone with the balls to stand up to these guys.' Monica tilts her head in Frazier's direction like the FBI is who Algood stood up to. Then Monica says to Algood, like she's begging or something, 'So let me go?'"

Laura leans back against the sofa like her role in the conversation is over. I scan the room, waiting for someone to continue. Everyone is silent.

"So then what happened?"

"That was it," Nate says. "They didn't discuss it anymore. They didn't pack anything. No masks. They didn't take water. Algood just waved the gun toward the door and followed Agent Frazier and Monica out into the parking lot."

I squint in Nate's direction. "I came up the road with Tristen. We didn't see them. Did they go down Middle Cottonwood?"

"I didn't follow them," Nate says.

"I did." Finally, Julie volunteers something. "That's why I was out there when you and Tristen came back. I watched them turn at the river. But before the bridge, not after."

"*Before* the bridge?" My voice comes out incredulous. Everybody in the room looks up at me. I realize none of them share my familiarity with this river. We had a Search & Rescue mission up this direction a couple of years ago and our teams had ample opportunity to explore both sides of the river. "They can only travel down the south side of the river for a mile and then they would have to cross over because of the cliffs. But there's no bridge to make the crossing."

"Maybe you can still catch them," Mike suggests, his first input to the conversation.

He has a point. If I stay on this side of the river, I might be able to corner them where the cliffs start. Or I might meet them coming back after they figure out they funneled into a dead end. But tracking down Algood and his party means leaving five people alone up here. Unless I risk taking them with me. I'm unsure how far the fire has spread, but I'm positive Algood's route is impassable. I can't leave the three of them out there either. Especially Frazier. Not just because she's law enforcement—but also because I need her. I can't do this alone.

I turn back to Julie. "So how long ago did they start?"

"Fifteen minutes before you got back," Julie says.

I check my watch and do some mental math. They've been gone forty-five minutes, but it would take them an hour to reach the part of the river where they would either have to find a way across or turn around. I can hole up at the bridge—that's my best guess for where they will end up crossing the river—but I have time. Time enough to find out more about Martin Algood.

CHAPTER 20

I catch Mike's eye and nod toward the kitchen. He turns for the door.

I turn to the rest of the group. "I need you all to stay in this room until I get back."

"What's up?" Mike says, after I close the kitchen door behind us.

"Is this place alarmed? Is there a security system that will tell us if someone tries to leave or get in?"

"Sure. But the company can't receive the alarm without Wi-Fi. And with the fires, it's not like the cops could respond even if they got the alert."

He's missing my point. "That's not what I mean," I say. "I don't care about the remote alarm. I want to know if the system can give an audible alert when breached. One that warns us—warns the people inside The Lodge."

"I get it. Yeah, that's easy. One switch on the alarm system. Then you just arm it."

I pause before speaking again. I've mulled over the possible ways Mike could be responsible for either the theft of the painting or the murder of Davis. I just can't see it. If he stole the painting, then why did he stay behind during the evacuation? And why would he kill Davis, a man he just met, after fires trapped us in The Lodge?

I can't get anything done without some help. Now that Agent Frazier is gone, I decide to put my trust in Mike.

"Set it up. Don't lock the doors. If Frazier gets away, I want her to be able to get in." I clap my hand on Mike's shoulder. "I'm going to do some looking around upstairs. I need to know if anybody tries to leave or get into the Lodge."

"I can watch everyone," Mike volunteers.

I nod, giving him a thin smile. "You going to threaten them with a spatula if someone tries to leave?"

Mike steps backward, pointing at the open kitchen. "I got knives. And not just butter knives."

"Great. Let me give you two scenarios: the first, Laura gets up and walks out the front door. You tell her to come back. She says 'Fuck off.' Are you going to stab her?"

Mike says nothing.

"The second, Martin Algood walks back through the door with that weapon of his drawn. You tell him to leave. He says no and points the gun at you. What's your next move?"

Mike steps toward the kitchen door. "I'll go set the alarm."

I climb the stairs to Algood's room. Halfway down the hallway, I pause in front of Tristen's door and knock.

"What?" Tristen's voice rings higher than normal. I suspect his pain hasn't improved.

"Just checking in. Need anything?"

"I need to get out of this place. I'm lying on my stomach with a burnt ass and a forest fire coming in our direction. You guys doing anything about that?"

"Working it," I lie.

I still don't know what to tell everyone about the forest fires. If they approach within several hundred yards, my plan is to take us all up Cottonwood Pass. With this crowd of misfits, it'll take us two days to reach the summit; the first place I can imagine us running into another vehicle. And that's if we're lucky–why would someone drive up the pass if this side is closed? Hiking is a last resort.

But Tristen's question reminds me I haven't thought through the evacuation plan. If we bolt out of here in a last-ditch effort to avoid the flames, we need to be prepared with food, water, and overnight gear. And right now, I have a lodge full of people with no purpose. As soon as I've looked through Martin Algood's room, I'm going to put them to work building emergency packs in case we have to evacuate.

Algood's room is trashed. Not like someone searched it before I did, but more like Martin Algood is a slob. I find this humorous since none of us were planning on spending the night, or came here with a suitcase or anything. White towels litter the floor. A terry-cloth robe dangles off the end of the unmade bed. An empty bag of tortilla chips sits next to a half-bag of pretzels resting atop an open satchel lying next to the bed.

Algood has a gun. My assumption is he also has a phone and a wallet. Not that we have cell reception or a place to spend money, but old habits die hard. I circle the room looking for any other personal items, saving the satchel for last. A shaving bag lies on the counter to my left as I enter the bathroom. Its contents litter the opposite side of the sink: deodorant, shaving cream, a razor, toothbrush, toothpaste. A plastic container of dental floss elicits a smile—after seeing how Algood keeps his room, I question his personal hygiene habits.

The shaving bag is unzipped, and I peer inside. I recognize a store-brand laxative, one I sometimes use myself. There's also a Viagra prescription, another thing I probably need if the opportunity ever arises. Of course, that would require getting past first base.

The orange of another prescription bottle flashes from the back of the bag. I use my pocketknife to roll it toward me so I can read the label.

Leaving my fingerprints will do nothing to help the investigation. Algood pulled a gun and forced someone to leave with him against their will. I'm no law enforcement officer, but I made it far enough through the Academy—and I've watched enough TV—to recognize this is a room of interest.

The pill bottle is empty. Ritalin LA 20mg. This is the stuff they give kids for ADHD. Stuff I've heard college students use to help them study. What's Algood doing with it? His name is right on the label. Whatever he's dealing with, some doctor seems to think Ritalin is the answer for it.

I flip off the bathroom light before returning to the satchel. Algood must have his clothes back at his Buena Vista hotel because the satchel only contains an extra shirt and a rain jacket. Except...I nudge the jacket to the side and spot a black case at the bottom. I pull out my knife again, performing my detective trick to get a better look at what I've found. It's an iPad; one of the bigger models with a large screen. There's a decent chance I could learn more about Algood if I can get on this computer. But my pocketknife isn't going to help with this one. I poke around the rest of the bag, hoping to find a keyboard. No luck. My guess is this thing is password-protected, and he uses the touchscreen. If I mess with it, I'll contaminate potential evidence. And still probably won't get in.

I imagine Agent Frazier out there with Algood, unarmed, and frustrated at him catching her by surprise. Monica is with them as well, but I'm less concerned about her. She chose to join Algood. He's not viewing her as a threat. But Frazier will seek an opportunity to gain the upper hand. She's in danger.

I'm only batting five hundred when strong women in my life are in danger. I got my daughter back. But not my friend Kristee. Fifty-fifty is OK in baseball. Not with the lives of those I love.

I reach for the iPad, then pull my hand back as Perez's words float in my memory: *I don't want you going around involving yourself in this case like you tried to do last time.*

Yet, here I am.

CHAPTER 21

Laura waits for me at the foot of the stairs. I glance to the fireplace where Nate and Julie still sit silently, as if they can overcome our situation through a commitment to silence.

"I want to look for *Broncho Buster*," Laura announces.

Behind her, Mike emerges from the kitchen. He gives me a thumbs-up, then raises his hands, curling and uncurling his fingers, in what I assume is a signal for *the alarm is on*. I nod his direction. Laura follows my eyes and turns toward Mike. He gives her a wave.

"Hey, Ms. Long."

Laura turns back to me, hands on her hips. "Based on your interrogation back there, I'm assuming you're in charge now. So, I'm letting you know I'm going to be searching. She hid it somewhere around here."

From the moment Laura told me that *Broncho Buster* had been stolen, my chest ached like the air in my lungs was sucked out. Laura calling my interview an *interrogation* hurts worse–like my chest has been filled with the smoke from the nearby fires. Our fledgling relationship can't survive this. Every time this woman sees me, she's going to associate me with our ordeal here at The Lodge: the theft of her most prized painting, the murder of the man who guarded it, and the man she was starting to date treating everyone as a suspect.

So I don't even try. I give it to Laura straight. "I don't think that's a good idea. Let's get out of here first. Let the police come back after it's all over."

"You mean after this place burns to a crisp with my painting somewhere inside?"

"You don't know it's here."

"You don't know it's not. And really—you think someone just picked it up? Carried it out to the parking lot during the evacuation without anyone noticing?"

She's right. I don't think that. I have no idea where her painting is, but it's probably not far away.

"You can search inside The Lodge. I don't want you outside now—not with Algood out there, and the fire, and…well, I just don't want you outside."

Laura's smile is thin. "Any other restrictions?"

Her voice is snarky—and sarcastic—and she's not expecting me to say yes. She's wrong.

"Yes. Stay out of Davis's room. And Algood's room. I'm sure I don't need to explain why."

Laura nods and turns. "I'm starting with the downstairs," she says over her shoulder.

"I'll help." My offer is automatic—a habit of mine—but not sincere. I need to get the rest of our people prepping supplies to leave. I'd rather intercept Algood's return at the bridge than risk him entering The Lodge. I don't have time to look for her painting.

Her shoulders stiffen. "No need."

"Laura?" Those same shoulders drop. She releases an exaggerated sigh as she turns, waiting for me to speak. "Let me know if you find any Wi-Fi router equipment."

I join Julie and Nate in the kitchen, helping Mike collect supplies in case we leave in a hurry. Mike empties an armful of empty daypacks he has retrieved from behind the reception desk onto the counter. Julie leaves, then returns with the remaining masks from the lobby.

"It's not like we'd be cooking over a fire, Mike," I explain. "Just enough dry food to get us through two days or so. Do you have anything like that?"

Mike shakes his head. "That's not normal menu fare for high-paying guests. There's hardly anything where you add water and stir. Maybe some pasta?"

"What about the concessionaire?" Julie says. "Do you have keys to that? My husband brought me here for an anniversary. I remember a midnight Twix bar run."

Julie's break from her silence surprises me. Not only has she spoken, but there's a trace of humor in her voice. We need that.

Nate must notice too. "Sounds like an anniversary to remember."

Uh oh. I doubt Nate knows Julie is a recent widow. I wince, anticipating her response. To her credit, she answers Nate with a genuine smile.

"It was, Nate. It really was."

Mike disappears around the corner as soon as Julie says *concessionaire*. He's already back with the key before she finishes speaking. "Great idea. Exactly what we need…I think." He turns to me. "Granola bars, Pop-Tarts, and candy bars work?"

"Right. We're not talking about long-term protein. Just enough to get us over that pass. Sugar is good."

Mike hands us each a bag and then grabs three for himself. "I'll fill up stuff for Tristen and Laura too."

I nod. It's hard to imagine Tristen traveling more than a hundred yards with his injuries. Adrenaline got him back to The Lodge. The back of his legs still weep from the fresh burns. Any movement will be agony.

I've been avoiding this dilemma. What will we do when the fire forces us to evacuate? I don't see how I can leave one of us here to die. But I can't put everyone in danger by keeping them here either. I need Frazier. I'd send her on the evacuation and figure out what to do with Tristen on my own.

Mike leads us down the hallway to the concessionaire, where he unlocks the door. He steps inside and we file in behind him, gaping over his shoulder. This is like trick-or-treating at an apartment complex. Easy pickings and nothing healthy. Mike surveys the small room before unlocking the counter window. "It'll just be easier if I hand it to you over the counter. Everyone back out."

I step back to let Julie and Nate back into the hallway. My name echoes from the lobby area. Laura. She calls again, using a voice loud enough for me to detect tension, but hushed in a way I can tell she's trying to hide it from someone.

"I'll be back." I jog toward the lobby. As I burst through the swinging glass doors to the hallway, Laura flinches beside the stairway.

"What?" I stride toward her.

"It's Algood. I saw him outside." She points to the window near the fireplace. "And then he looked through the window there." She points to the other window in the room's corner next to the parking lot.

"Did he see you?"

Laura shakes her head. "I don't think so."

"He's moving toward the front door." I pull my Glock from my holster. "Everyone else is halfway down that hallway. Go down there and tell them what you saw. Go into the office and don't come out until I say. Got it?"

Laura nods and disappears. I turn to the main entrance door. So much for leaving it unlocked for Frazier. I should have anticipated this. Once Algood and the women discovered they couldn't make it through the fire using this side of the creek, they'd have two choices: either try the other side, or return to The Lodge. Looks like they chose the second option.

Laura's vertical banner from the exhibition still stands to the side of the entrance. I use it as cover, hoping to surprise Algood when he enters. I'm just not sure how he will come in. With Frazier in a headlock as a hostage? Or with Monica in the lead? She left willingly. Has that changed?

I aim my Glock at the door, ready to react to Algood's entry. My heart leaps to my throat as The Lodge's alarm blares. It's the first time I've heard it, and I assume someone from inside The Lodge went out of the service entrance or another exit. That's why I've asked Mike to set it—so I'd know if anyone left.

Then it hits me. If I didn't have a gun in my hand, I would have slapped myself upside my head. Algood's probably set off the front door alarm.

I crouch to a knee, peering around the banner and scanning the foyer windows. No need. Algood is already through the front door, weapon drawn, and aiming for the lobby.

I stand and barrel across the entryway on what I hope is an intercept trajectory on Algood. Once I've cleared the banner, the man is in plain sight. I immediately see I'm off by three feet—Algood passes in front of me. Unless I adjust course, I'll be grasping at the thin air he's leaving behind.

Algood must sense the movement from his right, because he stutter steps and turns in my direction. The pause in his forward momentum slows him just enough to place him in my path. His eyes widen. He swings his gun toward me. I nail him chest-first somewhere around his right lung, my arms wrapping him up like a successful open-field tackle from my high school days. Instinctively, my legs churn, ensuring the impact of my hit. Combined with my consistent vector, I stop his forward movement and throw him off balance.

One thing I didn't do in high school was tackle anybody while I was carrying a handgun. When I nail Algood, the blunt force of the contact launches my Glock 26 from my right hand. As I scramble to wrap Algood's arms in my own, my Glock skitters across the stone floor.

Algood hits the floor hard, cushioning my own fall.

"Oomph." Algood loses whatever air he had remaining in his lungs. In the split second, before we hit the ground, I remember Algood's weapon. Forget football—it doesn't matter who tackles who. All that's important is who ends up with a gun pointed at the other. And since mine is now on the other side of the room, I need to win this next battle.

I release Algood as soon as we hit, running my hands up his right arm, searching for his pistol. I'm instantly aware of two things: Algood is much better at hanging on to his weapon in conflict than I am…and I don't need to panic. Algood lies on the ground like a rag doll. I wrench the pistol from his fingers, then roll him over. I scoot backward toward my own gun while training Algood's weapon on him. I slow when I realize Algood still isn't moving. His eyes are open. So is his mouth. He's got the wind completely knocked out of him. The Lodge's alarm still blares in the background.

Keeping Algood in my peripheral vision, I examine his weapon. A Walther PPQ, according to the lettering engraved on the barrel. I eye Algood one more time, confirming he's not going anywhere, before tapping the magazine release to find out what I've got for ammo. Which is a big bunch of nothing. The magazine is empty. Sure, there might be a round in the chamber, but I'm not familiar enough with the weapon to check that fast enough to get a loaded weapon trained back on Algood.

I glance at Algood. His eyes remain open, but they are tracking my actions. He just watched me check his weapon.

"You got one in the chamber?" I say, sliding backward again closer to my own weapon.

Algood finally sucks in a breath. I drop his weapon, wrapping my fingers around my Glock. I train the muzzle on him.

Algood gasps again. "Dead." His eyes drop to the floor.

The alarm drowns out his voice, but I read his lips well enough to understand.

"Not yet, I'm not." I retrieve Algood's pistol and tuck it into my waistband. "And you're not in any position to do anything about that."

Algood's eyes still aim at the floor. He starts shaking his head as he tries to pull in more air. His chest heaves twice before he raises his head. I move closer as he begins to speak.

"Not you, Zahn." He gulps another breath. "That agent. Frazier. And Monica. They're both dead. I came back to tell you."

CHAPTER 22

They're both dead.

I can't comprehend it. Then, when I do, I feel guilty. Because I'm more concerned about Frazier's death than Monica's.

"Zahn?"

A voice from the hallway, louder than the alarm, jolts me from my shock. I turn my head while keeping my weapon in Algood's direction. It's Mike. Probably leading the others to the lobby. If I can't process Algood's news about Monica and Frazier, there is no way Laura and Julie will be able to handle it.

"Mike?"

"Yeah. Is everything OK now? Can we come in?"

"No!" I shout. *Too panicked.* "I mean, yes, I got everything under control. I've got Algood in here. But I'm not ready for all of you. I need to interview him. Can you turn off the alarm? Tell everyone to stay in the hall."

"Hang on." A minute later, The Lodge falls silent. All I hear is Algood panting. And maybe the thud of my racing heart.

Mike's voice breaks the silence. "Julie and Laura are asking about Monica. Is she there? What about Frazier?"

I glance back at Algood, still lying on his stomach. His head tilts to meet my eyes, then shakes left and right. "Dead." His voice is barely audible.

"Shut up." I say. He nods.

I shift my gaze from Algood back to the hallway. Is it true? Are Frazier and Monica both dead? I need to find out exactly what happened from Algood. But I'm unsure whether I can trust him to tell me the truth. He had to have killed them. But why would he come back here? The fire?

This isn't something I can do alone. I need Frazier.

"They're not here," I answer. "We're discussing that right now."

"What—"

I interrupt Mike. "I need you to escort everyone back to the conference room while we finish our talk."

If Algood killed two of our party, do I automatically assume he's the one who killed Bruce Davis too? Without Frazier here, I'm going to have to make some educated guesses about who is on my side and who isn't.

"Did you hear me, Mike?"

"Already moving." His voice fades. They've started back to the conference room.

"After you get them there, I need you to join me back here." I'm still convinced Mike is uninvolved in all this. He can help me with Algood. Watch my back while I focus on the man. That leaves Laura, Julie, and Nate in the conference room and Tristen upstairs, lying in a similar position as Algood.

"Got it," Mike calls.

• • •

"How did they die?" My eyes drill into Algood.

We've moved to the lobby. I've got Algood in a chair between me and the entryway, allowing me to monitor the front doors and the staircase leading up to Tristen's room. Algood's bag with Frazier's gun inside, sits at my feet. Mike stands near the fireplace where he can also monitor Algood. Turns out Mike isn't a gun guy. I've given him a quick tutorial on Algood's Walther. Now Algood appears more nervous about Mike's shaking gun hand than he was about me.

Algood still wheezes, but he's regained his breath. He's easier to understand. "So you know we departed soon after you went looking for Tristen LaFrance."

I note his use of the verb *depart*, but I stay quiet. They didn't just *depart*. Algood kidnapped Frazier at gunpoint, then allowed Monica to go with him. Or at least that's the story I got from the others.

"So we didn't want to run into you on the way into town," Algood says. "I figured you wouldn't be too happy about me using my gun to get things moving, so we went down the river from this side. I knew the other side had the road, and the road was closed for the fire, so I guessed this side was our best chance."

"Do you even know where we're at on a map?" I say. "Or were you just winging it?"

"We're part way up Cottonwood Pass." Algood's head drops. "I didn't know about the cliffs on this side of the river. That you couldn't stay on this side."

I nod and say nothing.

"So we got to that section and realized we had to cross the river. It's kind of fast moving there."

Fast moving is an understatement. The creek turns into a full-fledged river at the bend where the cliffs start. I've seen it from the other side. Before Kristee disappeared, I used to joke with her about how she should try kayaking that section. She never laughed.

"How far did you backtrack to cross the river?"

"We didn't backtrack. That's where we tried to cross."

Now I can't stay quiet. "You forced those women across at gunpoint? At the fastest part of the whole river?" Algood is making this up. He's going to claim he didn't kill them. I don't buy it. I still believe that if the two women are dead, then Algood murdered them. If they're not dead, then they got away. But why would Algood come back here if they got away?

"It wasn't like that. I told them we'd backtrack and look for another spot. But Monica said it would be easy to cross right where we were. She had this plan to use the end of the tree that jutted out from the other side. She said that once she got to that, it would be smooth sailing." Algood meets my eyes with a look that almost comes across as sorrow. "She jumped from our side. Landed on the tree. But then she slipped…slipped off where the current pushed against the roots. It pulled her under." He leans forward and presses his knuckles to the side of his head. "I can still see it. It was like slow motion. Until she got sucked under."

"Did you try—"

"Of course we did." Algood jerks his head from his hands. "I was getting ready to go after her—I could see the color of her jacket in the roots under the water. Like she was stuck there or something." His eyes widen. Even though I still don't buy his story, it's becoming harder and harder to believe he's this good of an actor. His hands tremble. "I turned to tell Frazier I was going to save Monica. But she was already heading to the river. She didn't even ask me. She didn't even look to see if I was still pointing the gun at her." He shakes his head. "I wasn't, by the way."

Right. Because you were getting ready to go save her yourself. I don't say the words, but Algood is a piece of shit. I'm already furious.

"Frazier jumped out to the log. She yelled at me to get a stick, or a branch, or something, but I didn't want to leave the shore while Frazier was out there in the river, you know?"

Algood's expression is pleading. Like he needs verification of his actions. Or inaction.

I say nothing.

"So Frazier grabbed onto the parts of the roots above the water. She dropped her lower body into the river. At first, I had no idea what she was doing. But then I figured it out. She was giving Monica something to grab onto—to pull herself out of the water."

"Did it work?" Much as I disbelieve Algood, he's hooked me with his story.

Algood's back to shaking his head. "I don't know if Monica grabbed her, or Frazier lost her grip, but she fell." He looks at me. I swear the glistening in his eyes wasn't there before. "Gone. Both of them."

"How could you be sure? How do you know they actually drowned? Did you do anything to save them?

"I'm pretty sure Monica drowned by the time Frazier went under. You could see her body under the water. Hell, I can show you if you don't believe me. And Frazier?" Algood glances at Mike. I turn as well. Mike's mouth hangs open as if Algood's story has stunned him into shock.

Algood continues. "I couldn't go downstream. Because of the cliffs on my side. But I could see ten or twenty yards downstream. The smoke was too thick to see further. I waited to see if she came out from under that mass of roots. Never saw her."

"How long did you wait?

"About ten minutes or so."

"Then what? Why did you come back here? Why didn't you go upstream, cross to the other side, and try to get to town?"

"Jesus, Zahn. Cut me a break. I just watched two women die right in front of my eyes. When I came upstream, I knew I was close enough to tell you what happened." Algood's expression hardens. "I still think we should leave. You're going to let us all burn up in this place."

Algood's offer to show us Monica's body bothers me. Not the move a killer would make. Unless he killed the women. Left them in the water. He acts like the shocked bystander now, but he certainly didn't creep into The Lodge like an innocent man.

"Martin. You snuck up on this place, looking through windows and finally inching through the front door with your weapon drawn. You were aiming it at me when I tackled you."

Algood doesn't appear fazed. "Of course I was. I'm not stupid. I realize how this looks to you. That I forced Frazier out of here at gunpoint. You weren't going to welcome me back here with open arms. Hell, you probably don't even believe me."

"You're right about that."

Algood turns to Mike. "What about you?"

Mike tilts his head at Algood before turning to me. "I don't know what to think. But if you need someone to go check out his story about

Monica and Frazier, I can do that. Would take me less than an hour. I'm guessing you want to keep an eye on him?"

I'm silent for a moment, then nod. I can't leave Algood alone with everyone else in The Lodge, but I need to know what happened to the women he took. What if they aren't dead? What if they escaped? Or what if they are hurt? I look out the window. A wall of smoke presses against the panes. I can't tell if it's thicker or not.

"OK, Mike. You've got to play it conservative, though. That side of the river has pocket fires. If you start seeing more than that, get back here. I don't want you dodging through the fire, chasing after something that might not even be there." I pause. "And if the flames are that bad, we need to know that. You need to get back here and tell us."

"Got it. I'll grab the bag I was prepping. And a first aid kit."

Algood speaks. "I can go with you. I can show you where they are."

"Shut up," I say. "You're not going anywhere."

CHAPTER 23

Mike rustles up a pouch of zip-ties from the pantry. He helps me secure Algood's hands together behind his back and to the chair, then zip-ties the chair to the fist-sized baluster next to the bottom stair. I've given due process and innocent until proven guilty five or six seconds of thought. But what choice do I have? Mike's leaving, looking for Monica and Frazier. I need to check in on Tristen's wounds while monitoring everyone else.

So we tie him up.

Are the two women dead? I don't know. But I don't trust Algood. I don't believe his version of events. After we secure the chair to the stairway, I use additional ties on his ankles, one each around the thinnest part and then another one, tying the two together. He's not going anywhere.

Mike shows me how to work the alarm so I can reset it when he leaves. After he departs, I lock the front entrance door before flipping the alarm switch in the kitchen. According to Mike, the alarm will trigger if anyone tries to open the locked doors.

Laura, Julie, and Nate wait in the conference room for an update. I'm not ready to share Algood's story. Especially since I don't believe it. But I've got to tell them something.

"Algood left them. He came back here." Not exactly a lie, even if Algood is telling the truth. "I've sent Mike out to check the location

Algood gave me. I need you all to give us an hour to sort this out. Let us see if Mike finds evidence of their location. Then we'll talk. OK?"

Laura's having none of it. "If they split up, why would the guy who kidnapped them come back here alone? Why wouldn't Monica and Frazier come back here instead?"

She's got a point. But I need to talk to Mike before we get into it.

"Give me the hour, Laura."

She glares at me—not for the first time today. She opens her mouth to speak again, but stops when Julie lays her hand on her shoulder.

I take advantage of the pause to leave the room. Algood glowers at me as I pass him on my way up the stairs. Everybody's giving me looks today. When I check on Tristen, I find him sleeping.

I step back into the hallway and shut his door. Slumping to the wooden floor, I lean against the hallway wall, taking stock of our situation. I've got no communication with the outside world, and the fire—although seemingly stationary now—is close enough that I'm considering evacuation. But I've also got a man too injured to walk, and another who may have killed a third of our group. I could give a shit about Laura's stolen painting now. Small potatoes when viewed in light of our life and death situation.

Fatigue hammers me. My head nods forward. I jerk awake, trying to remember the last time I felt so weary. Between dragging Tristen's burnt ass back to The Lodge, and completing my first open-field tackle in thirty years, my body is spent. And I haven't slept. My head drops again. This time I don't fight it.

Laura's voice blares downstairs. My head snaps up from my chest, banging against the wall behind me. I glance at my watch as I climb to my feet. I've dozed for an hour. Where's Mike? Did he find the women?

"Where's Monica? Where did you leave her?" Laura's voice is crystal clear and directed at Algood.

I turn the corner at the upstairs handrail. Laura, visible through the balusters, has her hands on her hips, confronting Algood. Halfway down the staircase, I spot Julie and Nate several feet behind Laura, watching her interrogate her captive audience.

Don't tell. Don't tell. I don't say the words aloud—maybe if I think them hard enough, Algood will get the message. I'd rather give them my theory about what is going on than have Algood tell his story again.

"I'm sorry," Algood croaks. "She didn't make it. Her and the agent…neither made it."

I'm too late. At the bottom step, I pivot, grabbing Algood's shoulder. "I'll take it from here."

Laura peers around me, trying to decipher Algood's response to her question. "What does 'didn't make it' mean? What are you saying? She didn't make it back here?"

"She—" Algood starts.

"Stop!" I command.

Laura steps backward. I don't look back at Algood, but he stops speaking.

"Let's move away from here. Over to the sitting room and I'll explain."

Laura's mouth wordlessly moves. Behind her, Julie wipes her eyes. When Nate moves to the same seat by the fireplace as last night, the women follow. Creatures of habit.

I turn to Algood, pointing my finger at him. "I'm going to tell them what you told me. But I'm also telling them my thoughts on what you said. And you won't like that." I bring my finger to my lips. "But you'll keep your mouth shut. Do you understand?"

Algood has lost all the bluster from our first meeting. I don't know whether it's my open-field tackle, his bound hands and feet, or his potential role in the deaths of two women, but his head hangs, like he's lost all the fight that characterizes his abrasive personality. Maybe it's his empty Ritalin bottle.

When I turn to face the others, Laura has regained her poise. She points at me.

"What does he mean 'she's gone?'"

I'm prepared to repeat Algood's story, along with my thoughts, when the alarm blares again.

Julie screams. I whip my head toward the front entrance. Mike's figure fills the glass window next to the door. He waves, but his expression reveals nothing about what he's found. No one stands with him.

I open the door. Mike enters. He opens his mouth to speak, but I hold up my hand. He pauses, and I step around him to secure the door. The alarm continues wailing.

"Don't say a word. I'm going to turn off the alarm."

I dash to the kitchen, resetting the security system before returning to the lobby. Mike stands awkwardly at the door. The other three face him. Laura seems to sense the answers to her questions about Monica are standing right in front of her. She stays silent.

"Go ahead." I nod at Mike.

"Here?" Mike's eyes shift from me to Laura and Julie, then back to me.

"Here. They need to know whatever you found out."

"I didn't find Frazier. No sign of her."

My heart lifts. Just as quickly, it sinks. I don't know if Laura and Julie recognize the subtext of Mike's first sentence or not. He didn't open with *I didn't find the women.* Just mentioned Frazier. She might be alive. But Monica…

Laura remains mute. Julie is the one who asks the question. "What about Monica?"

Mike's eyes aim at his feet. He glances quickly toward Algood before returning them to the ground. "Like Algood said. She drowned in the river. I can see her in the roots under the log."

CHAPTER 24

I jolt awake, as The Lodge's alarm wails again. The first thought racing through my mind is why I ever asked Mike to activate it. I reach for my Glock 26 on the nightstand. Confusion clouds my thought process. It's not just the lack of sleep. Or the sudden rush of adrenaline from the alarm. It's the question niggling at me: who else out there would want to force their way into The Lodge?

I barrel down the hallway past the guest rooms. As I reach for the banister, the answer hits me. What if someone is trying to get out?

Spinning, I aim for Algood's room. Mike might have confirmed Monica is dead and trapped under the river obstruction, but I still have no reason to believe Algood is telling the truth about what really happened. That's why I have him secured in his room, ankles still zip-tied together and wrists secured with another plastic strip to the headboard. Sort of like the author held prisoner in Stephen King's *Misery*. I'm not torturing Algood—he can still sleep on his side—but there's no chance in hell I'm giving him free rein to move about The Lodge.

Except he's gone. When I open the door, I face an empty bed. I flip on the lights. No sign of Algood. Two broken pieces of zip-tie on the floor confirm he's moving freely now.

Shit.

"Zahn?" Mike's voice floats up the stairs, barely audible over the alarm. "Someone's trying to get in."

I step out of Algood's room. Nate stands in the hallway. Laura's head pokes out from her room. Julie's nowhere in sight.

"Stay here," I say to Nate. I point at the door. "Check on Tristen." I turn toward Laura. "You check on Julie and make sure she's OK." I head for the stairs, calling out to Mike. "It's Algood. He got out of his room. I think he triggered the alarms when he left."

I descend the stairs, Laura's voice calling out behind me, "Julie's fine."

"Tristen, too," Nate echoes.

I breathe a sigh of relief. I don't need to deal with Algood taking more hostages. He appears to have left on his own.

"Thanks. Stay upstairs," I yell, then turn to Mike.

"Did you check the front doors?" I nod toward the foyer.

"Yeah, they're shut. He didn't go out that way."

"How do you know he didn't just close the doors behind him?"

"Because he would have had to have keys to reengage the deadbolt." Mike points in the door's direction. "And it's deadbolted."

"Where else could he have gotten out? The kitchen, you think?" I walk that direction.

"Zahn."

"What?" I whirl toward Mike.

"We don't need to check all the doors. The alarm system will tell me where it was breached when I reset it."

Mike should be in charge. He figured out Algood didn't leave from the front door. Now he's saving me ten minutes of chasing my tail with a solution that shouldn't take a genius to figure out.

"You're right," I say. "I'll go with you."

We move through the kitchen, Mike in the lead, flipping on lights as we go. He pauses at the pantry door before turning to me.

"Have you been in this room tonight?"

"No. What's up?"

"Door's open. I'm pretty sure I closed up everything down here when you guys headed up to bed. I wouldn't have left this door open."

My Glock is still unholstered. I tug Mike's arm with my other hand. "Let me go first. Maybe Algood tried to shut off the alarm before he left."

"Maybe." Mike nods. "But then he wouldn't be in here, because we heard the alarm go off when he left."

"Maybe. But I'll go first, just in case."

I hit the light switch. The pantry is exactly what I expect. Shelves of canned goods. No strange men hiding. I work the perimeter of the room toward the alarm box in the rear. The system's panel hangs ajar.

"That door was already open," Mike says. "I left it that way."

I turn to ask Mike why, when I see motion cross the doorway—a shape creeping past the pantry.

"Move it." I push past Mike, pausing before the doorway. "Stop where you're at, Algood."

I flip the pantry lights off before peering around the corner. The kitchen is empty. Why Algood is still inside mystifies me, but I'm pretty darn sure he doesn't plan on staying. He's heading for the service entrance.

Mike's so close I feel his breath on my neck. I turn to him. "Go reset the alarm system. Stay back there. If it goes off again, tell me which door. Got it?"

"Got it." He turns back to the panel. I step into the kitchen, swiveling my head left, then right. The alarm goes silent.

Movement flashes to my right. I hold the Glock in the shooter's stance I learned in the Air Force and track the figure crossing the closest lobby window. Outside. How is it possible that Algood exited already? Did he get out during the alarm activation?

The alarm blares again. Mike's voice booms from the pantry door. "Rear loading dock!"

I swivel that direction, picking my way in the darkness to the rear door. A square of light shines on the kitchen floor. The rear door hangs open, but there's no sign of Algood. Big surprise. Why would he wait for me?

I charge through the door, ignoring any remnants of my military training, before abruptly skidding to a stop.

"Fuck!" The grunt comes from below me, where a shadow limps away. I remember why they refer to the platform as a loading dock. There's a four-foot drop off straight out the door with a staircase to the left. Looks like Algood missed the memo on that.

"Martin?" I call. "Don't make me chase you down. I left my mask inside." Maybe if I lighten the mood, it'll throw him off.

"I didn't kill those women!" Algood's voice sounds strained. As much as I'd like to believe it's from my flawless tackle earlier in the day, I suspect it's because he's hurt himself falling off the dock.

Algood knows I don't believe he's innocent. There's no use trying to lure him back with logic. "Fine," I call out. "But do you really think you can just run away? Everyone knows you were here. You kidnapped a law enforcement officer."

"You're a fucking idiot, Zahn. I'm not running away from what I did. I'm running from the fire. You guys should be too."

I aim for the concrete steps leading down the platform. "We don't know the fire's coming our way. The last thing they said before we lost communication was that it was a possibility."

"That's what *your* communications say." Algood's voice fades. He's moving away from me. "Not what mine are saying."

He's got communications? I move across the loading area, entering the trees where Algood disappeared. The further I get from The Lodge, the more difficult it is navigating through the underbrush. Ahead of me, branches snap. Obviously, Algood faces the same challenge.

"If you're talking to the outside, then why aren't you getting us out of here? Why aren't you sharing the information?" The phone confirms what I already know. Algood has something to hide.

"Because I don't like what they're telling us." Algood's voice is close. And ragged. He's having a harder time navigating than I am.

"That the fire is heading our way?" I spot an angular shape against a tree ahead. I advance with my Glock trained on the figure.

Algood spots me, his chest heaving. I plant my feet at a distance, keeping my weapon trained on him with one hand while pulling my headlamp from my side pocket with the other. I drape the elastic band of the light over the back of my head, pull the light to my forehead, and train the beam on Algood.

"Yeah," he breathes, squinting at my light. "I don't like the fact the fire is heading our way. But what I really don't like is them telling us where we need to go to get out."

Algood knows the escape route? "Where?" I say.

"I can't do their plan. That's why I'm running away." Algood nods his head over his shoulder. "This way."

"Where?" I repeat. "Where are they saying we need to go?"

Algood points his finger over my shoulder. "Mt. Yale."

I laugh. "Right. They want us to climb four thousand feet up a mountain because that's the way to get out of a forest fire? We're going to hike up Cottonwood Pass. It's a haul, but it's do-able and makes sense."

I watch Algood's head swinging back and forth in the dark. "They didn't say climb the mountain. They said use the trail to get above the treeline, then work our way north. There's nothing burning on the other side and there's less smoke. That's what they're saying."

"Cottonwood Pass makes more sense," I say.

"Nope. Everything that direction is socked in with smoke. And there's another fire down toward Taylor Park Reservoir. They can't guarantee they can get you out of there."

Now I'm the one shaking my head. "If you're the one with all the answers, how come you aren't using them? I don't get it."

Algood raises a hand to shield his eyes from my beam. Again, I'm struck at how believable this guy can sound. "I. Can't. Make. It. Jesus, Zahn—I can't even catch my breath running from you. That trip down the river wiped me out. I've heard about your fucking mountains out here. Mt. Yale is fourteen thousand feet high." He laughs. "I'd rather take my chances dodging flames than dying on the side of some god-forsaken peak."

"Give me your phone," I say, waving my gun.

"Sure." He eyes my gun trained on his chest. "I'm going to take off my pack and pull it out, OK?"

I nod. Algood stands, unslinging his bag from his shoulders. He unzips the pack and rummages around while I tighten the grip on my Glock. What are the odds he has another handgun in his bag? Did he bring an arsenal up here?

He pulls out an oblong shape, like a cross between a GPS and a cell phone. I step closer. A stubby antenna juts from the top.

"Sat phone?" I say, even though it's clear to me what he's got. "You come to an art exhibit with a handgun and a sat phone? What's your deal, Algood?"

Algood shakes his head before lowering his gaze. "Not what you're thinking. I don't travel unless I'm prepared. If you check my bag, you'll find $5k in cash as well."

I consider following up on his offer of a search. But even if he's telling the truth about carrying that kind of money, it doesn't matter. I know he's guilty. He claims he's not. The money wouldn't make a difference.

Algood shoves the phone toward me, extending his hand. I don't accept it.

"Turn it on," I say.

He smiles. Not maliciously, but almost like he's sad for me. "It's dead, Zahn. Useless."

I cock my head. We might not have communications back at The Lodge, but we have tons of electricity. "Now that you're through with the running away business, why don't we just head back and charge it up?" I wave my pistol toward The Lodge.

Algood's smile remains in place. "Can't charge it. No cable. It's sitting on a nightstand in my room at the Surf Hotel. I didn't expect to be here for an entire weekend."

"We got plenty of—"

"Regular phone chargers don't work. You need an Iridium charger.

"Let me see it."

Algood hands me the phone. I take it and I wave him back toward the tree. I don't want him anywhere close to me while I'm fiddling with this thing. The phone doesn't look too complicated. There's a power button—an etched white circle with a line bisecting it—in the same spot as my Garmin InReach. I mash the button and nothing happens. I glance at Algood. His smile has changed from sad to *I told you so.*

I flip the phone to check the battery situation, but it's set up like my iPhone, not my GPS—the batteries are internal and difficult to swap out.

Shit. I try to keep my face straight. I don't need Algood gloating over our mutual tragedy. I've got him. I won't let him escape again. He must know that.

But here's the important question: do I trust Algood's story about the safest way to get out of here?

CHAPTER 25

I consider perp-walking Algood back inside, one arm twisted behind his back, my gun trained at his head—but decide against it. He's limping from his loading dock leap, and his smart-ass smile after I discovered his sat phone was dead has disappeared. Algood staggers like a man defeated, resigned to the fact that he's lost any future chance of escape. So instead, I march him ten feet ahead of me while training my headlamp on the dense forest between us and The Lodge.

"Follow my beam."

My brain churns on the walk back. Is Algood blowing smoke—my daughter would be groaning at the way my dad-pun brain works, even under pressure—about the Mt. Yale escape plan? Something about his story niggles at me. When I asked him why he chose the wrong side of the creek with Monica and Frazier, he claimed unfamiliarity with the terrain. He said he didn't know about the impassable cliffs.

But tonight he's talking about climbing partway up Mt. Yale, then following the treeline to avoid the fire. He's given a perfect description of how you would get over to the next valley, one that he couldn't have known unless someone told him. What makes him even more credible is that he doesn't even want to take the route he's describing.

I let out my breath, loud enough for Algood to turn and see if I'm communicating with him. I wave my hand for him to continue walking. There's something else I'm missing. Something besides Algood's fire information.

Mike waits for me at the service entrance, the door held open. He glances at Algood and me, but then refocuses over our shoulder. I follow his gaze, but see nothing. I march Algood up the steps and into The Lodge.

"Everyone awake?" I say, after Mike locks the door behind us. "After all the alarms and everything?"

"Probably. I told them to stay upstairs. Believe it or not, they listened to me." Mike follows me into the lobby, moving toward the entranceway as I motion for Algood to take his familiar seat by the fireplace.

"Did you find the other person?" Mike says.

"What other—" I stop, confused. Mike meets my eyes before shifting them to Algood. He probably figures if I'm not going to keep an eye on our escapee, then he should.

The other person. That's what's been bothering me. We found Algood sneaking toward the service entrance inside The Lodge. He didn't set off the first alarm. That means that someone else tried to get out.

My brows furrow. Mike is way ahead of me again. We accounted for everyone in The Lodge. No one besides Algood was trying to get out.

Someone was trying to get in.

•   •   •

"I'm going back out," I tell Mike. "See what I can see. Maybe it's folks trying to help."

"What kind of helping people don't just knock? I mean, setting off a security alarm and running away doesn't really seem like the best way to provide assistance."

I like Mike. I'm guessing he's about twenty years younger than me. I know nothing about what he does besides his food catering gig, but the guy is funny. The kind of funny I'd like to share a beer with. And he's got a point about our intruder. Probably not here to help.

"Maybe they know we're having issues." I nod toward Algood. "You know—with him. If they think we're in some kind of hostage situation, they're not going to be knocking on the door."

"How would they know?"

"Not from me," Algood speaks for the first time since we've returned to The Lodge. "You think I told them I was going to force my way out of here with a weapon?" He snorts. "I might be desperate, but I'm not stupid."

Mike looks like he's struggling to stay quiet. Finally, he smiles. I've got a few choice words I'm holding back, as well—because if Algood isn't guilty, then he's definitely stupid.

Algood seems to pick up on our exchange. He looks from me to Mike. "OK, wise guys, if you're so smart, how is it I got away?"

Mike drops his smile. He glances at me. I nod at Algood. "You're right. That's on me. My mistake." I turn to Mike. "Can you remove his other shoelace?"

Mike freezes for a moment before moving to Algood's side and removing the one remaining lace from his shoe. He raises it. "He got out with the other one of these? How?"

"Go ahead, Algood. Tell him how you did it." I mentally kick myself for not anticipating this. Obviously, I'm not the only person who knows the secret zip-tie escape trick.

"Friction." Algood smiles at Mike. "All you got to do is get that nylon lace rubbing back and forth on the plastic. Eventually, it will burn through."

Mike nods. "But how did you get the lace out? Your hands were zip-tied to the bed post."

This is where I really messed up. I knew about the shoelace thing from my flight training days. We used to practice it in our resistance and escape classes. Sawing the shoelace back and forth and burning through the zip-tie plastic. It'd been so long since I'd had my training, I'd forgotten about it. Not only did I leave Algood with his shoelaces, I also didn't tie his ankles to the bed.

"I—"

Algood interrupts me, still riding his story of success. "I just did a crunch and rocked my ankles to my hands." Algood laughs. "I'm not in the best of shape, but good enough, right?"

Only an hour remains until dawn. I still want to check The Lodge's perimeter. Mike confirms he's not going back to bed anytime soon—he'll watch Algood. We use a fresh set of ties and secure him to the chair in the lobby. I take my Glock and a mask with me, but send Mike to the kitchen for a weapon before I head outside.

"Deactivate the alarm while you're in there," I say as Mike leaves the lobby.

He returns five minutes later. I've expected him to come back with a kitchen knife, or something else sharp. Instead, he wields a rolling pin, smacking it against his hand as he approaches.

"Disarmed. You can go out any door," he says. He sees me eyeing the rolling pin. "High school baseball. I don't have any experience in knife fighting, but I can swing a piece of heavy wood like there's no tomorrow."

I glance at Algood. He's not smiling.

I coordinate a signal—two taps-pause-two taps—for my return. Mike turns off the lobby lights so my departure won't be so obvious. Our caution might be overkill—the smoke is still so thick I doubt anyone outside can see over twenty feet. I leave from the main doors, my weapon drawn and my headlamp off. The nice feature of my Glock 26 is its internal safety. I don't have to decide whether to flip a switch or not–just whether to pull the trigger.

Crouching, I move down the walkway before turning left toward the pass. My plan is to circle The Lodge like the intruder would have, window to window, and door to door. If I don't find clues, I'll expand my perimeter search, looking for any signs we've had guests. I glance at the second story, where Nate instructed everyone else to hold tight. There's no obvious access to the second floor from out here. And I don't remember any stairs from the back. The fire evacuation for the second story is internal, not external.

I pause twenty yards from the front doors. Between the smoke and the dark, I'm unlikely to find anything. Not that I know what I'm looking for. I turn back toward The Lodge and squint. Tapping on my headlamp, I dim it to the lowest setting. I work my way around the west wing–where the conference room and Wi-Fi set-up reside–before turning toward the pond behind The Lodge. I point my headlamp toward the water and increase the illumination. The smoke hangs so heavy in this direction, it's like turning on my truck's high beams on a foggy night. The brighter my own light is, the less I can see. Dimming my headlamp again, I edge toward the lake shore. My weak beam reflects off the surface of the water. But there's nothing to see.

A hollow clang of metal-on-metal echoes from my left. I spin from the shore, swinging my Glock in the sound's direction, my headlamp beam still useless in the smoke. I switch it off while creeping toward the noise. Ten paces later, the dark logs of The Lodge's walls emerge. I orient myself, moving around the corner of the building. I'm approaching the loading dock and service area from the uphill side of The Lodge. The opposite side from where Algood tried to run away. The only things metal I remember in this area are the two dumpsters positioned side-by-side next to the outbuilding where Mike says the caretaker stores maintenance vehicles.

Another noise, this one dull and heavy, startles me. I work my way across the asphalt toward the dumpsters. Plastic sheeting trips me up and I stumble, my hands plunging forward to break my fall. As I pull back my hand to get to my feet, it comes back sticky. I've fallen on a torn bag of trash.

Five more steps. Visibility improves. The wooden gate to the dumpsters hangs open. I relax. I'm interrupting critters trying to get at the remnants of our dinner last night—not an intruder. Mike must have forgotten to latch the gate. I consider cleaning up the mess before deciding it can wait for daylight. Instead, I close the wooden gate, letting the metal latch drop in place. As the lever clicks shut, a snort sounds to my right. Swinging my Glock toward the sound, I use my free hand to mash the button on my headlamp.

A large black bear faces the door to the outbuilding. All I can make out is the green glow of its eyes turned toward me over a giant mound of bear ass. I catch my breath, considering my next move. Black bears aren't known for attacking humans, but none of our critters up here in the Rockies appreciate being surprised. The only thing worse than startling a large animal is cornering it.

As the bear wheels around, facing me, I wave my Glock. Then I step forward.

"Git!" I yell. "Move it, Bear." I've never herded cattle, but I've seen Bonanza reruns as a kid. If I had a cowboy hat right now, I'd take it off my head and slap it on my thigh while yelling. The bear grunts. Then paws at the ground. I wonder if my mask is throwing him off.

Shit. I train my Glock on the mass, slowing my breathing. Not my first choice. This is like taking a peashooter to a gunfight.

I step forward again. "Git out of here, Bear! Git! Git!"

The bear flinches like he's prepping for a charge, then bolts for the woods. Branches crash and pop as my would-be assailant escapes.

I release a breath, leaning forward with my hands on my knees, the gun pointed to the side. The post-adrenaline rush shakes me. I can't tell if my shaking hands are steadying my quivering legs, or if it's the other way around. Sure, I've never heard of a black bear mauling a human out here—unless it involved an idiot sleeping in a tent with his dinner— but that doesn't change the fact that I feel like I just cheated death or serious injury.

When I feel like my breath is under control and I've checked my pants for an involuntary discharge, I turn toward the dumpsters. I need to continue the search. Then I hear my name.

"Zahn?"

I whirl, swiveling my headlamp left and right, searching for whoever called me.

I stifle the first name that pops into my head. *Kristee?* Because it's impossible.

Instead I use logic. "Who's there? Laura?"

I heard my name being called. No doubt in my mind. None. It's not like I'm hearing things. It must be Laura. I can't imagine any of the sisters recognizing my voice just from me yelling at the bear. But then again, Laura calls me Tyler, not Zahn.

"Julie?" I try.

"In here. In the building," the voice calls.

I stride to the same door the bear found so interesting. My Glock points at the ready, and I reach out with my free hand to the handle. Then I freeze. I've got no reason to be afraid of Laura or Julie, but I'm still not sure it's the smartest move to silhouette myself in the doorway with my headlamp ablaze. Already made that mistake once tonight in my pursuit of Algood. What if the person calling is under duress? Someone could be holding them at gunpoint and making them call me.

I kneel next to the door and switch off my light. Algood's inside The Lodge, under Mike's guard. That leaves wounded Tristen or his buddy Nate. What the hell, though? I can't imagine either of them forcing one of the women out of the house. Even if they did, why hang out in the storage shed?

"Zahn? Is it you? Are you coming?" The voice is faint. But definitely calling from behind this door.

I reach for the handle, eager to help, before pausing again.

"Are you safe?" My question is useless. Like whoever is there will be able to answer truthfully if someone has a gun to their head. "Who am I talking to? Laura or Julie?"

There is a moment of silence, as if the person behind the door is processing my questions. Then I hear the voice again.

"Zahn, could you please get your ass through that door? I need some help. It's Frazier."

CHAPTER 26

Frazier is hypothermic. When I wrap a blanket around her in the lobby, she clings to me for just a second, shaking her head. Then she drops her hands. I send Mike upstairs to run a warm bath while I make sure she's comfortable on the lobby couch.

"Send down Laura or Julie to help get her wet clothes off."

I consider lighting the fire, but we haven't used the hearth since we arrived. I'm unsure that's the best use of our time right now.

Julie races down the steps to Frazier's side. I grapple with Algood's chair, turning him away while Julie helps Frazier with her clothes.

"Where's Laura?" I say.

"I thought she was down here," Julie says. "She's not in her room."

"Nate?" I frown.

"He's in talking to Tristen. I heard them."

What the hell is Laura doing? My first thought is that she might have left. But Nate reset The Lodge alarm. She can't be far.

"Why's he tied up?" Frazier's question is faint, like the move from the frigid outdoors to the warmth of the lodge has taken away whatever fight she had left. "Did he try to hurt you?"

I stare at Frazier over Algood's shoulder. Algood tries to twist her direction as well.

"I didn't—" Algood starts, before I interrupt.

"He snuck into the lodge brandishing a gun. He claimed you and Monica accidentally drowned in the river. What would you have done?"

Frazier says nothing.

I turn away as Julie reaches under the blankets to help Frazier with her clothes.

"Wait," Frazier says, and I turn back. Julie steps away from the FBI agent and looks from her to me. Frazier continues. "Monica did accidentally drown in the river." She shifts her gaze to the couch. "I tried to save her. And I fell in too. The river was too fast at that spot."

"This all sounds so familiar…" Algood's voice behind me drips with sarcasm.

"Shut up." I say over my shoulder. I turn back to Frazier. "That's how Algood described it. I didn't believe him."

"That's what happened," Frazier says.

"But…he didn't try to save you. He just left you for dead."

"Zahn, listen to me. I probably would have done the same thing. I got pulled under into the mass of roots. When I came up, I was snagged, with my head barely sticking out of the tangle. I couldn't see Algood. There's no way he could see or hear me. Even if he found me, he couldn't have gotten me out."

"So, how did you get out?"

"I hung on there as long as I could. I couldn't pull myself out. The water was too cold to keep hanging on. Eventually, I just had to push myself underwater and let go. Prayed I wouldn't get snagged by another root."

"I guess it worked," I say.

A puff of air releases from Frazier's lips. "Well, praying to live worked. Not the getting snagged by a root thing."

"What happened?"

"When I let go, it felt like I went about five or ten feet downstream. Then I got snagged again. I fought it for as long as I could and then—" Frazier chokes.

Julie lays a hand on Frazier's shoulder.

"Everything went black. That's all I remember. Next thing I knew, I was on my side in the shallows next to the bank. Coughing up water." She takes a breath. "I guess I drifted free from the root after I blacked out."

"But why were you in the shed?" I say. "I don't understand."

"Tyler," Julie's voice is firm. "She's shaking. Don't you think we should get her warmed up first?"

Frazier chuckles, but her voice is shaky. She still shivers. "Yeah, Zahn. I'm supposed to be doing the interrogations, not you."

I glance at Julie and nod, turning my back on the two women.

"Guess you can untie me now," Algood says. His voice is cocky, like every bit of humility he might have picked up in the last several hours has dissolved with Frazier's validation of his story.

"Guess you can shut up," I reply. "Unless you want to explain why I found her in a shed behind The Lodge instead of knocking on the front door."

"I can explain that." Frazier calls from behind us.

"Emma, let me finish," Julie says. "You're shaking so hard I can't get your pants off."

"Bath's ready!" Mike yells, from the top of the stairs.

•　•　•

Mike takes over watching Algood while Julie helps Frazier upstairs to the bath. I follow the women to the second floor and knock on Tristen's door.

"Enter."

Inside, Nate stands over Tristen's bed, inspecting his wounds. Tristen lies on his stomach. His face is pointed in my direction.

"How's it look?" I say to Nate. Tristen rolls his eyes. Nate glances in my direction.

The younger man shakes his head. "Depends on what you're going to ask him to do. Do you want to take a look?"

The last thing I need is another peek at Tristen's burned ass, but I need to know if he'll be ambulatory any time soon, in case we evacuate. I move next to Nate and examine Tristen's wounds. It's not pretty. And it's not really Tristen's butt that took the brunt of the burn—it's the back of his legs, across his hamstrings. When we first situated Tristen in the room, we had cleaned his wounds but not treated them with any ointment. Just let the air do its thing. The burns still flame red, weeping a clear pus from the skin. Jagged spears of crimson spike out from the sides of the burn, like it's trying to spread. Eventually, we're going to have to put something on them to corral an upcoming infection.

"Not pretty," I offer. "But not as bad as it could be." I lean toward Tristen. "What do you think? Could you walk if we needed to get you out of here?"

Tristen twists his head. "Hurts like hell when I get up to pee. Feels like the longer I lie here, the more it tries to scab over. But then when I get up, it rips them all apart." He attempts a head shake, but can't do it while lying on his stomach. "I might be able to move a little way. If we go more than a mile, I'm going to need some drugs."

I turn to Nate. "You got anything?"

"No. Mike gave us Tylenol. No one's got any painkillers. There are no antibiotics we could find on the premises." He pauses. "I have some edibles out in the car. Stuff I can't get in Texas."

Tristen grunts. "You shit—you've been holding out on me. Go. I'll still be here when you get back."

Nate looks at me, waiting for an OK.

I nod. "We have to reset the alarm. I'll walk you out." I turn to the window. Black has turned to gray as dawn breaks. The shroud of smoke enveloping The Lodge ensures the sun is nowhere to be seen.

Nate heads downstairs to wait for me while I move to Frazier's room. I knock on the door.

"It's Zahn. How's it going?"

Julie answers. "Come in."

I crack the door and poke in my head. Julie sits on the bed facing the bathroom door.

"She's still in the tub. I'm waiting…you know, just to make sure everything's OK."

"Everything's OK!" Frazier's voice penetrates the bathroom door, stronger than it was downstairs. "I've stopped shaking. Give me five more minutes and I'll be out of here."

I nod at Julie. "Any sign of Laura?"

"Nothing. Did you look around the first floor? She's probably still looking for the painting."

"Not yet. I'm going to walk Nate outside to get some meds for Tristen from their car. You need anything from yours?"

"No. Nothing."

I step through the doorway and call to the bathroom door. "Hey, Frazier. Did you know Algood's got a sat phone?"

Frazier doesn't respond right away. I'm just about ready to repeat the question when she finally replies. "No shit?"

I smile. "No shit."

"Have you used it? What's the status of the fire?"

"It's dead. He didn't bring the power cord, and it's non-standard." Silence. "Frazier?"

"What do you mean, non-standard?" Frazier finally says.

"None of our phone cords work."

"If it's an Iridium, I think I've got a cord. No phone, but I have a bag of cords and adapters with my computer. I'll check while you're outside and charge it up if I have one." She pauses. "I'll be downstairs by the time you get back."

Water sloshes. I assume Frazier has given up on her five more minutes.

Downstairs, Nate has already explained to Mike what we're doing. Algood's dozing, his chin on his chest. Mike looks exhausted. Actually, he probably looks the same as I do. Neither of us got much sleep last night.

"Need anything outside?" I offer.

Mike shakes his head. "Want me to ask him?" He nods toward the sleeping Algood.

"No." But it occurs to me I might as well take a look at what Algood has in his car while I'm out there. Hell, he had a gun and a sat phone with him inside The Lodge. Who knows what he might be packing in his vehicle that could tell us more about his motives? So he didn't kill Monica? That doesn't mean he didn't have something to do with Bruce Davis's death. He has moved no closer to my good-guy column.

I stride toward the reception desk where we've piled Algood's possessions. Grabbing the keys, I call back to Mike. "Frazier thinks she might be able to charge Algood's phone. Can you help her out when she comes down?"

"Got it." Mike replies.

I duck down the conference room hallway, poking my head inside the unlocked rooms for signs of Laura. Nothing.

Returning to the kitchen, I open the pantry door and step back to the security panel. The panel door hangs open. I pause at the flashing red lights. Steady green means armed. Flashing red means disarmed.

Stepping to the pantry door, I call out to Mike. "Did you reset the alarm after I brought Frazier in?" I attempt to keep my voice even. It's been a long night for both of us.

Mike walks my direction, stopping in the doorway between the lobby and kitchen. He squints like he's mentally rewinding his last three hours.

"Shit. No. You guys came in and you asked me to run that bath for Frazier. I forgot." Mike shakes his head. "Sorry, man."

I can't really be pissed at Mike, since I'm the one who sent him upstairs. If I wanted the alarm reset, then I should have remembered to do it.

"What's it matter now? Algood's in here. Frazier confirmed Monica's dead. There's no one else out there."

I nod but don't reply. Mike's right about keeping folks out of The Lodge. Who else could be out there? But now I've got a new concern. I'm worried someone got out. Where the hell is Laura?

CHAPTER 27

It takes only minutes to retrieve Nate's edibles from their car. I scan the parking lot—or what I can see of it—while Nate rummages around in the back seat. With the smoke still shrouding the valley, I barely make out the outline of The Lodge behind us. I turn toward Buena Vista, down in the valley, but have no better luck with visibility. At least I can't see flames through the smoke.

I drop off Nate at The Lodge, poking my head inside to remind Mike to reset the alarm.

"Got it." Mike replies. "Frazier's charging up the sat phone. She said it'll take a few minutes before you can use it."

I head back to the parking lot to check Algood's vehicle. Like the other cars we left at the bridge, it's unlocked. I open the driver's door and slide into the seat. Algood arrived in a rental. There's not much to check. The glove box holds a vehicle manual tucked into a Ziplock bag. A rental envelope containing receipts rests on top of it. That's it. I lean over and check under the passenger seat. Nothing. I reach under the seat I'm using. Nothing.

When I finish searching the entire vehicle, I slam the trunk closed. An echo of a closing door makes me jump. I whirl, scanning the line of cars behind me, trying to detect the source of the noise.

As I walk down the line of cars, something flashes in my peripheral vision. A female figure strides away from the remaining cars in The Lodge's parking lot. She has a small case in her right hand.

"Laura?"

The figure freezes, then turns my direction. A masked Laura waves and walks toward me. I meet her halfway.

"Where've you been? We've been looking for you."

Laura's eyes crinkle. I suspect the smile under the mask is fake. It's obvious my worry for her is the least of her concerns.

"I told you I was going to keep searching for *Broncho Buster*."

"In your car?"

"I looked in some of the outbuildings first. No luck. I was just grabbing my laptop before going back inside. You said we should prepare to leave. I want to take it with me."

This woman I think I'm getting to know? The one I might be starting to care for? She confuses me. I recognize how important her art is to her, even if I don't understand the mind of an artist. It's more than a hobby—I get that. But in the last 24 hours, we've had one man murdered, one man injured, and two people kidnapped—one of whom is confirmed dead. No matter how I turn our situation around in my head, I can't imagine a scenario where if I were in Laura's shoes, I would still be this worried about my painting.

I drop my eyes, trying to form the words to explain what I'm thinking. "Laura, I—" Then I stop. Laura's laptop case has two loops of cord protruding out of the side pouch. But that's not what catches my eye. Instead, it's the silver-handled metal handgrip next to the coils that looks out of place. "What's that?" I nod at the case.

"The laptop. I told you—"

"No. The metal thing sticking out."

Laura looks down at the handle, almost like she's forgotten she's carrying it. "It's for breaking the windshield." She pauses. When I don't reply, she continues. "And for cutting the seatbelt." She pulls it out of the bag and hands it to me.

I twist it in my hands. She's right. This thing is capable of doing both those things. But unlike the five-dollar specials with a hammer on one end and a protected seatbelt cutter on the other, this thing is more like a high-end utility knife with a titanium blade and case.

Laura extends her hand. "I'm taking it with us if we leave." Her mask twitches as if she's wrinkling her nose. "I don't have a gun like Algood."

I return the knife. I don't blame her—and I'm relieved she's thinking about her personal safety, and not solely about the missing painting.

"Let's get you back inside," I offer my arm. She ignores it. We walk back toward The Lodge, the gap between us a twelve-inch mile.

•   •   •

Inside, Frazier sits on the couch beside Julie. To my surprise, Tristen has hobbled his way down the stairs, standing with Nate by his side. I'm guessing he won't be sitting down anytime soon. It's almost like that first afternoon when we gathered to discuss our predicament—except this time there are fewer people and different circumstances. Now one of our party is severely burned. Another is tied to a chair. Maybe it's not like that first afternoon.

Frazier holds Algood's phone in her hand. She stands, looking from me to Laura, before giving a slight shake of her head. I'm not sure if it's because she's surprised I've found Laura, or she's confused about how much attention I shower on a woman who's clearly not the same one we met several days ago. Julie's reaction is different. She leaps from her chair, wrapping Laura in a hug.

"Where were you?" she says.

"Trying to find where Monica hid the *Broncho Buster*." Laura monotones, pulling her mask from her face. It's obvious she has no interest in continuing the conversation.

Julie steps back from Laura, glancing at the laptop case in her hand. "What's that?"

Frazier steps forward before Laura can answer, pushing the phone toward me.

"It's charged." Frazier's eyes shine bright. "Let's make the call."

I grab the phone and check the screen. "I'm surprised you waited for me. Don't you need to call your boss or something? Tell him what's up?" I told her we'd call Perez together, but that didn't mean I expected her to wait for me to even use it. She's the law enforcement officer here, not me.

"We just got enough charge to use it a minute ago. You go first. It seems like we need to figure out if we're safe from the fire first, before we get into all the law-and-order stuff."

I nod, examining the screen to figure out how to make a call. Unlike the sat phones we used in the military—large brown 5lb bricks—Algood's phone is about the same size as a regular cellphone, only a tad bit thicker, with a stubby antenna protruding from the top. Green symbols form a line across the screen's upper half. The battery icon is pretty obvious. I'm guessing the other symbol means we have satellite connectivity.

I press the phone icon and watch the screen switch to blank spaces. I instantly realize my problem. I don't have Perez's number memorized, and Algood won't have Perez in his contacts.

"Anybody have Rick Perez's number?" I shake my head. Why would they? "He's a contact on my phone, but my phone doesn't have service. This phone works, but he's not a contact." I twist the phone in my hand, feeling like I'm missing something.

"Uh, Tyler?" Mike speaks from the back of the group.

"Yeah."

"Does your phone turn on and off?"

"Yes. But it can't call out. All I can do is get the time and look at pictures." That niggling feeling again. "Aw shit. My contacts, right? I can get the number from my contacts?"

Nate, the only other person in the room under the age of thirty, smiles. "That or just look at your recent calls. Deputy Perez was calling you before we lost the Wi-Fi, right?"

I pull my phone from my pocket. It takes thirty seconds to boot up. Another thirty for Nate to show me which arrows to press. Then I'm dialing Perez's number.

It goes to voicemail.

"Send a text," Mike suggests. "Who knows what this number looks like when it shows up on Perez's personal phone? I probably wouldn't answer it either." He pauses. "Algood told us that when he was using the phone, he was talking with emergency services, not the sheriff."

I use a single finger and type out a message to Perez.

It's Z-man calling from a sat phone.

I hit send. Nothing happens. I turn to Mike.

"Give it a minute," Mike says. "Data can take longer than voice sometimes."

It only takes forty seconds.

"Zahn?"

"Rick? It's me. We've been comm out." I tap a button with a cone on it and Perez's voice comes out of the phone on speaker.

"No shit. Where are you?"

"We're at The Lodge. I've got some—"

"What the fucking fuck, Z-man? Dispatch was talking to one of your party on a sat phone. They clearly told him to tell you to move your party out of The Lodge and get your asses above the tree—"

I jab at the speaker button and move the phone to my ear before cutting off Perez. "This is the sat phone your guys were calling." I nod at Frazier to follow me, then aim for the kitchen. I stab the speaker button again, so Frazier can listen, then lower my voice. "The guy who owns it is tied to a chair in the other room. One of our group has been murdered. Another drowned in the river—Laura's sister, Monica. There's just a bit of shit going on here."

"Murder? WTF Zahn?" Perez's voice is muffled, like he's talking to someone in the background. Finally, he returns. "What about that FBI agent? What's she doing about it?" He pauses, obviously waiting for me to answer. When I don't, he continues. "I still don't understand why you didn't bug out when we told you to. The fire's going to hit you within the hour."

I've got a ton I want to say to Perez right now, but it all has to do with defending my actions. Explaining why we didn't know about their instructions. However, none of these excuses are worth delaying another second of our departure, especially based on Perez's last statement.

"I'll explain when we get out of here, Rick. Sounds like we need to move. Is the evacuation route the same? Up the Mt. Yale trail at Denny Creek until treeline, then skirt around to the other side?"

Perez says nothing, but his breath is heavy.

"Perez?"

"Yeah, I'm here. The route you described is still correct. But when we first gave it to you, you had loads of time to get to the trailhead." He pauses, and I wait. "Not anymore. You're going to have to move it."

CHAPTER 28

I've led rag-tag groups in my military days, but nothing quite like what's lined up before me today. After inventorying my SAR 24-hour pack, I join Frazier, checking knapsacks and bags, to ensure no one is lugging anything that will slow our evacuation. I'm discouraged. What's going to slow us down isn't the weight on our backs. It won't be the fact that half our party is hiking in the shoes—and clothes—they wore to the exhibition because they couldn't find anything else in The Lodge. It's Tristen LaFrance and his burned legs. Martin Algood claims to be out of shape, but I still have a hard time imagining him hiking slower than Tristen. Nate has pulled down a pair of wooden ski poles decorating the lobby wall. Tristen leans over them now. He's the only one of us not carrying anything.

After inspecting Nate's and Tristen's bags, I dig through what we allowed Algood to pack. Frazier checks over Mike, Julie, and Laura. It's not that I'm uncomfortable checking the women, but Laura still acts cold toward me. I figure my rummaging through her personal items will not improve that situation. I glance her direction. Frazier pulls the laptop from Laura's knapsack. They exchange words. Frazier shakes her head, and Laura stuffs it back in her bag.

Algood stands close to me, zip-ties removed, flexing his wrists. I still don't trust the man. Frazier thinks he just panicked when he forced her to leave with him at gunpoint. I disagree. The one thing I'm sure about is that he doesn't want to burn up in this resort. We're his best chance at staying alive. He won't make a break for it this side of Mt. Yale. I'll decide on the other side about reintroducing the zip-ties. If we make it to the other side.

Nate wears an actual backpack and has stuffed it with enough food for both him and Tristen, as well as extra clothing.

"You brought a backpack to an art exhibit?" My smile is tight.

"Found it upstairs in a closet. Do you think I should leave a note or some money or something?"

"I think you're fine." I'm all about leaving as much behind as we can to lighten our load, but I have little confidence after talking to Perez that this resort will survive the fire. So Nate leaving money makes little sense, either.

"Tristen." I nod at the injured man. I wonder if he understands how hard this will be, but figure I don't need to ask.

His eyes fixate on the door and he doesn't look at me when I speak his name. "Let's just go. The alternative is to end up like Bruce Davis."

Shit. I'm not proud of our decision regarding our dead security guard. I considered a brief ceremony and burying him. Better than burning up in his bed in The Lodge. But Frazier and Perez overrode me. I respect their reasoning. Davis's body and his room are a crime scene. As long as the remote possibility remains that the fire will miss The Lodge, then we need to leave the scene as we found it. Frazier secured Davis's cellphone so her team can run forensics—if and when we make it out of our predicament.

My law enforcement friends' rational explanation for not moving Davis doesn't change the fact that it feels as if we're leaving him to burn like a Viking on a pyre. I compartmentalize my guilt so I can concentrate on the now—like the military pilot in me has been trained to do.

Packs inspected, I confer with Frazier. We agree there's nothing left to do here. Mike passes out masks. Frazier taps out a text message to Perez on Algood's sat phone while I disarm The Lodge's security system. There's a time delay function that would reactivate the alarm after we leave, but I ignore it. Anybody approaching this lodge after we leave is here to save it, not break into it.

Frazier takes the lead, opening the front door and striding outside. Smoke curls through the lobby as we shuffle single file to the parking lot. I bring up the rear and close the door behind me. The click of the latch triggers conflicting emotions. Although I consider myself an outdoors person, there's something about the comfort of walls and a roof around you when things get tough. I'd rather be inside in a thunderstorm, a blizzard, and even—I guess—a fire. Right now, it feels like we're leaving the safety of walls and entering the danger of Mother Nature's fury.

I keep these thoughts to myself. Others in the party might note The Lodge hosted an art theft, a major burn injury, and two deaths in less than seventy-two hours. Maybe not so safe.

"Last call to get anything you need from your car," Mike says, pointing to the column of vehicles leading to the bridge. I wince. The last thing we need is people adding more weight to their bags. A flash of orange halos the line of cars and I hear a sound like a distant waterfall. I pause and step forward, squinting my eyes through the smoke. The light isn't coming from my truck, but from the woods beyond it.

"Frazier?" I call. She stops and turns. The line of people pauses behind her, all looking at me. I point at the flames, so close they're visible through the smoke.

Frazier nods. The good thing about teaming up in a crisis is we hardly need words now. "Hey!" she calls, and all heads swivel her direction. "This is good news. It means we got out of The Lodge in time." She pauses, and I'm unsure whether she's doing it for dramatic effect, or because she's unsure how to phrase her next words. "It also means we need to move our asses out of here. Let's go!" With that, she wheels and strides toward the bridge.

Tristen follows, gamely moving out on his makeshift crutches with Nate tucked in close in case he stumbles. Frazier turns at the bridge railing, surveying the gaggle. She probably realizes that as much as we need to put space between us and the approaching flames, it's only going to happen at the pace of our slowest member. Unless we split up. And I'm not ready for that…yet.

We pick our way across the bridge before maneuvering a hundred yards to the Cottonwood Pass highway where I found Tristen. Right is the route to Buena Vista, but the line of fire moving toward us from that direction is even more pronounced as we step onto the open road. Only a football field-length away, the conflagration emits a dull roar, interspersed with sharp pops as the flames find fresh wood. To the left, the road leads thirteen miles up to Cottonwood Pass, where another fire rages on the other side.

Our plan is to take the highway toward Cottonwood Pass, but only for two miles. Far enough to make it to the Mt. Yale trail where we can start up the mountain, aiming for the treeline without fear of the fire catching us.

The heat from the fire creates a wind at our backs as we turn uphill. Tristen is already stumbling, even with Nate tucked in at his side, propping him up. Algood breathes heavily, but keeps moving. I suspect the proximity of the fire is the only thing providing the adrenaline required to keep this pace. It's working right now. But what happens when the adrenaline runs out?

• • •

Fifteen minutes later, I find out. It's not like we're running up the road, but we're also not out for a stroll. The fire's noise fades behind us as we march up the road. A mile after we've started, the group is hacking, coughing, and gassed. I know they are, because I consider myself in decent shape—part of my reinvented self out here in the Rockies—and

I'm already breathing hard. The only group members who don't seem to struggle are Mike and Frazier. Mike, I understand. He's young and lives in Buena Vista. He might not be used to the smoke, but he's accustomed to the altitude. But Frazier's fitness? Wow. The Art Crimes Division operates out of Washington, DC, with an elevation somewhere close to zero. I could tell she was in shape from the moment I met her, but still—the altitude usually plays the role of the great equalizer.

As if she senses she's on my mind, Frazier turns in my direction. But her focus is on Nate and Tristen, limping twenty yards behind her. She shifts her eyes from the two men, down the line, and then settles them on me.

"Break?"

We're getting to the point where we don't need words to communicate. I nod. I consider responding, but decide there's no reason to let the others know how out of breath I am. They need a show of confidence at this point, not someone sharing their pain.

"Five minutes. Everyone find a place to sit and take a load off." Frazier eyes Tristen, whose head shakes as if in denial. "Or lay down. Whatever you need to do." She walks toward me, motioning that she wants to talk one-on-one.

"What do you think?"

I debate how honest to be with Frazier. It's not looking good. I wonder whether she expects me to be the upbeat leader, or give it to her straight. Her chest isn't heaving like mine. I decide Frazier's not going to be the one who needs me to play Mr. Optimism on our little hike. She gets it.

"The good news?" I say. "We've made a mile in fifteen minutes. Damn good pace."

"I already know the bad news."

"Go ahead."

"You're going to tell me we've still got nine miles to go and that last mile we did was the fastest one we'll see."

I nod. "Bingo. Except we've got closer to ten miles left and the real uphill doesn't start for another mile."

"You're not planning on sharing that with them, are you?" Frazier nods up the line. I follow her gaze. Algood is drifting our direction. Frazier looks back at me.

"I'm not going to do the mountain. I can't." Algood staggers as he stops in front of us.

I'm still pissed at Algood. Monica is dead because of him. We're delayed escaping The Lodge because of him. Now he's back to his "I can't deal with the altitude" whining. My tolerance level sits on empty.

Frazier must sense my growing rage, because she lays a hand on my arm before answering. "We're not climbing the mountain. We're using part of the trail to avoid the fire and then we're cutting down the other side."

She waters down the explanation to mollify Algood. We are climbing the mountain. We're just not climbing to the summit. We need to get above the treeline and then follow it down to the next valley where there's no fire. But the treeline is at twelve-thousand feet—only two-thousand feet below the Mt. Yale summit. I smile, but say nothing. Algood doesn't need to hear all that.

"It's too steep. I'm going to take the road up Cottonwood and look for a ride on the other side."

"There's a fire down that pass," Frazier reminds him.

"I'll take my chances. Good luck." Algood turns and walks away.

During the entirety of Algood's conversation, I've felt a twinge of pride in how I've restrained my anger at him. I kept my mouth shut and let Frazier do the talking. But now I feel that control slipping.

"Who's in charge of law enforcement in this group?" I murmur in a voice only Frazier can hear.

"What?"

I repeat myself, pulling my mask an inch from my face.

"Me," Frazier says.

"Who's in charge of getting us—all of us—out of here alive?"

Frazier pauses for a moment, then answers. "You. You know the terrain. You're qualified in all that rescue stuff. You're in charge of that."

I nod, rising to my feet. "Then I hope you understand that splitting up is not an option."

Frazier nods. "I'll back you up. Whatever you need to say to him to get him to stay with us, I'll support."

I pull my Glock 26 from my holster, the barrel pointed to the ground. Algood and I aren't going to sit down and have a debate. I'm done talking.

CHAPTER 29

Algood stays with our group. Big surprise. I suspect Frazier's none too happy with my method of persuasion, but after Algood and I had our come-to-Jesus meeting, I sense the only problem we'll have with him is his slow pace. Which is easier to deal with than worrying about him running away.

It takes another three quarters of an hour to reach the trailhead. We stop for our second break of the day. The parking area is empty. Not a surprise, considering the raging fires. Julie and Laura take advantage of the parking lot restrooms, while the rest of us pause at the Forest Service sign marking the start of the climb. Everyone sits, except for Tristen, who hasn't sat since we left The Lodge. He rested on his stomach at the first break, but the obvious pain he endured returning to his feet makes me think he might not try that technique again. We've climbed a couple hundred feet since leaving The Lodge. The smoke thins. We still can't spot the mountain above us, but at least we can see fifty yards up the trail instead of twenty feet.

The next leg of our journey is steep. Not like ropes on cliffs or anything—it's an established trail—but the climb to the summit includes over four thousand feet of vertical climb in only four miles. To reach our cut-off point at the treeline, we'll need to climb over halfway up the mountain. From there, we'll cut off the trail, working our way around Yale, just above the treeline. That leg won't be easy either.

Nate calls out. I turn toward his voice.

"Tristen, just wait." Nate's ten yards up the trail. Tristen staggers in front of him, another ten yards farther uphill.

"Hey," I call. "Wait for the bathroom crew, Tristen."

The injured man ignores us both, continuing to shuffle up the trail. I'm not concerned we'll lose him—he's not moving fast enough for any chance of that—it's just poor hiking etiquette. In Search & Rescue, hikers commonly make one or two poor decisions, resulting in over half our missions. The first is someone taking a shortcut. The second is splitting up. That's what Tristen is trying to do.

I lean toward Mike. "Keep an eye on Algood. I'm going to talk to Tristen."

"What, you want me to kick his ass if he tries to run away?" Mike laughs. "I got it. I think you scared the shit out of him back there. He's not going anywhere."

I stand, shouldering my pack. If I'm going to walk twenty yards uphill to Tristen, there's no sense coming back for my pack later. He's close to forty yards away from the trailhead by the time I catch him.

"Hey." I fall in beside him, slowing my pace.

Tristen coughs, but says nothing.

"I know you're hurting. I know you're having a hard time at our rest stops. But we've got to do this thing together."

Tristen pauses, turning toward me. Sweat trickles from under his mask, but instead of a flushed profile, the skin under his eyes is pale— almost white.

"I want out. This isn't what I signed up for."

I'm confused. Tristen doesn't look well. Maybe he's confused too. "What do you mean 'signed up for?'"

After Algood's kidnapping efforts, I pretty much dropped any suspicions that Tristen was involved with the strange events at The Lodge. After all, the only suspicious thing he did was take off for town without telling anyone. I'll admit it surprised me. But after Algood did the same, with Monica begging to go with him, I had decided the impulse to flee must not be as uncommon as I first thought.

"Is there something you need to share with me, Tristen?"

Tristen shuffles forward again, but stops at my question. "What are you implying?"

"When you say 'signed up,' it makes me think maybe you're part of a larger plan. You know, the *Broncho Buster* theft, the Wi-Fi router stolen, and you trying to run away? Are you involved in all this?"

Tristen squints at me before releasing a breath. "You haven't been listening. I told you Monica stole the painting." His gaze lingers over my shoulder, toward the others. "I can't speak for Martin, or why he added kidnapping to his list of undesirable personality traits. Listen, Zahn, when I say I didn't sign up for this, I meant that I just wanted to come out and see the spot where my life changed. Where my art was stolen. I only went to Laura's exhibit out of courtesy. Do you honestly think I would steal her painting? It's worth nothing." Tristen had just about caught his breath when he started talking, but now he's breathing hard again. "I came here for closure. Not a forest fire, burnt legs, and mountain climbing. I'm ready to get home. Bathroom breaks are keeping me from that." He nods toward the trail.

I follow his gaze and spot Frazier walking in our direction with Nate. Julie and Laura are just visible through the smoke, hoisting their daypacks on their shoulders. Tristen nods. I wonder if he's telling the truth. If he's just the victim in this entire thing—from the theft of his own art to the errant burning tree falling on him—or if he's involved in something much bigger than I can understand. I don't know him well enough to determine if he's hiding something.

Tristen turns, resuming his shuffle-stagger. This time I don't stop him. We've got almost three thousand feet of vertical climb in front of us. I'm not entirely sure we'll make it.

•   •   •

Three hours later, I'm even less certain. We've traveled a mile and a half. The good news is we've knocked fifteen hundred feet off our climb. The bad news is we're at a standstill. We've been taking a break every five hundred steps for the past hour. A snail's pace is a generous metaphor to describe our progress.

Frazier calls for yet another rest stop. I lean my pack against a tree just off the trail. The FBI agent walks in my direction and I head up the trail to meet her halfway. An unfamiliar ring tone blares behind me. I turn back toward my pack.

"That's my phone," Algood calls from behind me.

He's correct. I've tucked his sat phone into my bag; our group's only connection with the outside world. Algood's not getting it back until we're out of this mess. Not until the police are through investigating him.

I unzip my pack's top compartment to retrieve the still ringing phone.

"This is Zahn."

"Z-man, it's Perez. You guys need to move faster."

I've forgotten Perez and the others are tracking us through the phone. I can't help feeling embarrassed that my fellow SAR partner is watching how slowly we're moving.

"Come on, man. We've got one injured, one—"

"I don't care," Perez interrupts. "This isn't a morale call. You saw the fire on your way out, right?

"Uh, huh." This doesn't sound good.

"It's shooting up the valley. Not the one The Lodge is in, but the Cottonwood Pass one. The one you're climbing out of."

I turn away from our ragtag group, scanning the trail behind us. Although the smoke has thinned as we've climbed, it's still too thick for me to track the fire's progress below. All my fifty yards of vision tells me is the fire's at least fifty yards away. At least I don't hear it.

"Got it, Rick. I don't know if we can move any faster, but I'll let everyone know we're not out of the woods—so to speak—yet."

Perez snorts. "Dad jokes during a life-and-death situation. Nice."

I turn back to the group. Frazier stands right next to me. I raise my eyebrows at her and keep speaking on the phone. "Any chance you guys are sending some help?"

Perez says nothing.

"Rick?"

Finally, he answers. "Yeah, that's a tough one. Search & Rescue is chomping at the bit to go after you guys. Mainly because they want to flip you shit for the rest of your SAR career that they had to come save you."

"Nice. Tell them I love them too."

"No, seriously, what they want to do is get your burn victim on the litter and use a harness to help your out-of-shape guy move faster. They figure they can get you over the top and down to the beaver ponds. The smoke is clear enough over there to get a chopper in." His voice trails off, like he's got something else to add.

I like this plan. In SAR terminology, a litter is a medical stretcher used in the field. We can move it with people, ropes and pulleys, or even a mountain bike wheel. Why hasn't Perez assured me they are already on their way?

"And?" I say, prodding Perez to keep talking.

"And I won't let them. Technically, my boss won't let them, but I agree with him."

"What the hell, Perez?" My eyebrows raise at Frazier again, before realizing she can't hear Perez's side of the conversation. And I'm not really in a position where I want to put the phone on speaker.

My friend barely lets me finish my question. "Listen. I'm in SAR just like you. None of us can stomach the thought of one of our own out there alone. But as part of the Sheriff's Office, I'm also responsible for their safety. We're not letting anybody over that crest. The fire's too close. And that's where you are—over that crest. So you make it over that and SAR will be waiting for you. Got it?"

My heart begs to argue. Frazier and I can't get these folks out on our own. But my head knows Perez is right. Safety of SAR personnel takes priority over safety of the subjects. It's a volunteer organization. We don't have the right to put their lives at risk in this kind of situation.

"Got it."

"I'll check back in with an update in an hour, unless something changes before then." Perez's voice goes up an octave. "Get them moving, Zahn. Do it."

I punch off the phone.

Frazier says, "What's the deal?"

Laura, Julie, and Algood all sit close by. Their heads are turned our direction, waiting to hear whatever news I have to share. I step down the trail, nodding at Frazier to follow. Ten yards later, I stop.

"What?" Frazier says.

I share Perez's update on the fire, including his warning we are moving too slow.

"What did he say about the help? When do they get here?"

"They don't. They're not sending anyone down this side of the mountain." I point up the trail. "We don't have to make it to the top of the mountain, just over the ridge separating the valleys. They'll have people waiting for us there."

"So what do we tell these guys?" Frazier nods over her shoulder.

I pause for a moment. We need to share the news about the fire. They need to understand we're not out of danger, especially if we're going to keep them moving. The tough decision is the rescue information. If we give them hope—tell them rescue teams will meet us soon—then they might slow down, assuming the teams will help them when they arrive. If we tell them the truth—that they have to climb the ridge before we have any chance of rescue—they might give up. Neither is a good option.

"I'll brief them," I say.

•   •   •

"I guess I was too subtle when I warned you about getting mixed up with a Coker gal?"

I'm still riding the caboose on our climbing train. Julie has worked her way back in the line until she's walking directly in front of me. Laura hikes ahead of Algood. Both of them are twenty yards ahead of us.

When I met Julie, she rubbed me wrong. Warning me to be careful about my relationship with her older sister. Advising caution when dealing with her younger one. It all seemed a little over the top for our first conversation.

But everything Julie cautioned me about has come true. Since the theft of her painting, Laura has barely spoken to me. She spent her entire remaining time at The Lodge obsessively searching for *Broncho Buster*. My longest interaction with her sister Monica was at The Lodge during our attempted evacuation, and within eight hours she was dead.

Maybe I should have listened with a more open mind to the middle sister.

"I have to admit, I didn't pay much attention at the time." I quicken my pace, pulling alongside Julie. "But there's no way you foresaw all this. Everything that's happened?" I look at Julie, expecting a quick headshake.

Julie says nothing. She doesn't meet my eyes.

"Right?" I push a little harder. "You didn't anticipate this?"

Finally, Julie turns. She coughs, and then her eyes squint, hinting at a smile under her mask. "No. Of course not." She pauses before looking up the trail. I follow her gaze. Laura's head turns in our direction.

Julie stops and bends over to adjust a lace on her shoe. I wait.

She looks up at me before standing again. "I warned you for two reasons. The first is that anytime either of those two starts a relationship, the other tries to sabotage it. It's always been that way."

I nod. "And reason number two?"

"Maybe they're not distinguishable, but the second reason is Laura and Monica's relationship is toxic. The more Monica slides into addiction—the more depressed she gets—the more Laura brings her in under her thumb. You know what I mean? Paying rent, giving her an allowance, that kind of thing? When Monica tries to break out of her downward spirals by going sober, finding work, and cleaning up, she can't do it. Because she's completely dependent on Laura." Julie squints her eyes. "Sorry, Tyler. I'm talking like Monica is still alive. I just can't get used to it."

"That's normal, Julie. It sounds like Monica didn't have many options. But you're saying Monica didn't appreciate Laura trying to help?"

"It isn't help. These arrangements Laura makes are all about control. Monica knows it. She reacts the only way she knows how." Julie looks at me as if she expects a head nod.

I figure this is where I'm supposed to guess the answer. "By being angry at Laura?"

Julie shakes her head before standing up and facing me. The others have disappeared around a bend in the trail ahead of us. Her eyes carry a look of disappointment. I've failed to provide the answer she'd anticipated.

"Not just anger, Tyler. Rage. Each time it's gotten worse. Monica goes after whatever makes Laura happy. Men, her reputation, her art—Monica might be an addict, but she's no fool. She figures out what Laura covets. Then she either takes it, or destroys it." Julie points her finger at me. "Laura likes you—or at least she did before all this happened—and Monica knew that. All of us knew that. You could see it in her eyes. In the way she talked to us about you—like a star-struck teenager. That's why I warned you about those two. Because I knew Monica would go for you. Laura knew it too. I was concerned about what would happen to you stuck in the middle."

"But Monica never tried anything with me." I blush, as I say the words. I can't remember the last time *anyone* tried to flirt with me. I was so surprised at Laura's initial interest in me that our next two interactions left me practically speechless. I considered it a miracle when she agreed to a date. Certainly, if Monica began flirting with me, I would have noticed it.

I nod toward the others and start walking again. I don't want our party to get too far in front of us. The trail is still wide enough for two. Julie falls in beside me.

"I don't have it all figured out, but Monica was doing something. Remember, I said she would go after Laura's men—" Julie stops when I whip my head toward her. "Don't get me wrong, Tyler, there were only a couple of those."

"You think she was involved with the theft of Laura's *Broncho Buster*? Like Laura said? You think she stole it?"

"I don't know," Julie admits. "If Laura's painting was stolen up on that pass, I might have thought Monica was involved. I don't know why she would steal it at The Lodge. It seems too obvious."

I stop in my tracks, stunned, then step forward quickly to catch up with Julie. "How could you think Monica could be involved in an art theft involving millions of dollars? The thieves were after the Remingtons. You're saying if they would have taken *Broncho Buster*, you would have suspected Monica?"

Julie nods. "It's the whole Duane Dahl-Bruce Davis relationship. That's just too convenient for me. Duane's got a buddy that does art security. That guy just happens to be on the job that involves a major theft. Laura's painting is on board. Doesn't that all seem coincidental?"

I don't answer. But Perez's words from previous cases we've worked together swim in the back of my mind. *There are no coincidences.*

Julie continues. "But Laura's painting didn't get stolen. She got it back. And now it's more valuable."

"What do you mean?"

"I don't know if there's a term for it, but it's like appreciation by association. You know, like if someone stole the *Mona Lisa* and some other painting. Something obscure. Then the police catch the thieves and recover the art. The obscure painting would be worth more because it was part of the *Mona Lisa* heist. This is what's happening with Laura's painting. It's gone up in value because it survived the Remington heist. How do you think she attracted a buyer like Algood? He would have never come out here otherwise."

"And now Laura's painting is gone." This is another habit of mine. I often state the obvious out loud, not because it's useful, but because it fills space in the conversation while I think. I haven't heard of appreciation by association.

"Right. And wherever it is, it's even more valuable than it was last week."

"Why?" Then it hits me. "Wait. I see now. It's more valuable because now it's not just the painting that survived the Remington heist. It's also the painting that got stolen a week later. It's like a big art mystery, right? People won't believe two thefts in two weeks is a coincidence."

"Exactly." Julie bobs her head. "Of course none of that matters if The Lodge burns down, right? Then it's just a painting that was destroyed. No value."

"Not necessarily," I say. I might not understand art, but Julie's description of how the market deals with rumors and intrigue has a sort of logic to it. Julie waits for me to continue. "*Broncho Buster* only loses its value if it's confirmed destroyed in a fire that may or may not reach The Lodge. But if they can't forensically identify the painting after they get these fires under control, then who's to say the painting couldn't have been spirited out of The Lodge during the evacuation?"

"You mean Duane? Monica's boyfriend?"

"Maybe. But several people saw him leave. No one saw him carrying anything the size of *Broncho Buster,* even if he cut it from the frame. It could have been someone else that made it out. There were like thirty or forty more people at the reception that crossed that bridge before Duane crashed his truck into it. It's possible someone got it out."

Julie says nothing, both of us breathing heavily as the slope increases. I think through the other people I recognized at the exhibit, trying to guess who might have made off with the painting.

"I don't think so," Julie finally says.

"Don't think what?"

"I don't think it was someone else besides Monica and Duane. I think Laura is right."

"Explain."

Julie jerks her head in my direction. I realize I've been abrupt.

"Walk me through it, Julie. Tell me why you're convinced it's Monica."

Julie's eyes soften. "All this talk we've had about increasing value makes sense. But you have to have the right buyer. It's like stealing the Crown Jewels—you can't just turn around and publicly put them up for sale, right? They are stolen goods. So you have to have a buyer who is willing to pay, but will never reveal they own the painting. In other words, they'll pay a lot of money for the art's intrinsic value."

"I don't know people like that. Do you?"

"No. Neither does Monica. But Duane does. He and Davis and their contracted art security gigs automatically network them with buyers." Julie stops to catch her breath. "Here's why I think it's Monica and Duane. I doubt anyone else at the exhibit has the contacts Duane has. Except for maybe Tristen or Algood. And it's a win-win for Monica. If she's involved with Duane's scheme, she gets a cut of the profits at the same time she's screwing over Laura."

I peer up the trail again, unsuccessfully trying to spot Laura or Algood through the smoke. I point uphill. Julie sighs.

"You're lucky Monica's no longer here."

I can't even guess where Julie is going with this proclamation, so I don't attempt an answer.

She waits a beat, then continues. "What my sisters do to each other is a tragedy. But it's a Coker family tragedy, not a public one. If Monica wasn't dead, I'd never share these theories with you. Cokers take care of their own."

My heart sinks. I had almost changed my thoughts on Julie. Now she claims to be helping me solely because her sister is dead. Not because it's the right thing to do.

We pass an opening in the trees and I glance uphill. The smoke is too thick to glimpse the sheer cliffs on the face of Mt. Yale, but I'm just looking for a clearing in the trees—some sign that we're nearing treeline. Once there, we can finally work our way over the crest to find the teams sent to rescue us.

I don't plan on dying on the side of this mountain. I don't want to leave anyone behind. After my discussion with Julie, I have additional motivation to make it through this ordeal. When I sit down with Perez and debrief him on everything, I'm going to point him straight toward Duane. Perez still has me on his personal probation list. He trusts me as a friend, but the jury is still out on my investigative skills.

But here's the deal. If Perez doesn't take action to investigate Duane? To look into the scheme he had cooked up with Monica?

If he doesn't, then I will.

I'm not going through this literal trial by fire just to come out on the other side and go home. I'm going to find answers.

CHAPTER 30

It's dark. We're exhausted. A wall of flames glows in front of us as we skirt Mt. Yale toward the treeline, searching for the shallowest climb over the saddle. The fire is close enough to feel the heat. The sound is different from the roar in the forested valley. Now the fire emits crackles and pops as it reaches the treeline, searching for one last pine. Like a rifle company clearing the last city block of an Iraqi city.

The fire won't reach us here—we're above the trees and there's nothing to burn. The only option is up. A climb to the treeless saddle between Mt. Yale and an unnamed peak, where the Colorado Trail runs down the other side to the Silver Creek Campground and North Cottonwood Creek. The next hours will prove whether Perez's directed escape route is successful or not. One thing is certain: we have no other choice. Perez's sat phone call an hour ago confirmed the fire already passed the trailhead where we departed the highway.

We can't go back.

If we're lucky, the SAR team will meet us at the saddle and load Tristen on a litter. Several hours ago, I thought he might be able to walk it out. After all, he's been a trooper on the hardest leg of this journey. Now, I'm not so sure.

We huddle at the base of the incline, the first level spot we've encountered in the last thirty minutes. Everyone coughs. Most are peeling their masks aside and spitting whatever comes up. Algood gasps, his hands on his knees. Tristen lies over a boulder on his stomach, eyes closed, face locked in a grimace. Nate crouches next to him, his lips moving. Probably trying to encourage Tristen for the next push.

The entire party is exhausted, but only Algood and Tristen look like they're in medical danger. Frazier focuses on the slope's grade. I follow her gaze. There's no way to pick out the crest through the smoke, but I know from experience it's less than five hundred feet of vertical. If it was just me summiting a 14er, or joining the SAR team on a mission, we would clear this pitch in less than thirty minutes, easy. Today? We'll be lucky to make it at all.

Once again, as much as I'd prefer Frazier to run the show, these are my mountains. Escaping them is my wheelhouse, not hers. Not that I'm a ropes and gear guy, but this slope doesn't require that. It simply requires us to keep going.

"We're almost at the top of this thing. If we take a steady pace—say ten steps and a thirty-second pause, then ten more steps—if we take it like that, we'll be on our way down in an hour." I hear optimism in my own voice. I hope everyone else feels it.

"I'm done," Algood says. He moves from hands on his knees to sitting against a boulder, clasping his hands behind his head. "Bring in the chopper."

"You're not done." I turn toward Algood. Everyone else probably assumes I'm showing the man I'm listening, but really, I'm showing him the handle of my Glock—again. I'm reminding him he needs to be listening. "Look around. The chopper can't get through the smoke. Even if it could, it wouldn't be able to land here. I'm asking for an hour of effort. Can you give me that?"

"No." Algood shakes his head.

Nate's voice calls behind me. "I don't think Tristen can give you an hour. I can't wake him up."

I turn to Nate and Tristen. Frazier joins me at his side. Tristen's breathing is shallow, and I tear his mask off, before pinching his arm.

"Tristen! Tristen! Can you hear me?" This is Wilderness First Aid 101. Check subject's responsiveness.

Nate is right. Tristen is unconscious.

My eyes meet Frazier's. Neither of us speaks. We're less than an hour from medical assistance and a downhill route to a clear landing zone. So close. But there is no way this team can carry an unconscious Tristen to the crest. Hell, even the SAR team with a litter wouldn't be able to carry him up the slope. It's covered with scree—an erosion field of loose pebbles. SAR would have to perform a scree evacuation—a process similar to pulling a refrigerator up a mountain with ropes and pulleys while climbing over unfinished marbles.

We can't leave him. Well, maybe we can, but that would involve wrapping him in a blanket on the side of a cliff, and hoping someone saves him in a couple of days. I still feel guilty about leaving Davis's body in the bedroom at The Lodge. Monica's body remains snagged underwater in Cottonwood Creek—another ice-cold corpse we left behind.

I need to fix this.

"OK. Here's how it's going to go." I step away from Tristen, surveying our group. "You all are going to take care of Tristen. Wrap him up. Elevate his feet. Treat him like he's in shock. Monitor his breathing." Frazier nods, but the rest of them stay silent. Nate's mouth hangs open. He changed Tristen's bandages at The Lodge, but probably has no clue what to do if Tristen's breathing stops. "Agent Frazier is trained in first aid. You all will help her."

I'm moving on to part two of my decision when Algood interrupts. "Where the hell are you going?"

His tone pisses me off. He already knows I'm leaving, and he's as pissed as I am—just for a different reason. I'm doing what he wants to do, but can't. I'm dashing to safety. Saving my own ass.

But that's not my plan.

"I'm going to scout the route to the crest and see how we might use what gear we have to transport Tristen to the top." Calling our limited resources *gear* is a stretch. We've got three or four tie-down straps, and that's it.

"Let me guess." Algood's tone rings sarcastic. "If it doesn't look feasible, you're going to keep going to find help, right?"

Algood's not completely wrong. What I'm not sharing with my team—and that's how I'm starting to think of these guys—is that I'm hoping to find my SAR buddies waiting for me at the top. They have specific orders not to come down this side of the mountain. I hope once I explain our situation—a litter evac over scree on an incline—they'll disregard those orders. I think they will. But I'm sure as hell not going to tell these guys that SAR will rescue them from our current position. The moment I hint at an imminent rescue, they'll shut down. And I'll never get them over this ridge if it comes to that. Hell, even if I talk SAR into coming down this slope, everybody here except for Tristen is still going to climb it.

"No. I'm not. I'm not leaving you all here. I'm going to the crest. Then I'm coming back. We don't have other options. I'm going to find us the best route."

And pray my guys are waiting at the top.

•　•　•

Fifteen minutes later, I'm only a third of the way up the slope. That's my best guess. The smoke and angle keep me from knowing for sure. The footing is sketchier than I expected between the boulders. When I get in among rocks, I'm unable to just pull myself from one to another. The boulders are separated by enough space that it requires me to climb in and out of the crevices separating them. Plenty of places to anchor ropes for a litter scree evac, but near impossible terrain if we have to drag Tristen up by hand.

A voice calls out, "Didn't know you were hi-angle qualified, Z-man. And by yourself? You're breaking all the rules today, aren't you?"

For a moment, I'm certain the voice is my own. I look up and see that I'm wrong.

I've been so focused on the rocks beneath me, I haven't looked up in five minutes. Ten feet away, I spy a masked Chad Storms, harnessed up and heading my way. I shake my head—of all SAR members to come to my rescue, what are the odds it would be the same guy who partnered with Kristee on her last mission?

"What the hell, Storms? I thought you guys weren't allowed on this side of the crest?" I'm so damn relieved to see Chad and whoever's with him that I stop moving. I sink against a large boulder, spent. Not so out of it I can't flip Chad shit, though. "Never took you for a rule breaker."

Storms's eyes widen and I know he's grinning under his mask. I had him there for a second. "We've been set up on the ridge for hours. Dispatch is tracking you on that phone. They told us you all were stalled out down there, just a couple hundred yards away from us. Then suddenly—no idea how it happened—we somehow lost communications."

"Yeah, right."

"Right." The louder voice comes from behind Storms. Tom Powell, one of our organization's older members, works his way in front of Storms. "So we're doing our best to guess their intent. We think they would have wanted us to go get you."

I smile. I doubt that's what Dispatch intended, but I'm happy the communications problem is resulting in our rescue.

"What's the situation down yonder?" Powell nods down the slope behind me. "You all going to need a litter or not?"

I tell Storms and Powell about Tristen first, then brief the condition of the rest of the group, emphasizing Algood will need extra assistance.

The two men exchange glances before looking at me again.

"How're *you* doing, Z-man?" Storms says.

What the hell? I start to reply, then stop. What exactly is Storms implying? And how much does the SAR team know about what happened at The Lodge? They have to know something because Perez wouldn't have let them come up here without briefing them on the criminal element of the missions. That someone in this group might be a murder suspect. You don't just send SAR folks out looking for criminals.

"What are you asking? I'm halfway up this ridge, aren't I? I'm good." Maybe they're wondering if I'm worn out.

Powell nods. "Physical. Mental. The whole thing. You don't have to get into it with us Z—we just need to know whether to treat you as a subject needing assistance or as a fellow member of SAR we met out in the field."

"I'm good. I'm SAR—I mean, I don't need to tell you guys what to do, but, yeah, I can help with this whole thing." A wave of relief washes over me. I walked into this whole weekend with Perez's voice ringing in my ears. *Don't get involved in any of this art shit. It's out of your lane.* Yet here I am, neck deep in a theft, a murder, and a drowning. I'm so far out of my wheelhouse, I can't see straight. Storms and Powell offering me a chance to do something I'm qualified to do?

A smile spreads across my face. "Hell, yeah. I'm SAR."

•   •   •

The litter evac transporting Tristen up the scree takes over two hours. A long time if you're Tristen, or one of the others from The Lodge, but it actually runs smoothly. SAR has deployed nine members to the ridge, and as soon as we settle on an evac plan, five more members start up from the Silver Creek campground to help carry the litter.

My worries about SAR rescuing a criminally charged subject are unfounded. Two of Perez's guys from the Sheriff's Office, including Deputy Morrissey—first on the scene at the art heist—wait at the ridge to take Algood into custody. Unfortunately, it's a long wait. Algood is the last up the slope.

Tom Powell runs the scree evac, using a six-man team to pull the stretcher up the slope. The remaining three SAR members, plus me, join Frazier and the others. While the three SAR personnel help the others, I stick with Algood. He isn't going to try anything with me. We climb faster than Tristen's litter moves, but it still takes us over an hour to reach the crest.

When I finally top out on the wide swath of flat stone, the deputies take Algood from me. I stand to the side as Morrissey reads Algood his rights. When she's finished, she turns to me.

"What do you think? Should we cuff him?"

I'm flattered they even ask. Maybe Perez hasn't shared his thoughts with his coworkers about me getting too involved with all this. "I wouldn't. He's too exhausted to go anywhere, and the cuffs will just slow you all down." I turn to Algood. "That sound about right, Martin?"

Algood turns to the deputies. "I'm not going anywhere."

Morrissey nods. She and the other deputy tilt their heads down toward the opposite slope from the fire. Algood shuffles in that direction. Within twenty yards, he and the deputies disappear into the smoke.

Frazier taps me on the shoulder. "I'm going to catch up with the deputies. Talk to them a bit."

"See you down there," I say. "Nice job." I know our ordeal isn't finished. But suddenly I feel we might make it.

I turn to Powell, who's managing Tristen's evacuation from the ridge top. "I thought the smoke was going to be better on this side. Are we going to ground evac Tristen all the way out of the mountains?"

Powell peers down at his teams working the last twenty-yard stretch before turning to me. "You know the small lake about halfway down to the campground? With the meadows?"

I nod. I've been up this side of the ridge twice—once for a day hike out-and-back, and the other when Kristee and I...a lump forms in my throat...when Kristee and I summited Mt. Yale from the less-traveled east ridge route. Powell is talking again, so I just swallow until my throat stops hurting.

"When we passed through, the visibility was like five hundred meters. Good enough for a chopper to get in, I think. We've got more litter carriers on their way up in case the chopper can't make it. They're going to update the visibility when they pass through the meadows."

Powell's all over it. He doesn't need more questions from me. I walk across the crest and descend to a group of Bristlecone pines where the remaining SAR members force hot tea on Mike, Laura, Julie, and Nate. Sitting with their backs against the slope, wrapped in space blankets, they look like potatoes waiting for an oven bake. Nate and the two women are shell-shocked, their eyes blank, gazes fixed on the downhill slope in front of them.

Mike sips his tea, peering down the slope like he can't wait to get going again. He catches my eye and lifts his chin, indicating he wants to talk. "When you think we're going to move?"

I shift my eyes back toward the crest for any sign they've finished moving Tristen. I see nothing through the smoke. "Just waiting on Tristen."

"Why do we need to wait?

Mike's question surprises me. He's been nothing but a team player through this entire ordeal. Now that we're so close to safety, he's ready to leave us all behind?

CHAPTER 31

The *thunk-thunk* of the chopper's rotor blades echoes through the valley before we clear the trees at Silver Creek Pond. I carry the front right side of Tristen's wheeled litter—not because SAR doesn't have enough folks to bring it down, but because I'm tired of talking to the people I've been trapped with at The Lodge. Nestled in among my SAR folks, I'm immune to personal drama. I'm aware it's out there—I'm sure every SAR member has something going on at home. But we don't talk about that on missions.

The smoke dissipates as we descend the draw, but still blankets this side of the ridge. Even as we walk toward the sound of the engine, I don't see the helicopter until we're within five hundred feet. I suspect they might have broken a few required visibility rules to get to us.

On the far side of the chopper, a group of people dressed in SAR-red shirts wait for direction. Our additional SAR members who have hiked up to help get the rest of our group out. The chopper has just enough room for Tristen and a medical technician. The rest of us will continue the remaining mile-and-a-half on foot. One of our newer members, Nathan, joins me at the litter. He nods toward the reception party.

"Want me to take the last hundred yards? So you can talk to the Sheriff?"

I turn from Nathan toward where he's looking. Deputy Sheriff Perez stands with the small group of SAR members, pointing at me with an outstretched hand. I can't read his expression. Is he pointing me out to someone else, or signaling he has a bone to pick with me? Either way, he's definitely pointing at me.

I relinquish my spot on the litter, patting my hand on Tristen's shoulder before making my way toward Perez. I'm still not happy with Tristen's decision to bolt when things got rough at The Lodge, but I've pretty much determined he's harmless. Maybe clueless as well.

I catch movement to my left and turn. Algood strides past the stretcher, toward the helicopter. Under the trees, the deputies have their backs to us, giving directions to the others. They've lost the bubble on watching Algood.

I veer in his direction, grabbing his shoulder from behind. "What the hell are you doing?" I shout.

"Getting a ride! I don't have time to walk down. Business stuff."

Algood's arrogance rocks me like a sucker punch from a little old lady. This man honestly thinks he can kidnap somebody…and then just walk away from it.

"No, you're not. Someone's here to see you." I nod in Perez's direction. The deputy stands with his arms on his hips. Algood looks from me to Perez, then back toward the helicopter. He takes a step toward the chopper. I grab his shoulder again.

Algood whirls, shouting, "What are you going to do? Shoot me? I don't think so."

The man has no clue how close I am to considering his suggestion. But he's right. I'm back in society. Rules apply. Stopping Algood is no longer my responsibility.

Algood's eyes widen as he focuses on something behind me. I turn.

Perez strides our direction, wearing a look on his face I haven't seen before. Like he hasn't taken a shit in a week, and he's looking for someone to take out his frustrations on. I turn back to Algood, but he's already moving away from the helicopter and maneuvering in Perez's direction. I smile and follow.

Even after all we've endured, I don't imagine Perez wrapping me in a big hug when we meet. He proves me right. Algood approaches the deputy, hands wide at his side. Perez nods at me, then holds up a hand to stop Algood. I don't have to be a lip-reader to recognize the Miranda rights. He slips a set of cuffs on Algood and points to a tree. Algood nods and sits down with his back against the trunk.

By this time, the rest of our party has caught up with us. Most have removed their masks and I take mine off as well. I watch as they file past Algood, none of them looking down at him.

I turn to Perez. I have so much to tell him, but I'm hesitant. His reaction is important to me. Will he be grateful for how I handled things? Or pissed at how involved I was?

"Deputy Perez?" Agent Frazier breaks from the group, joining the two of us. "You have time for a debrief?"

"That's why I'm here," Perez says, then turns to me. "I'll catch up with you later, Z-man."

I figure he must not be too pissed at me if he's using my nickname. I start walking toward my group, allowing Perez and Frazier some professional time.

Frazier's question to Perez brings me to a halt. "Would you mind if Mr. Zahn stayed? I want to make sure I've got everything straight that happened back there—and as you know, I wasn't there for all of it. Zahn was—and I trust him."

I've assumed positive reinforcement is something that works best on the young. That's how it was in my Air Force days, motivating my 20-year-old airmen. Doing my duty is usually motivation enough for me. But Frazier's words literally create warmth in my chest.

"I'm good with that," Perez says. "I'm partial to the old guy myself. Even if he can't stay out of trouble."

I turn around at that. Perez gives me a sly grin. Frazier smiles at the deputy's ribbing. Although relieved I've avoided a public dressing down, I don't return Perez's smile. I want to. I want to return to the banter and interchange of our normal friendship. But everything that just happened at The Lodge feels like unfinished business. Like I can't allow myself to return to normal until we figure out what happened back there.

But I do have a burning question. And the answer may lighten me up a bit.

"Can I ask a question before we start?" I say.

"Shoot," says Perez.

"How's Amore? Everything okay with him?"

Perez laughs and points his finger. I turn to the group of SAR members less than fifty yards away and finally spot what I'd previously missed. My dog—well, Kristee's dog originally, but mine now—strains in my direction at the end of a taut leash. As soon as Amore realizes I've caught sight of him, he lets out a bark.

I've never considered myself a dog person, but damn it if Kristee's mutt hasn't won me over. I stride toward Amore. He tugs at the leash. Becky tries to keep control of him, and I recognize why she won't let him go. The helicopter with Tristen inside hasn't departed yet. A loose dog in the middle of a technical rescue with a helo extraction isn't standard procedure. I break into a shuffle, which proves too much for Amore. He lets out another bark, pulling free of Becky. We meet halfway, Amore's paws on my thighs, as I kneel to give him a hug. Half of me surrenders to the affection Amore pours on me. The other half is embarrassed at our clichéd reunion—like we're putting on a Hallmark movie with Lassie and Timmy making cameos.

Finally, I calm Amore and grab his leash. I nod my thanks to Becky before turning back to Frazier and Perez, who are already in conversation. They've stepped away from Algood for privacy, but I'm not sure he's noticed. He's got his head buried between his knees, his cuffed wrists resting at his ankles. I'm not sure, but I sense the cuffs might have been the clincher. Algood's arrogance seems to have disappeared, replaced with something else. I can't decide if it's remorse or resignation.

●　　●　　●

I listen as Frazier finishes debriefing Perez. She nails it. I can tell she's won over Perez. She went over the theft of *Broncho Buster*, the death of

Bruce Davis, her kidnapping, and Monica's drowning. Bureaucratic lines have been tentatively drawn with Frazier agreeing that the art theft will fall under the FBI, while the kidnapping and deaths belong to the Chaffee County Sheriff's Office. Normally, a small-scale art theft wouldn't register as a blink on the FBI's radar, but even Perez agrees the timing and proximity of the two thefts is unlikely to be coincidental. He doesn't argue when Frazier explains she intends to recommend to her superiors that the FBI maintain the lead in the theft.

Before she rejoins the others, Frazier offers me the opportunity to chime in with anything she has missed. I say nothing. I had considered pointing out Mike's reluctance to wait for Tristen's rescue before heading down the mountain. It had nagged at me during our descent, right up until he barreled across the trailhead parking lot and wrapped a young woman in his arms. Turns out one of the SAR team had told Mike his girlfriend knew about the planned rescue and was waiting for him at the bottom. I wouldn't have been too excited about waiting for Tristen either.

"I'm impressed the first thing you asked about was Amore," Perez says after we're alone.

"What did you think I was going to ask?"

Perez exhales in what sounds like a scoff. That's when it hits me. He knows what's been rattling around in my head through this entire ordeal—the Asian woman at the scene of the heist. But surely he doesn't think I'm naïve enough to drill him on this issue before we're even off the mountain? After all, the Kristee Li case is why Perez thinks I'm unreliable. Why he thinks I'm too likely to let my emotions overrule my logic.

Yes, I'm dying to ask him if he's found out anything more about the woman. Do I think it could have been Kristee? No. No way. Just because it's only five miles from where she disappeared doesn't make it possible. Kristee was declared dead over a month ago. I went to her memorial service. I watched a cell phone video of her disappearing under a landslide of boulders.

But yet…people of color are rare in our county. I've not seen behavior or inherent prejudices that would explain why this is the case. It's simply a fact. Out of our twenty-thousand-plus county population, I bet there aren't a hundred people of Asian descent. And Asian women in their twenties? Likely fewer than ten.

Perez seems to sense he can't bait me, and offers what he's got. "Someone else saw a woman that night of the heist."

My gut wrenches. It takes a conscious effort not to reach out and shake the story out of him. Perez jumps in with the backstory before I can speak.

"Anonymous call after we sent out the public service announcement for anything unusual spotted on Cottonwood Pass that night. Dispatch took it and tried to get their name, but they weren't willing to share. And we didn't try to geo-locate the call because at the time, we didn't think a woman on Cottonwood Pass was related to the heist. Unusual, maybe—that time of night—but not like criminal unusual."

"What did they see?"

"A woman with a pack. She looked disheveled—my words, not the callers. They said she looked like ass—not my words—with blood on her face and black hair. Wearing black pants or tights or something."

"Shit, Rick…Kristee had a pack. She was wearing—"

"Stop it, Z-man. I knew you were going to go there." Perez shakes his head. My face flushes.

We never found her body. How can he not entertain a hint of hope?

He continues. "They said it was a daypack, like a knapsack. And they didn't say she was Asian."

Perez knows as well as I do, Kristee carried more than a daypack on missions. She had a 35- to 40-liter set-up she hauled to ensure she had every contingency covered. We used to laugh because a 35-liter pack is pretty small…unless it's being carried by a 5'3" woman. Then it looks a little bigger.

"OK—they didn't say she was Asian. Did you ask?"

"Damn it, Z. I told you this was before we knew about the woman with the thieves."

I consider what Perez has shared. He knows me. He knows telling me about the woman will spin me up. So why is he doing it? We continue hiking down the trail, the rear guard of our rag-tag group of survivors, while I stew on Perez's intent. As we reach the meadow's edge where the trail descends to the campground, it hits me. Perez does care about the anonymous call. But he cares the same way I do. As a friend grasping on to an impossible straw. As a deputy sheriff, he can't seriously investigate reports of an Asian woman rising from the dead. Maybe he's throwing it my direction, so I'll offer to look into it.

"I'll do it." Perez hikes directly behind me. I turn my head as I speak. "Do what?"

"I'll look into the woman. On the sly. See what I can find out about confirming who she was. And, you know…who she wasn't."

"What the fuck are you talking about, Zahn?"

I chuckle, pausing on the trail and turn toward Perez, expecting a wink and a nod. That twinkle in the eye acknowledging he knows I know what he really wants me to do. Instead, Perez gives me a look like he's wondering if I've got a dick growing out of my head. I try one more time. "I get it. Not a Sheriff's thing, but you'd appreciate someone checking it out. Kind of like that stuff I did for you last year with the security video up at Winfield?" I pause, looking for understanding in Perez's eyes.

Instead, Perez's face reddens. "Fuck, Zahn. Every time I think you're back on your feet, getting yourself squared away, you keep coming up with this crazy shit. You thought I was asking you to investigate the woman?"

"Why else would you tell me?"

"Because I figured you'd hear it from someone else. I wanted you to know the facts instead of hearsay."

Shit. Perez's expression makes it abundantly clear I've missed the ball on our conversation. He's serious. And he's not done talking.

"Fact: she was carrying a daypack, not a backpack. Fact: no one mentioned she was Asian. If she was, don't you think they would have noticed? It's not like we're the poster-child of diversity in this county. Fact: she was walking up the side of the highway. Walking." Perez pauses and takes a deep breath. "I know what you're thinking. You've got this wild fantasy that almost a month after Kristee disappears, she magically acquires a new pack and is strolling home."

Perez must see me preparing to answer because he shuts me down. "You saw the same video I saw, right?"

I nod, but say nothing.

"Even if someone survived that rockslide, you know they wouldn't be walking. Even if they survived out there with no food or water for a month—which is impossible, and you know it—it's not like they could have healed enough to hike it out. You know that."

My eyes fill with tears.

Damn it—I do not need Perez talking at me like I'm crazy. Then watching me turn emotional.

Because he's right. A part of me imagines a miracle scenario where our friend lives.

And then what? She steals paintings?

CHAPTER 32

When we finally hit the trailhead yesterday evening, Perez had a bus lined up to run everyone to the Buena Vista medical center for an evaluation. Everyone except for Algood and Nate. He took Algood to the station, presumably to book him and give him the opportunity for a lawyer. Algood got a doctor visit in a cell. He dropped Nate off at the same hospital they flew Tristen to, only three blocks from the Sheriff's Office. The rest of us checked out fine and were told to wear a mask to mitigate the smoke. They scheduled us for law enforcement interviews the next day.

I tried talking to Laura at the clinic, but she was having none of it.

"Let's take a couple of days," she said.

I sleep like the dead. It's nine in the morning before Amore finally drives me out of bed, his tongue scouring my ear. I set the drip coffee brewing before sitting at my dining room table to catch up on the news I've missed in the last three days.

The coffee maker spits and I fill up my mug before returning to the table. The news makes me think I could disappear for a month and not miss a thing. A famous actress criticizes her equally famous actor son for posting pictures of his infected toenail on social media. Local news describes a squabble between two different organizers of the annual burro races held in Buena Vista, Leadville, and Fairplay. I finally find an article from yesterday about the art theft in which Perez's boss assures the county, "We're doing everything we can within our jurisdiction to investigate the crime, but the ball is really in the FBI's court." I wonder what Frazier would say about that.

The clock on my microwave reads 10 am when I push away from the table and head out for a walk with Amore. Normally, it would be a run—that's what the newly health-conscious Tyler Zahn had been doing since I took custody of Kristee's dog. But the events of the last seventy-two hours have worn me out. The near-summit of Mt. Yale yesterday has me thinking I'll delay running for a couple of days. I consider a walk around the loop for Amore, and he does a Tigger bounce when I grab the leash. Perez had asked the two middle-school brothers who live next door to get him out for walks, so I'm certain his excitement isn't from lack of exercise. He must have missed me. I glance at my watch and wonder if I could take Amore down to Salida when I go for my interview. I hate to leave him in the house alone—again—for another afternoon.

Perez and I left on an awkward note yesterday. He was none too happy with my reaction to the woman he told me about. I'm pissed he wouldn't at least keep an open mind about it. I expected him to give me the whole spiel about not running off investigating her again, but he didn't. It was definitely implied, though.

Perez is so adamant that Kristee is dead that I doubt he'll pay attention to any investigating I do. I understand Perez wanting me to stay out of the original art heist investigation. He told me that directly, and besides, the Sheriff and the FBI are all over that. He made it pretty clear when he scheduled us for interviews that he will not be needing any help from me on investigating the theft of Laura's painting and the two deaths. But I don't really think Kristee is on his mind. Which is a little ironic, since she was always on his mind before she disappeared. It's not like Perez hid his crush on her, even after she started dating a US Marshal out of Denver.

Kristee's mother, Lin Li, never left Buena Vista after Kristee disappeared. She had been living hand to mouth, driving for Uber in Denver. When Kristee left behind a condo, Lin Li had a place she could afford to hang her hat. Not only that, she got hired on as a receptionist at the same business Kristee had started with her raft-guide friend, Travis. When the co-owners ran into trouble—Kristee disappeared and Travis ended up in prison, Lin Li ended up as a one-third owner of the office space business while Travis's parents picked up the other two-thirds. The parents were understandably unhappy with their son's involvement in a drug network and how he treated Kristee, so they jumped at the chance to offer Lin Li employment. I can't imagine Lin Li has any new information about her oldest daughter, but she's the only one I can think who wouldn't think I'm nuts for bringing up Kristee's name.

My truck is still parked behind The Lodge. I may never see it again. I borrow a car from my neighbor June. By the time I reach for the door handle at the entrance to The Aerie, it's past noon, so it's not a surprise when Travis's father, Robert, explains Lin Li is at home for lunch.

"She should be back in twenty minutes, though, if you want to wait," Robert says. "She's like clockwork—leaves at 11:30 and back at 12:30. I've tried to get her out to coffee at the Elkhead or lunch at that new pizza place across the way." He nods out the window. "She's very polite. But not what you'd call sociable."

That's an understatement. Lin Li and I didn't exactly become close during the investigation of Kristee's disappearance. My own investigation discovered Lin Li had Kristee followed the day she disappeared, trying to determine if Kristee was in an improper—Lin Li's words, not mine—relationship. Then, while we were all searching for Kristee in the rugged Apostle peaks, Lin Li was back here sifting through paperwork to make sure she would get what she felt was her due if Kristee turned up dead. Not exactly Mother-of-the-Year.

Did she ever do anything of a criminal nature? Not that I saw. But Robert here has no clue if he believes Lin Li is simply polite and reserved. I don't like her.

"Has Karla been out to visit from school?" Karla is Kristee's sister—Lin Li's daughter—who attends school at Duke.

"Not that I know of. You'll have to ask Lin Li. I've never met her. Sure would like to, though."

Robert pauses, and it's an awkward one for me. Karla is in her early 20s. Robert is at least twenty years older than me, and married. Weird.

"Why's that?" I can't help myself. I need to know.

"What?"

"Why would you like to meet her?"

"Oh," Robert reaches for the receptionist's desk and straightens a stack of business cards, "She's on my list of people who had contact with Kristee. I'm just asking people on that list questions about The Aerie's business account."

"What are you talking about, Robert?"

Robert sighs. "I had to swap out The Aerie's debit cards last week because someone used it without authorization. Down in Arizona. I talked to Travis at the—well, you know where he's at, right?"

I nod. Prison.

"I talked to him and he said he didn't share the number or give out the card. Said just he and Kristee had them." Robert shakes his head. "I asked Lin Li. She had no idea what I was talking about. I mean, she has a card, but she was here the whole time—not in Arizona. I figure the only other person who could've got their hands on the card or the number was her sister." His eyes narrow in my direction. "Unless you know something I don't."

"No." I'm stunned at Robert's revelation.

"I didn't think so. I mean, it's not a huge deal. We're talking about a couple hundred bucks from a grocery store and the card company erased the charges when they canceled the card. But it's the principle of the thing, right? Who would do that?"

I say nothing, but my mind churns. Kristee would. If she needed food. And if the card was the only option? She would use it.

•   •   •

Lin Li walks through The Aerie's doors at 12:29. The weather's warm today—mid-eighties—but seeing Kristee's mother for the first time since the events of a month ago sends a shiver through me. I sit in a chair next to the window. Lin Li glances in my direction as she pushes through the door, then freezes. I stand.

"Mr. Zahn. How nice to see you. How are you?"

Lin Li's voice doesn't vary in tone or tempo. I suspect the *nice to see you* line is the same one she uses when she greets her dentist. The last time we saw each other, I had called the cops because Kristee's downstairs neighbor was harassing Lin Li for the money she owed him for following Kristee. There's no love lost between us.

"I'm fine, thank you." I'm unsure why I've matched her voice in my response. Perhaps I'm subconsciously mocking her? Why would someone who just endured what I did—climbing over a fourteen-thousand-foot mountain to escape a fire—tell someone they are fine?

I predict her next line as a Victorian, "To what do I owe this pleasure?" but I've forgotten that even after years as a university professor in Denver—before the scandal that got her fired—Lin Li still struggles with the English language.

"What do you need?"

Shit. I should've anticipated Lin Li's lack of subtlety. What I need to know is if she's heard from Kristee. But everyone thinks Kristee is dead. I still remember Perez's reaction yesterday when I hinted I wasn't so sure.

Nimble as always—not—I fly by the seat of my pants. "I just wanted to check how Karla was doing at Duke?" Karla and I worked together well in our efforts to find out what happened to Kristee—at least in the beginning. I really do wonder how Kristee's sister is coping.

Lin Li steps to the reception counter and sets her bag down before turning back to me. Her eyes narrow. "Did she tell you to do this? To contact me? Where is she?"

Lin Li's questions pepper me like a scattergun. It's all I can do to keep from crossing my arms in front of my face to block the barrage. I try to speak, but she doesn't give me a chance.

She strides toward me, stopping with her head six inches from my chest. She looks up, her finger almost touching my face. "Tell me where she is."

"I don't know!" I rush the words, in case she keeps interrogating me. Maybe asking her about Kristee instead of Karla would have been the smarter move. I wasn't expecting this. "I haven't talked to her since she returned to school."

I read confusion in Lin Li's eyes.

She takes a small step back. "That's the problem. She didn't go back to school. I checked. She told me she was returning to Duke, but after a week of no contact, I did some checking and discovered she never arrived. Never checked in."

"Did you call the police?"

Lin Li squints at me. "I thought that was your specialty."

If I wasn't so surprised at finding out Karla didn't return to school, I might have smiled at Lin Li's attempt at humor. Better than an attempt, actually.

Lin Li continues. "No. I didn't call the police. Karla is an adult. I knew she was upset at me for what happened here when I hired our neighbor. I just didn't think she was upset enough to give up school."

I don't bring up the fact that maybe Karla couldn't afford to go back to school, especially after the person paying for it—Kristee—disappeared. That's a sore subject in the Li family and will get me nowhere.

"When was the last time you heard from her?"

Lin Li looks at the floor. She's embarrassed, but I'm unsure whether it's because she's admitting all this to me, or because she knows she's something less than a perfect mother.

"I haven't heard from her. Not since she left. That's why I was asking you." She raises her eyes to me. "You said she was your friend, right?"

"Right." There's more to the story than that—Karla sort of threw me under the bus at the tail end of the Kristee investigation—but Lin Li doesn't need these details. "But evidently not good enough friends to stay in contact. I don't know where she is."

"Will you go talk to her if you find out? Ask her what her plans are? Maybe find out if she is still angry at me?"

Lin Li asking for my help is new. I shake my head. Not because I'm unwilling to help, but because I'm not sure now is the time for me to run off on another investigation while I'm still on the hook to be interviewed by Perez and his crew.

Lin Li looks over her shoulder as if checking to see if anybody is listening, then turns back to me and whispers. "I think she's in Arizona."

CHAPTER 33

The drive to Perez's office from Buena Vista takes less than thirty minutes. My friend seems to have forgotten our tense conversation from yesterday. Either that, or he's as good at compartmentalizing as I am, because he doesn't bring up the reported Cottonwood Pass woman again. Instead, he's got news.

"The fire teams made it up to The Lodge this morning. The winds shifted. They saw a window to work on a firebreak. Deputy Morrissey is with them right now, processing the scene. The FBI hasn't got here yet, but they are on their way."

"My truck?"

"It's fine. One of my deputies drove it down to the BV police station."

"You're saying we could've stayed right there? We could've been rescued today?" I can't stop asking useless questions. "We didn't have to climb over the mountain at all?"

Perez smiles. "Yep. Imagine my enjoyment when I told that to Algood in his cell this morning. Never seen anybody get so riled up."

"You should've saved that for me to watch." I can't help but smile at the thought of Algood discovering his slow plod up and over Mt. Yale was ultimately unnecessary. My smile fades, though, as I consider the risk we took with Tristen LaFrance on the forced march.

"How's Tristen?" I say, but Perez holds up a hand like he's working traffic cop duty.

"Not until I'm done telling you about the scene." Perez grins. It's obvious he has news. I want to remind him we just left The Lodge yesterday. No one else has been there. It's not like anything will have changed. But I've known Perez long enough to understand that will just make him more excited about telling me what they found.

"I'm guessing Bruce Davis didn't come back to life," I throw out, just to play along.

Perez leans back in his chair, holding a pen on each end with his fingers, head shaking. "Nope. We found him right where you said. Dead in bed. Morrissey got pics and made the time of death call." He pauses. "We used the time you passed on to us. We're moving the body out, rather than waiting for the coroner. Not willing to risk sending anyone else up there."

Perez pauses again, like he's going to give me another guess. When I don't bite, he tosses his pen on the table. "They found the painting. It never left the premises."

I can't decide whether this news surprises me. It's not like I spent a lot of time searching The Lodge for the stolen art. Too much other stuff took priority. Like people dying. But this is good news for Laura.

"Where?" Now that Perez has spilled the story, I might as well let him enjoy the rest of it.

"One of the cabins on the perimeter of the parking lot. The ones for families staying at The Lodge, but not actually inside the Lodge. Found it under the mattress of one of the double beds."

"Laura's going to be excited about that. She needs something to lift her up after her sister, you know?"

"She's not going to be happy, Z-man." Perez shakes his head like he's upset. I sense it's not about Monica's death. This time, he doesn't make me drag it from him. "The painting is destroyed. Absolutely ripped to shreds." Perez fixes his gaze on me. "I'm not an art expert, and I haven't seen it yet, but from the way Morrissey described it, there are at least seven long gashes crisscrossing the canvas. Like all the way through. She said it's not an accident. Not like someone ripped it while moving it. More like Jack the Ripper decided he didn't like art anymore.

I'm not even hearing Perez anymore, as I try to process what he reveals. Someone destroyed *Broncho Buster*. I recall Laura's adamant accusations that Monica was responsible for the theft—how I believed that as much as those two didn't get along, stealing your sister's painting seemed like extreme behavior. But this? Was Monica so furious at Laura that she stole the painting? Then came back and destroyed it? Or did she destroy the painting in a fit of rage and then try to hide it?

"Z-man?" Perez tries to catch my attention, but I'm already questioning my own assumptions. The only ones who are convinced Monica stole the painting are Laura and Tristen. Even Julie thinks putting blame on Monica is a little extreme. Maybe it was someone else? Was Tristen simply trying to shift the blame? I immediately dismiss that theory. Why would a man who owns Remingtons steal a no-name artist's work?

"Z-man?"

This time I answer. "Sorry. Does this change anything as far as suspects go?" I'm not sure how this latest discovery would offer any more clues, but maybe Perez has something else.

"No. But it's kind of tricky."

"Why's that?"

"Because the painting theft is the FBI's bailiwick. The murders are ours. If we move the painting from where we found it, the FBI is going to be pissed that we contaminated their crime scene."

"And if you don't move it, and the fire shifts, then it might still all burn up, right?"

Perez nods. "Morrissey's taking lots of pics, though. There's a chance we'll get the agent out there this evening. Either Frazier, if we finish here in time, or one of the others who came in yesterday." He tilts his head at me. "How do you think it went down, Z-man? With the painting."

I'm unable to wrap my brain around *Broncho Buster*'s destruction. "No clue."

"Nothing?"

"I still think it was someone trapped with us. I can't imagine a scenario where someone steals the painting, destroys it, then evacuates the premises. It makes more sense that someone stole it first and then destroyed it later." I shift in my chair. "But I still defer to Frazier and what she thinks. Have you told her yet?"

"No. She's coming in to talk in about an hour. We informed her headquarters about finding the painting. And that it was destroyed. Frazier might know by now." Perez picks up the pen again and leans back. "Enough about art theft. I need to work the murders. Start with Davis. Tell me everything you know about him, leading up to his death." Perez's eyes narrow. "That includes the visit you paid to him at the hospital."

I spend the next hour relating every minute detail I can share with Perez. I've spent a lot of time with my friend while he was on duty. He's a skilled investigator. But this is the first time he's interrogated me. He's good. Not like he's grilling me or making me feel uncomfortable or anything, but he's meticulous. When I describe the discovery of Davis's body, he questions me about everything in the room besides the body. He quizzes me on Monica's actions, from the time she screamed through the entire time we were together.

When we finish, Perez is quiet. Then he hits a button on his desk. "Is Agent Frazier here?"

A voice answers through a speaker. "Affirm."

"Tell her it's going to be another thirty minutes." He tosses the pen on the table. "Okay, Z-man…we've talked about Davis. Now tell me about you going after Tristen and everything you know about Algood taking Monica and Frazier."

CHAPTER 34

My truck can make it from home to the Denver International Airport in two hours and forty-five minutes if I plan around rush-hour traffic. That's why I've opted for the redeye flight to Phoenix. Well, that and ticket prices. Denver to Phoenix runs less than a hundred bucks on Frontier Airlines.

Winding down the Rocky Mountain foothills into the Front Range, a text message buzzes my phone. I check my mirrors, then gauge the traffic before tapping the message. A picture of Amore curled up on my next-door neighbor's couch fills my screen. June captions it: *He's found a new home!* I jab a partial reply before pausing when the road hairpins. At the second sharp curve in the road, I give up. I want to rib June about spoiling Amore, but am putting my life in jeopardy trying to respond to a funny dog picture. I'm turning into one of the idiots I complain about on this high-altitude highway.

Frazier knows I'm heading to Arizona, but she's the only one. I didn't tell Perez. I didn't let Lin Li know, even though it was her idea for me to find Karla in Arizona. But I'm only partially interested in tracking down her youngest daughter. My true motive is just a little crazier. Davis's description of the Asian woman in the art thieves' van niggled at me the entire time I was trapped in The Lodge. My conversation with Perez about the woman on the pass that night has now turned the niggle into an itch that won't abate.

My brain knows how Kristee disappeared. I saw the evidence. If people ask me, I agree she died. How can I not acknowledge it without appearing unhinged?

But my heart keeps singing a different tune. I won't stop hoping until they find her body. Before The Lodge, this maudlin belief only poked its head up during my second beer of a night alone at my dining room table. Even after five days of sobriety—between The Lodge and my return home—I still feel there's a chance.

So here I am—off to Arizona. Because who is the one person Kristee would reach out to if she was still alive, but hesitant to return home? That would be Karla. Find one sister, find the other.

I text June while waiting for the plane, flipping her shit about letting Amore on to her furniture. I haven't admitted to my neighbor that while Amore is banned from my couch, the same doesn't hold true for my bed.

Frazier is my next call. When I told her yesterday I was heading to Arizona for personal reasons, she didn't question me. I'm sure she wouldn't have minded taking a little time off herself after our ordeal. She probably assumes that's what I'm doing. Instead, we talked about the *Broncho Buster* theft, and how its subsequent destruction fit into her investigation.

Today I call for a different reason. Perez hasn't shared many details on the Sheriff's side of the investigations. I'm curious whether they have made any progress into finding out Algood's motives for kidnapping Frazier. Plus, I miss talking to Frazier.

"Nothing new," Frazier says. "Perez gave me a two-hour grilling and pulled out details I didn't even know I remembered." She pauses. "Did he do that to you too?"

"Yep."

"I misjudged him. I think I carried some prejudices about small-town law enforcement, but he's crushing those. He's impressive."

I say nothing. *Impressive* is almost an understated description of my best friend. The more time we spend together, the more talent he reveals. Of course, the longer I know him, the more of a pain in the ass he can be. His black-and-white investigative skills don't always mesh with the out-of-the-box perspective I bring to cases.

"And he found something of interest for the case," Frazier adds. "Or at least his guys did."

"What's that?"

"They retrieved Monica's body from the river. The fire's pretty much under control near The Lodge, so they're letting everybody in."

The only thing interesting about Monica's death would be if it wasn't accidental, but the woman who saw her perish is the same one I'm talking to on the phone. "OK. You're doing a Perez on me—just tell me what you got, Emma."

"She had an SD flash memory card on her. Took us a couple of hours to dry it out, but when we did, we got three photos off of it. All the same."

"Go on."

"Yeah, it was a picture of the stolen Remingtons.

"From the California museum exhibit?"

"Yep. But the pics weren't taken there."

"What do you mean?"

"These photos are time-stamped the day the paintings were stolen. You can see the packing crates at the edges of the picture. I think they took the pictures in the transport vehicle."

My mouth drops and I almost blurt out the first thought that comes to my mind. *Monica was with Davis and his partner in the van with the Remingtons and Laura's painting?* But as soon as the theory forms, I realize where I've gone wrong. An SD card in Monica's pocket doesn't mean she took the picture. It could mean she took the SD card.

"Davis," I say, "Davis photographed the paintings and Monica must have taken the SD card."

"That's what we're theorizing. We just haven't figured out why."

I say nothing. What would make a photo of the Remingtons so valuable that Monica might kill for it? Monica wasn't really on our suspect list for Davis's death. But this is the first genuine lead we have.

Frazier waits for my response—I assume. When I remain silent, she speaks again. "So now Perez and the team are looking at Monica for

Davis's murder. We're looking at it now too, since it appears to have something to do with the stolen art."

"Do you think Davis took the pictures as a keepsake? Like he was thinking 'Look at me, I'm guarding the most famous Western paintings in the United States?'"

Frazier's response sounds skeptical. "Do you?"

"Not really." I don't really think that's what's going on here. I just tend to spitball ideas as they come up. It's my way of processing. "Two reasons I don't think they took the pictures for fun. The first: if it was a souvenir pic, then why wouldn't Davis—or the other guard, because maybe Davis got the SD card from the other guard—be in the pic? Kind of like a famous art selfie?"

"Maybe?" I picture Frazier on the other end of the phone, nodding her head at my question. "What's the other reason?"

"Why take the picture in the truck where you have to unpack everything? Why didn't they just photo it back in the museum while they were packaging the paintings for travel?"

"Huh." Frazier goes silent for a moment. "That makes sense. Perez said he was going to run this by you, so I guess I beat him to the punch. He said you had experience putting yourself in bad guys' heads. That you're good at it."

I don't respond to Frazier's indirect compliment. She's right—it's worked before. Until it didn't. "You didn't tell him I was going out of town, did you?"

"I assumed he already knew. When he said he planned to talk to you, I mentioned something about you having time to think since you'd be sunbathing in Arizona."

I wince. "That's not why I'm going."

"I know. You said it was personal. You didn't tell me the reason, so obviously I couldn't share it with Perez." Frazier pauses. "He acted like he knew. You didn't tell him you were leaving?"

I don't answer.

"What's going on, Tyler?"

CHAPTER 35

My flight touches down at Sky Harbor International Airport fifteen minutes early. I take the shuttle to the rental car center, the road paralleling the construction of the new Sky Train intended to replace the bus I ride. Thirty minutes after landing, I zip down the freeway toward Los Angeles before taking the exit to Luke Air Force Base. The air conditioning in my pale blue Chevy Cruze combats the summer heat with a roar like the jet engines on my inbound flight.

My Phoenix frame of reference is based on twenty-seven-year-old memories of pilot training at the now-shuttered Williams Air Force Base southeast of the city. We would fly our asses off all week before spending weekends floating down the Salt River, swilling beer and decompressing from the most stressful year of our lives. I didn't explore much of the state during that busy year. I just remember the major landmarks—the Grand Canyon, the desert we trained over, trips to Tucson, and all the retirees—especially near Luke Air Force Base.

Robert, from The Aerie, gave me the address of the store where his company card was used. It's within five miles of the active fighter base.

I review my cobbled-together plan on the drive. It doesn't take long. All I know is that The Aerie credit account was used at a Fry's grocery store in Sun City twice before Robert canceled the card. So my assumption is that just because the card doesn't work anymore, doesn't mean the user stopped buying groceries. I'm going to watch the store.

I check into a Super 8 two blocks from the Fry's. Inside the room, I unpack my overnight bag. I don't have much: two changes of clothes, workout gear in case I have time to get a jog in, and toiletries. I haven't decided how I'll attack the surveillance yet—obviously I can't watch the store 24-7. Then again, whoever used the card probably isn't making midnight grocery runs either.

The walk to Frys only takes three minutes. I'm sweating within two. The obvious setup location jumps out at me like neighbors throwing a surprise birthday party.

It's perfect. The store hosts a gas station at the entrance, an Olive Garden, and a Waffle House. The Waffle House front windows offer a broad view of the grocery store entrance—and I like my hash browns smothered and covered. I'd been worried if I would need binoculars, but the Waffle House is close enough to pick out faces. I enter to a "Welcome to Waffle House" greeting and grab an empty table at the window.

I'm not dense—I'm stubborn. I recognize this escapade as a long shot. Some people might question my willingness to fly all the way to Phoenix at the request of a mother who hasn't hidden her dislike of me. But I'm not doing this for Lin Li. I'm doing this for me. Kristee has been on my mind throughout this entire ordeal. Following this lead is the only way I can think of that will ease my confusion about her ambiguous death. If a stranger stole The Aerie's account card, then I'm screwed. I'm counting on spotting either Karla walking up to this grocery store, or—in my little fantasy world—Kristee. I won't recognize anyone else.

My hash browns arrive with a smile and a "Here ya go, hun." I pace my eating, making them last fifteen minutes. Two cups of coffee and a small salad later, and I've been at my post for three hours, excluding two bathroom breaks. I've done surveillance before in the Air Force, but not with the *Mark-I* eyeball—a military term for using our own eyes. We always had equipment set up in the back of the plane—beeps and squeaks we called them—to monitor ground activity, and an accompanying team of operators who knew what they were looking for.

All I had to do was fly the aircraft in long ovals, tell bad jokes, and complain when my copilot let one rip. All of which was better than staring out a window for three hours.

The rest of the afternoon isn't much better. I break the monotony with laps around the parking lot, stretching my legs while keeping my eyes locked on the store entrance. By seven in the evening, I've had enough. Returning to my hotel, I change into my gym shorts and a t-shirt, stretch for two minutes, and head out for a jog. Within the first minute, I'm soaked in sweat, but my energy level is higher. That's when I remember the altitude change. I've been shuffling along at a jog back home at over nine-thousand feet elevation. Arizona's desert isn't that far off of sea-level. So my evening jog actually feels like a run.

After a shower, I check my phone for updates. Not that either Perez or Frazier consider me part of their team. Perez used to keep me up-to-date on cases he knew interested me. Before he accused me of going whacko whenever I got involved.

Frazier and I have just endured a near-death experience, so I feel a bond with her. Evidently my friends aren't reciprocating my love, because I have nothing from them in texts or emails.

I recline on my bed while dialing Laura. Straight to voicemail. I don't leave a message, but I wonder how she is processing our experience. I'm pretty sure we won't be getting together for that dinner date any time soon. But I also don't want her to think I'm ghosting her.

Snatching the remote, I power up the TV, and search for something more exciting than my Waffle House day. On AMC, Rocky fights a boxer from Russia or the Soviet Union—I haven't quite nailed down the timeframe—and I watch him train in Siberia for twenty minutes before I give up. *Hearts on Fire?* Maybe for Stallone. Not so much for me.

The clock reads eight thirty. I'm still wired. Sleep isn't peeking over the horizon, so I decide to aid that process. I walk across the Super 8 parking lot to the AM/PM convenience store to grab a beer. Through the glass refrigerator doors, the neatly bundled six-packs whisper my name. Ignoring their siren call, like the disciplined man I am, I choose a tall IPA from New Belgium Brewing and return to my room. An hour later and I'm sawing logs.

The next day looks like the first, except I finally hear from home. Frazier's first text pops in mid-morning while I'm tackling my second variation of hash browns, the peppered and capped.

Enjoying vacation? I've got Frazier in my contacts, so the texter's identity is no mystery.

Yup. Needed the time. I wanted to open with *What's happening with the case?* Or, *Find out anything new?* But I remember she's working with Perez. Who knows what he's shared with her about my tendency to go all in on cases like these?

Not sure if you wanted an update or not?

My daughter once explained to me that when I type a return text, the other person can tell I'm working on a message. I will myself to take five deep breaths before replying, so Frazier won't see an instantaneous bouncing dot.

I got time. I type. *What's the news?*

I answer my cell before the first ring finishes, figuring she already knows I'm right next to my phone.

"We've made progress." Emma sounds breathless, like I'm the first person she's called with this news. "Something connecting Laura's painting to the Remingtons."

"You mean a stronger connection than the paintings being inches apart from each other when they were stolen?" I can't help myself—and I figure I've got a bead on Frazier's brand of humor by now.

"Exactly. We did a deep dive on Bruce Davis's phone. Guess who he had been in contact with?"

"Who?"

"Duane—Monica's boyfriend. We've pulled some interesting text messages between the two."

Frazier isn't uncovering anything new with the Bruce Davis-Duane Dahl connection. I watched Duane exit the hospital room when I went to ask Davis about the phone. The guard told me Duane helped get him the art security job. This sounds like old news. I push my hash browns from one side of the plate to the other before answering. "I thought we already established they were acquaintances?"

"We did. But now we've found proof Duane asked Bruce Davis for photos of Laura's *Broncho Buster* with the Remingtons. The photos—like the one we found on the SD card, but with Laura's painting added—aren't there, but the texts are pretty damning. Duane set it all up."

"Why?" I'm missing the obvious here. "What's so important about these photos?"

"They were planning to make NFTs out of them."

I recall Nate's description of non-fungible tokens. These must be the NFTs to which Frazier refers. "What does that mean? Like they were going to mint an NFT of the photo?"

"Look at you." Frazier laughs. "You even got the verb right. That's exactly what they planned—an NFT of *Broncho Buster* with the Remingtons." She sounds satisfied, as if her explanation is clear. It's not. Not to me, at least.

"That painting was displayed next to the Remingtons in an art gallery in LA for a month. In perfect lighting. Why would they decide on the 'back-of-the-van' shot…?" My voice trails away as it hits me. What the difference in setting might mean. "Did the picture on the SD drive come with a time-stamp?"

"Perez said it was easy to underestimate you." Frazier doesn't continue right away, as if realizing she hasn't exactly said what she wanted to say. "I mean, not that I ever thought that way. You were great at The Lodge. You—"

"Got it," I interrupt. "So what we have is the last known picture of the Remingtons before they were stolen; perhaps never to be seen again, right? So if someone turned that into an NFT, then it's permanent. Like forever. And if they sell the NFT before the Remingtons are recovered, they're bringing in some serious change, right?"

"That's what we're thinking."

I'm still confused. I raise my eyes toward the Fry's entrance and spy the back end of a petite woman with black hair disappear into the store.

I stand from my booth. "But if Duane is behind the theft of the Remingtons, then why do you need the NFT? Aren't the paintings more valuable than the NFT?" The woman vanishes before I can discern if she is Asian or not. "So I guess you've arrested Duane?"

Frazier laughs. "No. He's still walking around."

"What?"

"Let me explain. You're right about the paintings being more valuable. Two things on that, though. The first is that the Remingtons would be incredibly difficult to unload. I mean, you have to find a collector that wants them so badly, they will buy stolen art. So if you didn't have a buyer, the NFT could still provide income. Hell, even if you had a buyer, you could sell the NFT because the buyer wouldn't dare disclose they had the paintings. The date-time stamp would prove the picture was taken before the paintings were stolen."

I slap a twenty on the counter, and exit Waffle House through the swinging glass door into the parking lot. "I'm having a hard time picturing Duane figuring all this out. He didn't strike me as the sharpest tool in the shed." I stride toward the grocery store entrance, eyes locked on the exit.

"That's the second thing. Davis's texts show Duane was just a facilitator. Duane knew something was going to happen. He's the one who recruited Davis for the guard job—but the times on the texts make it look like Duane was nowhere near Cottonwood Pass that night. We don't have enough to lock him up."

I enter the store and survey the registers, pondering what Frazier just shared. The customers and the cashiers are like a sea of gray; I'm finding it hard to identify anyone under the age of seventy. "Emma, I'm trying my hardest to be as smart as you seem to think I am, but I think I'm missing the big picture. Did you solve this thing or not?" I head for the aisles, but realize I might miss the person altogether. What if I choose baking needs and she departs the store from the soup aisle?

"Can I help you find anything, sir?" A shelf-stocker spots me standing between the registers and the aisles, head whipping back and forth like I've either lost my wife or my bearings. I doubt either is an uncommon occurrence around here.

"I'm fine," I whisper, and the shelf-stocker nods before turning away.

"Glad to hear it. Where are you, anyway?" Frazier's voice blares in my ear.

"Grocery store. So, did you solve it or not?" I ask again.

"Not. We don't know who stole the paintings or where they are. But let me give you our working theory on how the thing was set up." She pauses. My heart accelerates. "From the text messages, we know Duane hooked Davis into the job. He probably knew that Davis would be asked to take the picture before the robbery. Just of the Remingtons—for the people stealing them. You follow?"

"But you said the pic had *Broncho*—"

"Bear with me here, Z-man. You mind if I call you that? I've been hanging with Perez and his nickname for you is rubbing off."

So much for my hope that Perez and Frazier aren't talking about me. "Whatever."

"We think Davis took a pic with just the Remingtons and got it to the thieves. Then he probably took another with *Broncho Buster* to give to Duane."

It clicks, like the sound of the final segment of a 1000-piece puzzle snapping into place. "Wait. I got it. Because if Duane turned his pic into an NFT, it would increase the value of Laura's piece, right? The painting that wasn't stolen, sitting right next to America's most famous paintings, stolen hours later? Is that it?" I nod my head at my own logic, while turning to scan the aisles again. That's when I see the short, dark-haired woman walking out of Aisle 13. She is Asian. She walks straight toward me, pushing her cart. I step to the side so she can turn down Aisle 15. She smiles. The woman is closer to my age than Kristee or Karla's—and I read it as a smile of interest. When she dodges an old woman on a scooter, she turns to me and rolls her eyes. She's not interested in me—she's smiling because we're the two youngest people in the store. And she's not Karla.

"That's what we're thinking." Frazier agrees with my logic. "I mean, Duane's NFT wouldn't be worth the same as the Remington one, but it would definitely drive up the price of Laura's *Broncho Buster* if she was trying to sell it."

Ding. Ding. Ding. "She *was* trying to sell it. That was part of the reason Algood was up there. But no one was talking NFTs. Laura told me the price of *Broncho Buster* was up because of the LA exhibit and all the exposure. That, and the fact that it survived the theft." I snort as I exit the store aiming for Waffle House again.

"What?" Frazier says. I haven't done a lot of snorting around her.

"Laura and I disagreed on the Remington theft event raising the price of her *Broncho Buster*. I thought it would go up because it was the painting left behind. Laura thought the value would decrease because the thieves didn't think it was worth taking."

Frazier says nothing. I pick my way between the curb and the gas station while waiting for her thoughts.

She breaks the silence. "It didn't really matter which of you was right."

"Why?"

"Because once her painting—*Broncho Buster*—was stolen, the NFT value would skyrocket. The mysterious Laura Coker Long's *Broncho Buster*, photographed during the Remington heist. The painting that survives two weeks before it's stolen from its own exhibit."

And then finally torn to shreds. I keep that thought to myself.

I cut across to the entrance of the gas station convenience store, pausing as a customer exits.

"Excuse me." The man's eyes appear trained on the gas pumps behind me. He wears jeans and a t-shirt.

I turn toward the man as he passes. He strides toward a Dodge Charger at the pumps. I've seen this man before. Except last time he wore a polo shirt. And he was exiting Bruce Davis's hospital room with Monica's boyfriend, Duane.

CHAPTER 36

"Emma, I got to run." My voice drops to a whisper before I remember Frazier won't think that's normal.

"What's up? Everything alright?"

I don't have any reason to hide this information from Frazier. But talking to her while processing what I've just discovered exceeds my mental capacity.

"It's fine. I've just got to go. I'll call you back in a bit."

"OK, let me know—"

"See you." I punch off my phone, turning my back on the man. I push through the convenience store doors. Inside, I move right of the door toward the window. I swipe my phone into camera mode. The car moves before I can start snapping pictures, so I don't get any shots of the driver. But I get several photos of the California license plate hanging on the vehicle's rear end. As the car exits into the grocery store parking lot, I rush from the gas station. I pass a woman returning her empty cart to the cart stalls.

"I'll take that for you." I grab the handle from her.

The woman freezes. "Oh!" She smiles. "Thank you."

I move at a brisk pace, but not so fast I'll draw attention. At the lot's exit, the Charger turns left onto a main road. As soon as it disappears, I jog to the corner, still steering my cart as cover. In the distance, the Charger brakes at a stop sign four blocks down before continuing straight ahead. I keep my eyes on the vehicle until it vanishes.

I return the cart to a stall before trudging back to my hotel room. I try to process what I've just seen. The guy I saw in Bruce Davis's hospital room shows up in the parking lot of the same store where someone illegally used a credit card from The Aerie—an obscure business in a town of twenty-five hundred people?

I run through the facts. I'm in Arizona trying to track down a lead on Kristee's sister, Karla, that may or may not have to do with Kristee, who may or may not have been on Cottonwood Pass—or even inside the thieves' vehicle—the night of the heist. I just got off the phone with an FBI agent who has proven a connection between the art security guard Davis and the people who stole the painting. The man I practically bumped into at the gas station knows both Bruce Davis and Duane Dahl.

I pull out my phone and bring up the pictures of the Charger. Silver, with black trim. California plates: XFO-359. Tags are current. No bumper stickers. I can't make out anything but the silhouette of the driver inside the car.

I pull up Perez's number. He can run the plates. My finger hesitates over the green button. What am I planning on telling Perez?

I saw a guy who knows Bruce Davis at a gas station in Arizona.

And then the inevitable avalanche of questions from my friend.

Why are you in Arizona? Where is the guy now? This sounds like art stuff—why aren't you calling Frazier?

I don't want to lie to Perez, but if I tell him I'm tracking a lead on Karla that might have something to do with Kristee, he'll shut me down. I'll never get the chance to explain that this t-shirt guy is actually polo-shirt guy from Bruce Davis's hospital room. The one with Duane. I've pushed Perez's buttons too far on the what-really-happened-to-Kristee issue. If I share this information—and I'm wrong about anything—I'll never earn his trust back.

Playing out these questions in my head is like chair-flying before an important mission in the Air Force. I'd literally sit in a chair, one hand holding an imaginary yoke and the other imaginary throttles. It helped me identify potential problems before they arose. And that second question I imagine Perez asking? *Where is the guy now?* That's a problem. I need to find out where this guy is before I call in the cavalry.

I pop into my hotel room for a necessary stop after my three cups of Waffle House coffee, then climb into my rental car. Before leaving the parking lot, I pull up my current location on my map application. The neighborhood streets where the man disappeared loop around in curves and esses off the main highway like macrame knotted on a stick. I tap the screen on the spot where I last saw the Dodge Charger's taillights and head in that direction.

Fifteen minutes later, I've covered what feels like maybe five blocks. I spot exactly three California plates—none on a Dodge Charger. I can't count the number of garages I've passed, each capable of concealing the car I seek. I turn around in a cul-de-sac and spot a California plate on a VW Bug—the second one I've seen today…and the same color. I look at the wooden lawn ornament propped in the gravel showing the underpants under a checkered red skirt of the backside of a woman gardening and realize I've inadvertently returned to where I first started searching.

My app shows me where I'm at, but not where I've been. I have no doubt Big Data knows where I've been, but I can't see it on my screen. I pull over next to the sidewalk, grabbing my phone as I brake. I've got an idea.

I pull up my fitness app and hit the record button. I select *bicycle* then mash the START button. Success.

It's ten in the evening before I call it a day. The fitness app has kept me from retracing my steps. I've explored about three square miles of neighborhood. Every house. Every curb. But I still can't discount the garages. My mind is numb as I crash on my hotel bed. I don't even need the television or the beer to help me sleep.

My eyes pop open early the next morning, the clock radio's red numbers glowing 05:46. I consider a run before resuming my search from yesterday, but decide coffee is a higher priority. I use my rental car and aim for the same gas station next to Fry's. Because two blocks is a long way when you've just stumbled out of bed.

With a full cup of coffee wedged in the center console, I head for my hotel. Five minutes later, I'm only three hundred yards from the gas station, trapped in what must be Sun City's busiest intersection. Another three minutes pass, waiting for a green light, and I search for Dodge Chargers out of sheer boredom. I spot two of them, one with California plates, but neither is silver. I laugh—louder than normal, because it's just me and my coffee. More cars have passed by in the last three minutes than I saw in an hour last night on my search.

Across the intersection, a golf course sprawls green in the brown of everything else. The broad parking lot between the clubhouse and the street is practically empty. I make a command decision for a major change in tactics. When the light turns green, I cross the intersection and pull into the parking lot so the nose of my car faces the traffic. Polo shirt man used this road yesterday, heading toward the neighborhoods I've searched. My educated guess is this man will not sit in his house all day. This is the main thoroughfare. If he drives by here, I'll spot him.

After an hour, my coffee is drained and my bladder is full. The gas station has restrooms—and food. All I have to do is give up my post for ten minutes. Three minutes to get back through the intersection. Four in the store, and three to get back. My stomach rumbles.

I shift into reverse, glancing in the rearview mirror. When my eyes return to the front, a silver Dodge Charger passes from right to left in the far lane. No time for me to catch the front plate. I scan the driver's window while waiting to check out the rear plate. My breath catches.

The driver is Kristee Li.

CHAPTER 37

I whip out of the golf course parking lot, heading for the intersection. Kristee's heading in the opposite direction of where polo shirt man disappeared yesterday. She's already through the intersection, and is stopped at the next light while I wait at the red light on the cross street. As I tap my steering wheel, my focus shifts from my red light to Kristee's, five hundred yards away.

Screw this. I'm not losing her. I spot a gap in the traffic and barrel through my red light, joining the traffic flow in Kristee's direction. When her light turns green, I need to be on her tail. Horns blare. I hear the screech of tires as I force my way into the traffic flow. I expect the sound of metal on metal, but somehow the other cars avoid mine as I accelerate. The Charger is four football field lengths ahead of me, close enough to recognize, but far enough away that I doubt Kristee noticed my traffic shenanigans.

I close the distance between our cars, minimizing the chance I'll lose her on another light change. My foot eases off the accelerator when I'm within three car-lengths. Kristee won't recognize my car. I'm too far back for her to see my face. We travel in tandem for another three minutes, maintaining the space I've established, before she uses her right blinker and switches lanes. I do the same. A block later, the Charger pulls into an empty parking lot with a sign at the entrance reading KinderCare. Car surveillance isn't my bailiwick, but I've read plenty of police procedurals. If we're the only two cars in a child-care parking lot, I'm busted. I continue past the turn and pull to the curb, out of sight from where Kristee parks.

Child care? Kristee? I force myself to count to thirty—time enough for her to get out of her car and into the building. Then I maneuver my car back to the lot where she turned. The Dodge Charger is parked closest to the front door of the facility. I select a parking spot two rows back where I can watch the front door. I consider getting out and waiting for Kristee at the door, but I'm unsure why she's here. Did she bring a kid to child care? Picking one up? Or maybe even meeting polo shirt man here? My safest bet is to remain undetected until I figure out what is going on.

Three minutes later, Kristee exits the building and my breath makes that same hitching sound as when I first saw her.

It's not Kristee. It's her sister, Karla.

•   •   •

I reach for my door handle, my eyes locked on the sister of my closest friend, trying to rationalize how I could have been so wrong about who drove the car here. I've heard all the tropes about insular Americans who think all Asians look alike. I've never thought of myself as that guy. The Air Force sent me to live in Korea, work in Japan, and travel to China—I understand it can be hard to tell one nationality from another. The same way someone might not be able to distinguish a French citizen from a resident of Germany. But I've never had issues with my Asian friends. Kristee and I were close. I often described our relationship to others as paternal—pairing up with Kristee on a SAR mission was like doing a job with my daughter.

And Karla? I'm not even certain if we're still friends after we found ourselves thrust together investigating Kristee's disappearance; but we are close. Stress is strange that way—sometimes it can drive people apart; but it can also bring them together.

I crack the door and pause. Here's the deal—I'm uncertain how Karla will react when I confront her. She's come to Arizona for a reason.

She's here because this is where Kristee has come. And if Kristee is alive and not back in Buena Vista, it means she doesn't want to be found. By anyone. Including me.

If Karla panics, I can't force her to tell me where her sister is. I ease my door closed again, waiting for Karla to climb into her car.

Her car? Shit. In my euphoria at spotting what I thought was Kristee and then my disappointment at discovering Karla instead, I'd almost forgotten it's no coincidence that Karla is driving polo shirt man's car. That Kristee isn't the only connection to Colorado down here. Somehow the man exiting Bruce Davis's hospital room in Salida is involved with the Li sisters.

I'll confront Karla—after she leads me to the owner of this car. And—I barely allow myself to imagine the possibility—hopefully she'll lead me to her sister as well. And a bathroom. My need to compensate for my morning coffee is beginning to be a problem.

Three car-lengths are the most I allow Karla as I follow her to the highway. I might know the direction she came from, but I have no idea if she's returning to where she's staying. Hell, I don't even know why she stopped at the child-care center. I was turning around down the street when she entered the facility—I never got close enough to see if she was taking a kid into the place. She didn't walk out of the building with a child on her hip.

A mile and a half from KinderCare, Karla pulls into a strip mall. Exiting the Charger, she clicks the button on her key fob. The car lets out a honk before she turns and strides toward a store with a sign reading RoadRunner Shoes on the front. I settle into my seat, waiting for her to exit.

I spend the next hour in the parking lot, regretting my decision to forego a shower before starting my daily surveillance. Antsy at the lack of activity, I don a pair of sunglasses and my ball cap and stroll by the storefront. Karla is visible through the window, kneeling in front of a customer, helping them lace up a pair of running shoes. She works here.

I dash to the Subway across the parking lot and barrel into the men's room. I snag a bag of chips on the way out and return to my car. At

11:30, Karla exits the building and walks three stores down to a Chipotle. Ten minutes later, she returns to the running shoe store, bag in hand. As soon as she enters, I climb out of my rental. The gas station at the corner of the strip mall sells mixed nuts and coffee. Enough to get me through the day. I don't expect Karla to leave any time soon, but I keep the Dodge Charger in sight just in case.

Shortly after five, Karla is out the door and into the Charger. She points the car toward the child-care center. I'm unsurprised when she exits the center with a blond-haired toddler on her hip and a diaper bag over her shoulder. I'd already done the math and determined Kristee couldn't have a child here. And Karla wasn't pregnant when she disappeared. Someone else's child.

I play my follow-the-leader game back toward my hotel and the Fry's gas station where I first saw the Charger. Ten blocks later, Karla pulls into the concrete driveway of a house I recognize from my search the previous night. She stops in the driveway and waits for the automatic garage door opener to do its thing. I drive by and watch her pull into the empty two-car garage. No wonder I couldn't find the Charger last night. I stop three houses down, parking my car at the curb. I turn off the motor and rest my hands on the steering wheel.

Should I call Frazier and tell her I found polo shirt man from the hospital wearing a t-shirt in Arizona? Let her in on my suspicions about his involvement with the art theft? It's not like I'm one hundred percent sure he lives here, but I'm in the high probability range. But what if Kristee lives here too? Am I willing to roll the Feds in on her problems as well? I can't imagine how my friend—or her sister—could be involved in an art heist. Neither is a criminal. But I don't know what I don't know and I've already proven that I didn't know everything about my friend Kristee Li.

The curtain twitches in the house closest to where I've parked. I sigh. I've got to do something, or the neighbors are going to call the cops about a middle-aged man loitering in the street.

The heat radiating off the pavement blasts me as I step from my car, diminishing slightly as I stride up the concrete walkway. The house looks like every other sunbird residence on the street, with no clues hinting that even a child lives here, let alone two Asian sisters and possibly an art thief.

I ring the doorbell. Karla answers. Her mouth drops when she sees me and she slams the door shut. Surprise, I expected, but I'm unprepared for her to ignore my presence. I step back from the door and walk halfway down the walkway where I can watch the sides of the house. Karla's reaction has me worried she's going to make a break for it. Or warn Kristee so she can avoid me.

I wait a few moments, but see no indication of movement from the house. I ring the doorbell again. Nothing. It occurs to me that Karla probably isn't going to run away with a kid in tow. If she's the only adult in the house, there's no way she would leave the child.

"Karla! Tell Kristee I just want to talk to her. Can you do that?"

"What?" Karla's voice is muffled behind the door.

"Five minutes. Ask her if she can give me five minutes." It's not like five minutes is enough for Kristee to explain her disappearance in a way that will satisfy me, but I'll take what I can get and work it for more.

The door opens and Karla looks at me like I've lost my mind. "Tyler. What the hell? What are you talking about?"

I step forward. Karla swings the door like she's going to slam it again. I hold my palm up like a traffic cop before stepping back. Karla holds the door half-open. Sweat runs down my back.

"Is she here?" I say.

"Kristee?"

I nod. "Just tell me. Have you seen her?"

"Jesus, Tyler. She's dead. You know she's dead. You saw the video." Karla's eyes glisten. She steps back like she might invite me in, then seems to remember where she's at and steps forward again. "What's going on? Why are you doing this? Tracking me down and bringing up Kristee. Why?"

I've only spent time with Karla during Kristee's disappearance. I don't know her well, but I have seen her reactions in a time of crisis.

She doesn't look like she's lying. She looks like she's concerned I'm going to have a mental breakdown on her doorstep.

"I—" I pause, uncertain how to continue. "I heard about the charges on The Aerie's business account. I found out there was a woman on Cottonwood Pass a couple of weeks ago. Only five miles from the landslide. I—" But I can't continue. A tear rolls down Karla's face. I'm concerned about the moisture in my own eyes.

"I'm not letting you in, Tyler. I can't." She looks over her shoulder. I wonder if someone else is in the house. Someone besides the child. She sighs, as if she's made a decision. "Look. I'll answer a couple of those questions, but you've got to promise to go away. I can't deal with my mother tracking me down and starting in on me again. Can you promise me that?"

I nod in what I hope appears as a sincere manner. I can go away. I don't have any problem keeping Karla's location from her mother. Karla's an adult and I've spent enough time with Lin Li to understand why Karla might want distance from her. Something tugs at my conscience. I remember polo shirt man leaving Davis's hospital room. I might leave Karla, but I'm not dropping the lead I've found on the art thefts. I can't. That's not who I am.

"I promise."

Karla takes a breath, like she's preparing for a long story. She leans forward and pokes her head through the space between the door and the jamb and nods at the bench set up on the concrete walkway under the eaves. "Let's sit."

• • •

"It was me." Karla's hands lock into each other like she's trying to crack a walnut between them.

There are so many ways I can interpret this declaration that I'm unsure which question to start with. So I say nothing.

"It was me on the pass. Or at least that's what they tell me. I can't remember anything after finding Kristee's belt."

I've still got too many questions, but Karla's last statement floors me. "What belt?"

"I guess that's what you call it. The thing that you clip around your waist? The lower part of a backpack. That's a belt, right?"

I nod. "It's a waist belt. What do you mean you found it? Like in her condo or something?"

Karla remains silent, like she's giving me a chance at comprehension. It doesn't come. "Like out by the landslide. I found that part of Kristee's pack."

"What were you doing out there? With who? Did you find anything—?"

"Tyler," she interrupts. "Stop."

The questions tumble and I can't stop them. "But—"

"I'll tell you what I remember. Then you need to go, OK?"

I nod again.

"After you got out of the hospital, I stayed in Buena Vista. At Kristee's condo, with my mother." She takes a breath. "It wasn't easy. I was pissed at Mama Li after finding out she paid that neighbor creep to follow Kristee on the SAR mission. I was so angry. It was very typical of her."

I force myself not to nod, because I realize I'm looking like one of those Brett Favre Bobbleheads. But I'm worried if I stare at Karla, it might make her feel uncomfortable.

"And I was mad at myself for throwing you under the bus and lying to the cops about my computer."

"I'm not angry about that, Karla. I told you that already. Those guys threatened you. You didn't have a choice."

"I know. Thank you for saying that. Again. But I wasn't proud of myself." Karla crosses her arms across her middle like she's chilled. Or anxious. "I told Mama I was going back to school. I still had the semester left Kristee had paid for, and that's what Mama assumed I would do, so she wasn't surprised."

Kristee had financed Karla's college education after their mother's fall from grace at Denver University and losing her job. Karla's scholarship at Duke covered over half the expenses, but the rest of each semester was no small sum and influenced Kristee's faulty decisions leading up to her disappearance.

"But you didn't go." Master of the obvious, I throw out my statement just to keep Karla talking.

"I didn't go. I wasn't exactly sure what I wanted to do long term." She looks over her shoulder, then turns back to me. "I'm still not. But after the video came out of Kristee, I felt I had to go see where it happened."

"But we sent teams—"

Karla interrupts. "I wasn't trying to find her, Tyler. I just needed closure. To see the spot she was running toward." She pauses, as if gauging my reaction.

"Long hike," I say. "Did you spend the night?"

"I did. You know I stayed in BV for almost a month, right? Way too much time with Mama Li. Finally, I told her I had to get back to school. She put me on the bus to the airport with one of Kristee's old daypacks. She probably thought I was just taking it to remember her by. Then I got off at Fairplay and hitched back to Cottonwood Pass. Spent the first night down by Texas Creek, only about a mile from where it happened."

I'm surprised at this. Karla would be the first to admit she's not outdoorsy like her sister. The route she took in was mostly on the Colorado Trail. Some might argue that a downhill hike on a maintained trail isn't that challenging, but throw in Karla's inexperience with the fact that she started at over eleven-thousand feet of elevation and the narrative changes.

"The next morning, I worked my way up to the site. I recognized the stand of trees. It was where the video showed her running. I spent the morning there, just remembering Kristee and thinking about all the things she went through to help me. Even if it wasn't the smartest thing I've done, I'm still glad I did it."

"What happened?"

Karla squints her eyes as if trying to sort her memories. "I stayed there all morning and had lunch. I think I might have tried to figure out how to camp there, except for the afternoon thunderstorms rolling in. It happened, like, instantly. One moment, I was tucked in among the rocks—the next there was lightning and it started to pour." Her eyes widen as if she's reliving the storm. "Even though I was at the bottom of that mountain, it's still pretty high up. And the rain turned to hail. I bolted further down the valley and tucked in under a tree to wait it out." Karla gives me a guilty look and I refrain from telling her what she already seems to know—tree, lightning, human—bad combination.

"That's where I found the belt…the waist belt thing. It was under the tree and all torn at one end. Almost like it had been gnawed on."

My eyes widen. "Did you find any bones?"

She shakes her head. "I thought of that, you know, because the belt looked like it had been chewed off. But it was just the belt. I unzipped it and there was some of Kristee's stuff. Her little wallet with her credit cards, license, all that stuff. Her SAR ID. Toilet paper. And one of those battery packs for keeping a cell phone charged."

I can't hold myself back at this revelation. "So you find evidence confirming your sister died. You hike out of the woods, travel to Arizona, and start spending money you don't have using her cards? Did you ever think about contacting the authorities?"

I haven't taken my eyes off of Karla's during my entire diatribe and I watch as my outburst seems to shut her down. She stands up and walks toward the door.

"Thanks for that, Tyler," she says over her shoulder. "Who needs a mother when I've got understanding friends like you?"

Shit. Mouth precedes brain again. Shit. "Listen, Karla…I didn't—"

"You're asking *me* to listen? When you don't even have the courtesy to hear what happened next? So rich. Kristee said you were different, but I don't think so. You're like every other Boomer I've met. You've got all the answers."

Karla's not wrong. I assumed her next actions and judged them. Instead of listening.

I stand. When I step toward Karla, she flinches and reaches for the door.

"I'm so sorry, Karla." I briefly consider kneeling in apology. Her eyes bore into mine. "You are right. I am wrong. I'm ready to listen."

The first sentence gets her, not the second or the third. My guess is that no one has told her she is right in some time. Her eyes soften and she leans her back against the door.

"I got hurt. On my way out—I was picking my way down the next rock field below the tree and I fell. That's the last thing I remember."

I will myself to stick to my promise; to listen. Even though I want to scream, *when did you start remembering again? On the road to the pass? In the van with the thieves? After that?* Because everything Karla has just explained has destroyed whatever inkling of hope I clung to that it was Kristee on the pass.

The waist belt is almost definitive proof. Kristee is dead. Karla was the one on the pass, in the van, and now down here with someone I know is connected to the art heist.

But does Karla know what she is involved in?

CHAPTER 38

"So when your memory returns, you're in an old folks' neighborhood outside of Phoenix, living with some strange guy." I wave at the house. "And his kid?"

"It's not like this is permanent. I've got a job now. When I get enough money for a car, I'll move out and get an apartment or something." Karla's voice is firm and methodical, like she's rehearsed how she would answer this very question. "And you're making it sound like some amnesia thing. It wasn't like that. Shane said I was hypothermic. They got me warmed up, some soup in me. I was conscious of what was happening before we ever left Colorado."

"So why didn't you have them take you home?"

Karla glares my direction. "Really?"

It wasn't a brilliant question. Lin Li is a natural disaster of a mother. If I were in Karla's shoes—lying to my mother, running away, almost dying—I might not have rushed home either.

"They offered to drop me at the hospital. I refused. When they told me they were going to Arizona, I asked if I could go. By the time we got here, Shane and I had worked out an arrangement for me to live here. Help him out while I got my feet on the ground." Karla pauses, as if trying to read my reaction to her story. "It worked out well for him, too. He's trying to raise Justin by himself. His travel schedule for work makes that tough."

I bet it does. I'm guessing an art thief doesn't work a nine-to-five job in an office near his house.

My expressionless face must not sit well with Karla.

"What?" Karla's voice rises an octave. "Don't you dare judge me, Tyler Zahn. Not after what I've been through." She steps toward me, her finger out like she's going to stab me in the chest. She pulls up short and seems to think better of the finger, moving her hands to her hips. "If you have something to tell me, just say it."

So I do.

•　　•　　•

"No fucking way." Karla's eyes are dull. We've moved back to the bench, and she sinks onto it. I sit next to her. This might be the first time I've ever heard Karla swear. Her reaction seems genuine. Like she wasn't aware of what was happening on her journey to Arizona.

"Way."

"Are you sure? I mean, are you positive it was Shane and Chris?" Karla turns to me. "I knew it was paintings in the back. They told me. I mean, I even knew they were armed. That's what Shane does. Chris too. They're art couriers—they transport high value items and provide security at the same time."

"That's what they told you."

"That's what I believe."

"Let me ask you a question, Karla. When you arrived in Arizona, I'm guessing Shane—Shane's the one who lives here, right?" Karla nods. "I'm betting Shane left on another trip right away. Am I right?"

"He had another job—just a one-day job. I watched Justin."

"Where did he say he was going?"

"New Mexico. He said he had to finish business with the people who took delivery of the paintings."

I press my lips together before speaking. "I saw him two days after they picked you up on the pass, walking out of the hospital room of the security guard who survived the art heist." Karla squints, like she's skeptical. "Karla, it wasn't like I *thought* I saw him—I saw him. It was the same guy I saw yesterday driving that Dodge Charger."

Karla leans forward, resting her elbows on her knees. Instinctively, I reach to pat her back, before pulling my hand back. I'm still unsure if she believes my account of what happened to her. Besides, I've been around Karla before when she needed comfort. I've never seen anyone touch her in those moments. Instead, I lean forward, matching her position. And I wait.

Finally, Karla speaks. "Why are you here, Tyler?"

My answer would be simple if she would just reframe the question. If she asked, *Why did you come?* I could admit that I came to Arizona to find Kristee.

If she added specificity, asking, *Why are you here on this porch, right now?* The answer would change. I could tell Karla it's because I care about her. I'm concerned about her safety.

But I didn't find Kristee. And I've explained to Karla the situation she's in.

Suddenly, I realize why I'm still here. I've found the residence of at least one of the thieves who stole the Remingtons. I'm taking this information to Frazier.

"I'm going to the FBI."

I believe Karla's story—that she was clueless about the thefts. I might not know her as well as I know her sister, but she's not a criminal. I have a hard time imagining her helping those kinds of people. I'm going to Frazier—but Karla doesn't have to be part of the narrative.

"You need to leave tonight," I tell Karla. "If you need money, I can leave you some. But Shane's going to have to answer some questions. You don't want to be anywhere close when they pick him up."

Karla's fists clench and unclench. "What about Justin? He's just a boy. What's going to happen to him?"

I say nothing. Because I'm unsure what happens to an art thief's kid when he gets caught. But surely Karla understands she can't take the child.

Karla must recognize I'm out of ideas. "Shane's got a sister in Scottsdale. Will you help me get him there? Help get me out of town?"

"I can do that." When I said she had to leave tonight, I just assumed she'd drive away. But that would mean taking Shane's car. Frazier and the Feds would figure that out in a heartbeat. She needs more than just money from me. I nod toward the door. "But you need to move it, Karla."

CHAPTER 39

As soon as I'm done with Karla, I grab the first airline ticket available home. Twelve hours later, Amore tugs at the leash, dragging me uphill on my standard three-mile loop. We're two-thirds of the way up the slope. For once, I wish he would just stop and take a dump, so I'd have an excuse to catch my breath.

My cell phone vibrates. I skid to a stop, exhaling. *Frazier* flashes on my screen.

"Amore, heel." He ignores me, tugging at the leash. I'm unsure if Kristee taught any commands to Amore or not. He certainly doesn't understand mine.

"Zahn here."

"Z-man! It's Emma. I've got news!" Frazier's voice bubbles through the phone like she's calling from a bar to tell me a joke she just heard. My watch reads 10:30 am. Even if she's returned to the east coast, it's still a little early for that.

"I know."

"How? Did Perez already tell you?" Now she sounds disappointed.

"I mean, I know it's you. My phone tells me who is calling. Because you're a contact, and—"

"Z-man, if you're trying to impress me with your tech skills, it's not working." She pauses. "We got McGee, and he's talking."

It takes me a moment to process. McGee is Shane—aka polo guy and t-shirt-man. The guy Karla was living with in Arizona. Before I swooped in and got her out.

"He fessed up to the Remingtons. He gave us his partner, and we got a bead on the buyer. We're running a raid tonight."

"What about McGee's connection with Duane? Monica's boyfriend? You guys find anything to help Perez on Davis's murder?"

"That one's not as clear." Frazier's voice raises in pitch at the end of the sentence.

"Why? Those three guys were in the same hospital room. There's some kind of connection. There has to be." I might not be FBI-trained, but they always taught us in the military that *if it walks like a duck, and talks like a duck…*

"Right. We confirmed McGee knew the security guard Davis, and that Davis had prior knowledge the theft was going down. McGee said they paid Davis to take photos of the Remingtons for NFTs."

"I thought NFTs were Duane's thing? McGee's guys were into them as well?"

"McGee said they do this as a sidebar. They steal paintings for paying customers, and mint time-stamped photos into NFTs to sell on the side. Probably how Duane found out about it in the first place. Anyway, Davis's photo was the last picture of the Remingtons before the thefts. Except…" Frazier pauses.

"Except it wasn't," I fill in the rest of her sentence. "Because Duane got Davis to take one afterward with Laura's *Broncho Buster*, right?"

"Right. We can prove Duane hooked up Davis for the security job. And they had their own NFT side deal." Frazier pauses again. "But we have nothing solid tying Duane to McGee, or the Remington theft."

I nod, even though Frazier can't see me. "Did you quiz Duane on Davis's death? He's probably not talking, right?"

"He just laughed when we started asking questions. Of course, he's got the perfect alibi—he wasn't there."

"What did he say about Monica? She's the obvious suspect."

Frazier sighs. "Here's where it gets interesting. Monica's dead, so Duane has no reason to protect her, right?"

"Right."

"He's doing it anyway. He says she didn't have any motivation to kill Davis, because he had already delivered on the photo."

"How did he explain the SD card they found on Monica?"

"He didn't. We haven't shared that with him yet. He said Monica got the photo through a shared drive, downloaded it to her laptop, and deleted it on the shared drive." Frazier lets out a laugh. "Of course, he can't prove it, because the laptop is missing."

I recall standing in line behind Monica and Duane as they complained about the stolen laptop. "But the SD card you found on Monica proves Davis still had a copy of the picture, right?" I feel like I'm stating the obvious.

"Does it?" Frazier's voice sounds like she's admonishing me. I recognize my mistake.

"Oh shit. The one you found on Monica didn't have Laura's painting in it."

"We're looking at everything. But that's what I meant when I said the whole murder end of this investigation isn't moving as fast as the art theft."

"What about the new fire? Did Duane start that after he crashed his truck into the bridge?"

"We can't prove it."

I realize one more question I forgot to ask Frazier. The one Karla couldn't answer. "What about the Asian woman? Was she involved?" I know Karla didn't steal the paintings. But I don't know why McGee and his partner picked her up.

"McGee said she stumbled up to their car in the parking lot, right as the Remingtons were going down. They told her to sit in the back and they'd give her a ride to town. And that's what they did. I'm surprised they didn't shoot her like the guard. Thank God for miracles."

I say nothing for a moment. Frazier's explanation isn't exactly what happened, but it matches with what Karla told me. And might explain how she ended up with McGee.

Frazier fills the silence. "Don't go overboard with the enthusiasm, Z-man. We're a hell of a lot further toward solving this than yesterday at this time."

I divert the conversation away from Karla. "I know. I get it. I'm just trying to figure out how this all factors into Davis's murder. Perez's problem—not yours. I guess your boss must be happy about the art recovery."

Frazier laughs. "It's not recovered yet. Don't jinx us. But he's happy. Damn happy." She pauses. "He's grilling me, though. Like how it was you knew to go to Arizona. You have to admit, you heading to the Sun Belt for R&R and randomly running into our art thief at a Fry's gas station isn't cutting it, right?"

I say nothing.

"Zahn—if you can't explain yourself, we have to dig. You knew something. You acted on it. If you can't tell us what it is, then you have to see how it looks from our end."

"Frazier." If Frazier's suddenly going all last names-only on me, I can play along. "You can't possibly think I had anything to do—"

"I don't. But look at it from my boss's perspective. Hell, you were dating the artist whose paintings were in the same truck. You spent time with the security guard at The Lodge. Then, within a week of our rescue, you track down one of the thieves you claim you know nothing about by randomly spotting him in Arizona? I don't think so." She pauses. "Just tell me."

Her last command almost sounds pleading. "Are you recording me, Emma?"

Silence.

"Agent Frazier?"

"I'm not. But I could, you know. We can do all kinds of things."

Frazier's statement is not quite a threat, but it's pretty damn close. It stings. Partly because after all we've been through, I consider her a friend. And partly because she's right. If I'm going to get back to a normal life, I'll need to explain myself. I'm just not sure how to do it without implicating Karla.

"I'll tell you," I say. "But not on the phone. You get back out here. I'll explain in person."

CHAPTER 40

If so much hadn't happened over the last two weeks, I would almost consider this Groundhog Day—like the movie. Perez sits across from me at the Elkhead, munching on a slice of quiche. I'm working over a scone while sipping my black coffee. The only thing non-standard about our coffee shop meet-up is that I suggested it instead of Perez. He's still so busy with the Davis murder case that he almost turned me down.

"Frazier's coming in tomorrow, Z-man." Perez pulls his fork from his quiche, jabbing it my direction. "She wants to talk to you about that Arizona shit. I assume you want to dry run whatever it is you're going to tell her with me, right?"

Perez couldn't be more wrong. I hid my Arizona trip rationale from Perez so he wouldn't think I was still mentally wrecked about Kristee. Admitting I chased the lead he inadvertently provided would just confirm his suspicions. Besides, I'm not interested in sharing Karla's involvement with the art thieves with anyone. I don't even want to tell Frazier, but I'm worried the Feds will chase me like smoke from a campfire if I don't fess up and beg for discretion. I trust Perez—even though he's lost confidence in me. But sharing Karla's tangential involvement in the art heist does nothing to help solve his murder case.

"You already know why I was there. Cheap tickets and sunshine. Are you telling me you wouldn't take a couple days off if you'd been through what I had at The Lodge?"

Perez squints. "Bullshit, Zahn. You're retired. Every day is a day off for you. I'm in the same camp as the Feds—you recognizing this Shane McGee at a gas station in Arizona is bullshit. And you know how I feel about coincidences."

He's not wrong. More than once, I've reflected on Perez's maxim that there are no coincidences in law enforcement investigations.

The silence turns awkward. Then Perez breaks into a smile.

"That's OK. I'm not pressing you on this. You know why?"

"Why?" Now he has me curious. And nervous.

"Because if I push you, you're going to clam up. I'm still buried in this Davis murder. You were there. So I'm going to pretend I'm not pissed at you in the hopes that you might still be able to help me solve this thing."

I offer Perez a thin smile. Not from a lack of enthusiasm; I'm just unsure what help I have to offer. "So, what did you find out on the toxicology report?"

"Fentanyl overdose."

"Fentanyl? Again?" The first time Perez and I worked together involved a fentanyl case. One of the terrorists who died in the Dillon dam incident had been running a sidebar drug operation and cutting his product with fentanyl. "How do you know it was murder, then? What if he was a user?"

Perez nods. "That's possible. He could have overdosed. Killed himself on purpose. But we found no traces of other drugs in the room. No empty baggies, containers, residue…nothing. Don't you think it's unusual that if Davis did this himself, he would get rid of all the traces prior? Even if he was planning suicide, he would know the toxicology would show the fentanyl, so why bother with the clean up?"

"That brings it back to Monica, right? And Duane—except he wasn't there. Laura said they were both regular drug users. I heard that from Julie as well." I sip my coffee.

"That checks with us, too. Monica has…well, had…a record. She was a known addict. Duane doesn't have any criminal record involving drugs, but he has been crosswise with us before. And the guys he hangs out with have had drug issues."

"I assume you heard Duane's statement to Frazier and the Feds?"

"About Monica not having a motive because she already had what she needed from Davis?"

"Uh, huh."

Perez tilts his head and eyes me. "Riddle me this, Z-man. What about the SD card we found on her body?"

I nod. "I know—the assumption is she could've offed Davis and taken the card, right? But what if she already had the card? If she didn't take it from Davis?"

"Yeah," Perez says. "We've considered that. But it brings us back to motive. The only people who had plausible reasons to kill Davis were Duane and Monica…or the guys who pulled off the heist. And the heist guys weren't at The Lodge. We've done background checks on everyone else. None of the people you were stuck with had ever met Davis before the theft."

"What about the laptop?"

"What about it? Duane says it was stolen the day after the heist."

"Right. But did you lean on Duane to see who he thinks stole it? Whoever took the laptop knew what was on it. They likely knew who sent the photo—namely Bruce Davis. And maybe whatever they had on the laptop wasn't any good if Davis kept a copy."

"You're saying whoever stole it could have snuck into The Lodge—through a forest fire—and killed Davis?" Perez shakes his head. He's getting that same look he gets when I bring up my doubts about Kristee's disappearance. But he's misunderstanding me this time.

"No. I'm saying maybe the person who stole the laptop was at The Lodge the whole time."

CHAPTER 41

"Are you fucking kidding me?" Frazier says.

I'm certain I've surprised her because it's only the second F-bomb she's ever dropped on me. This one's not as endearing as the first. We're ensconced in the back corner of The Stray Cat coffee shop, because I'm worried Perez will barge in on us if we meet at the Elkhead. Frazier has an untouched bear claw pastry sitting on her plate. I'm already halfway through my second scone of the week. I started eating it as soon as we sat because I expected this reaction when I explained my Arizona visit to Frazier.

"The Asian girl in the van? *That's* the lead you ran with? *That's* what broke this thing open?" Frazier's head sways back and forth like a bull elephant. I can't tell if she's pissed at herself because I followed a lead she missed, or because she knows why I followed it—and can't believe it resulted in the art thieves' arrests.

"Just good detective work?" I try, but Frazier's on to me.

"You went down there because you thought your friend was still alive. That was the whole reason, right?" I've told her about The Aerie and the credit card, so she already knows how Arizona came up on my radar.

I nod and say nothing. I wish I could tell Frazier I left for Arizona with at least a single clue about the paintings. I like it better when Frazier thinks I'm a skilled investigator. In fact, I feel better when I know Frazier is thinking about me at all.

"You damn military guys and your 'leave no one behind' mentality. My twin brother's the same way. Except he's Army. Not Air Force."

"You've got a twin brother?"

"Forget it." Frazier shakes her head. "Focus, Zahn. So you didn't tell us because you were protecting the sister, right? Didn't want her to get in trouble for consorting with known criminals?"

I nod again.

Frazier's eyes haven't left mine, and they look hurt. Like she's trying to decide if trusting me was a mistake. But I also can almost see the gears turning in her head. Maybe because no matter how lucky I was, she knows they would have never recovered the art—which they secured in the raid two days ago—without me. After our time together at The Lodge, I sense Frazier respects me. I'm unsure I can say the same about Perez. That's why I'm sharing this information with Frazier instead of him.

"I have to talk to her myself, Z-man," Frazier says softly. My eyes drop to the table. I knew this would be her answer. But then she surprises me. "Here's the deal. I need to verify her claim she didn't know. If I can do that, I'll keep her out of the investigation. Out of my report. If I can't—"

"She didn't know," I interrupt. "If you find out she did, then take her in. I wouldn't be covering up her involvement if I honestly thought she knew."

"I know." She finally reaches for her bear claw and takes a nibble.

I pull a card for the local towing company from my wallet and scribble Karla's email address on the back before handing it to Frazier.

"Not going to tell me where she's at?" Frazier says.

"Can't you guys figure that out from the email?"

"Not if she's using a VPN."

"A what?"

"Forget it." Frazier sighs.

I smile.

•   •   •

"People have been asking after you, Tyler." Judith reaches across the library's front desk, grabbing my wrist. "Everyone heard about you escaping the fire…then you weren't around for a while. It's good to have you back."

Judith is the library matriarch, as well as my unasked-for matchmaker. I had told her about my planned date with Laura before the heist and I suspect it hurt her feelings that I found Laura on my own. I'm surprised she hasn't thrown questions at me about the status of our relationship. I know I have plenty.

"It's good to be back. Got anything for me?" I've been volunteering at the library since I moved here, usually going in two to three times a week and shelving books. It's a different kind of community service than Search & Rescue. My mother raised me on libraries and books and the smell of a library makes me as nostalgic for my childhood as the scent of fresh-cut grass does for my high school football days.

"Of course." Judith wheels a metal cart out with two rows of books. "Anything I should tell our interested patrons about your status?"

Here it is. The elephant in the room. I scramble to come up with a non-specific answer. "The fire was pretty dramatic. Laura and I are still trying to come to terms with what happened up there. She lost her sister. And her art. I think she'll be grieving awhile."

If Judith recognizes I've deflected a question about me to an observation about Laura, she hides it well. She gives me a warm smile, pats my hand, and points me toward the Adult Fiction section.

I'm working through the cart's second row of books in the Large Print aisle when my phone buzzes. I pull it from my pocket and see a notification for a text from Frazier. I press a button and read her message.

There's an NFT of Laura's Broncho Buster on the market from an anonymous seller. Just got the link.

I assume she's referring to the pic taken with the Remingtons, but I've been in trouble assuming before. I poke out a reply on my phone.

The shot with the Remingtons?

I see bouncing dots showing Frazier is typing a response.

Yep. Either the laptop thief put it out, or there's another copy.

She hasn't seemed to consider the other possibility, so I type it out.

Or you got a leak.

This time her reply is immediate.

I don't think so.

I consider ducking outside or into the bathroom to call Frazier for more details, but decide against it. They obviously don't know who is trying to sell the NFT. The laptop thief could be any one of Duane's network of losers that might have known about the NFT scheme. It could have been any one of the random people Monica would talk to when she got high.

Shoving the phone back into my pocket, I return to my shelving duties. I've arranged my next four Large Print titles in order on the cart so I can move down the aisle without backtracking. Charlie Donlea, Jennifer Hillier, Mary Kubica, Lisa Jewell. Who would've guessed so many Large Print readers loved thrillers? I remember Laura increasing the font size on Frazier's laptop at their Surf Hotel interview and smile. She needs to find this Large Print section of the library—or break down and buy reading glasses like mine.

I shelve the Hillier book and have the Kubica in my hand when it hits me. What Laura told Frazier and I at lunch when she was having problems showing me the missing art database on Frazier's laptop. *This is why I don't own one of these things.*

But Laura has a laptop. I watched her pull it from her car and carry it over the mountain when we left The Lodge. Unless it wasn't hers.

I laugh out loud, then turn toward the desk to see if anyone noticed. Judith smiles, waiting for me to explain. I smile back, raising the Kubica book like I've found it funny, then turn back to the shelf. Shaking my head, I stick the book in among Kubica's others. I guess when you're looking for a laptop and a thief, everyone is a suspect. Why would Laura steal her sister's laptop?

My heart pounds. Not like it wasn't beating before, but all of a sudden, I can literally feel the thumps in my chest. I return the cart to the front desk. Judith glances at the remaining books and raises her eyebrows.

"I'll finish later, Judith. Something just came up." I shake my phone at her and she opens her mouth to reply. I cut her off. "I'll be back."

Whirling toward the door, I force myself to walk instead of run. I'm so used to figuring things out in a sequential order that this sudden revelation is throwing me for a loop.

Did Laura know about Duane and Monica's plan from the start? Because if she did—if she knew they were going to make money off a *Broncho Buster* NFT, then she had every reason to steal Monica's laptop. And when her painting was stolen at The Lodge? The value of the potential NFT she stole from her own sister increased. The only thing that would make that NFT even more valuable is if it was the last picture ever taken of Laura's *Broncho Buster*.

Before it was destroyed.

CHAPTER 42

I should call Frazier. Or Perez. Instead, I drive straight to Laura's studio. A CLOSED sign hangs from her door. It's a weekday, and it's not lunch hour. Laura's normally working in the back. I walk around the building to the empty parking area.

On the drive to her house, I consider my theory. I've got all kinds of motive and not a shred of evidence. In fact, if character counts, people in this town would think I was nuts to bring these questions to Laura—a pillar of our arts community.

Did you kill Bruce Davis?

Did you steal a photo from your now-dead sister?

Did you destroy your own painting?

Maybe I am crazy. I chased the ghost of Kristee all the way to Arizona. And I was wrong. Well, I was wrong about Kristee. The rest of the trip turned out to be productive.

I pull between the posts marking Laura's driveway. My phone flashes with an incoming text message. Frazier.

Where are you now?

I grab the phone, slowing to a crawl as I fumble to answer. My tires leave the driveway's paved surface and I wrench the steering wheel until I'm back on the pavement. I stop, returning the phone to the cradle before rolling forward again. When I'm done here, I'll call her back. I need to have this conversation with Laura, before I put my reputation on the line–again–with my new theory.

Laura's driveway loops in front of the path to the front door. I park my truck and climb out. I take two steps toward the house before remembering my phone. While I don't want to be disturbed during our talk, it occurs to me that recording our conversation might not be such a bad idea. I lean into my truck, grab the phone, and swipe down to open my memo app. I hit RECORD and jam the phone in my pocket. When I shut the truck door and turn toward the house, I spot Laura in the living room window, with a phone pressed to her ear. When our eyes meet, she breaks into a smile and waves. I raise my hand and do my best to smile in return.

"Tyler!" Laura opens the door wide. The phone to her ear is gone. I'm surprised by her enthusiastic greeting. It wasn't like we left on the best of terms. I'd gotten the message loud and clear that our future date was permanently on hold. "Come in!"

"I just came by to…you know, to—" For someone who headed this way with such clear purpose, I'm stuttering like a high-schooler asking a girl to the prom.

"To talk?" Laura steps further back and I step forward. "Of course you did. Get in here." I take another step forward, and she closes the door behind me. She motions to the living room where I'd first seen her at the window. "I should be the one knocking on your door, the way we left things and all. Let's sit. Can I get you anything?"

My heart pounds as I imagine her asking the same question to Bruce Davis. There's no way I'm willing to accept anything she's offering. But I also recognize the paranoia in my own thoughts. Laura's making this whole conversation natural—like I'm here to figure out how we can restart our relationship, not to ask her about potential criminal actions at The Lodge.

"No thanks." I finally say. "I'm good. I can wait if you want to get something for yourself."

Laura grabs my hand, leading me to the couch. Her touch is warm. I wonder if she feels the contrast with my cold hands.

We sit. For a moment, neither of us says a word. I shift, turning toward Laura and preparing to speak.

Laura interrupts. "Are you here about what happened at The Lodge? I mean, it has to be that, right?"

I nod. Maybe this conversation will be easier than I expect. "I just want to ask you a couple of questions."

"Like why I shut down out there and acted so pissy to you? Why I haven't called since we got back? I can explain."

Part of me is desperate for Laura's explanation. Even with the trauma Laura experienced with the *Broncho Buster* theft, and then the tragic death of her sister, somehow, I had still hoped we could work through that. That I could be a comfort to her in a time of need. And when she had shut me off…it hurt. It still hurts.

But that's not why I'm here.

"Have you talked to Agent Frazier since you've been back?" I say, easing into my agenda.

Laura nods. "She interviewed me the same day I talked to Deputy Perez." She tilts her head at me. "Funny you asking, though. She called today requesting to meet up tomorrow. Do you know something I should know?"

The phone call in the window. Laura must have been talking to Frazier. Right after Frazier sent the text to me.

I take a deep breath. "Someone has an NFT for sale of *Broncho Buster*."

"Which one?"

At first, Laura's question surprises me. Most people would ask me what an NFT is. But I remember Laura's an artist. I should be more surprised if she's never heard about NFTs. But it's unclear to me where she's going with *which one*.

Laura must sense my confusion because she fills the awkward silence. "There are hundreds of *Bronco Buster* NFTs out there if you're talking about the Remingtons. Both for the painting and the sculpture. If you're talking about my *Broncho Buster*…well, there're not as many. But there are a few."

"How about an NFT of your *Broncho Buster* next to the Remingtons the night they were stolen—time-stamped to prove it?"

Laura pauses before answering. I search her eyes for a flicker of anything reflecting guilt. I detect nothing.

"I would say that was an NFT worth quite a bit of money up until…say…yesterday."

"Why's that?"

"Surely you heard they recovered the Remingtons, Tyler? It was all over the news. So there's no longer an NFT of the last picture of the Remingtons. They found them. The NFT would lose its value."

"Do you think so?" I tilt my head at Laura. "The biggest art theft in a decade. So what if they were recovered? The mysterious other *Broncho Buster*—yours—never was. It was destroyed. Ripped to shreds—right after the security guard from the theft was murdered and your sister died. In the middle of a forest fire. This NFT has a story, Laura. A valuable one."

Laura's eyes flick to the window behind my left shoulder. She stands. "Just a moment, Tyler. Someone's here."

I turn to the window. Julie Coker climbs from a Toyota Pathfinder. As she walks toward the front door, a tote bag in her hand, Laura cuts across the living room, aiming for the entranceway.

"We need to finish this conversation, Laura." I'm unsure what Julie knows about Laura's involvement in this, but I'm hesitant to keep grilling Laura with Julie here.

Laura pauses before turning back to me. This time her smile seems forced. "Don't you worry about a thing, Tyler. We're just getting started."

What the hell is she talking about?

"Hey, Jules. You ready for this?" Laura stands to the side of the door as Julie enters the foyer.

"Yes." Julie glances at me still standing in the living room. I tilt my head to the side. She looks uncomfortable. And there's something else. She doesn't appear surprised to see me.

"Did you bring what I asked?" Laura guides Julie into the living room to a chair across from me, before returning to her perch next to me on the love seat.

Julie nods at Laura.

I look from one woman to the other. "What's happening here?"

Julie opens her mouth, but Laura interrupts. "Jules, let me start OK?" She turns to me. "Tyler, our ranch—the Coker Ranchlands— we're in trouble."

"What do you mean? I thought you and your sisters had someone else running it."

"We do. We lease it to the McCormicks. You know Tom McCormick, right? And his brother, Luke?"

I nod. I've heard of Tom and I've met Luke at a Chamber of Commerce meeting.

"What does that have to do with what we were talking about?"

Laura sighs. "You're not a patient man, are you?" She glances at Julie, as if looking for agreement, but Julie seems almost frozen in her chair. "I'll just say it. It's money, Tyler. The McCormicks aren't turning a profit. They're not paying rent. We can't afford the combination of property taxes and loan payments for the inheritance tax without the rent income."

I squint at Laura. "Property tax is less than one percent. It's farmland. How hard can that be?"

"Coker Ranchlands was assessed at $10M when Daddy died. He zoned a portion of the ranch for residential. You know what's happened in this valley the last ten years."

Boy, howdy. I sure do. My landlord showed me the assessment for the house I rent. It's tripled in the last five years. Her $400K modular home is now worth—according to the county assessor—a whopping $920K. "Doubled?" I try.

"Tripled. Over $100K in taxes a year now, not including the little inheritance tax present Daddy left behind." Laura glances at Julie. "We're selling the NFT for the money. We need it to save the ranch. To get us through another couple years."

It's one thing to suspect Laura is involved in all this. It's another to have her admit she and her sister are both neck-deep in it. "But Davis…and Monica. You?"

Laura glares at me. "Stop it. We're not killers. It's Monica's fault Davis died." Julie sucks in her breath so hard that I turn my eyes from Laura to her.

"Fuck you, Jules. You know it's true." I've only heard Laura use that word with Monica. The sharpness in her voice draws my attention back to her. She fixes her eyes on me. "And Monica's death was an accident. Frazier was there. She confirmed it." She glances in Julie's direction. "It's not easy to lose a sister. Family is family. But Monica's death meant Julie and I had to work even harder to preserve what's ours."

"The ranch," I say.

"The ranch." Laura nods. "I'm not even sure the NFT will cover it, but we're trying to make it work. And if you can keep quiet about it, we'll figure out a way to reward you for that."

I'm confused. From everything Laura has shared so far, she and Julie are seizing an opportunity—picking up the pieces of a plan Monica and Duane botched up. If Laura and Julie knew nothing about the heist, or Monica's murder of Davis, then I'm not sure why they need to buy my silence. What have they done wrong?

"So, what do you think? It's not like we're doing anything wrong." Laura says, as if reading my mind.

Except they're trying to buy me off. I say nothing, my mind churning.

Tampering with evidence. That's what hits me like a line drive to the pitcher's mound in baseball. Perez and Frazier interviewed both these women. Neither shared all they knew. About Davis's death. About the NFT.

"I don't think I can. Keep quiet about it, that is."

Laura's eyes harden. She glances at Julie.

"Sorry," I say. "This is still an active case. You all have information you've kept from the authorities. You need—"

Laura stands up and shouts, "No!" She turns to Julie. "Pull it."

I follow Laura's glance. Julie bends forward, removing a handgun from the tote bag at her feet. She points the weapon at me without hesitation. My internal clock seems to slow. I register her practiced grip on the weapon and note her steady hands. This is not the first time she's used a pistol. I shrink back into the couch, raising my hands even with my shoulders.

"Hey, Julie. Not this. You guys don't want to do this. Not for messing with evidence." My voice quavers. "It's probably just a fine or something." I doubt my statement is true, but I'm desperate. "But the gun thing…I mean, if you use it. Do you really want to go there?"

Julie's eyes flick in Laura's direction, and then back to me. "Sorry, Tyler."

CHAPTER 43

My former almost girlfriend's voice barks, "Not on the couch. Let's take it to the garage. I'll grab some trash bags from the kitchen."

Julie doesn't move, or indicate she's heard Laura, so I don't move either.

"Jules. Did you hear me? Move it."

Julie jerks, as if she's just awoken. She nods in the door's direction. I stand and walk to the entryway, with Julie following. Laura straddles the entryway, hands on her hips, as if waiting to make sure Julie is functional before she turns her back on her.

"Open the door." Julie's voice is robotic. I follow her instructions, turning the handle and stepping through the doorway. I consider slamming the door behind me. Making a run for it. But when I turn, Julie is right there, crowding me onto the porch. Her eyes are suddenly alert, as if an alarm clock has rung.

I turn to the porch stairs as a door slams behind me. I glance back.

"Now go. Run!" Julie pulls the door handle with one hand and waves the gun toward the driveway with the other. "Go!"

I'm momentarily paralyzed. The woman with the gun is letting me go—I shouldn't be asking questions. But the handle she's pulling is already twisting from the other side. Laura bellows from inside.

"Let go of the fucking door, Jules. Right. Now." The vertical window next to the doorjamb shatters and the bottom end of a ceramic vase thrusts through the glass.

Julie looks at the vase only inches from her leg, then turns her head toward me, her eyes wide and her voice pleading. "Go!"

This time I do. I whirl, making a beeline for my truck. I dig in my front pocket for my keys while sprinting toward the driver's door.

Wood splinters behind me and I glance back. The door yawns wide, and Laura grapples with Julie on the porch. I pause. Two women wrestle for control of a loaded weapon, and my gut tells me to go back and break it up so no one gets hurt. I even take a step toward the house before shaking my head and sprinting to the truck.

I slide into my bucket seat and turn the key. My Tundra fires up and I shove it into gear to loop around the circular driveway and go for help. As I pass the walkway, two muffled pops make me duck. My passenger window and driver window simultaneously disintegrate. I glance across the cab at the house. Julie is down on the porch, swaying on her hands and knees, while Laura strides purposefully down the walkway, the pistol aimed at my truck.

Shit. Time slows as I realize I'm not out of danger. One or both of the bullets she shot crossed directly in front of me, taking out both windows. Like her sister, Laura seems plenty comfortable with the pistol.

I floor the gas. My truck fishtails toward the piñons at the perimeter of the driveway. Another two pops. When I try to pull out of the fishtail, the truck continues in the direction it's drifting, smashing through a stand of small trees. Laura hit one of my tires. But these trees aren't huge—I can drive with a flat. I keep the pedal pressed to the floor and attempt to plow through the fist-sized trunks filling my windscreen.

The truck slows as the first trees crumple under my hood. The vehicle jerks to a stop, the engine still whining but the tires finding no purchase. I'm caught up on the tangle of small trunks forming the base of the shrubs, and my Tundra is high centered. I jerk the transmission into reverse, instinctively checking the rear-view mirror. Laura steps off the driveway and walks toward my truck. Even in my panic, I note the deliberate and purposeful set of the jaw on this woman I thought I knew. She's coming to finish me.

I jam the accelerator again, this time not only to free the truck from the trees but also in the hopes I can back toward Laura. Throw her off target. I consider whether I should just mow her down with the rear bumper, but the whining of my engine indicates I'm going nowhere.

Shifting back to drive, I floor the accelerator. More whining. Back to reverse. My mirror shows Laura almost to my tailgate. I shift back to drive. This time, the truck gives me a foot of forward motion before stopping. Back to reverse. Laura's no longer visible in my mirror. Back to forward. I sense motion to my left and turn. Laura steps back from my window and lifts her weapon. I raise my foot from the accelerator.

"Laura—"

"Z-man!" Laura's lips aren't moving. She didn't say my name. Her eyes widen.

I dive across the center console like someone dropped a grenade on the passenger-side floor and I've got seconds to get rid of it. Two more gunshots reverberate in the closed cab. I ponder the thickness of my Toyota doors, the capacity of the magazine in Laura's handgun, and the glove box pressed against my face. The glove box. I scrabble at the glove box handle, wondering why I didn't think of my Glock before. My hands grope nothing but paper. My weapon is locked in my safe at home. The only things in my glove box are registration, proof of insurance, and the paperwork from when I had new tires put on a month ago.

My Tundra still runs, but the aftermath of the pops is such a contrast, it feels like silence. I consider continuing my slither out through the passenger door, but I'm unsure if the reason Laura isn't firing is that she's out of ammo or because she's working her way around to the passenger door of my truck for a better shot.

"Z-man? Tyler?" The voice is closer this time, and I recognize it. Frazier.

Laura already knows where I'm at, so silence doesn't protect me. "Stay back, Emma. She's got a gun, and she's using it. It's Laura."

I twist on the floor toward the passenger door handle. A shadow flashes over me and I flinch, shading my eyes toward the driver's window.

"You OK?" It's Frazier's voice, tense with worry. When I squint, I can make out her silhouette, head turned over her shoulder, facing away from my truck.

"It's Laura. Watch out for—"

"She's down, Z-man. I got her covered." Frazier's head turns away from the truck and her voice is fainter. "I need to know if you're OK. Could use some help here."

"Yeah." I roll from my back and open the passenger door. "I'm coming out."

As I stand, someone screams.

"Julie! Stop where you're at." It's Frazier's voice again.

I round the front corner of the truck and survey the scene. Frazier's still in a firing stance, her back against my truck's door. She's angled toward the house and I follow the direction her weapon points. Julie stands frozen in place, mouth agape, and her hands on either side of her face. Laura lies on the ground only a yard from Frazier's feet. She's on her back, eyes closed, with blood staining the right side of her chest.

"You killed her," Julie screams.

"Zahn. Direct pressure now." Frazier doesn't even glance my direction, her weapon still trained on Julie.

I move to Laura's side and kneel. The wound rides high on her right side. At first glance, I'd assumed a chest wound. But it's her shoulder. The blood isn't spurting, but rather pulsing from the hole. I thrust the palm of my hands over the wound.

"Let me help her," Julie pleads.

"Are you armed?" Frazier's voice is clipped.

"No. Look." I picture Julie raising her shirt or twirling around, or something. I don't have time to look up. The blood seeps around my palms. I release the pressure on the wound and rip off my shirt. All my senses are heightened. I feel the breeze on my bare back and the small tire around my gut spilling over my belt. I press my shirt against the wound and apply pressure again.

"You want to help, you can call 911," Frazier calls. "Can you do that?"

"Yes."

"Careful."

"My phone is in my back pocket."

A moment later, Frazier is at my side, Julie's hysterical voice yelling in the background.

"How did you know?" I say. "How did you know I was in trouble?"

"I didn't. I was scheduled to talk to Laura tomorrow. But then I started thinking about the motive. Who had what to gain? All of a sudden, I realized I had questions that couldn't wait. So I came out here."

The distant wail of sirens drifts through the trees. A small town means a quick response. We have five minutes before the ambulance arrives.

"Then I'm winding up this driveway and I hear gunfire." She pauses. "What the fuck, Zahn? What the hell happened out here?

CHAPTER 44

Frazier's query—what the hell happened out here—ends up being the easiest question of the day. Of the week, actually, because that's how long it takes law enforcement to figure out exactly what happened between the art heist and Laura getting shot.

Perez and Frazier no longer work separate investigations. As Perez consistently claims, there are no coincidences. It turns out his murder investigation has been intertwined with the art theft since the beginning.

I'm out of the loop. Not shut out like I felt after Kristee's disappearance—it's just that I have no badge, no more connection, and nobody needs my help with the investigation. I'm interviewed twice, once by Frazier, and again by Perez. My deputy friend doesn't even pursue his questions about Arizona like he did the last time we were together. I figure Frazier has tipped him off about how I was still chasing the dream that Kristee Li is still alive. Perez is probably avoiding the topic out of respect for our friendship—and a desire not to embarrass me.

Frazier calls twice the following week. She doesn't share theories, or results, but she does talk procedure. She's been re-interrogating Duane Dahl and Shane McGee. Martin Algood sits in jail, awaiting trial for kidnapping her–so a colleague takes over those interviews. She brought back a hobbling—but much more cheerful—Tristen LaFrance for more questions.

She says most of the information comes from Julie, which doesn't surprise me now. Two weeks ago, Julie would have been the last person, besides Laura, I would have guessed was involved in murder, theft, and fraud. But now, all I have to do is remember her practiced grip on that handgun. I believe she's capable of plenty of things I never imagined.

So, I'm stunned when Perez calls me up and invites me to the final out-brief—the meeting where Frazier summarizes the investigation's results to her FBI boss. All the key players are behind bars—well, except for Laura, who remains hospitalized under security, and Julie, who is out on bail. No part of the case under county jurisdiction remains open, so the brief is scheduled for late afternoon in Denver at the FBI office.

"Frazier thinks you should be there. I agree," Perez says. "You had boots on the ground for almost this whole thing. You deserve to hear about it before it's released to the media."

He invites me to join with him for the ride over Kenosha Pass to Denver, but I decline with the excuse that I plan to stop by Colorado Springs on the way to take my daughter Daria to lunch. I'm not lying. I haven't seen Daria since she checked in on me during the Kristee disappearance. I'm long overdue a visit. But I also don't want to spend three hours in a car with Perez until we've put some time between us and this case.

"I'll meet you there."

•   •   •

The drive to Colorado Springs takes just under two hours. My ex-wife, Sheila, lives on the south side, close to the Air Force base where she and her new husband work. Technically, Daria lives here as well, but she's only got a year of college left.

Sheila greets me with a hug and an extra squeeze. I step back, still holding her arms and tilt my head.

"I'm just so happy you made it out of that fire. Sorry." Her eyes shine before she lowers her gaze.

"I'm sorry I waited until the next day to let you guys know I was alright." I can't quite believe we're having this conversation. My cheeks begin to ache from the smile I can't keep off my face. Two years ago we still weren't talking. My wasted years after our son's death did nothing to enhance our post-marriage relationship. It's only since I've reconnected with Daria that Sheila and I began to be civil with each other. I don't blame her. The bad years were all on me.

I point to a Subaru Forester parked on the street. "New car?"

"Daria's got a friend here. You know her too."

I squint at Sheila, unsure why she doesn't just say the friend's name. Sheila leads me through the house, then out the sliding glass door to the patio. Two young women sit, their backs to me—my daughter with her mane of curly black hair pulled tight in a ponytail running down her back, and her friend, also sporting black hair but cut in a familiar bob.

The girls turn at the sound of the door. Daria's eyes light up as she steps forward to hug me.

I wrap my arms around her before looking over her shoulder at the other girl.

It's Karla Li.

Daria must sense my body stiffening because she releases me, stepping back and turning toward Karla.

"She's got some things to tell you, Dad. I hope you don't mind."

•   •   •

At Daria's suggestion, we delay our conversation until we arrive at our chosen location for lunch. It's Chinese—not out of deference for Karla, who was born in this country and probably eats more pizza than dumplings, and not for Daria whose school dining area has an entire Chinese buffet available every day. No, the Chinese food is at my request. We have one Chinese restaurant in Buena Vista and it's known more for providing comfort food than specialty cuisine.

Daria wants the inside scoop on the FBI brief. The one I haven't heard yet. I've heard the theories, but nothing confirmed, and assure her it will all be in the papers tomorrow. Karla appears to hang on my every word, hoping for more information. I know why. She was in the actual vehicle the thieves used to steal the paintings. I wonder if she's shared this with Daria.

But Daria has already heard rumors. "I heard it was all about Laura Coker Long trying to keep her ranch. And two people died." Daria's fork freezes between her plate and her mouth. "And you were dating this woman?"

I'm not sure how to correct Daria, or whether I should even try. Laura and I weren't technically dating, even though I had been working pretty hard to make that happen. I say nothing.

Daria's not completely wrong.

"Read the papers tomorrow. I'm sure they'll sum it up better than I have." My face is hot and I suspect it's flushed. "Except for the part where we were almost dating."

Daria turns to Karla and raises her eyebrows.

"I found something else in Kristee's wallet, Tyler. Something I didn't know about when I saw you in Arizona."

"Arizona?" Daria looks at Karla, then at me.

Whatever Karla and Daria have talked about before my arrival must not have included everything Karla's been up to.

Karla looks at me and nods toward my daughter indicating she doesn't mind if I explain. But I'm far more interested in hearing from Karla.

"I'll explain, Dar. I'd like to hear what Karla has to say first."

Karla reaches into a handbag and pulls out a plastic baggie; the kind mothers fill when packing snacks for their preschoolers. She opens it, pulls out a notecard folded in half, and hands it to me.

"I found it stuck on the back side of her SAR card."

I unfold the card and read: *GUC-IAH 6096*

"Any ideas?"

I contemplate how we've gone straight from talking about the FBI debrief to Kristee's disappearance. Karla hasn't offered a single detail about where she's been since we got her out of Arizona. Maybe she doesn't want me to know…and I certainly haven't asked. I know she trusts me, or she wouldn't have let me help her. But we're not friends. Friends would ask the kind of questions about Karla's life that I haven't.

I know exactly what these letters and number mean. Any number of my Air Force friends would recognize them, as well.

"The three-letter codes are for airports. GUC is Gunnison and IAH is Houston. The four digits are likely a flight number," I explain.

"Gunnison is in Colorado, right?" Karla says.

Daria and I both nod. "You remember Cottonwood Pass, where the guys picked you up?" I say.

Karla nods.

"If you go down the other side, it will take you to Gunnison. It's just over an hour drive from the pass."

Karla says nothing.

I look down at my plate.

Daria breaks the silence. "Gunnison is the closest airport to Buena Vista. You don't know how long that paper was in her wallet."

Daria's right. Kristee could have checked out this flight two years before while planning a trip through Houston to Cabo San Lucas or anywhere else in or out of the country.

I look up. Karla meets my eyes.

I wonder if she's thinking the same thought. Or whether she's considering alternative reasons Kristee might carry this information.

Maybe Kristee went down the back side of Ice Mountain because she had a plane to catch.

CHAPTER 45

Perez greets me at the FBI briefing room door. Over his shoulder, a PowerPoint slide projects a montage of photos on the wall-mounted screen, including The Lodge, one of the Remingtons, and Laura's painting.

"Look at you going all professional with the electronic brief." I point to the screen after shaking Perez's hand.

"Not me. Frazier did that." Perez looks at the floor, then back at me. "I just sent her pics and stuff. She'll be doing most of the talking. I'm just here to fill in details or answer questions. You know, like courtesy to the locals."

After talking to Frazier, I know better. She described Perez's integral role in tying the case together. He impressed the FBI with the work he's doing out in our valley. As she told me, "I didn't interact with the actual Sheriff much, Larkin, but if I were him, I'd be watching out for my job. Perez is an up-and-comer. And the public has seen a lot of him in the news."

She's right. Perez hates the bureaucracy and politics of large organizations as much as I do. It wouldn't surprise me to see him in the top law enforcement position in Chaffee County someday.

Perez directs me to a seat against the back wall. "Nothing personal, but I've got to sit up front next to Frazier. The table seats are reserved for the bigwigs taking the brief." I nod, grateful I even received an invitation. Perez moves to the front of the room, where he whispers into

Frazier's ear. She smiles and stands, but as she steps in my direction, two men and a woman enter from the main door, dressed in business attire.

I assume these are the FBI bosses. Frazier shifts her focus from me to them, and guides them to their seats. She introduces Perez and everyone else sits. Frazier nods toward me. I panic, looking over my shoulder in the hopes she's nodding at someone else. She is. A young man who looks about the age of my daughter reaches for a spot on the wall just behind my shoulder and the lights dim.

"Assistant Directors Jamison, Walters, and Park—thank you for joining us today. I know you all have received the written version of our report. This briefing provides an executive summary of the results and allows you to ask me or Deputy Perez any questions you might have about the case. Would any of you like to say anything before we start?"

The lone woman in the group raises a finger.

"Director Jamison?" Frazier says.

"The three of us had breakfast before we arrived. We discussed the media release for this afternoon. I'll be at the podium for the release. I want to make sure we are in sync with the locals from Choffy County."

"That's Chaffee County, ma'am," Perez says. "Pronounced Chafe-ee, like if you've been in a saddle all day and your nether regions are chafing." Perez's voice almost has a drawl to it. He's having fun with this.

"Chafe-ee County. Got it, Deputy Perez. Thank you." Jamison keeps her eyes on Perez. "We are very interested in what happened at The Lodge and with Ms…" Jamison glances down at her notes, "…Laura Coker Long and her art. However, we want to focus the press briefing on the Remington thefts on Cottonwood Pass. Do you know why, Deputy Perez?"

"Because everyone's heard of Remington and no one cares about the Coker sisters?" Perez straightens in his seat and drops a little of the drawl.

Jamison smiles. "I like you, Deputy, even if you're not completely correct. The reason is that this is good press for our Art Theft Division—the recovery of a well-known artist's works. It provides us an opportunity to look good while our recent budget increase request remains under review." Jamison pauses. "How's that for transparency?"

"Sounds just like politics back out in Choffy—just kidding, ma'am—Chaffee County. I got no problem with that. The Coker sister involvement will get plenty of press out where we live, no matter what you do." Perez gives a snort. "And it will just sound like Jerry Springer redneck stuff if you dwell on it at the national level."

Jamison nods, still smiling. It's obvious Perez has won over the FBI leadership. Frazier appears uncharacteristically confused. I'm unsure whether it's because she's never seen this side of Perez before, or because she's too young to remember chairs flying across a stage in a Jerry Springer episode.

"OK, then." Jamison nods at Frazier. "Let's get started."

• • •

"So you're saying this Mr. Davis, the guard, was in on the theft, right up until the time the shooting started?" Deputy Park's question is the first from the assistant directors.

Frazier nods, then stops. "Sort of. Duane Dahl—Monica Coker's boyfriend—was the first to get a hint of what was going to happen when he was contacted about whether he wanted in on the operation. Duane had been skirting a little close to the law already, and didn't want to be involved. He recommended his contact, Bruce Davis." Frazier points to the screen where four pictures are presented: Duane, Monica, Bruce Davis, and the slain security guard.

"Duane claims no knowledge of how the theft would go down. Says he didn't even know they would just take the Remingtons and leave the Laura Coker Long art behind. But he did admit he asked Davis to unpack the crates back in LA and take pictures of all the art together in the van. When Davis asked why, Duane told him his suspicions—that there would be a robbery."

Park laughs. "Bet he nearly shit his drawers when the bad guys started shooting at him."

Frazier chuckles, but her smile looks artificial, like she's unsure how to react to good-old-boy language from upper management. "Right." She aims her laser pointer at Davis's profile. "Davis has already taken the picture by the time he escapes the robbery. But when the night is over, Davis is lying in a hospital room in Salida with no phone."

Park nods. "And he needs the phone to send the picture to Duane."

I lean forward, shifting my weight. This is where I enter the picture. Not my incident command work rescuing Davis, but the part where I tell him we've found his phone.

"No," Frazier says. "He took the picture on an SLR camera. Saved it on an SD card. So he could control when it went online. When Duane Dahl came to the Salida hospital, Davis gave him the card." Frazier pauses. "But the picture was password protected, and the password was on Davis's phone."

"He couldn't remember his own password?" Park doesn't look like he's buying the story.

"Actually, this was one of the smarter things these guys did. The password is complicated—a mix of letters, symbols, and digits. Davis had it stored on his Notes app on his phone.So the phone is found the next day. Search & Rescue returns it to the Sheriff's Office after a brief detour by the hospital."

Oh shit.

Jamison interrupts before Frazier can continue. "What detour?" Perez looks at the director before glancing toward the back of the room. I grip the chair arms, preparing to rise and admit my error.

"The Search & Rescue representative stopped by Davis's room to let him know we'd found the phone. You'll remember that at this time, the Davis rescue was considered a completed mission for SAR, not a criminal case. Unfortunately, Davis used that opportunity to send the password to Duane Dahl."

"How does that get Davis killed?" It's Jamison again. I release an almost audible sigh, lowering back into my chair, when we don't go down the path identifying who the SAR representative was. Obviously, Perez and Frazier know, but don't consider the information relevant enough to throw me under the bus. Perez might be pissed about a lot of things I've done, but I doubt he'd have invited me to the debriefing if he was planning on throwing me to the Feds like meat to wolves.

"He blind-courtesy-copied himself on the email and deleted the email he sent from his phone. So he had the password on his email account in case he never got his phone back." Frazier shakes her head. "He had another SD card with the picture."

"So Davis was killed for this other SD card?" Jamison says. "Because the report wasn't exactly clear at this point."

"Let me catch you up to Davis." Frazier makes a quick glance in my direction, before continuing. "Duane Dahl and Shane McGee were seen coming out of Davis's hospital room before the SAR rep went in. McGee isn't talking, but Dahl says that McGee showed up in the room after Davis gave Dahl the SD card with Laura Coker Long's art. McGee had co-opted Davis to take pictures from the robbery as well. Not for Laura's *Broncho Buster*, but for the Remingtons. Dahl stayed in the room to make sure Davis didn't tell McGee about the Laura Coker Long side gig."

"So there are separate NFTs for the Remingtons? Last-known pics before they are stolen?" Jamison says.

"We can't prove that. Davis's phone doesn't show that. McGee isn't talking. Dahl could be trying to shift some of the blame, but it offers an explanation why Dahl and McGee were in the same room."

Jamison nods and spins her hand, indicating Frazier should continue.

"So, this is where everything gets a bit wonky." For the first time since she has started, Frazier's voice sounds a little tentative. Not like she's unsure what to say—I've gotten to know her well enough to recognize she wouldn't give a brief without knowing her script—but more like she's not sure her bosses will believe her.

Jamison looks like she's noticed too. She leans forward to say something, but Frazier plows ahead.

"The Coker sisters, ma'am. They're the wonky part." Frazier's voice gets louder. She flips to a slide, showing a triangle of women's faces—

Laura Coker Long at the top; her sisters Julie and Monica at the base. "Not a postcard picture of sisterly love here. They were a family with strained relationships."

Frazier spends the next five minutes running through the Coker family history in the Upper Arkansas Valley. She concludes with the death of patriarch Dwight Coker, his legacy, and the tension the ranch created between the sisters.

"Here's how the situation with the sisters stood, the night of the Cottonwood Pass heist. Monica Coker—confirmed drug user who knows there's going to be a robbery. She and her boyfriend, Duane Dahl, plan to profit from it with the NFT of the paintings. Laura Coker Long—she knows about the impending heist as well-"

"How does she know?" Park interrupts.

"Sir, I promise I'll explain after I get through this. Is that OK?"

Park nods, and waves his hand for Frazier to continue.

"Laura Coker Long knows the heist is going to happen, and she also knows about Monica's NFT plan. But Monica doesn't know Laura knows. Julie Coker Keller—Laura's other sister-claims she knew nothing about the robbery. When Laura confides in Julie later, it's about the cameras and the NFTs-not the robbery." Frazier pauses and gives the directors a thin smile. "Julie believes Laura didn't know about the robbery because when Laura's *Broncho Buster* gets left behind, Laura's feelings are hurt."

Frazier looks at Park. "Sir, back to your question. Laura had been using these little audiovisual cameras—like stealth nanny cams—from Amazon for months to monitor Monica's behavior. Long before the robbery, Laura was worried that Monica's drug habit would affect the status of the ranch. That Monica would try to use Coker assets to support her addiction."

"Holy shit," Park says. "And the other sister knew about this? Ms.—" He shuffles his papers.

"Ms. Julie Coker Keller. Yes, sir, she found out about it at The Lodge. You'd have to understand the dynamics between the sisters to understand why Julie was OK with this."

I hold back a snort. Good luck trying to figure out the Coker women. I walked into the Coker sisters' lives with fair warning. I left, shaking my head at how I'd underappreciated Julie's warnings to stay away from them. Even now, the idea of Laura using cameras to spy on Monica and Duane seems overboard.

"So, after the robbery, you've got Duane and Monica with the SD card from Davis and the follow-on password sent through email. They upload the picture to their laptop, leaving the SD card in the laptop slot," Frazier says.

"But—"

Frazier interrupts Park. "Sir, please remember what I said about the lack of geniuses in this operation." She waits until Park nods, then continues. "Ms. Long knows all this is happening—she's watching it on the cameras. She knows the file is on the laptop and she knows there are sleeping drugs in the laptop case."

I nod, recalling standing in line at Rocks, Rapids, Eats, and listening to Duane and Monica's conversation. Right before Julie took me parking down by the river. I don't remember hearing anything about drugs, though.

"I saw this in the report." Jamison says. "*Sleeping* drugs? That's what everyone who's talking is saying, right?"

Frazier nods. "Duane and Monica suspected Davis had a copy of the picture. They knew they were going to see him at the exhibition at the lodge. Their plan was to drug Davis at the exhibit as an excuse to drive him home early. After he was knocked out, they would go through his stuff and try to retrieve the picture. Their plan fell apart when Laura Coker Long stole the laptop containing the picture, the SD card, and fentanyl. Not sleeping drugs like Duane claims. Fentanyl." Frazier shakes her head. "Monica and Duane's plan—whether you believe them about the sleeping drugs, or not—fell apart. Monica stole her sister's painting out of spite and hid it. She took down the Wi-Fi to keep the authorities in the dark. Laura Coker Long had no doubts who took her *Broncho Buster,* so she decided to execute Monica and Duane's NFT plan on her own painting."

Jamison turns to Park, who shrugs.

"These kinds of NFTs are all about scarcity," Frazier explains. "She had the laptop with the picture of *Broncho Buster* with the Remingtons. That made her actual *Broncho Buster* more valuable. But when it was stolen, the only thing of value she had was the NFT—and it was even more valuable because every painting in the picture was now missing. Scarcity."

"So Laura Coker Long drugged Davis with fentanyl that she thought was sleeping pills. She killed him." Park nods like this makes sense, but I'm blown away. Laura killed Davis? She was the one leaving Davis's room the night he died? I struggle to keep my face expressionless. I don't see how the FBI leadership can. Then I remember, they've all scanned through the written report already. I'm the only one hearing all this for the first time.

Frazier starts to answer, but Park holds up his hand while shuffling through his copy of the report. "It says here, you have confirmation from Duane that there were drugs in the laptop case and you have confirmation from the sister Julie that this was Ms. Long's plan. What's Ms. Long saying?"

"She's not talking. But her sister says that Ms. Long never found the photo everyone thought Mr. Davis had," Frazier says.

I remember Monica's discovery of Davis's body. I thought she could have faked her shock because she was involved in his death. Now I'm not so sure. She must have been surprised to find Davis dead. But not so surprised that she didn't search for the SD card. Monica must have found it, either on Davis or in his room, before she let out her *dead-body* scream. Monica died in the river with an SD card that wasn't even the one she was looking for—the one with just the Remingtons that Davis was supposed to give to McGee.

Suddenly, I don't need the rest of the report. I know how this story ends. Duane bolted from The Lodge because he was going to search for the laptop he suspected Laura stole. Monica took the SD card Davis was keeping from McGee, but died before she could get it back to Duane. Her death really was an accident. Laura retrieved the laptop from her car before we evacuated—the laptop that contained the original copy of the *Broncho Buster* photo. All she had to do was pay someone to do keystroke forensics on the laptop and she would have the password to the picture. The two women waited two weeks before minting the photo and putting it on the market.

I examine the pattern of the conference room carpet, Frazier's voice a gentle buzz in the background. All of this—two people dead, lives in ruins, taxpayer dollars funding this massive investigation. For what? For maybe a couple hundred thousand dollars if the NFT market held up?

Yes, the NFT would undoubtedly have made more money than selling Laura's painting. But if they were looking for the big bucks, they should have just stolen the Remingtons. Why waste their time on these digital forays?

Director Walters speaks for the first time and when he does, I look left and right, wondering if I had been talking out loud.

"Why didn't they just steal the Remingtons themselves? Why all this for what can't have been a ton of cash? Relatively speaking, that is?"

Jamison turns to Walters, raising a finger to Frazier as if to say, *I'll take this one.* "That's the thing about big-time art, Robert. You need a buyer ahead of time if you're going to steal something well-known. You just can't put it out there online to the highest bidder because that anonymity thing won't work at that scale." She turns toward Park, who nods. "McGee had a plan with the New Mexico buyers. Ms. Long didn't have a plan beyond stopping her sister from using NFT profits to buy more drugs. When the shit hit the fan, Ms. Long saw an opportunity to get the family out of some trouble. Her pain-in-the-ass, drug-addicted sister was dead. She saw a chance to save her family's land, and she took it. And she just brought the other sister—Julie—along for the ride because she knew she would go along with whatever she said." Jamison turns to Frazier. "That sound about right?"

"Ma'am, that's it. Laura Coker Long has been released on bail. The list of charges against her are included in the report." Frazier reaches down and hits a button. The screen behind her goes blank. "Any questions?"

Jamison looks down the table for further input from her colleagues. They all nod in apparent approval. But Jamison shakes her head like something still bothers her.

"Agent Frazier, a man sits in jail right now for allegedly kidnapping you. Why isn't this a part of your briefing?"

Frazier's face flushes, and she opens her mouth to speak.

Jamison holds up a hand. "Relax, Emma. I've read the details and I'm not trying to call you out for this. He had a gun on you. You couldn't use yours. You did the right thing in complying, and your efforts to save Monica Coker were nothing short of heroic. I'm just trying to nail down how Algood was involved and why that info is missing."

I lean forward. I'm curious about this as well.

Frazier appears relieved at Jamison's rephrasing of the question. I know from talking to her, she's still embarrassed about Algood abducting her.

"Ma'am, there is no evidence linking Martin Algood to the theft of the Remingtons, the theft of Laura Coker Long's *Broñcho Buster,* or anything with the NFTs. He is guilty of kidnapping me, but not Monica. We all saw Monica choose to go with him."

"But why?" Jamison wrinkles her nose.

"I can give you what he's saying. And I can give you my opinion."

"Go ahead."

"Algood says he was claustrophobic and under the influence of drugs. That's what caused his aberrant behavior."

Drugs? Then I remember the empty Ritalin bottle I found in his gear. Maybe he *was* all amped up. But kidnapping?

"And your opinion?"

Frazier glances in my direction with a thin smile, then back to the directors. "Ma'am, pardon my language, but Martin Algood is an asshole who thinks of no one but himself. I can't speak to his claims about why he acted in the way he did, but based on my short time with him, his actions, while extreme, were not totally out of character."

When Frazier dropped the *asshole* label, I had to choke back a laugh. I still find it crazy that Algood had nothing to do with the case, but I agree with Emma's assessment.

Jamison must feel the same way. "Agent Frazier, this is incredible work. Your casework is meticulous, but your actions at The Lodge? That was above and beyond the call of duty. You can be sure I'll be submitting you for additional recognition.

"Thank you, ma'am," Frazier says. "I had a lot of help."

"I know you did. We'll be letting Deputy Perez's boss know about his work, as well. And the governor, too."

I smile, warmth blossoming in my chest. Part of my happiness is because I'm proud of my friends. But most of it is because the entire time Jamison speaks, Frazier's eyes are focused on mine, not with the glow of friendship and respect like Kristee used to provide, but with what might possibly be the start of something new.

Am I imagining it? I'm in no hurry to pursue romance again, and I've got things to do. The paper Karla found in Kristee's wallet intrigues me. I owe it to Karla, and yes, even to Lin Li to follow up on that. Without telling Perez.

A week ago, I wouldn't have mentioned it to Frazier either. I don't want her thinking I'm crazy. But maybe I could meet her and discuss some theories about Kristee's case. After that look she just gave me, I need an excuse for another cup of coffee with this woman.

Crazy? Maybe a little.

ABOUT THE AUTHOR

Over a 30-year Air Force career, best-selling author Cam Torrens delivered combat supplies and personnel across Europe, the Middle East, and Africa. He piloted the first mobility aircraft into Iraq during the Iraq War, served as the United States Air Attaché at the US Embassy in Beijing, China and spent four years as the Professor of Aerospace Studies at Virginia Tech.

Father of six, Cam and his spouse live in Buena Vista, Colorado where he serves as the Vice President of Central Colorado Writers and volunteers with the Chaffee County Search & Rescue team.

Scorched is his third Tyler Zahn novel.

OTHER TITLES BY CAM TORRENS

NOTE FROM CAM TORRENS

Word-of-mouth is crucial for any author to succeed. If you enjoyed *Scorched*, please leave a review online—anywhere you are able. Even if it's just a sentence or two. It would make all the difference and would be very much appreciated.

Thanks!
Cam Torrens

We hope you enjoyed reading this title from:

www.blackrosewriting.com

Subscribe to our mailing list – *The Rosevine* – and receive **FREE** books, daily
deals, and stay current with news about upcoming
releases and our hottest authors.
Scan the QR code below to sign up.

Already a subscriber? Please accept a sincere thank you for being a fan of
Black Rose Writing authors.

View other Black Rose Writing titles at
www.blackrosewriting.com/books and use promo code
PRINT to receive a **20% discount** when purchasing.